RANDOM
HOUSE
LARGE
PRINT

# Ghosts

# Ghosts

### a novel

Dolly Alderton

RANDOM HOUSE
# LARGE PRINT

Copyright © 2020 by Dolly Alderton

All rights reserved. Published in the United States of America by Random House Large Print in association with Alfred A. Knopf, a division of Penguin Random House LLC, New York. Originally published in hardcover in Great Britain by Fig Tree, an imprint of Penguin General, a division of Penguin Random House Ltd., London, in 2020.

Front-cover photograph by ViDI Studio / Shutterstock
Cover design by Kelly Blair

The Library of Congress has established a Cataloging-in-Publication record for this title.

ISBN: 978-0-593-46024-5

www.penguinrandomhouse.com/large-print-format-books

FIRST LARGE PRINT EDITION

Printed in the United States of America

10  9  8  7  6  5  4  3  2  1

This Large Print edition published in accord with the standards of the N.A.V.H.

**For Mum and Dad,
for never disappearing**

# Ghosts

Prologue

On the day I was born, 3rd August 1986, "The Edge of Heaven" by Wham! was number one. Since I can remember, an annual tradition was playing it as loud as possible as soon as I woke up. I remember all the birthdays of my childhood through the sound of George Michael's defiant "yeah, yeah, yeah"s in the opening bars—jumping on my mum and dad's bed in my pyjamas, eating sprinkle sandwiches for breakfast. It is why my middle name is George—Nina George Dean. This mortified me throughout my adolescence when my flat chest and certain jaw gave me a masculine enough energy without also being named after an ageing male pop star. But like all abnormalities and embarrassments of childhood, adulthood recalibrated them into a fascinating identity CV. The weird middle name, the birthday breakfast sandwich spread thick with margarine and dipped in hundreds and thousands of sprinkles—all of it strung together to form my own unique mythology, which I would one day speak of with bewildered pride to airtime and intrigue.

Mortifying oddity + time = riveting eccentricity.

On my thirty-second birthday, 3rd August 2018, I brushed my teeth and washed my face while playing "The Edge of Heaven" from the speakers in my living room. Then I spent the day on my own, doing and eating all the things I loved the most. For breakfast, I had a poached egg on toast. I can confidently declare at thirty-two years old that there are three things I can do flawlessly: arrive anywhere I need to be on time with five minutes to spare; ask people specific questions in social situations when I can't be bothered to engage in conversation and I know they'll do all the talking (**Would you say you're an introvert or an extrovert? Would you say you are ruled by your head or by your heart? Have you ever set anything on fire?**); and poach an egg to perfection.

I checked my phone and found a grinning selfie of my parents wishing me a happy birthday. My best friend, Katherine, WhatsApped me a video of Olive, her toddler daughter, saying "Happy birday, Aunty

Neenaw" (she still couldn't get it quite right despite extensive tutoring from me). My friend Meera sent a gif of a luxurious-looking long-haired cat holding a Martini in its paw with the message "CANNOT WAIT FOR TONIGHT, BIRTHDAY GAL!!!!!," which meant she would certainly be in bed before eleven. This is what happens when people with children get too worked up for a night out—they tire themselves out with anticipation, set themselves up for a fall with their bravado, get stage fright then ultimately go home after two pints.

I walked to Hampstead Heath and went for a swim in the Ladies' Pond. On my third circuit, the inoffensive lick of summer rain began to fall. I love swimming in the rain and would have swum for longer had the matronly lifeguard not ordered me to get out for "health and safety reasons." I told her it was my birthday and thought this might grant me an off-the-record bonus circuit, but she informed me that if there was lightning, it would directly strike me in the open body of water and "fry me like a rasher of bacon," not a mess she wanted to clean up—"whether it's your birthday or not."

I came home in the afternoon, to my new flat and the first home that I'd bought. It was a small one-bed in Archway, on the first floor of a Victorian house. The estate agent's generous description of the property was that it was "warm, eccentric and in need of modernization"—it had a carpet the colour and texture of instant coffee granules, a peach-tiled eighties bathroom replete with abandoned bidet and two broken doors on the pine kitchen cupboards. I was sure it would take as long as I lived there to afford to do it up, but I still felt lucky every morning I woke and looked up at the swirly crusts of my Artex ceiling. I never imagined I would ever be able to own a flat in London—the actualization of this once-impossible dream alone made it the best place I'd ever set foot in.

I had two neighbours: an elderly widow named Alma who lived above me, whose hallway small talk about how best to grow tomatoes on a windowsill and generous donations of leftover homemade kibbeh were both delightful; and a man downstairs, who I hadn't yet met despite having moved in a month ago and made a number of attempts to introduce myself. I'd knock, but there was never an answer. Alma said she'd never spoken to him either, but she did once talk to his female flatmate about the building's electricity meter. I only heard him—he came in from work at six o'clock and made virtually no noise until midnight when he cooked and ate his dinner and watched TV.

I scraped together the money for the flat with savings, the royalties from my first book, **Taste,** and the advance on my second cookbook, **The Tiny Kitchen. Taste** was a recipe book, inspired by my family's cooking, my friendships, my only long-term relationship, my travels and my favourite chefs. It also had a thread of memoir spun in between the recipes. There was an overarching theme of discovering my own tastes in life as I learnt about my culinary ones—what I liked and what satisfied me. It told the story of how I'd balanced a night-and-weekend occupation as a supper club owner with my day job as an English teacher at a secondary school, and how I eventually saved enough to quit and become a full-time food writer. It also touched on my relationship and ultimate amicable break-up with my first and only boyfriend, Joe, who was supportive of my decision to write about us. The book was a surprise success and off the back of it I got a column in a newspaper supplement, a number of soul-destroying but bank-account-enhancing partnership deals with food brands and a further two-cookbook deal.

**The Tiny Kitchen,** which I had just completed, was about what I'd learnt from cooking and entertaining in a rented one-room studio flat with no kitchen storage space, an oven the size of a Fisher-Price cooker and only one hotplate for a hob. It was my first solo home after Joe and I broke up. I preferred to talk about my third book, a temporarily unnamed project about seasonal cooking and eating, which was in its proposal stage. I'd now learnt from years and years of writing that the very best version of a piece of work was when it was still just an idea and therefore perfect.

I ran a bath and put on a long-loved iTunes playlist that was called "Pre-lash" in my twenties, which

I'd renamed "Good Times" in recent years, to mark a move away from reckless, bodily abandon and towards mindful, considered pleasure. I created the track-list to listen to before a night out when I was a first year at university and the shape of its journey played out in full was always in tandem with the same tireless rituals of feminization I had been following for fifteen years: wash hair, dry it upside down and try to increase its volume by ten per cent, pluck upper lip, two layers of mascara, second drink, walk into two spritzes of perfume—by the time the penultimate track came around ("Nuthin' but a 'G' Thang") a cab was always waiting outside while I cut my legs to ribbons with a disposable razor over the sink because I'd forgotten to shave them in the shower.

My hair was back to its natural dark brown and cut to shoulder-length. There was a recent addition of a fringe to hide the new creases in my forehead, as light as concertinaed tissue paper, but visible enough for me to want to not think about. Luckily, I saved time when it came to make-up. My face had never worn make-up well. I was grateful, as I already felt grooming took up far too much time and was a constant source of feminist guilt, along with my total disinterest in all DIY and all sports. Sometimes, when I felt despondent, I liked to calculate how many minutes of my remaining life I would spend removing upper lip hair if I lived until

I was eighty-five and think about how many languages I could have learnt in that time.

I wore a high-neck, low-back black dress to my birthday drinks. I didn't wear a bra, simply to show off that I don't have to wear a bra, which is a paltry consolation for having such small breasts. But I didn't mind any more—I had become mostly indifferent to my body. I was an irritating size 11, totally average height at 5 foot 4 and happy that big arses had come back into fashion, so much so that I had observed with pride that we now occupied more than two categories on any given porn-streaming platform.

There were a number of people I didn't invite to the birthday drinks this year. In particular, my ex-boyfriend. I wanted Joe to be there, but inviting Joe meant inviting his girlfriend, Lucy. Lucy was harmless enough, despite the fact she owned a handbag in the shape of a stiletto shoe, but Lucy always felt like there were unsaid things between us. Once she'd drunk her three glasses of specific rosé ("Is it **blush**?" she'd ask the weary barman, the 134th white woman to do so that day), she wanted all the things to be said. She'd ask if I had a problem with her, or if I sensed awkwardness between us. She'd tell me how important I was to Joe and how special he thought I was. She would give me a series of hugs and repeatedly tell me that she hoped we'd be friends. We'd met at least five times, and she and Joe had been going out for over a year, yet she still believed there were declarations we had to make to each other in quiet corners of social situations. I had thought about why she did this a lot and, rather generously, had come to the conclusion that Lucy was a woman who'd watched too many structured reality TV shows. She evidently felt a party wasn't a party until two women in peplum dresses clutched hands while one says: "After you slept with Ryan, I stopped liking you as a friend, but I will always love you like a sister."

There were, in total, twenty guests who came to the pub, made up of mostly university friends, a couple of school friends, old colleagues and a handful of people I was currently working with. There were also a couple of friends who I saw precisely twice a year—once at their birthday drinks, once at mine—and there was a new-found mutual understanding that while we didn't want to let go of the friendship altogether, we had absolutely no interest in investing time in it beyond these biannual meet-ups. I found this unsaid pact to be both sad and cheering in equal measure.

Etiquette demanded I invited partners and spouses. These were mainly well-meaning men whose charismatic conversational prowess I had long given up on and instead knew they'd spend the evening sipping pints on a bench, saying nothing other than "happy birthday" every time they passed me to get to the loo until they got tired and whingy and made their girlfriend go home. I was fascinated by the men all my friends had chosen to merge their lives with, particularly how they all interacted with each other. When I was with Joe, the girlfriends and wives of all his friends came together at every gathering with something akin to the Blitz spirit. We talked, we listened, we learnt about each other, we gradually grew closer every time we intersected by way of our boyfriends. I had noticed over the years that a group of male other halves do the absolute opposite to this when they find themselves shoved together. Time and time again I observed that most men think a good conversation is a conversation where they have imparted facts or information that others didn't already know, or dispensed an interesting anecdote, or given someone tips or advice on an upcoming plan or generally left their mark on the discourse like a streak of piss against a tree trunk. If they learnt more than they conveyed over the course of an evening, afterwards they would feel low; like the party hadn't been a success or they hadn't been on good form.

The thing they liked the most were instances of trivial commonality. I watched them do it at every one of my friends' birthday drinks—search for a crossover of thought or experience as a way of feeling instant connection with a fellow man without having to make any effort to get to know or understand him—**Oh yeah, my brother went to Leeds uni too. Where did you live? YOU'RE JOKING,**

**oh my God okay so you know Silverdale Road, right by the Co-op? Like, to the left of the Co-op. That's the one. My brother's friend's girlfriend owned a house there! Such a small world. Have you been to the pub on that corner? The King's Arms? No? Oh, you should, it's a great pub, really cracking pub.**

The one other half I adored was Gethin, who was the long-term boyfriend of my university friend Dan. All three of us were close and had spent some of my wildest nights and most brilliant holidays together. But, in truth, they had disappointed me recently. I'd thought I could always rely on Dan and Gethin to flout tradition, but they had begun making the most conventional choices of anyone I knew. They had "closed" their relationship, which was a let-down because their respective sexual escapades made for riotous stories and I held them up as the only successful example of non-monogamy I had encountered. They'd created an incredibly complicated alcohol-restriction schedule, which meant they were allowed to drink on certain weekends but not other weekends and they definitely couldn't drink during the week. They'd stopped coming out because they were always saving money for something. They had just begun the adoption process. They had bought a two-bed in Bromley.

Dan and Gethin stayed for two lemonades, told me about the nightmare they were having with an overgrown tree in their neighbour's garden, which was overspilling into their garden, then left before eight to "make it back to Bromley" like it was a quest to Mordor.

I received a number of thoughtful presents from people, indicating to me that who I was and how that manifests in my taste and lifestyle choices had been received loud and clear. There was an early edition of **The Whitsun Weddings** by Philip Larkin, a brand of smoky hot sauce that I love and can only be bought in America, a Chinese money plant that doubled up as a house-warming gift and a lucky mascot for my new book. The only rogue contribution was from my former boss at the school I worked at, who bought me a framed print of an illustrated 1950s woman doing the washing-up, with the caption: **If God wanted me to do housework, he would have put diamonds in the sink!** This was not the first time I had been given a gift of this ilk, and I decided that it was my prolonged state of singledom plus my fondness for a Vodka Martini that had made people think that I like this sort of kitsch vintage sloganism, which made light of women being drunk, desperate, childless, chocoholics or overspenders. I thanked her.

I was offered a line of cocaine by my friends Eddie and Meera, who were desperate to have their "first proper night out together in eighteen months" because in that time Meera had been pregnant, given birth and had just stopped breastfeeding, which meant she could now fill herself to the brim with booze without passing it on to the baby. Eddie and Meera had a feral look in their eyes that I had come to recognize in new parents on their first night out. I politely declined. I didn't mind them taking it at the party, but I was very aware of how much Meera talked about the need for paternity leave when high, especially the phrase: "the default patriarchal constructs of parenting." Eddie did a lot of restless shuffling from foot to foot—he couldn't get settled—and they both continuously spoke about Glastonbury like they were its founders.

My Only Single Friend, Lola, took me to one side and twitchily told me she felt very judged and isolated by all the married people. She was wearing red lipstick and a very strange up-do which involved a number of tonged segments of hair half pinned up and half down, not unlike a barrister's wig. She only ever did these sorts of hairdos when she was very hung-over and overcompensating. She admitted to me that she'd had a bit of a heavy one the night before—a date that began in a canal-side pub at seven p.m., moved on to dinner, then a bar, then another bar, then back to hers at three a.m. It was clear she hadn't been to bed. My Only Single Friend Lola worked in events, but at the time I would have described her as a freelance dater. She'd been single for ten years and was desperately searching for a relationship. She was my closest friend from university and none of our extended group of mates had

ever been able to work out why she couldn't get beyond a handful of dates. She was charming, funny,
beautiful and had greedily looted the genetic bank
by being the proprietress of not only enormous tits
but enormous tits that didn't need a bra. She told
me she was "wigging out" about her date from the
night before. I made a joke about her hairdo reflecting her state of mind. She said she was going to
get the tube home. I told her that Eddie's younger
brother was arriving shortly who was single, twenty-
six and a trainee vet. She said she might have one
more prosecco for the road.

Katherine, my oldest friend who I'd known since
my first day of secondary school, asked me what I
wanted from the following year. I told her I thought
I was ready to meet someone. She responded with
unbridled glee—I think she felt that my decision
to search for a relationship was once-removed approval of her choice to get married and have a baby.
I'd noticed this was a thing that people did when
they got into their thirties: they saw every personal
decision you made as a direct judgement on their
life. If you voted Labour and they voted Lib Dem,
they thought you were voting Labour specifically
to let them know that their politics were incorrect.
If they moved to the suburbs and you didn't, they
thought you were refusing to solely to prove a point
that your life was more glamorous than theirs.
Katherine had defected to long-term monogamy in

her mid-twenties when she met her husband, Mark, and, since then, she wanted everyone to come and join her.

I had been inactively single—single and not dating—for two years since the end of my relationship with Joe (together for seven years, lived together for four, our lives and friendship groups were completely conjoined, I began to notice him say things like "on the morrow" instead of "tomorrow" and "the book of face" instead of "Facebook"). After we broke up, I tried to catch up on all the sex I hadn't been having in my twenties with a six-month promiscuity spree. But a "promiscuity spree" for me meant sleeping with three men, all of whom I tried to make my boyfriend. After self-diagnosing as a co-dependent, I decided to stop dating before my thirtieth birthday and see what really being on my own felt like. Since then, I'd lived on my own for the first time, travelled on my own for the first time, made the transition from teacher and part-time writer to full-time published writer and generally unlearnt all the habits accumulated in a near-decade of cosy, comfy monogamy. Recently, I'd started to feel ready to start dating again.

It was last orders at eleven o'clock. Katherine left shortly before then because she was pregnant. She hadn't told me she was, but I could tell by the way she kept eating pickles—she picked gherkins off everyone's burgers and then ordered a plate of cornichons. She craved intensely savoury food all through her pregnancy with Olive. I asked if her craving of umami is what inspired the name of the baby—she didn't like that. I'd learnt a lot about what pregnant women and new mums don't like over the last few years and one of them is when you have any questions or comments about their baby's name. One friend stopped talking to me when— I thought rather helpfully—I let her know that Beaux is a French plural and she should spell her son's name Beau instead. It had already been registered. Another got cross when she had a daughter named Bay and I asked if it was in reference to the herb, window or parking space. They particularly didn't like when they told you their baby names "in confidence" and you accidentally told someone else and it got back to the mother.

But the worst faux pas—the asking-someone-how-old-they-are, belching-in-public, eating-off-your-knife no-go—is when you can tell a woman is pregnant and you ask her if she's pregnant. You also can't say you knew all along when they do finally tell you they're having a baby—they **hate** that. They like the touch of theatre that comes with the big reveal. In all honesty, I understood and would probably be the same. You've got to get your thrills from somewhere if you're not allowed a cocktail for nine months. Which is why I nodded along and said nothing when Katherine left the party with a made-up reason of "having to get the car fixed" the next morning.

At around ten p.m., there were mutterings of heading to a twenty-four-hour club in King's Cross, mainly from the newly arrived trainee vet, who Lola was already talking to and twirling her wig at, but come 11:15, no one followed through. Eddie and Meera had to get back to relieve the baby-sitter and, on their behalf, I dreaded the twitchy, sleepless night that lay ahead of them as I watched their jaws rhythmically jut from side to side. Lola and the vet went to go find "a wine bar," which meant somewhere dark where they could talk some drunken nonsense at each other until one of them made the first move and they could dry-hump on a banquette. This suited me just fine as I was ready for bed. I hugged the remaining guests goodbye and told them, not entirely soberly, that I loved them all.

When I got home, I listened to half an episode of my current favourite podcast, which was a light-hearted romp through the history of female serial killers, and I removed my mascara, flossed and brushed my teeth. I put my new old copy of **The Whitsun Weddings** on my bookshelf and placed my Chinese money plant on my mantelpiece. I felt unusually and perfectly content. On that August evening, in the first hours of the second day of my thirty-third year, it felt like every random component of my life had been designed long ago to fit together at that very moment.

I lay in bed and downloaded a dating app for the first time in my life. Lola, a veteran of online dating, told me that Linx (with a silhouette of a wild cat out on the prowl as its logo) had the highest yield of eligible men and the best success rate for matching long-term relationships.

I filled in the About Me information boxes. **Nina Dean, 32, food writer. Location: Archway, London. Looking for: love and the perfect pain au raisin.** I uploaded a handful of photos and fell asleep.

My thirty-second birthday was the simplest birthday I ever had. Which was a perfectly lovely way to begin the strangest year of my life.

ONE

"It is our imagination that
is responsible for love,
not the other person."

MARCEL PROUST

LIVING IN SUBURBAN North London was nothing but an act of pragmatism for my parents. Whenever I asked them why they chose to leave East London for the suburbs when I was ten, they would refer to functionality: it was a bit safer, you could buy a bit more space, it was near the city, it was near lots of motorways and close to schools. They talked about setting up their life in Pinner as if they had been looking for a hotel that was close to the airport for an early flight—convenient, anonymous, fuss-free, nothing special but it got the job done. Nothing about where my parents lived brought them any sensory pleasure or cause for relish—not the landscape, nor the history of the place, not the parks, the architecture, the community or culture. They lived in the suburbs because it was close to things. They had built their home and therefore entire life around convenience.

When we were together, Joe often used his northernness in arguments against me, as a way of proving he was more real than I was; more down to earth and therefore more likely to be right. It was one of my least favourite things about him—the way he lazily outsourced his integrity to Yorkshire, so that romantic implications of miners and moors would do all the hard work for him. In the early stages of our relationship, he used to make me feel like we had grown up in separate galaxies because his mum had worked as a hairdresser in Sheffield and mine was a receptionist in Harrow. The first time he took me home to his parents' house—a modest three-bed in a suburb of Sheffield—I realized just what a lie I'd been told. If I hadn't known I was in Yorkshire, I would have sworn we were driving around the pebbledash-fronted-leaded-window gap between the end of London and the beginning of Hertfordshire where I'd spent my adolescence. Joe's cul-de-sac was the same as mine, the houses were all the same, his fridge was full of the same fruit-corner yogurts and ready-to-bake garlic bread. He'd had a bike just like mine, to spend his teenage weekends going up and down streets of identical red-roof houses just like I did. He was taken to PizzaExpress for his birthday like I was. The secret was out. "No more making out that we've had completely different upbringings, Joe," I said to him on the train home. "No more pretending you belong in a song written by Jarvis Cocker about being in love with a woman in a tabard. You no more belong in that song than I belong in a Chas and Dave one. We grew up in matching suburbs."

In recent years, I'd found myself craving the familiarity of home. The high streets I knew, with their high density of dentists, hairdressers and bookies, and total lack of independent coffee shops. The long walk from the station to my parents' house. The women with matching long bobs, the balding men, the teenagers in hoodies. The absence of individualism; the peaceful acquiescence to mundanity. Young adulthood had quickly turned into just plain adulthood—with its daily list of choices to confirm who I was, how I voted, who my broadband provider was—and returning to the scene of my teenage life for an afternoon felt like a brief holiday back in time. When I was in Pinner, I could be seventeen again, just for a day. I could pretend that my world was myopic and my choices meaningless and the possibilities that were ahead of me were wide open and boundless.

MUM ANSWERED THE DOOR like she always answered the door—in a way that demonstrably made the point that her life was very busy. She did an apologetic wonky smile as she opened it to me, portable landline pressed up to her ear on her shoulder. "Sorry," she mouthed, and rolled her eyes. She was wearing a pair of black jersey-fabric bottoms that didn't look assertive enough to be trousers, weren't tight enough to be leggings and weren't slouchy enough to be pyjamas. She wore a grey marl round-neck T-shirt and was decorated in her base-coat of jewellery: thick gold bracelet, one gold bangle, pearl stud earrings, snake chain gold necklace, gold wedding band. My guess was she was coming from or going to some form of physical exercise—my mum had become obsessed with physical exercise since she turned fifty, but I don't think it changed her body by even half a pound. She was wrapped in a post-menopausal layer of softness, a small bag under her chin, a thicker middle, flesh that now spilt over the back of her bra, visible through her T-shirt. And she was gorgeous. The sort of big-bovine-eyed gorgeous that is not hugely exciting but evokes familiar magnetism in everyone—like an open fire or a bunch of pink roses or a golden cocker spaniel. Her espresso-brown bob, although sliced with grey strands, was lusciously thick and her golden highlights shimmered under the light of the overhead IKEA lamp. I inherited almost nothing of my looks from my mother.

"Yeah, fine," she said into the phone, beckoning

me into the hallway. "Great, well, let's do coffee next week then. Just send me the dates. I'll bring you that teach-yourself-Tarot kit I was telling you about. No, not at all, you can keep it actually. QVC, so easy enough. Okay, okay. Speak then, bye!" She hung up the phone and gave me a hug, before holding me at arm's length and examining my fringe. "This is new," she said, looking curiously at it, like it was 3 down on a crossword.

"Yes," I said, putting down my handbag and removing my shoes (everyone had to remove their shoes on arrival, the rule was more stringent here than at the Blue Mosque). "Got it before my birthday. Thought it would be good for covering my thirty-two-year-old lines on my thirty-two-year-old forehead."

"Don't be silly," she said, flicking it gingerly. "You don't need some mop on your head for that, you just need some effective foundation."

I smiled, unoffended but unamused. I had got used to the fact that Mum was disappointed by quite how ungirly her daughter was. She would have loved a girl with whom she could have gone shopping for holiday clothes and gossiped about face primer. When we were teenagers, and Katherine came round, Mum would offer her all her old jewellery and handbags, and they'd sift through them together like two gal pals at a department store. She fell deeply in love with Lola the first time they met, purely on the basis that they both felt particularly passionate about the same face highlighter.

"Where's Dad?" I asked.

"Reading," she said.

I looked through the French doors of the living room and saw the profile of my dad in his bottle-green armchair. His feet up on the footstool, a large mug of tea on the side table next to him. His strong chin and long nose protruding—the chin and nose that also belong to me—as if they were competing to get to the same finish line in a race.

There was seventeen years' difference in age between Mum and Dad. They had met when Dad was the deputy head of an inner-city state school and Mum was sent there by her secretarial agency to be the receptionist. She was twenty-four, he was forty-one. The gap between their personalities was as large as their age gap. Dad was sensitive, gentle, inquisitive, introspective and intellectual—there was almost nothing that didn't interest him. Mum was practical, proactive, logistical, straightforward and authoritative. There was almost nothing she didn't involve herself in.

I took a moment to take him in from behind the glass doors. From here, he was still just my dad as he'd always been, reading the **Observer,** ready to tell me about where rubbish goes in China or ten things I may not have known about Wallis Simpson or the plight of the endangered falcon. My dad who could instantly recognize me—not the face of me, but everything of who I was—in a nanosecond: the name of my childhood imaginary friend, my dissertation subject, my favourite character from my favourite book and the road names of everywhere I've ever lived. When I looked at his face now, I mostly saw my dad, but I sometimes saw something else in his eyes that unsettled me—sometimes it looked like everything he understood had been cut into pieces and he was trying to configure them into a collage that made sense.

Two years ago, Dad had a stroke. It only took a couple of months after he had recovered for us to realize that he wasn't entirely better. My dad, always so sharp and cerebral, had slowed down. He'd forget the names of family members and close friends. His easy confidence and ability to make decisions dwindled. He'd regularly wander off on days out and get lost. He often couldn't remember the road he lived on. Initially, Mum and I wrote it off as an ageing brain, unable to face the possibility of something more serious. Then, one day, Mum got a call from a stranger to tell her that Dad had been seen driving around the same large, busy roundabout for twenty minutes. Eventually, someone managed to get him to pull over—he'd had no idea where to turn off. We went to the GP, he did a range of physical tests, cognitive assessments and MRI scans. The possibility we were dreading was confirmed.

"Hi, Dad," I said, walking towards him. He looked up from the paper.

"Hello, you!" he said.

"Don't stand up." I bent down to give him a hug. "Anything interesting to tell me?"

"There's a new film adaptation of **Persuasion,**" he said, holding up the review to me.

"Ah," I said. "The thinking man's Austen."

"Correct."

"I'm going to go help Mum with lunch."

"All right, love," he said, before reopening the newspaper and arranging himself back into the repose I knew so well.

When I went into the kitchen, Mum was chopping broccoli florets that were collecting next to a pile of sliced kiwis. From a speaker, a woman was talking loudly and slowly about conforming to male sexual desire.

"What is this?" I asked.

"It's the audiobook of **Intercourse** by Andrea Dworkin."

"It's . . . what?" I asked, turning the volume down a few notches.

"Andrea Dworkin. She's a famous feminist. You'd recognize her, quite a big girl, but not much of a sense of humour. Very clever woman, she—"

"I know who Andrea Dworkin is, I meant why are you listening to her audiobook?"

"For Reading Between the Wines."

"Is that your book club you've told me about?"

She sighed exasperatedly and took a cucumber out of the fridge. "It's not a book club, Nina, it's a literary salon."

"What's the difference?"

"Well," she said with a slight curl of her lip that couldn't conceal the glee she felt at having to, once again, explain the difference between a book club and a literary salon. "Me and some of the girls have decided to start a bi-monthly meeting where we talk about ideas rather than just the book itself, so it's much less prescriptive. Each salon has a theme and includes discussions, poetry readings and personal sharing that relate to the theme."

"What's the theme of the next one?"

"The theme is: 'Is all heterosexual sex rape?' "

"Right. And who is attending?"

"Annie, Cathy, Sarah from my running club, Gloria, Gloria's gay cousin, Martin, Margaret, who volunteers with me at the charity shop. Everyone brings a dish. I'm making halloumi skewers," she said, transporting the chopping board to the blender and piling the assortment of fruit and vegetables into it.

"Why this sudden interest in feminism?"

She hit the button on the machine, letting out a cacophony of buzzing as the mix pulverized to a pale-green gunk.

"I don't know if I'd call it sudden," she shouted

over the top of the electronic roar. She turned the blender off and poured the fibrous-looking liquid into a pint glass.

"That sounds great, Mum," I relented. "I think it's really cool to be so engaged and curious."

"It is," she said. "And I'm the only one who has a spare room, so I've said we can use it for Reading Between the Wines meetings."

"You don't have a spare room."

"Your dad's study."

"Dad needs his study."

"It will still be there for him, it just doesn't make sense to have a whole room in this house that's only occasionally used, like we're living in Blenheim Palace."

"What about his books?"

"I'll move them to the shelves down here."

"What about his paperwork?"

"I've got everything important on file. There's a lot of stuff that can be thrown away."

"Please let me go through it," I said with the slight whine of a stroppy child. "It might be important to him. It might be important for us further down the line when we need as much as possible to jog his memory, to remind him of—"

"Of course, of course," she said, taking a sip of her smoothie with her nostrils flaring in displeasure. "It's all upstairs in a few piles, you'll see it on the landing."

"Okay, thank you," I said, offering her a muted

smile as a peace offering. I took a deep, invisible yoga breath. "What else has been going on?"

"Nothing really. Oh, I've decided to change my name."

"What? Why?"

"I've never liked Nancy, it's too old-fashioned."

"Don't you think it's weird to change it now? Everyone knows you as Nancy, it's too late for a new name to catch on."

"I'm too old is what you're saying," she said.

"No, I'm just saying a more appropriate time to workshop a new name would have been your first week at secondary school, probably not in your fifties."

"Well, I've decided to change it and I've looked into how to do it and it's very easy, so my mind's made up."

"And what are you changing it to?"

"Mandy."

**"Mandy?"**

"Mandy."

"But," I took another deep yoga breath, "Mandy isn't all that dissimilar to Nancy, is it? I mean, they sort of rhyme."

"No they don't."

"They do, it's called assonance."

"I knew you'd be like this. I knew you'd find a way to lecture me like you always do. I have no idea why this should cause you any trouble, I just want to love my name."

"Mum!" I said pleadingly. "I'm not lecturing you. You must be able to see this is quite a strange thing to announce from nowhere."

"It's not from nowhere, I've always told you I like the name Mandy! I have **always** said to you what a stylish and fun name I think it is."

"Okay, it is stylish and fun, you're right, but the other thing to consider," I lowered my voice, "is that this might not be the best time for Dad to get his head round his wife of thirty-five years having a completely different first name."

"Don't be ridiculous, it's a very simple change," she said. "It doesn't have to be this huge thing."

"It's just going to confuse him."

"I can't talk about this now," she said. "I'm meeting Gloria for Vinyasa Flow."

"Are you not eating with us? I've come all the way here for lunch."

"There's loads of food in the house. You're the cook, after all. I'll be back in a few hours," she said, picking up her keys.

I went back in to see Dad, still engrossed by the paper.

"Dad?"

"Yes, Bean?" he said, turning his head round to me. I felt the glow of relief that came with him using his childhood nickname for me. Like all good childhood nicknames, it had had many nonsensical and convoluted iterations—what was once Ninabean turned into Mr. Bean, Bambeanie, Beaniebean, then finally just Bean.

"Mum's gone out so I'm going to make us some lunch in a bit. How do you feel about a frittata?"

"Frittata," he repeated. "Now what's that when it's at home?"

"It's a tarty omelette. Imagine an omelette on a night out."

He laughed. "Lovely."

"I'm just going to sort through some things upstairs first, then I'll make it. Do you maybe want a piece of toast to keep you going? Or something else?" I looked at his face and instantly regretted not making the question simpler. For the most part, he was still completely capable of making quick decisions, but occasionally I could see him get lost in potential answers and I wished I'd saved his confusion by saying "Toast, yes or no?"

"Maybe," he said, frowning slightly. "I don't know, I'll wait a bit."

"Okay, just let me know."

I dragged the three boxes into my bedroom, which hadn't changed since I moved out over a decade ago and looked like a museum replica of how teenage girls lived in the early to mid-noughties. Lilac walls, photo collages of school friends on the wardrobe and a row of frayed, greying festival wristbands hanging from my mirror that Katherine and I had collected together. I sifted through the papers on the floor, most of them marking time and plans but no feelings or relationships: wedges of Filofax pages of dentist appointments and term times from the late nineties, stacks of old newspapers containing stories that must have caught his interest. There were letters and cards that I took off the scrap heap: a garrulous postcard from his late brother, my Uncle Nick, tightly packed with complaints about the food being too oily on Paxos; a card from one of Dad's former students thanking him for his help with his Oxford application, and a photo of him beaming on graduation day outside Magdalen College. Mum was right, he didn't need these relics of mundanity, but I understood his inclination to hold on to them. I too had shoeboxes of cinema tickets from first dates with Joe and utility bills from flats I no longer lived in. I'd never known why they were important, but they were—they felt like proof of life lived, in case a time came when it was needed, like a driving licence or a passport. Perhaps Dad had always anticipated, somehow, that he should download the passing of time to papers, Filofax pages, letters and postcards, in case those files inside him ever got wiped.

Suddenly, I heard the piercing cry of the smoke alarm. I rushed downstairs, following the smell of burning. In the kitchen stood Dad, coughing over a smoking toaster, removing charcoal-edged pages of the **Observer** from its slots.

"Dad!" I shouted over the thin, shrill beep, flapping my hands to try to break up the smog. "What are you doing?"

He looked at me with a jolt, as if he had snapped out of a dream. Ribbons of smoke rose from the singed piece of folded newspaper in his hand. He gazed down at the toaster, then back up to me.

"I don't know," he said.

HE CHOSE THE PUB. This was an enormous relief. Lola had been giving me a crash course in modern dating over a series of drinks and emails since my birthday and had warned me of all the impending disappointments to expect. One of them was that men were completely incapable of choosing or even suggesting a place for a date. I found this sort of apathetic, adolescent, can't-be-arsed, useless-intern-says-he-still-doesn't-know-how-to-use-the-printer attitude an immense turn-off. Lola told me to get over it, because otherwise I'd never confirm a date and the rest of my life would be spent in a sexless semi-coma on my sofa, sending the message "Hey, you still free tomorrow? What time? What do you fancy?" back and forth on Linx to men I'd never, ever meet.

Max told me where we were going to meet within an hour of talking.

"Dive bars and old-man pubs okay?" he wrote.

"They're my favourite," I replied. "No one wants to go to them with me any more."

"Me neither."

"I feel like everyone loved them when we were students, but now they don't because they're no longer ironic."

"I think you're right," he replied. "Maybe they think we're edging too close towards being the old man to enjoy the old-man pubs."

"Maybe old-man pubs only bookend a person's drinking life. Ironically when we're teenagers, then earnestly when we're retired," I typed.

"And in between we're stuck in a hell of gastro-pubs serving £9 sausage rolls."

"Totally."

"Meet me at The Institution in Archway at seven o'clock on Thursday," he wrote. "There's a darts board, an old Irish landlord. Not a Negroni or in-dustrial light fitting in sight."

"Perfect," I wrote.

"And there's a dance floor I can throw you around on if all goes well."

I had been on Linx for three weeks, but my drink with Max was my first date. This was not through lack of trying. I had, in total, twenty-seven conversations on the go with twenty-seven different men. Which sounds like a lot, but given that I had initially spent approximately four hours of each waking day on the app, green-lighting hundreds upon thousands of men, to know just twenty-seven of them wanted to match me back seemed meagre. I asked Lola if this was normal. She said it was and informed me that her matches halved when she turned thirty, as lots of men put their preferred age limit to thirty and under. She said once she found that out, she was much more accepting of how few matches she got. For a while, she said, she combed Reddit threads for her name because she was convinced there was "a rumour" about her online that was rapidly mutating without her knowledge and was putting men off. I thought Lola's "rumour on the dark web" theory was quite a self-aggrandizing paranoia to have about yourself, but I was reminded that she also was long-convinced she would die by "assassination" and I didn't have the heart to tell her only famous people get assassinated. Normal people just get shot in the open.

For the first few days, I was totally enamoured with Linx. I fell under its enchantment. I'd cheated the system of romance—all these handsome and interesting men, just waiting for me in my pocket. For years, we'd been told finding love was like an impossible quest of endurance, timing and luck. I thought you had to go to awful pop-up events and specialist bookshops; keep your eyes peeled at weddings and on the tube; strike up conversation with other solo travellers whenever you were abroad; get out of the house four nights a week to maximize your chances. But none of those strategic man-hours were needed any more—we didn't have to put in the time like we used to. As I flicked through prospective love interests on the tube, on the bus, in the loo, I realized how time-efficient this method was. Looking for love didn't have to be factored in to my schedule in the way I'd dreaded—I could do it while watching TV.

Lola told me this was a completely normal reaction for a first-time dating app user—that the dreamy haze would plateau in a couple of weeks and then dull to a despondent ennui and ultimate deletion of the app in about three months' time. She said it worked in this cycle until you met someone. Lola had been on and off dating apps for seven years now.

She also warned me that the way the apps initially hook you in was by offering up their best produce to new users. She seemed to think there was an algorithm that determined this—the most-ticked people were offered up as bait for the new user's first month, then they leave you with the rest of the riff-raff. She said it worked because you'd wade through the bottom-dwellers indefinitely, always holding out hope that you'd find the chest of buried treasure again.

The most common type of conversation I'd had on Linx was stilted chit-chat as insubstantial and fleeting as a summer breeze. They always began with an anodyne: "Hey! How's it going?" or an emoji of a waving hand. There was a minimum of three hours' delay in their response; three days was more common. But the anticipation was never rewarded with quality of content. "Sorry, been insane at work, food writing that's cool. I work in property" was all the long silence afforded. These conversations also revolved a lot around the mention of days—**How's your day going? What does Tuesday look like? How's Thursday treated you? What are you doing this weekend?**—which didn't carry much topical relevance anyway as the day he was referring to or I was asking about was only addressed a full week later.

I had also quickly identified another, very different, type of nuisance, but a nuisance none the less. This was a type of man I labelled "pretend boyfriend man." Pretend Boyfriend Man used his profile to push an agenda of a dreamy, committed reliability. His photo selection always included an image of him holding a friend's baby or, worse, stripping wallpaper or sanding a floor with his top off. His profile included supposedly throwaway phrases such as "on the lookout for a wife" or "My dream evening? Snuggling on the sofa while watching a Sofia Coppola film." He knew exactly what he was doing and I wasn't having any of it.

Equally as useless, but earning slightly more respect from me, were the men who were unabashedly forthcoming about the fact they wanted a night of sex and nothing more. I had one of these virtual encounters early on with a bespectacled primary school teacher called Aaron who I exchanged pleasant small talk with for half an hour, before he asked if I wanted to "go on a date tonight." It was half eleven on a Tuesday. I asked him if he meant a date or whether he just wanted me to come over to his flat. "I suppose I could force a quick pint down," he replied sulkily. That was the last of mine and Aaron's dialogue.

There were a number of effete subgenres of language employed by many of the men I spoke to. "Good evening to you, m'lady—doth thou pubbeth on this sunny Saturday?" one asked. "If music be the food of love, play on, but if a food writer love both love and music—shall we go out dancing next week?" another wrote in an incomprehensible riddle that reminded me of those questions I got in my GCSE maths papers (**Shivani has ten oranges, if she gives the square root of them away, how many does she have left?**). It was a unique style of seduction that I hadn't come across before—wistful and nostalgic, meaningless and strange. Humourless and impenetrable.

Some, on the other hand, made a spectacle of their tonal plainness. "U ENGLISH??" a red-headed mechanic asked as his opening gambit. A few of the men's messages had the manner of an unedited, tedious, all-day stream of consciousness, with ramblings such as: "Hey how's it going just had a cold shower so annoying the boiler's broken!! Oh well now on my way out for coffee might get a bacon sarnie you only live once. Later going for a swim was planning on meeting my friend Charlie for a drink but he's having issues finding a dogsitter, the pub we want to go to doesn't allow dogs how's your day xx." "Fantastic profile, Nina" was the opening sentence from one man, in the manner of a headmaster handing out end-of-term reports.

And the more men I saw, the more I pieced together categories of humans that I never knew existed. There were the men who were incredibly excited about the fact they'd once been to Las Vegas. There were the guys who were obsessed with the fact they lived in London, which made me nervous that they would forgo a pub or bar for a first date and instead choose hiking up the Millennium Dome or abseiling down the Natural History Museum. I kept seeing Festival Man—a bloke who worked in IT by day, wore glitter on his face by night; who saved up all his holiday allowance to go to five festivals a year. There were the men who lived on canal boats, enjoyed fire poi, had had a taste of harem pants and looked like they wanted more. There were the hundreds of men who feigned indifference to being on Linx—some of whom said their friends had made them do it and they had no idea why they were there, as if downloading a dating app, filling in a profile with copious personal information and uploading photos of yourself was as easy to do by accident as taking the wrong turning on a motorway.

There were the men who wanted you to know they'd read and continued to read a lot of books, and not just the ones by Dan Brown—**real** ones, by Hemingway and Bukowski and Alastair Campbell. There were graphic designers—Jesus, there were so many graphic designers. Why had I only ever met a handful of graphic designers in real life and yet I had seen at least 350 of them on this dating app?

The saddest category I'd noticed was the Left-Behind Guys. They would not have been aware that they gave off any particularly melancholic personal brand, but they did. They were normally in their late thirties or early forties, with big grinning faces betrayed by their half-dead eyes. Photos showed them giving a best man's speech or reverently beholding a friend's baby during a christening. Their fatigue and longing were palpable. They came up, on average, every ten clicks, and each one broke my heart afresh each time.

The most simultaneously reassuring and unsettling discovery I made in those first few intense weeks of compulsive right- and left-clicking on Linx was just how unimaginative humans are. None of us would ever fully grasp the extent of our magnificent unoriginality—it would be too painful to process. I-like-the-outdoors-also-like-the-indoors I-love-pizza-I'm-looking-for-someone-who-can-make-me-laugh-I-just-want-someone-to-come-home-to-and-feel-wriggling-next-to-me-in-the-middle-of-the-night unoriginality. There was the evidence, in all these profiles, where who we really are and who we'd like everyone to think we are were in such unsubtle tension. How clear it suddenly was that we are all the same organs, tissue and liquids packaged up in one version of a million clichés, who all have insecurities and desires; the need to feel nurtured, important, understood and useful in one way or another. None of us are special. I don't know why we fight it so much.

Here's what I knew about Max before I met him: Max had hair that was a shade between sand and caramel and was cropped but just long enough to show its loose, messy curls. He was 6 foot 4, a full foot taller than me. His skin was surprisingly tawny for someone with fair colouring—he was tanned from being outside, which his photos made a point of declaring he did a lot. His eyes were moss green and gently sloping in a way that suggested he was benevolent and might have an elderly, incapacitated neighbour who he sometimes bought groceries for. He was thirty-seven. He lived in Clapton. He grew up in Somerset. He liked to surf. He looked good in a chunky roll-neck. He grew vegetables in an allotment near to his flat. We'd established the following shared interests, experiences and beliefs:

the Beach Boys' **Pet Sounds** was the soundtrack of our childhoods; we loved churches and hated religion; we liked to regularly swim outdoors; we agreed strawberry was the best and most underrated ice-cream flavour due to its obvious nature; Mexico, Iceland and Nepal were next on our respective travel wish lists.

I showed Lola Max's profile and she eagerly said she'd "seen him on there," which I didn't love. I had thought of these men as offerings from Mother Destiny—hand-selected possible partners, chosen especially for me ("It's not cock couture," Lola said). While speaking with pictures of my potential soul-mate, I had forgotten that hundreds and thousands of other women were assessing their prospective futures from their sofas and commutes too. Lola told me this was a classic reaction of a co-dependent monogamist who hadn't properly dated before and that if I wanted to get anywhere in dating apps, I'd have to toughen up. "It's cut-throat," she informed me. "You can't personalize this process. You've got to be in it to win it. You need to be fighting fit and stay focused. It's why it's a young man's game." She told me that Max could be something of a Linx Celebrity, which she had encountered a hand-ful of times—dastardly men who were prolific on apps thanks to their good looks and pre-packaged charm (she once discovered she and her colleague were dating the same one: all the messages from him had been copied and pasted). They wouldn't commit to anything substantial, she explained, because they wouldn't stop being single until they'd finally run out of options and they knew that women would never, ever stop right-clicking on their profile.

Max was ten minutes late. I hated lateness. Being late is a selfish habit adopted by boring people in search of a personality quirk who can't be bothered to take up an instrument. I tried reading my book, a detailed but digestible account of North Korea, but I was so nervous, my eyes kept flicking up from the page in search of Max and I couldn't absorb any of the words.

"Hello!" I finally texted him after fifteen minutes had passed. "I'm at the bar. What are you drinking?"

"Got us a table outside so I can smoke," he replied. "Pint of pale ale would be great, thank you." This slightly annoyed me, not only because he had not checked whether I smoked before planting us outside on what was quite a cold evening but because he hadn't sent me a text to let me know he was sitting outside. Was he waiting for me to do a full external recce of the site to happen upon him before our date could begin? How long had he been waiting there? I was reminded that the behaviour around dating had its own set of rules and standards, which all the participants had to seem overly relaxed about at all times. It was completely different to having a drink with a friend. How strange it would have been for Lola to have done this if we'd agreed to meet at a pub she suggested that I'd never been to before.

I ordered a gin and tonic and a pale ale and took one last glance at my face in the mirrored panel that lined the back of the bar behind the bottles. I had put on some token mascara and little else, and my fringe was on its best behaviour. I walked out to the beer garden, which was empty other than for Max, who was sitting on a bench reading a book. I wondered if he was reading it, or just pretending to read it like I was. He wore a white T-shirt, blue jeans and brown leather boots. The first thing I noticed were his very, very long legs, one of which stretched out to the side of the picnic table.

I walked towards him and he looked up and smiled at me in recognition. He glowed like an ember—his eyes shining, his beard golden brown, his skin burnished from sunbeams. His tousled hair looked like it had been washed in the sea and dishevelled by the windy afternoon. There was dirt on his boots. There was dirt on his jeans. He was as solid as a Sequoia, high as a Redwood and as broad as the prairie. He was earthly and godly; elemental and ethereal. Both not of this earth and a poster boy for it.

"Hey," he said and stood up to tower over me. His voice was low and soft; the distant rumble of thunder.

"What are you reading?" I asked. He kissed me on both cheeks and held up the cover for me to see.

"What's it about?"

"It's a story told from the perspective of a man on his deathbed looking back on his life and reflecting on what he's learnt. It's all about the passage of time, which I used to find moving and I now find terrifying."

"The passage-of-time stuff is the **worst,**" I said, sitting down and placing the drinks on the table, hoping he hadn't noticed the nervous warble in my voice. "My favourite genre of literature used to be old-person-inches-towards-death-and-thinks-about-the-past-with-epiphany. I can hardly bear it now."

"Me too," he said.

He looked older than thirty-seven in the flesh. His pictures hadn't captured the strands of grey in his hair that laced through strands of white blond, streaked by the sun. The camera also hadn't caught the creases, crinkles and lines of his skin, in which I could see cigarette smoke, late nights, sunshine, hard soap and hot water. This softened his sturdiness and made me like his face even more— I wanted to know all the pleasure and pain that had left his features rumpled. I also resented how much the visibility of his ageing seduced me—had it been worn by a woman, I might have found it haggard rather than weathered. Only a species as accommodating and nurturing as women could fetishize the frame of a sedentary middle-aged man and call it a "dad bod" or rebrand a white-haired, grumpy pensioner as a "silver fox."

He rolled a cigarette and asked if I wanted one. I told him the truth, which was that I was desperate for one, but I hadn't had a cigarette in three years since I gave up. As I spoke and he rolled, he glanced up at me from time to time in a gaze that made his irises seem all the more verdant. In the milliseconds in which he licked the edge of the tobacco paper he looked me in the eyes.

I asked him about his job. Job stuff is the first thing you talk about on Linx—it's the first thing you talk about in life. I hated talking about my job. I'd noticed that anyone who has a job that could be perceived as even vaguely glamorous (art, media, food, writing, fashion) cannot talk about their work at all without everyone thinking they're being self-important, so I've found it best to just avoid it. Also, everyone has an opinion on food, so when I tell someone what my job is, it's rare that we can then move on and talk about something else. I am normally lectured on where to get the best dim sum north of the river, or which classic French cookbook is the most reliable, or the best nuts to put in brownies (I don't need to be told this, it's chopped hazelnuts or whole blanched almonds).

I was delighted to realize that by the time Max and I asked each other about our respective jobs, we'd been talking for a week on Linx and fifteen minutes in the flesh. Max was an accountant, which I hadn't expected. He said a lot of people said that. He'd ended up accounting by accident, because he was good at maths and it's what his dad did, and he'd wanted to impress his dad. When he mentioned his dad, his words were jostled with a tone of either resentment or regret. I knew it would be a subject we returned to at some point when we were drunker and more comfortable with each other and we'd steer the conversational tone until we sounded like Oprah doing a tell-all televised interview, in which we'd take turns to be the guest.

He said he'd been in a cycle for the last ten years of accounting, saving money, then taking a large chunk of time off to travel. He loved to travel. Recently, he'd become restless. He hated the daily slog of his job and dreamt of a simpler life—teaching surfing, working on a farm, living in remoteness—but he was realistic about the fact he'd probably miss his salary. He couldn't work out which gave him greater freedom: earning enough money so he could disappear whenever he wanted, or earning no money and choosing a life of semi-permanent disappearance. He said he'd felt untethered in recent years—unsure of the sort of life that would make him happiest. He felt like he had to escape something, but he didn't know what and he didn't know where to go. I told him I thought that was the sensation commonly known as adulthood.

I told him about **Taste,** which he said he'd seen in bookshop windows. I told him about **The Tiny Kitchen** and he seemed genuinely fascinated by the concept, asking to see photos of my old studio flat where we did all the book's photography. He'd read my weekly food column once or twice and told me that he'd messed up a recipe for Canadian glazed gammon—he had friends round for lunch and they'd had to order Chinese.

He asked me if I'd like another drink, I said yes and he said: "Single or double?" I smiled and he winked. We were in this together now, two comrades on a mission.

When he went into the bar, I grinned to myself and realized I was already tipsy. When he came back from the bar, we talked about Linx, which was inevitable but somehow it felt gauche to talk about the dating app that was the very reason we were on the date. It struck me that the only event where it's appropriate to talk about the reason you're at the event is a funeral.

Max had been on Linx for six months. It was his first time on a dating app. He said he'd initially found it fun, but the hollowness of the encounters had made him feel jaded. He'd been thinking about deleting it.

"Thanks for squeezing me in before the deadline," I said.

"Yeah, but look at you," he replied. "How could

I not?" It was the first of a few disingenuous, dashed-off compliments and I adored every single one of them. I told him he was my first Linx date—we both made lots of bawdy jokes about him taking my app virginity which weren't that funny at all.

He insisted on buying the third round and when he emerged back into the beer garden, I felt a strangely historic connection to him; a sense of pride and belonging; of long pre-established togetherness with this man I'd met two hours ago. When he sat down, I wanted to touch his face, which looked like it belonged to a Viking warrior. I sat on my own hand to stop myself. As he rolled another cigarette and turned to ask someone for a lighter, I noticed the unapologetic strength of his profile, particularly the slight curvature of the bridge of his nose. I wanted to put him on a coin.

I asked for a drag of his cigarette. The act of it felt good, but it tasted horrible. I'd almost forgotten how to do it, and the smoke sat in my mouth and did nothing but feel toxic and hot. My second drag tasted better. The ritual felt shared and I loved passing something back and forth between us with adolescent excitement.

"I feel like I've corrupted you," he said. I told him not to worry as he hadn't—I was bound to have a drag of a fag at some point. He told me he'd like the opportunity to corrupt me, if that was okay. I laughed in a knowing way.

He went back in to order us another round. We talked about our plans for the upcoming weekend— he was getting out of London, as he nearly always did, this time by himself to camp in Sussex. I asked how he was getting there and he said he was taking his beloved car, which was a red 1938 MG TA named Bruce. I couldn't believe that was his car, and told him the personality hybrid of accountant who drives a classic sports car, wears muddy jeans and swims in lakes at the weekend was almost incomprehensible. He said, "But those are the best things about a person—the contradictions," with a faraway look in his eyes. I knew that very second that if I ever had a reason to hate Max, if he ever treated me badly, I would return to this sentence as proof that he was the worst person alive. But for now, I was able to nod dreamily and agree.

"Are you cold?" he asked. I was, and I wanted another drink, so we went back into the pub. A muttering old man wearing two hats (flat caps, one on top of the other) and drinking Guinness on his own started talking to us. He talked a lot about the gentrification of Archway and how he could barely recognize his road any more because of all the blocks of new-build flats. We both listened patiently, nodded along and said things like "Shocking, isn't it?" Max bought him a pint, which I saw as an act of goodwill but also a definite full stop to our interaction with him. But he was having none of it. He shuffled his bar stool closer to us and relayed a protracted personal history of all the local MPs that had governed the constituency over the course of his lifetime. I was keen to end the conversation, and I could sense Max was too, but we were both proving a point to each other about how down to earth we were. We asked questions we didn't want to know the answers to and feigned total absorption in his twenty-five-minute description of a particular pub in Kentish Town that he used to drink in that was now closed. We did it because we wanted to earn each other's admiration and trust: **Look how kind I am, look how curious I am. I care about local business and local libraries and the welfare of the elderly.**

As Geoff (his name was Geoff) launched into a detailed account of where the old post office used to be on Highgate Hill, I felt Max's hand on my waist. At first, I thought this was just a signal that he too wanted this rambling monologue from Geoff to cease. But then his fingers reached underneath the fabric of my top and he slowly and lightly doodled on my bare skin. He did it all without looking at me. Just a few centimetres of flesh, only for a few minutes, then he retrieved his hand to roll another cigarette. Why was that always the most exciting bit? I knew, at some point, I would be naked with this man, our bodies interlocked. That my legs would be wrapped round his waist, or over his shoulders, or that my face would be burying itself into a pillow with the force of him behind me. And yet—I knew this physical sensation was the greatest one he'd ever be able to give me. The sexiest, most exciting, romantic, explosive feeling in the world is a matter of a few centimetres of skin being stroked for the first time in a public place. The first confirmation of desire. The first indication of intimacy. You only get that feeling with a person once.

We went outside to share another cigarette and we talked, through guilty laughter, about Geoff. He took off his denim jacket and draped it around my shoulders because I was cold. I could tell he was just as cold as I was, but I didn't want to stop his big show of masculinity. How could I? I'd bought front-row tickets to it. I wondered how much of his behaviour this evening had been dictated by a pressure to perform his gender in such a demonstrative way. But then again, what was I doing? Why was I wearing a pair of four-inch heels that gave me blisters? Why was I laughing knowingly twice as much as I normally do and making half the amount of jokes?

I went to the loo, rearranged my fringe and texted Lola: "I'm on the best date of my life. Don't text me back because he might see your reply. Love you."

When I returned to him in the bar, he'd ordered us another round and a shot of tequila each.

"The music sounds so good," I said as I watched drunken students descend into the basement club, Martha and the Vandellas wailing loudly beneath us.

"It is, they play the best songs."

"Shall we dance?" I asked and realized how stiff I sounded.

"Let's dance," he replied.

We paid one pound each for entry and our hands were stamped with the words THE INSTITUTION in black ink. Initially, I felt self-conscious on the dance floor. Watching how we moved our bodies felt like an audition for the inevitable. I never used to feel anything but total liberation when dancing, but something had changed recently. I was at a wedding of a university friend a few months ago when "Love Machine" by Girls Aloud came on, and all of us rushed to the dance floor. When I looked around the circle of women, the women I'd been dancing with since I was a teenager, I suddenly saw us as completely different people. Lola in her strapless jumpsuit, using a glass of prosecco as a microphone. Meera moving her hips rhythmically around her clutch bag on the floor. We didn't look free or wild or mysterious, we looked like pissed-up thirty-something women pointing at each other to the beat of the music we grew up with that would now be played at a nostalgia club night.

But the mix of gin, tequila and lust loosened me up enough to shimmy off my inhibitions. We danced for about an hour—sometimes comically, away from each other, with over-the-top moves. Sometimes campily, with Max twirling, spinning and dipping me, much to the chagrin of other revellers on the tightly packed dance floor. Then I heard it. The percussion of George Michael's bassy **donk donk donk donk** and finger clicks.

"THIS SONG!" I shouted.

"SO GOOD!" he replied.

"IT WAS NUMBER ONE THE DAY I WAS BORN!"

"WHAT?"

"IT WAS NUMBER ONE THE DAY I WAS BORN!" I repeated. "IT'S WHY MY MIDDLE NAME IS GEORGE."

"NO!" he bellowed, his eyes wide in disbelief.

"YES!" I shouted.

"I LOVE THAT!" he shouted back, grabbing me by the waist and pulling me into him. His T-shirt was damp with sweat and he smelt like the warm earth as the air rises after a summer storm. "FUCKING WEIRDO." He craned his head down towards me in a smile and we kissed. I draped my arms around his neck and he pulled me closer to him, lifting me off the ground.

We left the pub in search of a chippie. As we walked down Archway Road, we were side by side and he moved me so he was standing on the outside of the pavement. I was reminded of how annoyingly delicious these patronizing traditions of heteronormativity could be. Of course, the rational part of my brain wanted to tell him that he was no more capable of receiving the oncoming blow of a crashing car than I was, and his act of supposed

chivalry made no sense. But I liked him standing on the outside of the pavement. I liked feeling like I was a precious and valuable thing to be
guarded, like a diamond necklace in transit with a
security guard. Why was a sprinkling of the patriarchy so good when it came to dating? I resented
it. It was like good sea salt—just a tiny dash could
really bring out the flavour of the date and it was so
often delectable.

In the kebab shop, we ordered chips and we
drowned our polystyrene containers in burger
sauce. We established that we both suffered from
condiment anxiety—a fear that the sauce will run
out on the walk home. We found a bench, finished
our chips, then we kissed some more. The kissing
was rigorous and exhaustive—we encompassed
every teenage tradition in our medley. There was
neck-kissing and dry-humping and ear-nibbling.
There were all the things we used to do to make just
one thing—kissing—as exciting as possible, before
the act of sex distracted us all.

"Your neck smells of bonfire," I said, nuzzling
into it.

"Does it?"

"Yeah, it smells of burning leaves. I love it."

"I built a bonfire a couple of days ago, I must have
been wearing these clothes," he said.

"No you didn't."

"I did, near the allotment."

"Shut up," I said, before kissing him some more.

We walked back up to the pub, now dark and locked up, and he stood by his bicycle, which was chained on the railing outside. He asked how I was getting back (bus) and told me to text him when I got home (another **delicious** patriarchy seasoning).

He unchained his bike, then turned to face me. "I've had a lovely night, Nina," he said, and held my face in his hands as if it were as unexpected as a pearl in an oyster. "And I'm certain I'm going to marry you."

He declared it quite plainly and without a note of sarcasm or comic hyperbole. He hoisted his bag over his shoulder and mounted his bicycle. "Bye." He pushed off the pavement and cycled away.

And do you know, for about five minutes as I walked to the bus stop—I believed him.

3

IF THERE'S ONE VISIBLE warning sign that a friendship has become faulty, it's the point when you realize you only ever want to go to the cinema with them. And not dinner and the cinema— I mean meeting outside the Leicester Square Odeon ten minutes before a specifically late showing of a film, then having a "quick catch-up" during the trailers and an excuse to leave as soon as it's over because all the pubs are about to close. It is the platonic version of no longer wanting to have sex with your long-term boyfriend. It is the lingering, looming sense that something is no longer working, pervaded by a reluctance to fix it. I had started, for the first time in over twenty years of friendship, longing to only meet Katherine at the cinema ten minutes before a late film began.

But I couldn't, because Katherine had a toddler and I'd found that trying to get her out of the house was always more of an effort than sitting on the Northern Line for an hour to get to her place near Tooting Broadway. And neutral ground seemed to have become an intimidating place for her—she used every environment as a way of justifying and defending her life to me, when I had never asked for justification nor defence. When she came to my flat, she'd make comments on how she couldn't own half the things I owned because Olive would break them, as if a set of mismatched whisky tumblers off eBay made my dingy flat a boutique hotel. When we went out for dinner, she'd talk about how she never got to go out for dinner any more and empha-size what a treat it was for her, no longer making it feel like a treat for me. And when we met up for a drink, she'd talk about her "former life" of "drink-ing" that felt like a "distant memory" as if she were a recovering addict giving an educational talk in schools, rather than a woman who worked in re-cruitment and enjoyed two-for-one Mojito night at her local.

I walked to the Cotswold green-grey door and rang the bell. Katherine answered, and the smell of used coffee machine pods and an expensive woody candle smell I could instantly and depressingly identify as "fig leaf" wafted out.

"Thank you so much for coming, my darling!" she said into my hair as we hugged. "This must be so much earlier than you normally wake up on a Saturday. Really appreciate you coming all this way at the crack of dawn."

"It's ten a.m., mate," I said, taking off my denim jacket and hanging it up on a hallway hook.

"No, I know!" she said. "All I meant was, if I didn't have to wake up so ridiculously early for Olive, I would sleep in every day."

"There's the small matter of my job, though," I said pedantically. Why couldn't I just let it go? Why couldn't I let her think my childless life allowed me to rise at noon and lie in a warm bath of milk and honey all day while being fanned with dodo feathers?

"Yes, yes, of course!" she laughed. I had been in her hallway for less than a minute and was already thinking about the dark, cosy silence of sitting side by side in the cinema for two hours.

We exchanged small talk about the intensity of this August's heat while she made us coffee, then went into the living room. The components of Katherine's interiors made up a completed game of middle-class-London-zone-three bingo, but I always loved being there. There was something so reassuring about all the strategically placed low-light lamps and the deep, squishy sofa and the creamy-beige colour palette as easy to digest as a plate of mashed potato or fish fingers. Instead of prints and posters there were photos that charted every step of their relationship: Katherine and Mark when they first started dating, drinking plastic pints of cider at a London day festival. The two of them on the steps of their first rented flat together. Their wedding, their honeymoon, the day Olive was born. There were hardly any photos in my flat. I wondered if this breadcrumb trail of a couple's history became important when they had a child—a way of tracing back who they were before they became co-wipers of a face and arse. The reassuring evidence was always there on their mantelpiece.

"Olive, what's nursery like?" I asked her. I had picked up some miniature chocolate cakes from a bakery on the way over, and she was already cresting a sugar high. One of my favourite things about my goddaughter was how utterly obsessed she was with food—it made it very easy to make her love me.

"Olive," Katherine said brightly and loudly. "Tell Aunty Neenaw about nursery." Olive continued to ignore us both, her fingers jabbing into the cakes with a smile on her face, while she chewed the first two she had stuffed in her mouth before the plate had even reached the coffee table. Katherine sighed. "Are you going to tell her about your friends?"

"How old are you now, Olive?" I asked, bending closer towards the apple rounds of her cheeks in profile. She turned her face to me—the same alabaster skin as her mother was smeared with brown buttercream.

"Chocklit cake," she said slowly and surely, like a child about to undergo an exorcism in a horror film.

"Yes," I said. "And how is nursery?"

"Chocklit. Cake," she repeated.

"Okay and what's your favourite colour?"

She turned away from me, already bored by this game, and picked up another miniature sponge, stroking it like a pet hamster.

"Chocklitcake."

"Imagine if happiness was as easy in adulthood," I said, sitting back up on the sofa. "Imagine if that level of divine contentment were that accessible to us."

"I know."

"It must be good to know you can completely control another human with sugar. Enjoy this phase because as soon as she's a teenager, it will be money."

"It's bad, though," Katherine said, tucking her bare feet underneath her impossibly long legs and blowing on the steaming mug. "I've started using cakes and biscuits as a way to buy some conversational time with my friends when they come over. It keeps her distracted, but I don't think it's proper parenting."

"Every parent does it."

"Yes, and I actually think we're much better than most," she said briskly, the tireless performance of perfect motherhood resuming after a sentence-long interval of humility. I took a long glug of my coffee.

"How are you?" I asked.

"I'm good, I have some news actually," she said, leaving a dramatic pause. "I'm pregnant."

I feigned total surprise—squealing sounds, face agog, put my cup down, the lot. "When is it due?"

"March."

"How exciting."

"You're going to have a little brother or sister, aren't you, Olive?" Katherine said.

"Ice cream," Olive replied flatly.

"No, no ice cream," Katherine sighed.

"Cake!" I said, picking one up and waving it under her face. "Look, yummy yummy cake. Have you told work?"

"Not yet. I've actually decided not to go back after I have the baby and take my mat leave pay, so I'm going to have to play it all very delicately."

"Oh, wow," I said. "That's great. Are you looking for other jobs?"

"No, we're actually thinking of moving out of London." There was a brief silence as I quickly replayed all the conversations we'd had over the last year to remember if she'd ever mentioned this before. "Which will give me a chance to properly think about what it is I want to do once I have both kids."

"Really?"

"Yeah, we've been talking about it a lot—Olive,

don't eat the cake casings, honey, that won't taste good." She reached over and pulled one out of Olive's grimacing mouth. "And we could get somewhere bigger while reducing our mortgage and the kids could have a proper childhood."

"We grew up in London, do you not think we had a proper childhood?"

"We grew up in the very furthest edges of the suburbs, which is barely London."

"We've discussed this—if there are red buses, then it's London."

"There was a man outside Tooting Broadway station the other day selling blocks of hash before midday. Olive tried to grab one because she thought it was a biscuit."

"BISSKIT!" Olive suddenly shouted, Lazarus returning from her sugar coma.

"No biscuits, you've just eaten four chocolate cakes."

"Bisskit, Mummy, **please,**" she said, her squeaky little voice and rosebud mouth beginning to wobble.

"No," Katherine replied. Olive marched into the middle of the living room and threw herself on the floor like a grieving Italian. "MAMA, PLEASE!" she wailed. "NEENAW, PLEASE, BISSKIT. BISSKIT. **PLEASE.**" She began to cry.

Katherine stood up. "It's just never-ending," she said. She returned a few seconds later with a custard cream. Olive's sobbing ceased instantly.

"Where would you move to?"

"Surrey, I think, near Mark's parents."

I nodded.

"What?" she asked.

"Nothing."

"I know you have all those opinions about Surrey."

"I don't."

"Yes you do."

"Do you know anyone who lives there?" I asked. "Apart from Mark's parents."

"We do, actually—do you remember Ned, Mark's best friend from school, and his wife, Anna?"

"Yes, I met her at your birthday last year and she spoke exclusively about her kitchen extension."

"So they're in a village not too far from Guildford, and she says there are lots of mummy friends around there who she'd happily introduce me to."

**Mummy friends.**

"Okay, that's great," I said. "I just don't want you to be lonely."

"I'll hardly have a chance to get lonely, London is a half-hour train journey away. It would take me as long to get into central London as it would you, probably."

"That's true," I said. I didn't think it was true at all, but I was familiar with this defensive heat in her voice and I was keen to throw a bucket of ice on it. "And we'll always have the phone."

"Exactly," she said, playing with Olive's dark, soft tendrils of hair. "This all began on the phone."

"Do you remember what we even talked about? I

still don't understand how we could have spent all day at school together, then two hours on the phone every night of the week for seven years."

"That bloody landline. It's all me and my mum used to argue about. I always remember your dad coming to pick you up from mine and he'd printed out pages and pages of his BT bill. He and my mum sat at the kitchen table with two sherries trying to work out what they were going to do about it, like a meeting between two heads of state."

"I had forgotten about that."

"How is your dad?" she asked.

"He's the same."

"Has he not got any better at all?"

"It doesn't really work like that, Kat," I said, quite unfairly, because I also hoped she wouldn't ask me how it did work.

"Okay," she said, putting a hand on my arm. I was grateful for Olive, who could act as a conversational worry doll when I was with Katherine. I too started curling her soft strands of hair around my fingers. "Have you seen Joe recently?" she asked.

"No," I said. "I must see him. I assume he's still with Lucy?"

"He is."

"**She's** from Surrey."

"Is that why you don't like her?"

"No, I have at least fifteen reasons why I haven't warmed to her other than the fact she's from Surrey."

"Like what?"

"Like she once told me she finds air travel 'glamorous,'" I said. "Or that she still boasts about the fact she got her Mini Cooper custom-painted a specific shade of duck-egg blue."

"They were here for dinner last week."

This annoyed me, even though it shouldn't. Mark and Joe became friends when the four of us used to hang out and we agreed when we broke up that we were allowed to each keep our respective half of Katherine and Mark.

"How was it?"

"It was good," she said. "I like Lucy, she's very . . . creative."

"She does PR for a bubble tea company."

"Don't be snooty."

"I'm allowed to be snooty about bubble tea."

"I always thought you'd end up back with Joe."

"Did you?"

"Yes, Mark and I both did."

"Why?" I asked.

"I don't know, you just always seemed like such a good fit. And it made life so easy."

"What, you mean easy for you and Mark's social plans?" I said, sounding snappier than I meant to.

"Well, yes, sort of."

"You can invite Joe and me both round for dinner, you know. We're still really close."

"I know, but it's not the same."

"I've started seeing someone," I said reflexively.

"Have you?!" she yelped, with more surprise than I would have liked.

"Yes. Well, just one date. But he's brilliant."

"What's he called?" she asked, her pupils—I swear—dilating. I knew she'd love this—I was speaking her language now. Dates, man, love, potentially someone for me to bring round for Mark to talk about rugby and traffic with.

"Max."

"Where did you meet?"

"Through a dating app."

"I think I would have loved those apps."

"Would you?"

"Yeah," she said. "Although I do feel lucky that I never had to use them." Another fleeting moment of self-awareness. "What's he like?"

"He's tall and intense and clever and fascinating and a bit . . ." I browsed for a word I'd been looking for in the days since I met him, trying to piece together his face from my woozy, boozy memories. "Twilighty. You know?"

"No."

"There's something dark and magic about him, while being wholesome. Wholesome in an essence-of-man way. He's sort of biblical."

"Essence of man?"

"Yes, like it's all stripped back so he's just . . . instinct and hair. I can't explain it."

"Is he funny?"

"Kind of," I said unconvincingly. "Not like Joe funny. But I don't think I could be with someone Joe funny again."

"Really?"

"Yeah, it got a bit tedious all that 'Is it just me or have you noticed this weird thing about deodorant' stuff. I don't need to feel like I'm at the Royal Variety Show in my relationship any more. I'd quite like to be with someone a bit serious."

"He sounds great," she said, grinning. "When are you seeing him next?"

"I don't know, I haven't actually heard from him yet."

"You should text him," she said. "Say: I loved meeting you the other night, when shall we do it again?"

"I want to, but Lola says that's not how this works."

"Lola has never had a boyfriend."

"Yes, but she's dated a lot. You and I haven't dated at all, really."

"But isn't the point of dating to find a relationship?"

"You make it sound like a sport," I said. Katherine always made me feel like I was taking part in a competition I couldn't remember entering.

"Do you want more coffee?" she asked. I looked at my phone. I had to stay for at least another hour and a half.

Resetting the factory settings of a friendship is such a difficult thing to do. I knew it would take a long and uncomfortable conversation for us to say all we wanted to say and I couldn't think of a time it would be convenient for us both to do it. I could count at least three elephants now omnipresent in the room of our friendship from my side, and I'm sure Katherine could count at least three more of her own. I couldn't deduce how many elephants a friendship could withstand while still being able to function normally and when, if ever, they were going to stampede across us.

After exactly ninety more minutes had passed, I kissed Olive's chocolatey cheeks goodbye. I hugged Katherine, congratulated her again on the pregnancy and told her I'd love to help her look for houses in Surrey if she needed another pair of eyes, which of course I didn't mean. As I turned away, I felt the same sense of relieved satisfaction that I get when I clean my fridge or finish my tax return. I was pretty certain, from the other side of the door, I could hear Katherine have exactly the same thought about me.

When I arrived home, I knocked on the front door of the ground-floor flat for the fourth time that week. I'd missed a parcel and a piece of paper informed me it had been left with Angelo Ferretti downstairs. I'd tried to catch him when I heard he was leaving or entering the building, but somehow, I'd miss him. This time, to my surprise, the door opened after two knocks. A tall man appeared in the door frame. He had olive skin and brown hair that fell to his shoulders—which suggested a former hobby of small-warrior-figurine painting or a current hobby of weekend bass-playing in a band with some sad dads—paired with a counterproductive receding hairline. I would guess that he was a few years older than me. He wore a resting expression of incredulity.

"Oh, wow! Hello," I said, with an awkward, flustered, jolly laugh that I hated. "Sorry, I wasn't expecting you to answer. I'm Nina, I live upstairs. I moved in a couple of months ago." He blinked twice. Silence. "I tried to knock a few times when I first moved in, just to introduce myself, but we seemed to keep missing each other. Well, I seemed to keep missing you." More blinking, more silence. "Is it just you here?"

"Yes," he said, his accent sprinkling thickly over his vowels.

"Oh. Alma—she lives upstairs, she's lovely—seemed to think you had a flatmate?"

"She go," he said.

"Ah, right."

"About three months ago, she leave."

"I see."

He continued to administer silent blinks, indicating that the conversational portion of this exchange was officially over.

"I think you might have a parcel for me?"

"Yes, why they leave here?"

"Because I was out."

"But why they leave with me?"

"Because I said they could leave it with a neighbour. Is that okay? You can always leave your packages with me if you're out."

He shrugged and turned back into his flat. With his harshly carved features and lolloping, dislocated movements, he looked like an old-fashioned puppet being pulled by invisible strings. He returned and passed me the cardboard package. He had his hand on the door now—he wanted me to leave.

"So. Angelo. Is that Italian?"

"Why you know my name?"

"On the missed parcel slip," I said. "It said it was left with you. Where in Italy are you from?"

"Baldracca."

"Never been. Where is it?"

"Look it up," he said, before closing the door.

I stood in the ringing echo of the slam and hoped that was the first and last time I would ever have to have a conversation with Angelo Ferretti from downstairs. In my flat, I opened my parcel, flattened the packaging for recycling and looked up Baldracca on Google Maps. Could not be found. I typed the word into a search engine. Its translation appeared immediately. **Baldracca—Italian noun: whore (mostly used as an insult)**.

LOLA WAS WAITING FOR ME on a bench outside the gym that evening. She had booked us in to do a class called "Body Boost," which combined "weightlifting and tai chi to the soundtrack of eighties dance classics."

"Can you be bothered?" she drawled as I approached, pulling me towards her and kissing both cheeks. She was wearing a stunningly strange workout combination of leopard-print leggings, a billowing cheesecloth top, aviator sunglasses, hoop earrings that were so big they rested on her shoulders and a silk jewelled headdress that looked a bit like a turban. She was drenched in the heavy, sweet warmth of her signature oud perfume.

"Haven't you already paid for it?"

"Yeah, obviously we'll do it, but I'm just checking if you still wanted to do it."

"**You** persuaded me to come."

"I know, it's just—" She gestured at an enormous carton of cranberry juice she was swigging from in a performative fashion and rolled her eyes.

"The vet?"

"All night. And he stayed the next day. Think we shagged for twelve hours."

"Lola, that's got to be a lie."

"I wish it was," she said wearily, pulling a Twix out from her enormous tan leather handbag, which had her initials monogrammed in gold. Lola liked everything to be monogrammed, from her phone to her washbag. It's as if she was worried she would forget her own name.

"Are you going to see him again?"

"I don't think so," she said, through indelicate, hurried chomps.

"Why not?"

"He's nice, but . . . I don't know. He did a couple of things that cringed me out a bit. He's the sort of man who lies in bed after you've had sex and waits to catch your eye and says 'Hey.'"

"Oh God, that's bad."

"Unforgivable," she said. She took the final bite of the Twix and put the wrapper in the bag, before pulling out a Kit Kat and a Twirl and unwrapping them both.

"You all right?"

"Yes, why?"

"What's with all the chocolate?"

"Oh yeah, sorry. I went to a nutritionist because, you know, I sometimes get those stomach cramps after I eat? Anyway, she said the problem is, I shouldn't be eating sugar after six, so I'm just getting these in now." She glanced at her digital watch, informing her it was 5:59 p.m. "Anyway, I'm done with these men who use me for the night to make them feel like they're the star in some . . . mumble-core romcom, you know what I mean?"

"I think so." The truth was, I very rarely knew what Lola meant when she said "you know what I mean?," but I found her so entertaining, I never wanted to signal at a platform where her train of thought could stop.

I'd met Lola in the loo of a club in our university town in freshers' week. I heard a girl crying in the cubicle next to mine and when I asked her if she was okay, she wailed that she'd had sex with a boy earlier that week and asked him the next morning to text her. He said he wouldn't be able to because he had no credit on his phone and he'd run out of money. She drove him to a local cashpoint, took out twenty pounds, gave it to him to top up his phone and said she couldn't wait to hear from him. The text never arrived. I asked her to come out of the loo to talk to me, but she said that half her make-up was down her face and she was too embarrassed for anyone to see her. I told her to lie down. And there, in the crack between the cubicle wall and the purple plastic floor, I saw Lola for the first time. Her huge aquamarine eyes leaking mascara tears down her face that was as orange and downy as a peach from too much cheap foundation. I reached out and put my hand on hers. The bass of "Mr. Brightside" vibrated through the floor and on to our cheeks.

"I miss home," she said.

I didn't know anyone who was more different to me than Lola. Most noticeably, she was a pathological people-pleaser—hell-bent on making sure every single person she came into contact with not only liked her but adored her and felt sensational about themselves in her presence. And not just people she knew—she put in the same effort to woo total strangers who she would only be in contact with for a few minutes. We once went on holiday to Marrakech and when "haggling" for a vase in the medina she offered the man 250 dirhams more than he originally asked for. Another time she withdrew the last thirty pounds in her bank account on a night out, gave it to a homeless man and sat down to talk to him about his life. He, quite understandably, told me he'd give me the thirty pounds if I would take her away from him.

Sometimes I found this habit of hers slightly pathetic and frustrating; other times I had admiration for it. I was regularly envious of the patience Lola could exercise in the face of other people's inanity and incompetence. She was fantastically good at small talk; at listening to people blither about something I knew she wasn't interested in; at complimenting women on their ugly shoes at a party because she could tell they were in need of a compliment. I was often accused of being irritable or short-fused, whereas she never got angry about anything—which wasn't just down to her benevolence, she was mainly too busy either daydreaming about herself or worrying about everyone liking her. She was both the most tragically insecure and beguilingly confident person I had ever met.

And she loved fun, which was infectious. Her pursuit of new experiences was a preoccupation, and her permanent state of being single had given her the time to make an ongoing project of her own life. In the time I'd known her she'd learnt calligraphy, photography and origami; how to make her own ceramics, yogurt and essential oil blends; attended classes for martial arts, Russian and trapeze. She'd undergone five tattoos, crowbarring a fake meaning on to every fey, insignificant doodle; moved flats seven times and jumped out of a plane twice. I had come to realize this was not evidence of Lola's frivolity but was instead her tribute to what she saw as the one great opportunity of being alive.

"I'm so stressed about the summer coming to an end," she said, pulling out a half-empty packet of menthol cigarettes and withdrawing one with her teeth.

"Why 'stressed'?"

"I'm worried I haven't made the most of it."

"You've been to four music festivals."

"I've **got** to get to Burning Man next year." She shook her head worriedly as she lit up. The early evening sun bounced off every ring on each of her fingers holding the white-tipped cigarette and she inhaled deeply. "And you've got to come with me, it might be our last chance."

"No. I don't know how many times I have to tell you."

"Please."

"You burn if you want to, the lady's not for burning. Also, what do you mean it will be our 'last chance'?"

"The summer afterwards I will probably be

pregnant," she said. I'd known that would be her answer, but I wanted to hear her say it explicitly. Her illogical optimism about the exact trajectory of her life never failed to make me glow with fondness for her.

"It'll be dark at four o'clock every day soon," she said. There was no reasoning with her when she was this deep into her stupor of fun-panic I had become so familiar with. "And everyone will be in every night with their partner and children, eating stilton and broccoli soup, not wanting to hang out with me."

"You do this every year."

"It's already started happening. People don't understand what it's like to be us. No one wants to do anything any more, everyone just wants me round for dinner. Which is nice and everything, but I don't want to spend my Saturday nights on a happy couple's sofa. How am I ever going to meet anyone like that? I've never heard of anyone meeting the love of their life because they wandered through their friends' living room in Bromley."

"But you can't plan your social life around opportunities to meet men," I reasoned. "That's so grim."

"Yes, I know that, but I also would just like some of our friends to appreciate that while their search is over, mine is still on. And I have supported them every step of the way on their search. I've written them poems for their weddings—"

"Which, in fairness, I don't remember any of them ever asking for."

"I just need them to help me achieve my dreams in the same way I supported theirs."

"I don't think we ever really stop searching."

"Oh, stop it."

"It's true. I don't ever spend time with married people and think they're significantly less restless than single people."

"Nina, I'm going to tell you something that you're not going to like hearing. And loads of people think it, but everyone's too scared to say it. And it's not about feminism, and it's not about men and women, it's just a fact about life. Loads of people aren't happy until they're in a relationship. Happiness, for them, is being in a partnership. I am sadly one of those people."

"How do you know if you've never been in one though? What if you're pinning all your hopes and planning your entire life on finding this one thing and then it disappoints you?" I asked.

She stubbed out her cigarette, pulled out another one and lit it.

"And what do you mean, 'what it's like to be us'?" I asked.

"Single," she said. We passed the cigarette between us.

"Do you want to go to the pub?" I asked eventually. "I know there's one round here that does a really spicy Bloody Mary and it's full of miserable suits looking to flirt."

"Yeah, go on then, yeah," she said, before adjusting her turban.

ON OUR THIRD BOTTLE of white wine, I began to feel drunkenly maternal towards myself four hours previously, putting on a pair of leggings and trainers, truly believing I was going to spend the evening in a "Body Boost" class. Bless her.

"What happened to your man mountain, by the way?" Lola asked.

"Haven't heard from him."

"How long's it been?"

"Three days."

"DON'T cave first," she said, pointing her finger at me and focusing her bloodshot eyes on mine. One of her enormous hoop earrings was now missing.

"Is that definitely necessary? Because I just really, really want to call him."

"Look, three days of not hearing from a man is not all that bad. I've got something for the Schadenfreude Shelf," she said. The Schadenfreude Shelf was a shameful, private ritual we'd developed a few years ago, in which we collected stories of other people's misfortunes to make us feel better about our own. The idea was, we would always have a selection of relevant anecdotes for us to reach for in any given situation that would put our disasters into perspective.

"Do you remember a woman in my office called Jan?"

"Is she the one who competed in the Microsoft solitaire championships?"

"Exactly. So Jan had been with her husband for thirty years. Never wanted kids, was just the two of them. They were really happy—lived in a flat in Brixton and went on all these cruises to Iceland, listened to all sorts of jazz scat albums and had a Cavalier King Charles spaniel with one eye called Glen."

"Right."

"So Jan's out in Brockwell Park one day with Glen."

"The husband?"

"No, the **dog,**" she slurred exasperatedly. "And she sees this man, much younger than her. He's very tall, Spanish, a sort of Tony Danza type. He comes over and he's all 'cute dog' and she's like 'thanks' and then he's all 'the owner's even cuter' and bless Jan, bless her, she hasn't been chatted up since the seventies or whatever, so she's beside herself. They go for some shisha, get to know each other, he's called Jorge, he's a locksmith, he's from Girona, they exchange numbers. Long story short, they start this affair."

"Wow."

"I know."

"Who meets in a park these days?"

"Well. That's it, isn't it? So Jorge is telling her he loves her, he wants her to leave her husband, he wants the two of them to start a new life together—with Glen as well—in Cardiff."

"Why Cardiff?"

"Dunno. And she's thinking, this could be my last great chance at a great, passionate love affair. I want to feel that one more time."

"But what about her lovely husband? And the cruises to Iceland?"

"Lust," Lola said knowingly. "It makes fools of us."

"What happened?"

"She packs two bags, one for her, one for Glen."

"She did not pack a bag for Glen."

**"I SWEAR TO GOD,"** she shouted. "One of those miniature backpacks you get on the back of a teddy bear. She writes a letter to her husband explaining everything and apologizing from the bottom of her heart. Tells him she will always love him. Thanks him for the happiest years of her life. Leaves it on the table, then goes to Victoria coach station where she'd agreed to meet Jorge."

"And?"

"Jorge," she said with a deep in-breath. "Never. Showed. Up."

**"No."**

"Yes. She waited there for ten hours."

"Did she call him?"

"Went straight to voicemail."

"Went to his flat?"

"He'd disappeared."

"What did she do?"

"She went back home, tried to beg for forgiveness, explain that she'd temporarily lost her mind. But her husband wouldn't let her in."

"Oh no. Oh no no no."

"Yup. Wouldn't speak to her. He'd even changed the locks."

"And the locksmith was probably . . ."

"Jorge," she nodded. "We'll never know if they ever crossed paths. Or what was said. It's a question mark that hangs in history."

"Where's Jan now?"

"She lives on a canal boat," she said, with a funereal tone. "You'll see it sometime, next time you go for a run along the towpath. It's called **The Old Maid.** There's a painting of a one-eyed spaniel's face underneath it. And you can smell it a mile off, because she's always home-brewing kombucha, says it's the only thing that makes the nights pass faster."

"Surely," I said in horror, "surely any name but **The Old Maid**?"

"She thought it would be funny. I said, 'Jan,' I said, 'you cannot make your life a joke, you have to start again.' But she wouldn't listen. I think she's punishing herself."

"That's so awful."

"I know. The locals around her mooring call her 'The Sad-eyed Lady of the Lock.'"

"Really?"

"Probably," she said with a shrug.

"You're right," I said, clinking her glass. "That's a very, very useful addition to the Schadenfreude Shelf. Thanks, mate."

"You're welcome," she said, turning the wine bottle upside down, dribbling the last drops into our glasses. My phone, lying face up on the table, pinged. The screen illuminated with a message notification from Max. Lola's startled eyes locked with mine.

"Oh my GOD I'm going to be SICK," she bellowed. Concerned drinkers on the bench next to ours turned to look at her.

"She's fine, don't worry, she's just excited."

Lola grabbed my phone, tapping in the passcode with the familiar intimacy of two women who have spent countless nights together in a pub, showing each other messages. She stared at the screen.

"Oh fuck, it's good, it's really good."

I grabbed the phone out of her hand.

I just listened to The Edge of Heaven five times in a row and you're still not out of my system. What have you done to me, Nina George Dean?

4

I COULDN'T REALLY REMEMBER what Max looked like. My brain had grabbed hold of just four specific details of him. I had spent the week since we'd last seen each other circulating those memories around my mind like four separate plates of canapés at a party. Once I'd had enough of memory platter one, I'd take a bite from memory platter two. When I was satisfied with that, I'd switch to another one and so on and so on. Not only were these four memories just enough to satiate my daydreams, working out exactly why my memory had clung on to the specific vignettes also fascinated me.

**Memory number one.** The angles of his face

as he went in to kiss me. Particularly the strength of his nose, the hoods of his eyelids and the knowing half-smile as his mouth opened slightly right before his lips touched mine.

**Memory number two.** Very, **very** specific. There was a point in the evening when we were talking about a female TV chef, and I was saying, both quite tipsily and remorsefully, that I didn't think her recipes worked. As I was saying it, he said "Miaow!" in a fairly camp way, and half raised his hand like a paw scratching, but decided to not really commit to it when it was already aloft. I could tell that whole thing was a bit mortifying for him, and I think my brain held on to this for a very specific reason, which was to stop the version of Max I would build in my head from becoming too perfect. I needed some bumps and chinks for the sculpture my imagination would make of him. It reminded me that he was real—existing in this realm and completely within my reach.

**Memory number three.** When Max laughed, the perfect severity of his face was briefly screwed up and discarded, revealing a goofy mouth, swimming eyes and a nose that slightly crinkled at its sides like a cartoon bunny. It was the only trace of the adolescent I could see in him—everything else seemed so entirely formed. When he laughed, I was reminded that he had been a dorky boy in a classroom, a student dressed up in a Hawaiian garland and a teenager in a hoodie watching **South Park**

with a homemade bong in his hand. His laughter was, so far, my only crack of light through the door and into his vulnerability.

**Memory number four.** The feel of his white cotton T-shirt on his warm body as we danced. His T-shirt was velvety with the fuzz of someone who uses fabric softener. My suspicions of fabric softener use were confirmed when I smelt the dampness of his skin rise through his top, lifting the scent of soapy lavender with it to the air. It was the only slightly synthetic thing about him. It made me think about his domesticity, otherwise so concealed, and picture him in his flat in Clapton on his own, doing chores and sorting things out. I imagined he did his laundry on a Sunday evening, with a Dylan live album playing. I spent some time wondering if he owned a tumble dryer (ultimately decided no) and whether he bought his household items in bulk online (ultimately decided yes, and that his friends were the sort of well-meaning, awkward men who might take the piss out of him for it, exclaiming, "You got enough loo roll here, mate?!" as they opened his bathroom cupboard).

THE DAY AFTER HE MESSAGED, when I'd sobered up, I replied. I wanted to just call him, but Lola told me that was tantamount to turning up at his flat unannounced and throwing rocks at his bedroom window. I didn't understand why a messaging process was still so necessary after you'd already met—it slowed everything down to a frustrating pace. Max's texting style was quite antiquated in that he liked to address every point I had made in my last message and respond to it—he also usually left four hours between reading my message and replying to it. This meant it took three days of this staggered back and forth chit-chat about what we'd been doing over the week before we even broached the subject of when we would see each other again.

He suggested a walk and a few drinks on Hampstead Heath after work. I was nervous about walking on the Heath—it was where Mum and Dad used to take me at the weekends when we were still living in Mile End and being there could make me feel violent grasps of nostalgia unexpectedly. I thought I was in direct contact with all my memories from this time—the funfair they took me to near the Kentish Town entrance, the dinky tub of strawberry ice cream I ate on a bench outside Kenwood House, as I glanced down at a ladybird crawling up my five-year-old arm. It's so hard to trace which memories are yours and which ones you've borrowed from photo albums and family folklore and appropriated as your own. Sometimes I took a wrong turn on the Heath and ended up in woodland or a field and felt the unique disorientation that comes from involuntary memory, like I was standing in a half-finished watercolour painting of a landscape. Returning to it gave me the same satisfaction as finally remembering a word I'd been searching for, then haunted me with a sinister sense that there were important things I couldn't remember and never would. Hundreds of black holes in who I was, as bottomless as a night spent drinking tequila.

I walked to the Lido in my navy-blue linen sundress and brown leather sandals, carrying a bag of cheap white wine and overpriced olives. Had it been my way, I would have packed a whole picnic, but Lola advised me that it was best to go low-key at this stage. I hadn't realized quite how much of early-days dating was pretending to be unbothered, or busy, or not that hungry, or demonstratively "low-key" about everything. I wondered if Max felt the same pressure. I hoped this phase would be over soon so I could ask him about it.

As I approached the brick-wall entrance of the Lido, I saw his instantly recognizable shape. I scanned his face and body, to quickly remind me of the man I'd been inventing for the previous week. I'd forgotten how long his legs were, how wide his shoulders; how cartoonishly masculine his frame—like the silhouette of a superhero drawn by a child with a crayon. He was reading the same book, and he looked up from its pages with the same familiarity he had done when he saw me on our first date.

"Slow reader," he said, gesturing at the paperback as I walked towards him. We hugged, quite awkwardly, and he rubbed my back in a way that made me worry he thought of me as more of a sad friend at the pub after their football team lost, rather than a potential girlfriend.

"Oh, me too," I said. "I basically can't read a book now unless my phone is switched off and in another room."

"We're all fucked."

"I know. I remember being little and being so absorbed by a Peter Pan picture book that I hid a torch under my mattress so I could read under the covers after I'd been put to bed. I was one of those annoying little girls who just wanted to be a boy. I had my hair cut short when I was seven and I refused to grow it until I went to secondary school." He smiled, his gaze breaking away from mine and roaming inquisitively across my face, as if it were a painting in a gallery. "What?" I said, feeling the pinpricks of self-consciousness on my cheeks. I was nervous and talking too much.

"Nothing," he said. "Just the thought of seven-year-old you, with short hair, reading a book by torchlight. Makes me smile." I felt my knees unhinge.

"Shall we walk?" I asked, jarringly formal and clearly not at ease.

We walked side by side towards Parliament Hill, talking as we went, as I tried to keep up with his long-legged strides while not running out of breath. I was used to doing this with Katherine, who had been statuesque since we were teenagers and always loved pointing out on her iPhone how many fewer steps she'd taken on a walk we'd done together (all tall people are smug, whether they know it or not). Walking meant I could take him in with stealth side-eye; correcting the mistakes I'd made in my mind's composite sketch. The distraction of navigating and looking ahead was also welcome, as a daylight activity date heightened all possibility for embarrassment. One of us could trip over a stick, or get shat on by a passing pigeon, or have our crotches sniffed by an overenthusiastic labradoodle at large. Every possible decision made me self-conscious.

As we paced up Parliament Hill, we talked about the city. I told him about the few memories I have of growing up in Mile End—looking up at palms three times the size of me on Columbia Road Market on a Sunday; the pub my dad used to read the newspaper in while I was allowed to eat chips and take sips of his beer; the bike I learnt to ride around the square we lived on. He told me how confused he'd been when he first moved here in his early twenties—how he'd assumed city-living meant a flat above a Chinese restaurant in Soho or a bookshop in Bloomsbury. He was surprised when he discovered all his graduate salary gave him was a matchbox-sized room in a six-person house-share in Camberwell. He told me about the domestic eccentricities of these strangers-turned-housemates, but I found it hard to not let my mind drift to what Max must have looked like as a twenty-three-year-old arriving in London—as fresh and rosy as a Somerset apple, his belongings boxed up on a Camberwell street, a Red Hot Chili Peppers poster rolled up in his backpack.

When we reached the summit, we sat on a bench that overlooked the sprawl of London's central nervous system. Around us were a couple of groups of students drinking tinnies and being showily extroverted the way students in parks always are, and a few sets of couples who all looked like they'd met on Linx. Max and I tried to deduce at what point in their burgeoning relationship they all were. We agreed that the couple comprising a woman in a pair of large cork wedges, carrying a pearl-studded clutch bag and a man in a pair of utility shorts were definitely on date one and he'd surprised her with the location. The pair on the grass whose legs were tangled up like messy wires underneath a telly had definitely seen each other naked for the first time very recently—perhaps even the night before—and we concluded they'd bunked off work to stay in bed together all day and were taking their sexual compatibility out for a public spin. We decided the two men holding hands and grinning at the city skyline while talking about what they remembered of "life before the Shard" had the comfortable, inane-but-devoted cosiness of two people teetering on the verge of saying "I love you." I liked being a commentator and co-conspirator with Max. I could have done it all night.

We walked further north, on winding paths and through woodland scattered with sunset slices through gaps of branches. We managed to keep in step while always staying about ruler-width away from each other as we talked. I was fascinated by how he responded to nature—instinctively touching bark as he passed tree trunks and holding his face to the lethargic sunlight.

We emerged at the field beneath Kenwood House and found a patch of grass to sit on. I opened the wine and olives and we lay back on our elbows— I forgot to pack glasses, so we took turns to drink from the bottle. It was nearing mid-evening and the walkers and drinkers were disappearing. A little boy in a yellow sunhat scuttled across the field with the speed of a wind-up toy on a laminated floor.

"ORLANDO," a marching man barked behind him. "Orlando, come back here NOW." The little boy picked up pace and his grin widened, the hat flew off his head.

"Lando!" the man bellowed again, chasing the errant hat. "Lando, I mean it, stop running RIGHT NOW or there will be NO MORE MEDIA all week."

**"No more media,"** Max hissed into my ear despairingly.

"Do you think you can be a parent and not be a bad-tempered tosser?" I turned to ask him, our faces close to each other.

"No," he said.

"Look at him. He's fine. He's having fun. He's in a field. He's not running into a road. What's the problem?" We both watched Orlando, who had thrown himself on the grass and was rolling around like a hound, breathless with hysterical giggles. He definitely would not be enjoying any more "media" for the foreseeable future. "It must be so sad, watching yourself become someone who is wound up and stressed out all the time. I don't think there's any way of avoiding it."

"Not having children?"

"Yes," I said. "That's true."

"Do you want to have children?" he asked. Lola had warned me this happens when you date after thirty—she said what was never mentioned before is now usually brought up within the first month. Katherine told me to let them know before we'd even met up.

"Yes," I said. "I do."

"Me too."

"But I'm dreading it as much as I'm excited about it. I think watching my friends have babies has made me want them more and less in equal measure."

"I feel exactly the same," he said, taking rolling paper and tobacco out of his pocket.

"I remember once seeing my goddaughter, Olive, hit her mum round the face while she was having a tantrum. Full-on whacked her across the cheek, left a bruise on her cheekbone. Three minutes later, she was in the bath, holding a rubber duck to her mum's lips and saying in the sweetest voice I've ever heard: 'Mama kiss ducky.'" He laughed. "She's going to have another one. My friend, Katherine. I always think that makes the strongest case for having a kid. If it were so bad, then people wouldn't want to do it again."

"Why didn't your parents have another one?"

"I don't think my mum ever really wanted to be a mum," I said. "I think she thought she did, then she had me and realized she didn't."

"I don't believe that for a second."

"No, no, it's okay. I'm weirdly fine about it. I don't think it was anything particularly to do with me, I think I could have been anyone and she would have been disappointed. I feel sorry for her, actually. It must be terrible to have a child and then realize it's not the right decision for you. Particularly as you can't say it out loud, so it's a secret she's had to keep for all my life." Max finished rolling his cigarette and lit it. "My dad, on the other hand—I think he would have had ten if he could."

"Did that cause problems between them?"

"I don't think so. He was just happy he finally had a family. He was in his forties when he married my mum."

"Are they happy now?" he asked.

I took the cigarette from him and inhaled deeply.

"I'm smoking again and it's all your fault, Max. I

actually bought a packet last week, which I haven't done in years." He looked at me expectantly. "It's complicated," I relented. "My dad's ill."

"I'm so sorry," he said. I took another drag and shook my head as if to tell him not to worry. He knew that what I meant was not to ask me anything more.

At the end of the bottle of wine, he pulled another out of his satchel. He stretched out on the ground and I lay beside him, watching the sky darken.

"What's Linx like?" I asked.

"You know what it's like."

"No, I mean, for you. What are the women like?"

"Oh." His fingertips reached out to my hand and the warm palm held mine firmly. "They're all different."

"Well, obviously, but you must have noticed some patterns. I won't think you're being sexist, I promise. I'm genuinely curious."

"Okay, well"—he stretched his arm out and scooped me into him, so I rested on his chest—"I've noticed there's this big thing for gin. They all say they love gin."

"Interesting," I said. "I've noticed women using gin as a personality replacement before. There's an implied sophistication with gin. A woman who is of another time."

"Yes, they're usually the ones whose photos are all in black and white." The depth of his voice reverberated through him and hummed on to my cheek.

"Do you know what the personality replacement is for men?"

"What?"

"Pizza."

"Really?"

"Yes, they all think pizza is way more of a lifestyle choice than it is. Every other Linx profile includes a reference to pizza. 'How do you like to spend your Sundays?' **Pizza.** 'What is your ideal first date?' **Pizza.** The other day, I saw a man put his current location as **Pizza.**"

"What else?" he asked.

"They all say they love napping. I don't know why. I don't know who told all these grown men that what women really love are giant pizza-guzzling babies who need sleep all the time."

"Heterosexual women should be decorated like war heroes just for loving us," he said with a sigh, his fingers gently separating the strands of my hair. "I don't know how you all do it."

"I know, bless us," I said. "We're really putting our shifts in and it's such a thankless job."

He turned on his side so we were face to face and kissed me, soft and tentative, then pulled me closer towards him by my waist.

"I can't stop thinking about you," he said. "I think about this curve where your neck meets your shoulder. And the shape of your mouth. And the backs of your arms. That's next-level fancying, isn't it? Wanting to kiss the backs of someone's arms."

"Top-tier fancying," I said indifferently, deciding not to tell him about the platters of memory canapés or how I'd imagined him at home doing his laundry.

"The last girl whose arms I remember wanting to kiss the backs of was Gabby Lewis. She sat in front of me in chemistry. She had a ponytail that swung every time she turned from side to side. Which she did a lot. I think she did it on purpose actually, I think she knew it drove me crazy."

"You sound like an incel."

"She had these perfect arms, like yours. And I used to stare at them, counting every freckle. I actually blame her for my D, I was predicted a C."

"I think that's adorable."

"Bit creepy?"

"It would be creepy if I didn't find you so hot. The rules of attraction are so unfair."

"I was very much not hot."

"Come on."

"I wasn't, honestly. I was a huge hairy teenager with no friends. I played chess with my grandpa after school every day. He was the only person who wanted to hang out with me."

"So that's why I like you so much. Accidentally hot people. They're the best."

"What were you like as a teenager?"

"I was nearly exactly the same as I am now."

"Really?"

"Yes, it's so boring. Same height, same face, same

body, same hair, same interests. My level of attractiveness was fixed at thirteen and has never really gone up or down."

"I've never met anyone who's said that before."

"Can I tell you my theory?"

"Go on."

"I know it's much more compelling to have a story of transformation. But I think having twenty years to get used to how you look is no bad thing. I think about the way I look much less than my friends who are still striving to be beautiful, waiting for the final stage of their transition."

"You are beautiful."

"I'm not saying it to be modest. I don't think I'm unattractive. But I have never and will never be a great beauty. And it's freed up a lot of energy to be other things. Also," I said, then paused for a short while to wonder if I was talking too much. "I think that's why I've been doing quite well on Linx so far."

"Why?"

"I think men are all so insecure that too much beauty overwhelms them. I think they probably see a profile like mine—sweet face, very unremarkable hair, sense of humour—and they feel like they're home." Max laughed loudly, tipping his head back into the grass. "You know what I mean though, don't you?"

"I suppose you do have a . . . welcoming quality, but not for the reasons you think you do."

"I'm like a service station on a motorway. They

know they can stop in for a cup of tea and a cheese sandwich. They know what they're getting with me. It's familiar. Men like what's familiar. They don't think they do, but they do."

When we'd finished the bottle, we walked back towards Archway through the cool, dark summer sunset. We stopped at the gates of the Ladies' Pond and peered in, along the dirt path. The black silhouette of delicate branches spread across the indigo sky like a chinoiserie plate.

"I wish I could take you in to see it. We could break in, I suppose." I said it weakly because I am not and never have been a rule-breaker.

"No, no," he replied. "You'll just have to describe it to me."

"So, that"—I gestured to the left—"is where everyone leaves their bikes. Further down this path on the right there is a patch of grass everyone calls the meadow. That's the bit that feels like a scene from a Greek myth. It's magical in the summer. A carpet of half-naked women languorously drinking tins of G&T. Then further down on the right, there's the pond."

"How deep is it?"

"Really deep—you can't see or feel the bottom. And it's always cold, even in the summer. But lots of women pretend it isn't. In the spring, the ducklings are tiny and they swim alongside you. We swam here in the spring on Katherine's hen do. And on solstice last year, my friend Lola made me come here at the crack of dawn and do a ceremony."

"Is she a pagan?"

"No, just neurotic," I said. "It's my favourite place in London. If I ever have a daughter, I'm taking her here every week as an education on women's bodies and strength."

"See—this is why we're so frightened of all of you."

"Are you frightened of us?"

"Of course we are. That's why we've always tried to keep you quiet and lock you up and bind your feet and take away all of your power. It's because we were so scared of what would happen if you were as free as we were. It's pitiful."

"What's there to be frightened of?"

"All of it. You can communicate and synchronize with each other in a way men never will be able to. You have tides within your own body. You're nurturing and magical and supernatural and sci-fi. And all we can do is . . . jizz on our own stomachs and hit each other."

"And make small talk in car parks."

"But barely, though."

"And change fuses."

"I can't even do that."

**"Girl,"** I whispered, my face closing in on his.

"I fucking **wish,**" he said, pushing me against the railings and kissing me. The wet, weedy smell of earth and wild water drifted out towards us—the English scent of Special Brew cans floating on canals and lily pads floating on lakes.

We walked hand in hand all the way home, which I hadn't done since Joe and I were students. I had been transported back to a time of promise and pleasure. I was a teenager again, but with self-esteem and a salary and no curfew. I had discovered a second type of life that could happen with Max—a life that could run parallel to the everyday one with the ill dad and the disintegrating friendships and the monthly mortgage payments. I thought about reality—the sciatica I'd developed the year previously, the physiotherapy I couldn't afford, the black damp in between my shower tiles that no amount of scrubbing could remove, all those news stories I'd never fully understand, all those local elections I never voted in, the incessant emails from my accountant that always began with: "Nina—you appear to be confused." As I felt the warmth of Max travel up into me through our hands, I felt like I was uncontactable. Reality could try as hard as it liked—it could text, email and call me—when I was with Max, it wouldn't be able to get in touch.

He walked me into my building, up the stairs and stood in the communal corridor with its stained petal-pink carpet, peeling wallpaper and dirty yellow light from the bare overhead bulb. I didn't know whether it was an act of chivalry or seduction—or

maybe both those motives hoped for the same out-
come. I leant against the frame of my front door.

"I am obviously desperate to invite you in," I said.

"You don't have to."

"I just think, maybe, you know. We should be
grown up. Wait." This was only partly true—I also
knew there was a pile of laundry on my bed. And
possibly some gusset-side-up knickers in the bathroom. There was no milk in the fridge for tea in
the morning. And most probably a tab open on a
search like: **How many hairs on nipple normal
for woman 32??**

"We've got time."

"How are you getting home?" I asked.

"Bus." Silence hung between us. "Goodnight," he
finally said.

"Goodnight," I replied. He leant down and placed
his mouth against my bare shoulder, then kissed
along the back of my right arm to my wrist. He
held me by my hips as he pulled himself round to
the other side of my body and slowly kissed along
the back of my left arm, as if taking its measure-
ment with his mouth. My skin felt as thin and
transparent as cling-film and I was sure he could see
the insides of me. He turned to leave and I instinctively pulled him back by his hand. He pushed me
up against my hallway wall and kissed me like I was
the only thing that could satiate him.

Only now do I realize that the first night I spent

with Max, I was looking for evidence of past lovers. I wanted him inside me so I could search for the ghosts inside him. In the absence of any context for who he was, I was gathering forensics from the inerasable fingerprints that had been left by those who had handled him. When he pressed his palm over my mouth, I could see the woman who fucked him to feel freedom in disappearance. When he held a handful of my flesh in his hands, I could tell he'd loved a body more yielding than mine. His lips running along the arches of my feet let me know he had worshipped a woman in her entirety— that he had loved the bones of her toes as much as the brackets of her hips; that he had known her blood on his skin as well as he'd known her perfume on his sheets. He held me like a hot-water bottle when he slept and I knew that night after night after night he had shared a bed with another body and together they'd constructed an oasis from just a mattress.

In the morning, he woke up early for work. He didn't shower, because he said he wanted to wear me like aftershave. He kissed me goodbye, stood up and left. As I groggily stretched across my sheet— filthy and feline—I heard him walk along the corridor and close the heavy front door to the building. But I could still feel him there—invisibly surrounding me like water vapour. Max arrived at my flat that night and he didn't leave for a long time.

## 5

WE MOVED THROUGH the milestones of the following month with a new, easier pace. We stopped sending each other measured texts that needed to be analysed and annotated, Lola acting as my CliffsNotes, and we started calling each other instead. The communication between us became regular—an on-off week-by-week conversation in which we knew what the other one was doing and checked in on how we were. We saw each other three or four times a week. We kissed on the back-row seats of the cinema. We learnt how we both liked our tea. I met him at work for his lunch break and we ate ham and piccalilli sandwiches in the park by his office. We walked round an exhibition, and I took in nothing of the art but instead marvelled at the spectacle of what it was to hold hands in broad daylight. I saw his flat—mostly white, mostly tidy and completely lived-in, with faded, frayed rugs from travels, stacks of records on the floor and towers of paperbacks on every surface. There were comedy mugs in his cupboards from well-meaning but estranged aunts, given as Christmas presents. There were piles of shabby equipment for adventuring—walking boots, wetsuits and helmets. There was just one photo in his entire flat—a close-up black-and-white image of a smiling, closed-eyed man with his nose leaning in to smell the head of a little, white-haired boy. I asked about him only once, then never mentioned it again. Max and I edged around our respective locked rooms marked "dad" and we both understood how important that was, without ever acknowledging it.

At night and first thing every morning, we journeyed through the new lands of each other's bodies, marking our territory wherever we went. We colonized each other and I always left Max knowing exactly where he'd been for days afterwards—where he'd kissed and pinched and bitten. I couldn't ever imagine getting to the end of him.

I sat in the reception of my publisher's office and pressed the barely visible bruise he'd left a few nights before on my right wrist as he had held me down. It had turned light yellow, like a piece of gold jewellery. I gazed at the books on the shelves that lined the Soho townhouse that the company occupied as its office, the hundreds of books they'd published, and spotted **Taste**'s sage-green spine. I felt the same sense of belonging I'd felt since I came in for my first meeting with my editor, Vivien—a feeling of security that I knew was naive. I was the publisher's product, not their child, and the fate of products was even more unpredictable than children.

"Nina?" a scratchy, lethargic male voice called. I turned round to see a slouchy man in his early twenties with an ironic mop-top haircut died copper orange, wearing a short-sleeved Hawaiian shirt tucked into tracksuit bottoms and a pair of sliders. His lids hung heavy over his eyes like a pair of half-drawn venetian blinds.

"Yes. Hello," I replied.

"You here to see Vivien?" he asked. I could see the chewing gum roll around his mouth like a ball in a lottery draw machine.

"Yes."

"Come this way," he said, jerking his head to beckon me. He barely picked up his feet and shuffled towards the lift like his shoes were cardboard boxes.

Vivien was sitting in a glass-fronted meeting room, her shoulders rounded and her head lowered intently towards a piece of paper. She had a shoulder-length, messy-fringed shaggy blonde haircut that implied a former life of lots of parties. The sort of hair that suits a woman of her age, but also would look completely appropriate on an iconic ageing male rock star. She was in her mid-fifties, which you could see in the gentle sag and folds of her face and the milky blue of her irises, but she had the energy of the most powerful and popular girl at school. She was decisive, exacting, confident and mischievous. She liked scandal, gossip and salaciousness. She orbited in high glamour—well connected, well versed in style and taste—while being decidedly unglamorous herself, which made her all the more intriguing. She was bookish and bespectacled, always in black trousers and an androgynously cut simple shirt, no matter where she went. Her glasses were square and cartoonishly thick-rimmed, her earrings were always large and geometric—you could tell that all her accessories were chosen on account of being "funky."

But the most compelling thing about Vivien was the spell of guruism she cast on whoever she met while being unaware of her own addictive didacticism. She would utter throwaway thoughts that would become fundamental truth to whoever heard them. She once told me to "always order turbot, if turbot is on the menu" (I always order turbot) and that "all scents are tacky other than rose" (I have since only worn rose perfume). I had never met a woman surer of her own thoughts and instincts, and it was an invigorating thing to behold.

Vivien stood up when I entered the meeting room and gave me a kiss on both cheeks.

"Nina the Brilliant," she said in her deep voice of full vowels and sharp consonants, as she gripped me firmly by the shoulders. "So much to talk about. Now, Lewis," she said formally, turning to the man who accompanied me, "I'm going to have to ask you to listen very carefully. We would like two coffees, please, from the shop downstairs not from the ghastly machine here. Nina likes a flat white, not skinny, I like a double espresso, no milk. Can you remember that?"

"So just, like, black coffee?" he said, leaning against the door frame.

"Well, yes, but don't say a black coffee because otherwise they will give me something completely different to what I'd like. And get one for yourself."

"I've actually given up caffeine, I've read it's the silent killer—"

"All right, Lewis, thank you," she said briskly, before turning to face me with a weary smile. The door closed and he sloped off. "I've only ever hired earnest girls with bobs and lots of canvas book bags who love Sylvia Plath, so I thought I'd try something different for an assistant this time."

"Is he good?"

"Disaster." An earnest-looking girl with a bob and leather brogues tapped on the glass door. Vivien turned to her. "Yes?" The girl stepped in, nervously tucking her hair behind her ears.

"Vivien, I'm so sorry, no one was actually allowed to book this meeting room for the next three hours."

"Why not?" she asked.

"Because every employee in the building has been asked to go to the 'Take the Stairs Week' talk."

"What is a 'Take the Stairs Week' talk?"

"It's a government initiative that we're backing. We're encouraging people to take the stairs rather than the lifts to improve cardiovascular health." Vivien looked at her blankly, awaiting further explanation. "And we have someone here telling us all about it."

"Out of the question," she replied plainly, turning back to me. The girl hovered in the doorway for a few moments, then took her cue to leave. "You wouldn't believe some of the guff they make us do here. I am convinced it's what finally drove dear old Malcolm away. Our best designer."

"Oh no, has he gone for good?"

"Yes, he's had a breakdown. He's sold his house to go live in Belgium. But I've always thought Belgium would be a rather splendid place to go mad in, so good for him." Another phrase I knew I would adopt as my own. One day, someone would tell me about Belgium and I would say confidently: **a splendid place to go mad in.**

"So. **The Tiny Kitchen.** The campaign is coming together nicely, we're sending all the information to you in an email this week."

"Brilliant," I said.

"And **Taste** continues to sell, your numbers were up last month, which is fantastic."

"I just really hope this book isn't a disappointment for anyone who liked **Taste.**"

"No, no," she said, flapping her hand dismissively. "It's your voice, which is exactly the same voice from the first book, tackling a very common issue for a lot of households, which is entertaining and cooking and storing food with no space. It's a winner."

"I hope so," I said.

"I know so," she said, nodding reassuringly. "Now. The not-so-fun news."

"Go on."

"Book three. I read the proposal over the weekend."

"You didn't like it."

"I'm afraid to say I didn't."

I was grateful for Vivien's straightforwardness. I couldn't bear the pandering language of feedback in publishing and journalism. It had taken me years to work out that when a magazine editor says "lots to love here" they nearly always meant "very little we can do with this." Mine and Vivien's working relationship was efficient, thanks to our honesty.

"Go on," I said.

"Boring. Unengaging."

"Okay."

"And just rather . . ." She searched for the right word. "Fussy. Who wants to check all their ingredients against a calendar? It's a hobby of someone with too much time or money on their hands."

"I was thinking of giving it more of a home-grown angle. How to source all your food from your country by keeping in sync with the seasons."

"Bit UKIP."

"Is it?"

She flared her nostrils in disdain. "Bit."

"So seasonal is out?"

"I think so. I think we need to go back to the start and think of a new theme."

I was disappointed—the research and writing of the proposal had taken over a month. I took out my notebook to write meaningless words on that I'd never return to, as a gesture of enthusiasm.

"What are you thinking?"

"Well, quite unhelpfully, I don't have anything specific in mind yet. I just know your readers want something personal. Something passionate."

"I don't know if I can do much more public catharsis after writing about my life in **Taste,** Viv."

"No, no more ghastly catharsis. We just want something human."

"Human. Okay."

"Have a think. Have some conversations. Live some life, then come back to me."

**Live some life,** I wrote down at the top of the page and underlined it twice.

"I will."

"What else are you working on at the moment?"

"I'm still writing my weekly column, I've just finished a big piece on flexitarianism. I'm now working on one about UK-produced wines. Oh, and I've just signed another soulless brand partnership deal to pay the mortgage."

"How soulless are we talking?"

"Condensed milk," I replied repentantly.

"Oof."

"So now I have to find ten genuinely delicious and ingenious ways of using condensed milk."

"Key lime pie," she said. "With many more limes than you think. They'll lick the plates. And no-churn ice cream."

"You have the answer to everything."

"Right. To the actual business: how did the online dating venture go? I've been desperate to know."

"It went well! I've ended up with a sort-of boy-friend from my first ever date."

"You're joking?" she said.

"I think I have to accept I'm terrible at casual dating."

"Perhaps you are. I always rather liked sleeping around. It was all a lot of harmless fun as far as I can remember, apart from the odd bit of disease, but that was no bother really."

"I don't think I'm built for it, sadly. I've tried."

"Well, lucky you've found someone then. What's he like?"

"He's an accountant. He's very outdoorsy."

"What does he look like?"

"Tall, broad, sandy-blond hair. A bit like a caveman-surfer in a suit."

"Oh, heaven," she said.

"I was going to ask your advice, actually."

"Go on," she said, looking pleased.

"I'm about to have dinner with my ex—"

"That charming little bear of a man I met?"

"Yes. You know we're still very close?" She nodded. "Do you think I should tell him I'm seeing someone? We always said we'd be honest about it, but I don't know if that seems sort of . . . presumptuous, to announce it to him, like he'd be bothered."

She leant back and ran her hands through her sexy sheepdog hair ponderously, as if summoning the part of her brain that dispensed love and life advice on tap.

"Yes," she said after a few moments. "You should tell him."

"I thought I should."

"But be very sensitive. Men always have to keep a low flame burning for every ex. It will be flickering in there for him, even if he doesn't know it is. Whereas women always have to extinguish it."

I WAITED FOR JOE outside the cinema. He was nearly fifteen minutes late. We were seeing a late-afternoon screening of **The Appaloosa,** starring Marlon Brando. Westerns had always been our mutual obsession, and we had no one else who would watch them with us other than each other. We both liked the simplicity of good guys or bad guys and the lack of moral ambiguity—it felt like comfort food. **The Appaloosa,** about a man stealing another man's horse because it's sexy, was a particular favourite. You can replace the word "horse" with "gold," "gun" or "wife" and you've got the plot for every single Western ever made.

We had managed to carry almost all of our relationship into our friendship post break-up. We still watched Westerns together, we still spoke to each other first when something went disastrously wrong at work, we still bickered about the correct details of a shared memory—our dynamic was unchanged other than the fact we didn't have sex. And the last part of our romantic relationship was so sexless, it had acted as a transitional period to prepare us for a platonic one.

In the long two-day sit-in in our flat that was our eventual break-up conversation, Joe and I did a full enquiry into where the sex went to. I don't think it's that we stopped finding each other attractive, I think we stopped seeing each other as gateways to a place of excitement or stimulation. We became each other's portal to comfort, familiarity and security, and nothing else. For years, the person I wanted to have new experiences with, stay up with, discover things with, was Joe. Incrementally that changed, and he was no longer the person with whom I wanted to live life. He was the person I wanted to report back to as we ate Thai takeaway. I wanted him to be the post-match commentary, rather than the main event. I wanted him to be the photo frame, rather than the photo. And that was when we stopped having sex.

I saw Joe's compact but bulky frame lumbering towards me in one of his lightweight shirt-jackets that I've always hated, and I was struck by how different he was to Max in every way possible. Max was confident and withholding with his enthusiasm, Joe was puppyish and keen to entertain. Max was serious, Joe would do or say anything to make people laugh. Joe was soft and round-cheeked, Max was solid and sculptural. Joe was as safe and comforting as a teddy, Max was leonine, dangerous and majestic. Joe looked like he was eagerly awaiting someone to make a joke about him around a pub table, Max looked like a leading man.

"You're late," I said as he arrived, out of breath.

"I know," he said, giving me a clumsy hug. "I'm sorry."

"What's the excuse, come on, say it quickly before you can make one up."

"Don't have one," he said, scratching his gingery-brown beard, always so flummoxed by his own inefficiency. "Faffing about this afternoon."

"Were you playing that football Xbox game thing?"

"A bit, yeah."

"Does Lucy mind you being late for her?"

"I'm never late for Lucy, Christ."

"So you're only late for me?"

He looked at me with a patient smile as he removed

what he called his "shacket" and rolled his eyes. "Don't be needy," he said, self-consciously pulling his khaki T-shirt down over his round tummy.

"I'm not being needy, I just find it interesting that your current girlfriend gets the benefit of all the tellings-off I gave you over the years, whereas your ex-girlfriend still has to put up with the same old shit."

"Oh, come on," he said, putting his arm around me, the smell of his armpit as evocative to me as a late grandmother's perfume. "I'll buy you one of those unfathomably big Cokes that you only let yourself drink at the cinema, how about that? And you can drink it all in one, like you always do, and piss everyone off getting up and down to go to the loo, like you always do." My shoulder sank into his armpit, and I put my arm around his back.

After the film, we went to a Vietnamese place nearby that I had heard did some of the best pho in London, which I was writing my column about that week. Joe, positively monarchic in his enthusiasm for feasting, always loved joining me on these culinary investigations.

"How's work?" I asked, in between slurps of soupy noodles.

"Work's fine, as rewarding as sports PR can be."

"Are you still looking at maybe going to another agency?"

He wiped at his mouth with the napkin he'd tucked into his T-shirt like a baby's bib. "Maybe," he said. "I think something happens in your thirties where you slightly let go of this idea of the perfect career. I have so much fun outside of work, maybe it's enough that it's just fine. It pays okay, I get on with my colleagues. At the end of the day, it's just ye olde day job." What a relief it was for Joe to make these Chaucerian jokes now and it not pose a threat to my desire for him. "How are you?" he asked. "What's new?"

"Nothing really, still settling into the flat, have to take my time making it my own as I don't have any cash and there's lots that needs doing to it. But I suppose it's nice to think of it as a long-term project."

"Yeah, course," he said, slightly zoning out as he signified to the waitress that he wanted another beer.

"And I'm excited about the new book coming out."

"I can't wait to read it."

"And I'm seeing someone."

He looked at me, slightly open-lipped. "Since when?"

"Month and a half?" I said, trying my best to seem unbothered by this announcement. "Around that."

He nodded, plunging his chopsticks back into his bowl to dig around for hidden noodles. "That's good, you're seeing someone. I was worried for all that time that you weren't."

"Why were you 'worried'?" I said, annoyed at his attempt to patronize me and conceal it as compassion.

"It was just that you seemed to be not dating any-one for a really long time."

"I did that on purpose, I was getting my career on track. Leaving teaching, going fully freelance, writing a book, buying a flat on my own. Quite a lot to do while trying to be some girl about town dating."

"Where did you meet . . . ?"

"Max," I replied.

"Max," he said, trying the word on for size.

"On a dating app."

"I never thought you'd do that."

"You don't really have a choice any more, people don't meet in real life. Look at Lola."

"Yeah," he laughed fondly. "Dear old Lola. How's she doing? I haven't seen her for a while."

I'd noticed that "dear old" had become almost a permanent prefix when people referred to Lola. "She's good, still dating."

"So what's he like?!" he asked with reluctant parental enthusiasm.

"He's . . . tall," I said. "Very tall."

"I thought you didn't like tall people."

"What an insane thing to say, why would I have ever said that?"

"You're always complaining about them blocking your view at gigs and taking the front seat of a car. I specifically remember you saying you'd never fancy a lanky guy."

"He's not lanky, he's very broad." I could see Joe

instinctively puff his chest out. His napkin bib was splattered with brown broth.

"Doesn't sound like your type at all."

"That's what I've always thought about Lucy," I said, instantly regretting how bitter it sounded.

He smiled, put his chopsticks down and adjusted the bamboo placemat ceremoniously. "I'm proposing."

"What?!"

"I know!"

"When?"

"This weekend."

"Wow, that's unexpected," I said.

"Is it?"

"I suppose it isn't. We're in our thirties, you've been together for quite a while. Sorry, I don't know why I'm quite so shocked."

"I've known I was going to do it for months. I designed the ring."

"Chill out, Richard Burton," I said, passive-aggressively spooning chilli sauce over my bowl, previously unaware that I could dispense condiments passive-aggressively. "What do men even mean when they say that: **designed the ring**? You can barely pick out your trousers in the morning."

"I mean, I sat down with a jewellery designer and told him the sort of thing she'd like. Look," he said, taking out his phone and showing me a photo of a small round diamond surrounded by other smaller round diamonds. I don't think I've ever seen an engagement ring I could remember.

"That's beautiful, Joe," I said. "Really well designed."

"Thank you," he said, missing the light sarcasm in my voice.

"I didn't think you were that keen for marriage," I said. "We always talked about kids but never getting married."

"Yeah, but that was with you," he said.

"Cheers."

"No, I mean, the future you decide with a person is different for every person, isn't it? It's not like you decide what you want, then someone else fits into that. We decided we wouldn't have got married. Lucy and I discussed quite early on that we would get married."

"How early on?" I asked.

"Early, I think. Within the first few dates."

"Was that the date when she took you to a bridal fair?"

"It wasn't a **bridal fair,**" he said impatiently. "It was to help her sister pick her wedding shoes."

"Hot," I said. "I don't know how women like Lucy do it. Every heterosexual woman I know is emotionally paralysed in relationships by this fear of 'scaring men off.' Then you have your Lucys of this world, these total anomalies, who know what they want and say: 'I'm the boss, here are the rules, do as I say.' And so many men seem to love it. Like it's a relief, or something."

"Yeah, well, it worked for me," he said. We drained the remaining soup with our wooden ladles, silent but for slurps.

"I'm really happy for you both," I finally said. "I can't wait to see you get married. If I'm invited to the wedding."

"Of course you'll be invited."

"All these things we thought about each other," I said. "Doesn't like tall people, wouldn't join dating apps, never wanted to get married. Funny how wrong we were."

"We weren't wrong," he said. "We were growing up."

ON THE BUS BACK HOME, longing for something unchangeable, I made the mistake of calling Mum and Dad.

"Hello?" Mum barked as she picked up the landline, harried and hassled, as if I were a PPI salesman calling for the fifth time in an hour.

"Hi, Mum, it's me," I said gently.

"Oh, Nina, hi."

"How are you? Everything okay?"

"Not really, no."

"What's up?" I didn't know when this started happening, when I would turn to my mother for comfort and find myself very quickly being her counsellor.

"I am having a nightmare evening. I was meant to be at a local production of **A Doll's House** and—"

"Where on earth is there a production of **A Doll's House** in Pinner?"

"It's at the Watford Community Theatre. Gloria's am-dram group are doing it and I've been excited about seeing it for weeks. Tonight was closing night. The cast are going out afterwards to that local nightclub, and we were all going to go dressed up as persecuted women from history. I've been working on my costume all week."

"What happened?"

"I get a call this evening from Mary Goldman, telling me she's received a condolence letter from your father about the death of her husband, Paul. Pages and pages, it went on for, about all their memories watching the football together and how he thought he hadn't been himself or looked well for a number of years. How sorry he was to lose such a special man."

"What's wrong with that?"

"Paul Goldman hasn't bloody died."

"Oh," I said.

"He isn't even bloody ill, he's fine."

"Okay, that's obviously not great. But it's clearly just a mix-up. Has someone else called Paul died?"

"No," she said.

"Has someone else died recently that you've told Dad about?"

"Err," she said hesitantly, annoyed at my line of rational inquisition when she was in a mood to rant. "I mean, Dennis Wray died this week, but Dennis is nothing like Paul. Dennis is an old colleague of your dad's, we've been friends with Paul and Mary for thirty years."

"It will be that then. He just got muddled, he gets muddled with details and timelines, you need to make things as clear as possible, he isn't being difficult. It's like he knows the shapes of things, but he sometimes gets the colours confused."

"Mary doesn't care about all that, she's just beside herself. It really upset her."

"Well, Mary Goldman is a twat."

"Nina."

"She is. She's a twat for making such a fuss when it's clear Dad made an innocent mistake and had such lovely things to say about her boring old husband, even if he wasn't dead. Why don't you ring a minicab and go join the after-party? It's only nine o'clock."

"I can't now, it would take me ages to get into the costume and by the time I arrive I wouldn't have long."

"What's the costume?" I could hear Mum rattling with impatience at the end of the phone— simultaneously desperate to tell me every twist and turn of this non-existent saga, while being irritated by my questions.

"It's Emily Davison. But I have to get into all the petticoats, then attach the big toy horse on the back of the dress, and I just can't—" I heard a voice in the background. "I'm on the phone to Nina. Would you like to talk to her? Fine. Nina, your dad wants to talk to you."

"Hello, Bean," he said.

"Hi, Dad. Is everything okay? Sounds like there's been a lot of drama about nothing today." I forced a chuckle, keen to placate the situation into relaxed normality.

"Paul died. Paul Goldman. Such a lovely bloke. We once all went to the Lake District together and we saw a deer. He hadn't been looking well for a while, but these things still take you by surprise." I heard Mum groaning in the background. "Are you coming for dinner today?"

"Not today, Dad, I'm coming in a few weeks."

"Is it a few weeks **already**?" he said with surreal dismay, like a character in a suburban **Alice In Wonderland.** "Blimey, blimey. How time flies."

"Don't worry about what Mum's saying about Paul and Mary, she's just cross she doesn't get to go on her big night out." I heard Mum call his name.

"I better go. I think your mum wants me."

"Okay, Dad," I said, resolutely cheery. "Lovely talking to you and I'll call you again tomorrow."

"All right, Bean. Bye, love."

I kept the phone to my ear and heard the loud, flat beeps of Dad jabbing at keys that weren't the button to hang up. Then I heard Mum's voice, weary and waning, edge closer to the phone. "It's this one, Bill," she said, then ended the call.

I put my mobile in my jacket pocket and pressed my face against the bus window, which was speeding over Hungerford Bridge, willing London's sparkling outline to distract me from the curdle of emotions in my stomach. I had never known a feeling as unbearable—as sour, wrenching and unshakeably sad—as pity for a parent.

I WENT TO BED as soon as I got home. I had never had trouble with sleep—it was something I was increasingly grateful for as I watched friends battle through nights of shallow-breathed tossing and turning or the repetitive servant's-bell ring of a hungry, wailing baby. Unusually, I was woken up two hours later by the sound of loud male laughter coming from the garden below me. I drew the curtains and saw Angelo and another man sitting on plastic chairs, smoking, drinking beers and speaking in Italian. I lifted the window ajar.

"Excuse me," I hissed. "Would you mind keeping the noise down? I was asleep, you woke me up." They both stopped talking, looked up briefly, then returned to their conversation.

"Angelo," I hissed again. "Angelo." They continued to talk. "Angelo, it's half twelve on a Monday night. On a Saturday I could understand, but it's Monday. I've got a really early meeting tomorrow. Can you talk inside?" They began laughing again, so loudly it became an orchestra of wheezing hi-hat cymbals and honking horns. Angelo's friend slapped him on his knee from the sheer hysteria of it all. "Excuse me!" I pleaded. They raised their voices, trying to rub out my voice like a pencil mark. "ANGELO!" I shouted. He snapped his head up at me with the sudden pep and fixed expression of a marionette.

"Do not. Shout at me. Like a dog," he said with a light garnish of threat.

"Go talk inside."

"No," he said, turning his head away from me again. I closed the window with a bang, put on a jumper, coat and a pair of trainers.

AFTER A PHONE CALL and a taxi, I stood outside Max's front door and the breeze bit my bare legs, alerting me to autumn's arrival. Max opened it and I smiled apologetically. He pulled me into the warmth of his hallway and body.

"This is a lovely surprise," he said as I pressed my face into his chest, my arms wrapped pathetically tightly round his middle like a child meeting a character at Disneyland.

"You don't have a woman here, do you?"

"Three of them," he said into my hair. "They're all very cross you've prised me away from the bed."

"Weird dinner with my ex," I said, looking up at him. "Then sad conversation with my mum and dad. Then run-in with my horrible neighbour."

He kissed me. "Do you want to talk about it?"

"No."

"Do you want a glass of wine?"

"A gallon." We walked to his kitchen and I pulled myself up to sit on his counter as he retrieved two glasses from the cupboard.

"I've never knowingly had a dinner with an ex that wasn't weird," he said.

"I know. I thought Joe and I had nailed it, but maybe we haven't."

"Did he beg you to come back to him?" he asked, pouring red wine into two glasses. "Because you know that's not allowed."

"No, no. He's getting married, which took me by surprise. We always said we'd never get married."

"How did it make you feel?"

"I don't know. Not jealous or sad or anything. He said this thing that I can't stop thinking about—that you decide what you want from your future anew with every new partner."

He gave me my glass, then took a sip of his own. "I think he's right, isn't he?"

"I suppose he is, I just hadn't thought of it that way before. I thought we decide what we want, then find someone who wants to do it with us." I reached down to my plimsolls and unlaced them. They dropped to the tiles and I pulled my feet up on the counter, my chin resting on my knees.

"Look at your sexy socks," he said, moving towards me and tugging at my feet. "Bare legs and socks on you does something to me." He stood between my thighs and I clamped them around him. I thought of the perfect moment we had found ourselves in, entwined on a kitchen counter on a weekday evening—the ephemeral period of a new relationship when everything domestic could be erotic. When watching someone pour milk on their cereal or towel-dry their hair was more entrancing than the ocean. When smelling their morning breath or unwashed scalp was exciting because it took you one step further into their high-walled palace of privacy, where you hoped only you were allowed to roam. Sexed-up to saturation point, therefore trying out the novelty of being humdrum. If this turned into a long-term relationship, one day we'd be only humdrum and we'd have to revisit the novelty of being sexy again—arranging "date nights" and putting on our best clothes for each other and purposefully lighting candles. We trick ourselves into being close until we really are close, then we trick ourselves into seeming distant to stay as close as we can for as long as possible. Sometime soon, our socks would no longer be seductive, they'd be a source of an argument (not rolled up, left on the radiator, left in the washing machine). For now, our socks were symbols of something secret and sacred.

"God, I love this bit," I said. "This bit where you melt over my socks. How do we keep it in this bit? How do we freeze this in time? There must be a way of tricking all the laws of monogamy. There must be some sort of gaming hack."

"No, no, no," he said, pushing my fringe back off my face and kissing my forehead, then my cheeks, then the end of my nose. "We need to keep going. We need to keep pushing through to all the next rounds. Your socks are only going to get sexier, I know it."

I'LL HAVE THE BURGER, please, with a gluten-free bun and mac and cheese on the side." Lola registered my confusion. "What?"

"Your order makes no sense."

"Why?"

"Because there's gluten in the macaroni."

"Yeah, but at least then I'm halving my gluten intake."

"But you're either allergic to gluten or you're not," I said. "It's not like fags, it's not a bit of gluten is better for you than lots of gluten. Flour is just an ingredient."

"You can opt for wheat-free pasta?" the waitress suggested.

"Blurgh, no thanks," Lola replied, tossing her menu on the table. I stared at her, unsure of where to begin.

"Burger with cheese, jalapeños and fries," I said. Lola's phone rang.

"Hang on," she said. "I left my cosmic shopping list at the library." She picked up the phone. "Hello? . . . Yes, we spoke earlier . . . well, I definitely left it there, so I'd appreciate it if you could look one more time . . . it's just a piece of A4 paper with a list of words on it like 'twin daughters' and 'my own events company' . . . okay . . . appreciate it, thank you." She hung up.

"Lola."

"What?"

"Why can't you just write another one?"

"Because, my life coach and I did a whole ritual with that specific list and I can't afford another session to do it all over again. I know you might think this stuff is silly, but it's very easy to dismiss it when you're all . . . loved up." Our drinks hadn't yet arrived and she had already said the thing she'd been wanting to say to me for weeks.

"That's got nothing to do with it, I thought you were loopy when we were both single."

"That's true," she said. "Thank you for coming to this thing with me tonight. I know you hate singles events. And I know you're not technically single any more."

"Don't be silly, I'll always come to them with you."

"I got ghosted last week."

"What does that mean?"

"It's when a person just stops speaking to you instead of having a break-up conversation."

"Why's it called ghosting?"

"Number of schools of thought," she said, with the command of an academic. "Most commonly, it is thought to have come from the idea that you are haunted by someone who vanishes, you don't get any closure. Others have said it derives from the three grey dots that appear then disappear when someone is writing you an iMessage and then doesn't send it. Because it looks ghostly."

"I see. And which guy was this?"

"Jared. Works in the charity sector."

"Oh no!" I said. "He seemed great."

"Yeah, well, they always do."

I wished, more than anything, that I could buy a Durex for her heart.

"Didn't he say he wanted you to meet his parents or something?"

"Yep," she nodded. "The last time I saw him he said: 'If you fancy a weekend away from London, I'd love for you to come meet my parents.' Then he kissed me goodbye and I never heard from him again. It's been three weeks. I've sent nine messages, ten was my limit. So I'm saving it up to compose a really good one, I'm going to really give him a piece of my mind."

"Let's write it together," I said.

"You are the only one who I could talk to about all the stuff we talk about." Lola closed her eyes and flapped her hand gently, a pre-emptive dismissal of comfort as her eyes filled with tears.

"Sweetheart," I said, my hands reaching for hers across the table. "What's the matter?"

"I am so happy that you've met someone, I really am, I promise," she said. "But now I really am all on my own. I've been left behind by everyone. I'm going to have to become that woman in the office who befriends all the graduates."

"No, you're not!" I said. "First of all, I'm exactly the same person and we can still do exactly the same things and talk about the same things and hang out just as much. And secondly, who knows what will happen with Max and me. It's not like once someone is in a relationship, they're sorted for ever."

"No, but I want it to work out for you two. I don't want to be one of those single women who resents the happiness of her friends, that's not who I am. Oh God, I don't know, maybe it's—" Lola turned her phone over, opened the cycle-tracking app that every thirty-something woman I knew now seemed to be obsessed with. "No," she said, defeated and sniffing. "Not even premenstrual." The waitress arrived with our bottle of Pinot Grigio and poured it, while Lola dabbed her eyes with the frilly cuff of a strange Edwardian shirt she was wearing, replete with diamanté buttons.

"Where are you taking me to tonight?"

"An astrological matchmaking event. Everyone gets their birth charts done and then we get paired up with our most compatible partner, horoscopically speaking."

"Okay," I said, happy to have distracted her. "And what are you?"

"Your classic, middle-of-the-road, straight-down-the-line Pisces. We're so predictable. I can spot one anywhere. I met my friend's beagle the other day, and I guessed instantly that he was a Pisces, and he was!" She was clearly fragile, so I let this one go without mockery.

"How interesting."

"Ideally, I'm looking for a Cancer, but they can be a bit too home-orientated and weirdly I've noticed often have psoriasis, which isn't a problem of course."

"Mmm."

"You're a Leo. What's Max?"

"I have no idea."

"I hope he's a Libra," she said, crossing her fingers excitedly. "I've always wanted you to be with a Libra. Relaxed but fiercely loyal, that's what you need. And they have whopper shlongs!"

"Lola, come on."

"They do."

"I've already seen his cock, his cock isn't going to suddenly enlarge once I discover he's a Libra."

"It's strange," she said, wrinkling her nose slightly. "I've always been so unconvinced you're a Leo."

I knew this was an insult, despite knowing nothing about horoscopes. "In what way?"

"You're just a bit . . . fussy."

"Thank you."

"No, in a good way. You have much more of a controlled Virgo energy."

"Do you think, maybe . . . **maybe** . . . it could be a lie?"

"Your birthdate? Could well be, actually. Could well be. I've heard of birth certificates being a few days out."

"No, not my birth certificate—star signs."

"Oh." Her eyes squinted slightly as she conjured this thought as a possibility. "No."

THE NEXT MORNING, with the sort of hangover that makes you google ashrams, I found myself ten and a half miles away from my sofa and once again on Wandsworth Common against my will. The original plan was for Katherine to come to my flat to help me choose a paint colour for my bathroom, then go for a walk and lunch nearby, but at the last minute she said she couldn't do the journey because of a childcare glitch. I was totally unsurprised—such is the superior trump card of motherhood that she once cancelled dinner with me an hour before we were meant to meet via a text explaining she had to "wake up in the morning etc.," as if being childless gave me an option of not existing for the day.

"And did she get any matches?" she asked as we strode beneath the tupelo trees, their amber leaves flickering like flames in the October wind.

"No," I said. "We turned up, and it was thirty-five women and five men."

"How poorly organized."

"I know, she was so disappointed. And the five men were all air signs, which apparently are the worst matches for Pisces, so we decided to cut our losses and we went to the pub instead."

"What's she going to try next?"

"I don't know," I said, my black lace-up boots pressing through ochre leaf mulch. "We decided to widen her Linx location preference from ten miles to fifty miles, as she's heard some rumours of there being single farmers in the Home Counties. It just all feels so overwrought and I'm starting to finally see her patience run out. Like she might give up."

"I'm trying to think if Mark has any nice friends," she said. I could tell her in one short answer: **no, no he doesn't.** But Katherine couldn't pass off an opportunity to act as The Gatekeeper To All Things Matrimonial. "Dear old Lola, I do worry about her." There it was again.

"How's the baby?"

"Good!" she said, stroking her small bump swathed in the grey wool of her coat. "Did I tell you we've found out the sex?"

"And?" I yelped excitedly.

"We've decided to keep it just between us," she smiled.

Ten and a half miles, I had travelled that morning. Ten and a half miles. "Why's that then?" I asked flatly.

"Just something for the family, you know?"

"Mmm. Cool."

"But, yeah, we're pleased," she said enigmatically, as if she were a Hollywood starlet in an at-home shoot and I was a pushy journalist for **Time** magazine, following her around with a notepad. I could see the spread now, her dripping with diamonds and lounging on the sofa in a housecoat. The headline: **My Weekend With Katherine.** "So now we're starting conversations about godparents," she said.

**"Starting conversations,"** I said. "And how many of the UN are involved?" I watched the inner conflict manifest on her face, trying to decide whether to jump on the joke and be a satirist with me, or defend her pomposity and be an arsehole.

"Oh, we're at the General Assembly next week," she said. "Expect to see it on the front of the **New York Times.**"

I laughed, begrudgingly. My best and oldest friend, stuck somewhere between her former earth-bound self and a new life, floating up and away from self-awareness and a sense of humour, to a place I couldn't reach her. **You don't get to be both,** I wanted to say to her. **Which are you, Katherine? A satirist or an arsehole?**

WE WENT BACK to her place for lunch. It was two o'clock and Mark was asleep—it turns out the "childcare glitch" was that he was too hung-over to look after his daughter and she'd had to be taken to Katherine's mum for the morning. He had rung the doorbell at four a.m. because he was so drunk he couldn't find his keys, and when Katherine answered the door and told him he had woken up Olive, he replied: "Who's Olive?" Katherine told the story with a sort of rolly-eyed, boys-will-be-boys joviality she often employed when talking about her husband. Not for the first time upon looking in on my friends' long-term relationships, I marvelled at how a marriage ironically seemed to provide men of my generation with even more of an excuse to not grow up. When Olive was still a newborn, Mark once spent the day at Twickenham with some colleagues and got so drunk he passed out in a friend's wardrobe and woke up soaked in his own urine. They still talk about the incident with the warmth of a family anecdote to be passed along the generations. If Katherine had done the same, either social services would have been alerted or at the very least she would have been spoken about as a new

mother free-falling into self-destruction and parental neglect. For Mark, it was just a big day out at
the rugby.

Mark emerged halfway through our lunch. His
ten-quid-at-the-barber standard brown haircut was
dishevelled like a schoolboy's, his chin dusted with
stubble. His pale face looked both plump and de-
flated, like a faulty airbed dragged out from the
attic. His small grey eyes were sticky and bloodshot.

"Big night?" I asked, the note of judgement in my
voice as bright and sonorous as a middle C.

"A bit, yeah, a bit," he said, leaning down to give
me a kiss on the cheek. "Was out with Joe."

"Oh yeah, what did you guys get up to?"

"Was meant to be just a few at the pub, but things
got a bit out of hand. He ended up losing a bet and
eating twenty quid."

"Eating it?"

"Yeah, two ten-pound notes," he said, laughing to
himself. Katherine shook her head and closed her
eyes, in mock dismay. "Then he was sick outside
the Duck and Crown and he tried to see if he could
find the pieces in the vomit and stick the notes back
together again to buy another round!"

"The one that got away," I said.

"We were celebrating his engagement," he said
pointedly, before getting up to go to the fridge.

"Did he tell you?" Katherine asked.

"Yes, he told me he was going to propose. Then
I saw it on Instagram." It had been impossible to

miss the press-release photo and statement Lucy
had issued of the pair of them, like it was news from
Clarence House. Mark and Katherine had been the
first to like and comment enthusiastically. Married
people loved doing this to newly engaged people—it
was how I imagined celebrities must reverently nod
at each other across a posh restaurant.

"Has Kat showed you the house?" Mark boomed
from behind the fridge door.

"No?"

"Oh," she said, reaching for a piece of paper from
a drawer in the sideboard. "We've made an offer."
She pushed the picture and description of the house
towards me.

"Starting to get really excited about getting out
of this hellhole of a city," Mark said, transporting a
plate of crisps, carrot batons and cocktail sausages
to the table along with a giant tub of hummus and
a tin of sweetcorn. I longed to point out that he
seemed to think this "hellhole" was more than suitable when he wanted to use it as a giant playground
to destroy with other fellow man-babies on a Friday
night out.

The house description showed a four-bed modern
home in a commutable Surrey village, crassly made
to look like a red-brick Georgian cottage. The asking price was written in bold at the top, as over-
blown as the building itself. I thought about how
sensitive I had been to Lola when I had bought my
tiny one-bed flat, which I knew was something she

might never be able to do; how I had hidden the price from her, how I had downplayed the perks of home ownership and reminded her of how freeing renting could be. This was not a courtesy that Katherine felt obliged to show. I could sit an A level in the details of Katherine and Mark's life together over the last decade. Every asset, every purchase, every detail of their wedding, every potential baby name. Tradition dictates that metamorphoses belong to the married—the rest of us exist in a static state.

"It looks lovely," I lied.

"It's got a great garden for the kids," Katherine said.

"So brilliant," I said, already running out of adjectives.

"Joe said you've got a new bloke," Mark said, using a large crisp as a ladle from which to shove a cocktail sausage in his mouth.

"Oh yes! How is he?" Katherine asked.

"A bloody big bugger, according to Joe!"

"Joe hasn't even met him," I said.

"He's found a photo of him online. Says he looks like Jesus crossed with the Incredible Hulk. He's seething about it, absolutely seething. It's hilarious."

"That's ridiculous," I said.

"Oh, you know him. He's a loveable but insecure child." Mark said this while mashing a dollop of hummus directly into the tin of sweetcorn.

"When can we meet him?" Katherine asked.

"Soon," I said. "He's got to meet Joe first."

"Can I come watch?" Mark asked.

I SAW JOE A FEW WEEKS LATER. I decided to meet him an hour before Max was due to arrive, to avoid doing a catch-up chat in front of Max and potentially making him feel alienated. We agreed on a centrally located pub, as centrally located pubs are the apolitical socializing territory. Everything had to be as neutral as possible—I could tell that Max felt nervous about spending time with the man whom I'd been in my most significant and longest relationship with; a man who was still such an important part of my life and friendship group. And I could tell Joe felt uncomfortable at the thought of potentially being replaced as my most significant relationship. Neither had said so explicitly, but, like so many other times in my life, I had been presented with a man in a muddle of feelings and I had found the correct vocabulary to match it. It was also down to me to manage and marshal those feelings in a way that made them feel as safe and comfortable as possible. Being a heterosexual woman who loved men meant being a translator for their emotions, a palliative nurse for their pride and a hostage negotiator for their egos.

"How's wedding planning going?" I asked Joe, who was wearing the grey denim shirt he had obviously forgotten he'd called his "slimming shirt" for all the years we were together. The buttons strained across him, the dark, downy hair of his belly visible through the gaps.

"I've sort of let Lucy get on with that," he said, avoiding my gaze by staring into his pint. "She's really got the eye for design, you know?"

There's nothing I loved more than watching a man merrily surrender to full-blown emasculation via wedding planning. "When's it going to be?"

"Spring."

"Wow, that's fast."

"Yeah. I've got something I want to ask you."

"No, I won't marry you, you should have asked me when you had the chance."

"Nina."

"Sorry."

"As you know, you're a very important person in my life. Probably the most important person in my life, other than Lucy."

"Right," I said, uncomfortable with this unusual tone of sincerity from Joe.

"And Lionel Messi!" he said, with a nervous chuckle.

"Okay."

"Anyway, I want you to be a part of the wedding. Originally, I thought I'd ask you to do a reading, but I know you'd find it cheesy, and I also want you to be there with me the morning of."

"Right."

"Will you be one of my ushers?"

"Yes!" I said, relieved that I wouldn't have to stand at a lectern in a pastel-coloured dress I'd never wear again bleating "love is patient, love is kind" for the 754th time in my life. "I'd love that. It would be an honour. Oh, Joe, that's so lovely of you. Do I get to wear a suit?"

"Yes. Or whatever you like."

"Can I come to the piss-up the night before?"

"Yes! You can stay in the pub with me and the best man and the other ushers."

"And can I come to the stag?"

"Er, no, actually."

"What?!"

"I know, I know, it's a bummer," he said. "But it's Lucy's one request. She's fine with you being usher, but she doesn't want you on the stag do."

"Why not?"

"Nina, my future wife is letting me stay in the room next door to my ex-girlfriend the night before my wedding because I need you for emotional support. I think she's being very understanding. I think we should give her this."

"Okay," I said reluctantly. "I can't wait, Joe. I'll do the best ushering you've ever seen."

"Will Max be okay with it, do you think? He'll be invited, of course."

"Oh, definitely," I said. "He likes that we're so close. He thinks exes being friends is elegant."

"How's it going with you two?"

"Great!" I said. "I think. Obviously, I have very little to compare it to. But it feels fun and easy, which I think means it's going well."

"Are you two exclusive?"

" 'Exclusive,' " I parroted. "I don't think I've heard that word since school."

"You know what I mean, are you just seeing each other?"

"I haven't felt the need to ask that. I thought it was just a given."

"Have you said you love each other?" he continued.

I left a slightly too long pause.

"Why are you talking about my relationship like some nosy teenage girl?"

"I'm not!"

"Yes, you are. 'Are you exclusive,' 'have you said you love each other.' You'll be asking me what base we've got to next."

"I'm just trying to gauge how serious it is."

"It's serious," I said. "Otherwise I wouldn't have arranged this."

MAX ARRIVED ON TIME, with his curls jostled from cycling in the wind. I waved at him across the pub, the door of which I had been nervously watching while trying to listen to Joe speak in a bit too much detail about his most recent parking ticket and the subsequent argument with the council he had found himself embroiled in. It was a disorientating moment when Max smiled at me and I realized that the person I felt closest to was the one walking towards me, not the one sitting next to me at the table. I never thought anyone would be able to eclipse the familiarity I had felt with Joe, and yet there I was, sitting at a pub, my insides radiating in response to Max's arrival. Something had shifted—dynamics of power always rearrange themselves when you're not watching them. We kissed on the lips, politely and briefly.

"Max, this is Joe; Joe, this is Max."

"All right, mate," Joe said, giving him a handshake. "Nice to meet you."

"Same, mate, nice to meet you."

**Mate.** Male conversational currency as widely effective as the euro.

"What can I get you?" Joe asked.

"Oh, don't worry, I'm up, I'll get it. Pint of . . . ?"

"Lager," Joe said, the slight chest-puff returning. "Thanks, mate."

"And a G and T for you?" he asked.

"Yes please."

"Double?"

"Yes please," I said.

"Atta girl," Max said, before kissing the top of my head and going to the bar. Joe and I resolutely continued to discuss our various gripes with our respective local councils as Max ordered drinks, both determined not to comment on the strangeness of the situation we found ourselves in.

When he returned, Max was the first to initiate the formalities of the pair of them getting to know each other.

"Nina said you work in sports PR?"

"That's right," Joe said.

"Anything you specialize in?"

"Football, mainly."

"Oh, awesome."

"You a football fan?"

"Not really, more of a rugby guy."

This was the first in a series of conversational fly-swats that the pair of them did to each other. Someone would float a topic in the air that could open up at least five minutes of pleasant chit-chat, and the other would whack the plastic swatter over it, killing small-talk potential in seconds.

"Who do you support?" Max offered as a condolence.

"Sheffield United."

"Ah," he said, then shrugged. "I mean, means nothing to me."

"Nina's a supporter."

I laughed. "Well, I'm not sure about—"

"Yeah you are. You loved those matches I took you to. Once you got over the bad catering."

"Nina George Dean," Max said, with gentle surprise. "You told me you hate football. In fact, we talked at length about it on one of our first dates."

"I hate the **culture** around football. And the

noise. And I hate those horrible pasties. But I don't mind the matches."

"Don't mind them? You went mad for them!" Joe enthused. "I couldn't keep you in your seat!"

"They can be fun in a live setting," I said swattingly, for some reason desperate to move on to something else.

"Or maybe you just loved them because you're so competitive."

"Are you competitive?" Max asked, his face wrinkling quizzically.

"Oh Christ, yes," Joe continued. "I think we broke up, what, maybe five times during a game of Scrabble?"

"I like rules," I relented. "Joe has a very weak grasp of spelling and grammatical rules."

"And you had a very firm grasp around my neck, that one time I landed a triple word score for flapjack!" Joe finished with an excitable, climactic look on his face—the one he got when he thought he'd "won" the conversation with wit. There was a brief silence while everyone sipped their drinks. This was the sort of Joe joke I would normally appease with a laugh, but that felt like a lie in front of Max. There was a daftness that I shared with Joe, and a seriousness that I shared with Max. Both were parts of me and both were true, but both seemed so in conflict with each opposing representative present. I hadn't anticipated that this merging of people meant this merging of selves—it made me think anxiously about myself in a way that was unfamiliar.

"How's **The Tiny Kitchen** going?" Joe asked.

"Good! The proofs arrived this week."

"Exciting! What's it like?" Joe looked expectantly at Max.

"What's what like?" he asked, having obviously been distracted with another thought.

"Nina's new book, what's it like?"

I was both intrigued and apprehensive about his answer. I had left proofs of **The Tiny Kitchen** and copies and translated copies of **Taste** in the flat over recent weeks and had noticed that Max hadn't so much as picked them up to read the back of them.

"I haven't read it yet."

"Oh, right," Joe said. "Did you read **Taste**?"

"I haven't actually yet, mate, no," he said, this particular "mate" laced with the paternal passive aggression of a tired father wanting his annoying teenage son to shut up. I had never seen him impatient. I had never seen him anything but relaxed and charming. I realized that, in over three months, I'd never really seen him with anyone. Sometimes bar staff, sometimes passing dogs in the park. But mostly I had only seen Max exist in reaction to me.

"You've got to read it, Max!" Joe said, making me both love and hate him in equal measure.

"I will."

"If I started dating someone who'd written a

memoir, I would have read it within the first month. Maybe I'm just nosy."

"I thought it was a cookbook?"

"It's both, it's a memoir with recipes. Or a cook-book with memoir chapters, depending on how you spin it," I said, glancing back and forth between them, conscious of not weighting my gaze towards one man more. I felt like a flying trapeze artist—one of them was the jumping-off platform, the other the catcher, and I was desperately trying to keep things swinging without a fall. We were only one drink in and I was exhausted.

"I'm keen to get to know Nina as Nina," Max said. "Rather than an author everyone else gets to know, if that makes sense?"

"I see, I see," Joe said. I could tell he couldn't "see" at all, but I appreciated his diplomacy. "Where are you from, Max?"

"Somerset."

"Nice one," Joe said meaninglessly.

"Do you know it?"

"I went for a weekend away near Taunton once, but otherwise no," Joe replied. Swat. "Are your parents still based there?"

"My mum is. My dad lives in Australia."

Australia? Why had Max never told me his father lived in Australia? I tried to keep an unwarranted look of betrayal from my face.

"Oh yeah? How long has he lived there?" Joe asked.

"He left when I was thirteen."

"I see. Do you get out there to see him much?"

"No, it's not really that kind of relationship."

"I'm sorry," Joe said.

"Not your fault, is it?" Max replied. It was the sort of sarcastic comment from a man that I hated—aggressively literal and belligerent. "Another round?"

"YOU DIDN'T TELL ME your dad moved to Australia," I said as Max and I got into my bed after what felt like the longest three drinks of my life.

"I told you my dad left when I was a kid."

"Yeah, but you didn't tell me he left and moved to the other side of the world."

"Oh, didn't I? Well, he did."

"Is that why you never see him?"

"To be honest, I think that's how much he'd want to see me if he were here," he said, plumping my pillows with unusual force.

"Okay," I said, sliding under the duvet next to him. "Do you want to talk about it?"

"Do I want to talk about my absent father right now? Right before we go to sleep and before my nine a.m. presentation tomorrow? No, not really."

"Okay."

"Do you want to talk about your ill dad right now?"

"Not really," I replied, bristling at his pettiness.

"Good," he said, turning off the lamp on his side of the bed. "Let's talk about it another time then."

"Fine," I said, turning the lamp on my side off.

"You didn't seem yourself tonight," he said, turning me on to my side and wrapping his arms around my stomach. "You seemed very eager to please."

"Is that not who I normally am?"

"You never seem keen to please, no, it's what I like about you."

"Don't say that. Don't give me a subtle warning that I've got to behave exactly as you'd like me to otherwise you'll go off me."

"Nina, come on, I'm not saying that."

"It was an awkward situation for everyone."

"No, I know, I know," he whispered, lifting my hair to kiss the back of my neck. "As long as you're fine."

"I am fine," I said, touching his feet with mine.

I COULDN'T SLEEP THAT NIGHT. I stared at the magnolia paint of my bedroom wall and felt the heavy weight of Max's body holding on to me. I couldn't stop thinking about all the gaps I'd seen over the course of the evening. Between Joe and Max. Between who Max was with me and who he was with other people. Between the cottage in Somerset where I thought Max's dad lived and the flat in Australia where he actually lived. Between who I was with Joe and who I was with Max. As I tried and failed to get to sleep, I imagined all the gaps filling up with dark, sticky, tar-like liquid and it made me feel inexplicably ashamed. I wondered if Joe and Max had thought of all the gaps in their lives and relationships and selves as they had fallen asleep that night. I wondered it as Max snored, peacefully and loudly, in my ear.

## 7

Dᴀᴅ ᴀɴsᴡᴇʀᴇᴅ ᴛʜᴇ ᴅᴏᴏʀ. He was wearing a pale-blue shirt underneath the navy cable-knit cardigan with brown buttons that I bought him for his seventieth. He only wore two jumpers on rotation per decade. His face was pale and the skin under his eyes looked thinner and lightly marbled with berry-coloured capillaries. Or maybe they'd always been there, I was just studying his face harder these days, looking for the tiniest marks of deterioration.

"Dad!" I said, giving him a big hug.

"Oh, Bean," he said, sighing into my hair as he hugged me. "It's been quite a week here."

"Where's Mum?"

"She's out," he said, walking towards the kitchen. "She's not speaking to me."

"Have you two had an argument?"

"I'm afraid so," he said. "This morning. A right barney."

"What happened?"

Dad stood over the dining table, which was covered in the silverware that was only taken out for Christmas. There was an open bottle of polish.

"Why are you doing all this? Have you got people coming over?"

"No, we're meant to be going away," he said, rubbing the prongs of a fork with the cloth. "That's what the argument was about this morning."

"Where are you going?"

"An opportunity has come up to go to Guinea."

**"Guinea?"** I said, dismayed that Mum hadn't brought this up on one of our many weekly phone calls in which she would list everything she had bought from Sainsbury's and how she intended to use it all.

"Yes."

"When?"

"We are meant to be setting sail through the seas next week, but Mum has other ideas."

"Is it, like, a cruise?"

"Yes."

"Is it the same company you guys and Gloria and Brian used when you went to the Canary Islands?"

"No, no, Gloria and Brian aren't coming," he said. "God, that'd be a sight. No, just your mother and I. It's me they want really, I'd be happy to go on my own."

"But Mum doesn't want to go?"

"No, she thinks it's too dangerous and she's worried about the weather."

"Well, that's a fair enough concern," I said. "Maybe you can go at a later date."

"No, it has to be next week, even if there's a storm."

"What are you doing with the silver?"

"We'll need it," he said. "For the trip."

"I'm sure they have their own cutlery on board."

"No, no, not for eating," he said, laughing at my suggestion. "For selling! Why pass up the chance for your mother and I to be merchants at last?"

**Why pass up the chance for your mother and I to be merchants at last?** Only Dad could come out with a sentence like that and it be unclear whether it was factual or fantastical. Nearly everything about my dad was still utterly recognizable to me—the East End edges of his vowels, the softness of his voice, his laugh, his vocabulary voluminous with the low-key language of chit-chat-with-the-neighbour ("a right barney") and poetic meanderings ("setting sail through the seas"). I had read over and over again when researching Dad's condition that what loved ones of sufferers experience is a sense of living grief—that the person you knew fades into an unrecognizable state. But I, so far, had found the opposite to be true in his case. It's what made the reality of his eventual fate even more difficult to process. His illness was making his personality more technicolour—more eccentric and exaggerated—than it had been before, rather than giving him an entirely different one. He was Dad concentrated—like a human stock cube—stronger, undiluted, boiled down, less filtered. He was harder to have a relationship or even a conversation with, but he was definitely still there. At times it felt like the trueness of his self was emerging more than it ever had.

I heard a car pull up outside the house and I went to the front door. Mum was getting out of Gloria's silver Toyota (every car in the North London suburbs was this shade—the roads looking down from outer space would be gilded with silver). Gloria saw me standing at the door and waved. I waved back. Mum was carrying a rolled-up yoga mat and wearing a lilac tracksuit.

"Bye, Glor!" she shouted as she walked away from the car. "I'll see you at Mingle and Mindfulness."

"Bye, Mandy!"

Mum approached me and gave me an exacting and prissy kiss on the cheek.

"Is that really catching on?"

"Yes."

"Everyone is fine with suddenly calling you Mandy?"

"No one has a problem with it other than you."

"What's Mingle and Mindfulness?"

"Exactly what it sounds like," she said, walking past me and going upstairs. I followed her to her bedroom. "Take the mickey all you like, Nina," she said, sitting on the edge of her bed and taking off her trainers as I stood by the wall watching her. "It's not going to embarrass me."

"Sorry, I'm not taking the mickey."

"Where's Dad?"

"Downstairs. He said you had an argument."

"Oh, it wasn't an argument, it was just a tiff," she said, moving to her vanity table, where she re-applied her gold jewellery.

"About a cruise or something?"

"A cruise?" she said, her face contorting in confusion.

"What was it about?" I asked.

"All I asked was for him to be a little less abrasive when we're out and about at social occasions."

"He's the least abrasive man alive, what do you mean?"

"We went for lunch at Gloria and Brian's last weekend and halfway through the meal he stood up to go to the loo, then just didn't come back."

"Where did he go?"

"We found him walking around their cul-de-sac half an hour later."

"Right, and what else?"

"We were at a drinks party last night and he was

rude to an acquaintance of ours in conversation, then sat in the hallway on a chair with his coat on for the rest of the night, making it obvious he wanted to go home. I was mortified."

"Okay," I said. "Do you remember what triggered it?"

"It was just normal conversation."

"Yes, but do you remember exactly what was being spoken about in both instances?" Mum thought for a moment with a frown—once again annoyed that I was using interrogation rather than tirade to try to solve the problem.

"At lunch, we were talking about Picasso, I think," she said. "Yes, that's right, Brian had been watching a programme the night before about Picasso."

"And what about at the party last night?"

"The man asked Bill what his favourite texts on the syllabus were when he was an English teacher."

"And what did he say?"

"He said, 'Mind your own bloody business,' and walked off."

"Right," I said, trying hard not to laugh at the thought of Dad the social anarchist in a cream-carpeted living room—the Punk of Pinner. "It's completely obvious to me what's happening here. Dad loves talking about art and he loves talking about books—he's so well informed on both of those subjects, but—"

"Nina—"

"Mum, please. Just listen to me, I'm not having a go at you, I'm trying to understand him." Her mouth tightened and she turned from the mirror to speak to me rather than my reflection. "I think Dad is at a stage where he's aware that something isn't right in himself, but he doesn't know what it is. He's pushing people away and isolating himself as self-protection. Think about who he is—he would prefer people to think he's rude rather than stupid." Mum stayed quiet, fiddling with the rings stacked on her wedding finger. "He's currently downstairs polishing all the silver, by the way."

She laughed weakly and closed her eyes in an expression that looked something like tiredness. It was the first small, visible sign of defeat I had seen in her for months. "A perk at last."

"You know, there are so many ways we can get some support," I said. "I've already started looking at how we could get a bit of help or advice—"

"I can't think about this now," she said brightly and suddenly, turning back towards the mirror. "Tell me how you are."

"I'm great," I replied, knowing not to push her any further today. "I've got proofs of my new book for you in my bag."

"Oh, I can't wait to see them!"

"And I'm in a relationship."

"NO!" she said, turning back to face me. "With who?"

"A lovely man called Max."

"What does he do?!"

"He's an accountant," I said. "But he sort of hates it."

"Accountant, that's a good job, very decent job," she said, assessing everything I said out loud that should be assessed in her head. "Where did you meet?"

"On a dating app."

"Sarah's daughter met her husband on a dating app. He's a personal trainer, runs marathons. No shame in it."

"I didn't say there was any shame in it."

"We've got to meet him. When are we all having dinner?"

"Would you like to?"

"Yes!" she squeaked. "Of course!"

"You don't think Dad might find a new person a bit overwhelming?"

"No, no, he'll be fine, leave him to me."

"Great," I said. "Right, do you like condensed milk?"

"Why?"

"I've got a load of it going spare, so I've brought a few tins here on the off-chance you'd like some."

"Is this for one of your blogs?"

"Mum," I said, already hating myself for the fragility of my ego, "I haven't written blogs since I was in my mid-twenties. I'm working directly with the brand to come up with recipe ideas and help advertise the product."

"All right, all right. No thank you, I won't eat it. Your dad will. I remember Grandma Nelly saying that condensed milk on bananas was his favourite thing to eat when he was a kid."

I cut up a banana and put it into a bowl along with half a tin of condensed milk and took it in to Dad, who was still happily clattering about as he polished the silverware.

"Here you go," I said. "Unorthodox elevenses."

He put down the polish and cloth and examined the bowl. He took a spoon from me and cautiously ate a mouthful. As he chewed, his face animated with recognition.

"I ate this with Uncle Nick when we were kids. Mum would give it to us as a treat, she used it as a bribe to make us do chores around the house. Once, I drank a whole tin thinking she wouldn't notice. I got **walloped,**" he said. "Christ, it's delicious. I'm amazed I have any teeth left in my mouth."

"Good!" I said, delighted that he was speaking of coherent, verifiable memories. "I've left a load of tins for you to get through."

I walked into the living room and saw, splayed on his armchair, a copy of **Robinson Crusoe** opened in its middle. The earlier conversation we'd had suddenly made sense, and I felt both unsettled and relieved. I was glad that, of all the books on his shelf, he had chosen to read that one that morning. I was glad he was about to set sail to Guinea on a swashbuckling adventure. If I were him, that's exactly where I'd like to be as well. I'd want to go as far away as possible.

WHEN I GOT HOME, I knocked on Angelo's door, like I had fruitlessly every day since our argument from my bedroom window in the middle of the night. This time, however, he answered. His hair and face looked creased and turned over, like an unmade bed. He squinted and rubbed his eyes, adjusting to the hallway light. The lamps were off in his flat and the curtains were drawn. It was four o'clock in the afternoon.

"Hi," I said.

"Hi?" he said.

"I wanted to talk about the other night." He stared at me—sand-specks of sleep in his eyes, his full lips even poutier than usual from just-awoken dehydration. I waited for him to speak before relenting. "Right, I'll start then. How you behaved the other night was not cool." **Not cool.** There I was again, in the interest of neighbourly diplomacy, employing parlance I had only ever used when I was a teacher who'd lost control of a GCSE classroom.

"When you shout at me like an animal?" he said, picking the yellow crumbs from his tear ducts.

"I didn't shout at you, I very politely asked you a good few times to stop talking so loudly at half twelve on a weeknight."

"If you wanted us to be quiet, you should have come down and knock on the door."

"You never answer your door."

"Do not shout at me."

My long-contained frustration was seeping out of me and making my skin tingle. "Stop saying that, it doesn't make any sense. You were the one who was shouting."

"No I wasn't."

"Can you not just apologize? That's all I need. Then we can move on."

"No," he said, his face expressionless.

"What?"

"No," he bleated as he closed his front door.

MAX AND I went for dinner that night—I was reviewing a newly opened pub and I took him with me. Now, more than ever, I needed the secret door of his company to take me to the fantastical place it had been taking me from our very first date.

"Let me look at that cover again," he said at the bottom of our second bottle of wine, reaching for my phone and bringing up the photo of **The Tiny Kitchen**'s book jacket. "I can't wait to see it on the shelves. You clever, clever thing." I felt myself lean towards his praise like it was the warmth of sunlight. I realized how much I had wanted Dad to say the same thing—I had decided to keep the proofs in my bag earlier that day and give him a copy another time. I hadn't wanted to cause any more confusion.

"I've had an idea," I said, placing my glass on the bar. "For my next book. I haven't told anyone yet and I wanted to tell you first because I know you'll tell me if it's bad or not."

Max straightened his spine and shook his face to sober himself up. "I'm here. Pitch."

"So, I saw my dad today, who was in a pretty disorientated mood. Getting things confused, imagining conversations, mixing up things that had happened with things that he'd read. I made him something to eat because I had a bunch of condensed milk with me—you know I'm doing that weird job with the condensed milk company?" He nodded. "So I made him condensed milk and bananas, because Mum said it was his favourite when he was a kid. And honestly, when he ate it, it was like a switch to his old self had been flicked back on. It was brief, but so immediate."

"How interesting."

"It made me think about food and memory. How much our eating habits are dictated by nostalgia. Looking into what it is about taste and smell that sparks involuntary memory. It would be a book of recipes, stories and science. Viv wanted me to write something human. I can't think of a more human way into food than talking about how it connects us to our past. What do you think?"

He pushed my wayward fringe wings to the side of my face. "I think it's great."

"Do you?"

"Yes. I love it. **Proustian Cooking with Nina Dean,**" he said. "No, that needs work."

"And I'll interview psychologists about why exactly certain tastes are linked to certain feelings."

"And you should research what the comfort foods are of every generation."

"Exactly—the historical context of why post-rationing war babies love bananas. And why our generation love hamburgers."

"Free toy with a Happy Meal."

"Free toy with a Happy Meal," I agreed.

"It's brilliant," he said, leaning into me like something he wanted a bite of. "You're brilliant."

We contemplated a third bottle of wine, and as light, silly tipsiness slid towards full-blown, slack-jawed drunkenness, the bell of a thousand soon-to-be-first-shags rang. "Last orders!" echoed down the bar.

"I'm not done drinking," I said.

"No, you're not," he said, a filter held between his lips as he rolled a cigarette. "Now, what's next on the agenda, Nina George? What else have we got to fix, because I can't bear seeing you sad and wallowing with your pretty little mouth all downturned and sulky."

"The nightmare neighbour downstairs."

"I think I should just go talk to him," he said. "He sounds like he might be one of those awful men who only listens to other men."

"No," I said, laying my palm against his shoulder and stroking the soft brushed cotton of his navy shirt. "I have to deal with him on my own."

"No, you don't."

"I do," I said, draining my wine glass. "I know that sounds petulant. But it's important that I manage this situation without the help of a man. I need to know I can operate efficiently on my own."

"But—" He stopped himself mid-thought and put his tobacco back into his pocket. He tucked the cigarette behind his ear. "You're not on your own." Max often disarmed me in seemingly unromantic conversation with these grand, surprising statements about our relationship. It felt like a test. I never knew the correct way to respond.

We staggered out of the pub with our arms around each other and spilt into the East London street, with Max promising that there was an ornately carpeted, decidedly inelegant, sweaty pub that I would love nearby with late hours and a pool table. I followed him as he took a twisting route through the streets, stopping at every corner and assessing which way to turn, like he was on a quest.

"I used to drink here every night between the ages of twenty-seven and thirty," he said.

"You between the ages of twenty-seven and thirty. I wish I could meet every single Max from every single year since birth. I want them all lined up for me."

"Right," he said, standing still in the middle of the silent, residential road, the heat of his breath forming clouds as he spoke. I imagined a furnace inside him, generating every word and thought. He took his iPhone out of his pocket and opened Maps. "I hate that I'm too drunk to navigate without this, but it turns out I'm too drunk to navigate without this."

I looked around the street we found ourselves on and felt the threat of déjà vu build momentum from a distance and come towards me like a crashing wave.

"Max. Where are we?"

"I'm just finding out, Nina George."

"I think we're near the flat."

"Which flat?"

"The first flat I lived in. Are we near Mile End?"

"Yes, the station is about ten minutes' walk away."

I felt myself being drawn towards one end of the road and I followed it like iron to a magnet. "Are we near Albyn Square?" I asked.

"Hang on," Max said as I carried on walking ahead of him. "Hang on."

"We are, I know where we are."

I got to the end of the road, turned right, walked

past the pub where Dad and I used to eat our weekend chips together and turned left on to Albyn Square. My body responded with more than my senses—I felt it in my cells. It was biological and visceral, prehistoric and predetermining. There in the middle was the garden square, perfectly kept in accordance with every angle my memory had captured. Every plant, every path and every tree looked exactly as it did since the last time I was here over twenty years ago. I walked towards the railings and looked into the garden. I wrapped my hands around the cold, shiny black metal poles and, as I looked down at them, remembered the fleecy mittens I used to wear.

"Max, this is it," I said. "This is the square I grew up in." Without thinking, I put one foot on to the latitude of the railings and heaved myself up to stand on it. I jumped off the other side and stood in the garden. Max followed behind me.

"This is where my dad and I came together every weekend. This is where I learnt to ride my bike. This is where they took me in my pram when I was a baby. This is the first place they took me to when they brought me home from the hospital." I pointed at the bench on the outskirts of the grass. "There's a photo of me and Mum sitting there when I was a couple of days old." In the top right-hand corner of the square towered a tall mulberry tree. "That tree—" I could sense I was garbling now, as I hurriedly walked towards it. "I used to sit under it. I used to pretend I was in a forest. Mum would make me sandwiches and I'd take my toys out here and play under it for hours. I fell out of it once. I had to have stitches on my knee. Maybe it wasn't for hours. I never know if what I remember as an hour when I was a child was actually ten minutes in reality."

"Wow," Max mustered. I wouldn't know what to say to someone being swallowed up by a vortex of nostalgia either. For Max, this was just a London square—a collection of roads, a patch of grass, a handful of street lights. For me, it was the source of my existence. I had been conceived here, carried here; learnt feelings and faces and words here.

"I've just realized something," I said. "This exact tree is what taught me what the word **tree** is. Any time I've said that word, or stood by a tree, or thought of a tree since I could speak, I've seen this one. In the bottom of my brain, there are all these pictures of the objects that taught me what the world is. I'm not even aware they're there, but they are. It's like this tree is inside me, some-how." Max watched me place my hand on its trunk and lean closer to it. "Sorry, I know I'm talking total fucking bollocks." I touched my forehead against its bark as the branches brushed the top of my head. "I feel really sick." He put his arm around me and we walked to the bench and sat down.

I folded forward, holding my head between my knees, and Max rested his hand on my back.

"I think my dad knows what's happening to him."

"Why do you think that?"

"I can just tell. I know him better than anyone. And he knows that something is changing inside him. He knows he's losing easy access to parts of himself and his memories. I wish I didn't know that was the truth, but it is. I wish I could let myself believe he's blissfully unaware, but I can't. How awful and confusing for him, Max. He must be so scared. It must be completely unbearable." He ran his hand up and down my back as we sat in silence.

"This is a beautiful place to live," he finally said. I sat back up and looked at the imposing row of giant doll's houses across from us.

"It's perfect, isn't it? I wonder if I knew how perfect it was when I was here."

"I want us to live on this square."

"We're priced out. Like the rest of the world."

"One day," he said. "I will find a way for us to live on this square. Even if it's just in someone's garden shed. I can see us here."

"I think everyone can see themselves here," I said. "I think it's like really attractive people—everyone thinks they belong with one. Everyone thinks the hottest person in the room is their soulmate."

"No, I really can see us here."

"Can you?"

"Yes, Nina," he said. "I love you."

I held his face like a Magic 8 Ball. I brought it inches away from mine and peered into his eyes to try to see all the pictures of streets and squares that lived inside him.

"I love you too," I said. The mulberry tree stood tall and proud against the moonlight, casting a shadow on our bodies wrapped up in each other.

## 8

**New message from: Nina**
**20 November 10:04**
My hero—thank you for cheering me up
after such a rotten day. You left this morning
before I got to lovingly force-feed you and
your hangover toast. Hope your head isn't
too sore. Have a good day at work x

**New message from: Nina**
**21 November 16:27**
How's your day? X

**New message from: Max**
**21 November 23:10**
Long and cold. No worries about cheering
you up, was lovely to see you as always x

**New message from: Nina**
**22 November 11:13**
Just saw a seagull swallowing a dead rat whole
outside Tufnell Park station. Hope your week
is going well, it can't be grimmer than that x

**Missed call from: Nina**
**25 November 19:44**

**New message from: Nina**
**25 November 19:50**
Don't worry about calling me back,
wasn't ringing about anything important,
just wanted to check how you are x

**New message from: Max**
**25 November 20:16**
All good this end, Nina George.
Hope all's good with you x

**New message from: Nina**
**25 November 20:35**
All fine. Writing a piece about how to
make perfect caponata, so I'm up to

my neck in aubergine. Wanna come
round and be my official taster?

New message from: Max
25 November 21:01
Wish I could but working late tonight x

New message from: Nina
25 November 21:13
Oh poor you. Hope work isn't too hectic.
Let me know when you're free x

New message from: Nina
27 November 9:07
Morning! Fancy the cinema tonight? X

New message from: Max
27 November 14:18
Would love to but have dinner plans I'm afraid.

New message from: Nina
27 November 16:05
OK—will leave it to you to let me
know when you fancy hanging out.
Hope things aren't too stressful.

**New message from: Nina**
**29 November 12:15**
That weird Peruvian bar we love has started
a bottomless pisco sour night. Shall we see
how far we can push the limits of the deal?

**New message from: Nina**
**1 December 11:00**
Morning. Slightly feel like I'm pestering you.
Totally understand if you don't have loads of
time to chat or hang out at the moment, but
can you let me know that everything is OK?

**Missed call from: Nina**
**1 December 15:02**

                    **New message from: Max**
                        **1 December 15:07**
                Hey—I'm at work. Are you OK?

**New message from: Nina**
**1 December 15:10**
Really not trying to distract you from
work—just wanted to check you're
OK, as per my message above.

                    **New message from: Max**
                        **1 December 18:39**
            Fine—things just so busy at the moment.

**New message from: Nina**
**1 December 19:26**
Is there anything I can do to help?
Don't like thinking of you stressed.

**New message from: Nina**
**4 December 10:54**
Morning. Hope work is easier and you haven't
been staying late too much. Fancy a drink
this week? Or if you've got early starts, I can
come to yours and cook or you could come
to mine? Whatever's easiest for you x

**New message from: Nina**
**5 December 14:40**
Get the feeling something is up. I
would really appreciate chatting on the
phone to you, even if it's just for five
minutes. Let me know when works.

**New message from: Nina**
**7 December 08:11**
I really hate feeling like I'm harassing you.
It's making me go a bit insane. Please
can you just let me know you're OK?

**New message from: Max**
**7 December 09:09**
Sorry if I've made you feel that way. I
don't feel like you're harassing me.

**New message from: Nina**
**7 December 09:17**
Thanks for your response. I guess I'm just
worried you're not being honest with me
about something. If you really are busy with
work, that's totally fine and I don't want to
be another burden/pressure on you, but I
need just a bit more communication so I know
that you/we are fine. It's odd to have been
seeing each other so regularly and speaking
every day to have not spoken to you in three
weeks. I hope you have a good day at work x

**New message from: Nina**
**12 December 12:01**
Hiya. Not sure if you remember but we're
meant to be going round to my mum and dad's
tomorrow night for dinner. 1) Do you still
fancy it? 2) If you do, Mum wants to know if
there's anything you don't eat? As a warning:
she nearly always does some undercooked
rice stuffed in something overcooked. So if
you're not in a rice mood: let it be known
now or for ever hold your peace x

**New message from: Nina**
**13 December 10:05**
I assume you're not coming for dinner tonight.

**New message from: Nina**
**13 December 22:17**
I don't understand why you suddenly don't
want to talk to me, Max. It seems strange that
the last time we saw each other you told me
you loved me for the first time, then you went
completely silent and lost all inclination to see
me or even pick up the phone when I call. I hope
you can see how confusing that is. I'd really
appreciate an explanation when you're ready.

**New message from: Nina**
**19 December 11:10**
Another week of no contact from you. I don't
really know what else I can do at this stage. I'm
really, really hurt at how you've behaved and
I hate that you've made me feel like I'm being
intense and demanding and weird, when it's your
actions that are strange. If you don't want us
to see each other any more, that's OK, but you
have to be honest with me about it. You can't
just disappear. It's staggeringly cruel and (unless
I've been totally wrong about you over the last
three months) I don't think you're a cruel man.

**Missed call from: Nina**
**19 December 20:14**

**New message from: Nina**
**19 December 20:33**
Max—please just call me back and tell
me what's happened. Then you never,
ever have to speak to me again.

## 9

I DEDICATED MY PRACTICE to you and Max in hot yoga yesterday."

"I don't know what that means, Lola."

She was lying across her sofa with her feet on my lap, eating chocolate raisins and wearing a navy polo neck that had NO PHOTOS, PLEASE emblazoned on it in cerise sequins.

"Yoga is most effective when you focus on a cause or a person who you want to send all your energy and focus out to," she said. "So when it gets really hard, you think of that person, and you almost feel like you're doing this work for them. So, when I was in Dancer's Pose yesterday and I thought my back was going to break in two—I just closed my eyes and imagined Max coming to your house."

"Okay, well it hasn't worked." I pulled the sofa throw over us. Lola's flat always had a very specific and irritating temperature—that of a house with all the windows open and the heating on full-blast.

"I know this isn't a comfortable thought," she said, tentatively reaching up to stroke my ponytail, "but is there any possibility he could have died?"

"I have wondered that."

"Let's try and trace him," she said, sitting up. "We'll need to go full Miss Marple. Oh God, I do love this bit!"

"What 'bit'?"

"Trying to work out if a man who is ignoring you is dead or alive." She opened up her laptop. "What's his Instagram handle?"

"He's not on Instagram."

"Okay, what's his surname?" She brought up Facebook.

"Max Redmond."

She typed his name into the search bar. Up came a teenager in Derbyshire proudly holding a mug with Chewbacca on it and an elderly, topless man in a bandana from Idaho. "Any of these?"

"No."

"Oh."

"I don't think he's on Facebook. I don't think he's on any social media."

"Okay, how about WhatsApp? How do you message each other?"

"Just texting."

"Ah-ha!" she said, one fluorescent-orange fingernail held aloft. "He'll definitely be on instant messaging service and that will tell us when he was last online." She typed his number into her phone and brought up two instant messaging apps. She frowned at her screen. "How weird. He's not on one."

"He's a sort of hippie," I said, loathing myself for speaking his own propaganda.

"Yeah, but nearly everyone I know is on at least one. Even my gran and I talk on one."

"Have we run out of options?"

"Give me your phone," she said. She went to the app store and downloaded Linx—I had deleted it about a month ago as it was doing nothing on my phone but inhabiting storage space and collecting occasional likes from plain-faced men with job titles I didn't understand such as "brand behaviours." She passed me my phone back and I logged in. "Scroll down to find the conversation you had with him. We can go on his profile and see when he last updated it." I scrolled down to the very bottom of my matches—they hung there morbidly, encased in cryonic ice—dead but perfectly preserved and ready to be desperately revived.

"He's not here. He's gone. What does that mean?"

"It means he either deleted the app and his

profile . . ." Lola said, fiddling with the pearly ear-cuff that sat like a miniature tiara on her cartilage.

"Or?"

"Or he's unmatched you."

I put down my phone and stared ahead at Lola's framed print of her own face made to look like a Warhol silkscreen.

"I think he's done this before," I said.

"Why?"

"Because he's gone out of his way to make himself as untraceable as possible. Who else is this untraceable nowadays? It's strategic. He doesn't want women to be able to find out where he is or what's going on after he vanishes."

"That can't be true. He knows you know where he lives and works. That's hardly an effective vanishing act."

"Yes, but he also knows that I would never ever go to his flat or his office for an answer. He's safe there. It would be too humiliating for me. He knows that I would hate to seem that mad. I'm strong-armed into silence by the fear of being called mad. So instead I just have to go actually mad with no answers."

"Do you want a glass of wine?"

"How have you done this for a decade, Lola?"

"Rioja?"

"It's eleven in the morning."

"It's an emergency, I think." Lola stood up and walked to her kitchen counter to retrieve a bottle from the wine rack.

"This is only fun for the boys," I said.

"What is?"

"Dating in your thirties. The boys are all in charge. We have no control in any of it."

"Don't make this political, it's not political."

"It's true," I said. "If you're a woman in your thirties and you want a family, you're at the behest of the impulses of flaky men. They make all the rules and we just have to obey. You're not allowed to say what you want or what has upset you because there's always this undetonated bomb underneath the relationship that goes off if you seem too 'intense.'"

Lola poured the wine into two glass tumblers. "But you weren't intense."

"Of course I wasn't! He told me he wanted to marry me on our first date. Can you imagine what would have happened if a woman had said that on a first date? He would have alerted the authorities. Why does he get to say that? Why does he get to be the one in charge of saying 'I love you' first, then ghost me?"

"In my experience, that's when ghosting is most likely to happen."

"Why?"

"Okay, so here's my theory," Lola said, sitting back on to the sofa's mountain of velvet cushions, clearly delighted that her PhD in dating was finally being put to good use. "Men of our generation often disappear once they've got a woman to say

'I love you' back to them, because it's almost like they've completed a game. Because they're the first boys who grew up glued to their PlayStations and Game Boys, they weren't conditioned to develop any sense of honour and duty in adolescence the way our fathers were. PlayStations replaced parenting. They were taught to look for fun, complete the fun, then get to the next level, switch players or try a new game. They need maximum stimulation all the time. 'I love you' is the relationship equivalent of Level 17 of **Tomb Raider 2** for a lot of millennial men."

I took a large gulp of Rioja that tasted more sooty than earthy when mixed with the lingering taste of my morning toothpaste. I thought about the hours that I had spent in my and Joe's flat with the grey background noise of his football videogame permeating through the walls of the living room, dark with the curtains shut. I thought about Mark passed out in a cupboard and pissing himself in his sleep, while his wife breastfed their newborn baby in the lonely silence of the dawn. I thought about Max playing hide and seek—watching me through a crack in the wall and giggling at my disorientation in the game I didn't know I was a participant in. I thought about all these men in their thirties—ageing on the outside with receding hairlines and budding haemorrhoids—running around a nursery, picking up and putting down women and wives and babies from an overflowing trunk of toys.

"Can we talk about something else?" I said. "Literally anything else."

"Of course," Lola said, giving my knee a squeeze. "I think if my split ends get any worse, I'm going to have to throw myself in the River Thames."

"Lola."

"What?"

"You can't think about your split ends that much. Surely they can't be causing you more than a second's thought a year?"

"I do," she said, holding the end of her hair between her two fingers and studying the strands forensically. "I think about my split ends I would say for thirty-eight minutes every day, mostly on my commute."

"How is this still the reality of our lives?" I said, gulping the rest of my wine in one. "Waiting for men to call us and reading our own hair like it's a book. I feel so grim to be a woman. That's not how I'm meant to feel."

"For God's sake, Nina. This isn't about being a woman. Most people are self-obsessed, gender regardless. Most people pretend they care about single-use plastics more than they care about their own split ends, but they don't. I'm just not scared to be honest about it. And THAT'S feminism." She said it with a camp flourish, like it was a gameshow host's catchphrase. I leant down to put my head in the cradle of my palms and closed my eyes. Lola soothingly played with my ponytail.

"I know this is so awful right now," she said. "But you just have to trust me when I say: you shall not pass."

"What do you mean?"

"You shall not pass," she repeated sagely, giving me a gentle smile.

"Pass where?"

"It's a phrase my mum always used to say to me when I was sad. It means: this will end at some point, then you'll be happy again."

"**This too** shall pass."

"Yes, exactly, it will."

"No, that's what you're meant to say."

"Is it? Why do I know the proverb 'You shall not pass'?"

"It's not a proverb, it's what Gandalf says in **Lord of the Rings.**"

"That's it!" She clicked her fingers, as if finally proven correct.

"I feel very comforted," I said, patting her hand. "Thank you."

WHEN I LEFT LOLA'S HOUSE in the late afternoon, with a foreign type of hangover from a mid-morning drink, I was ready to go home, turn off my phone and get straight into bed. As I walked to the tube station, the four letters that I increasingly dreaded seeing most on my phone screen appeared: HOME.

"Hi, Mum."

"Hi, Ninabean. How are you?"

"Fine. How are you?"

"I'm okay. Quick one—has Dad called you today?"

"No, why?"

"He's missing."

"Since when?"

"Since this morning."

"What time?"

"About six. I heard the door go, and I assumed he was just going to have a wander about in the garden, so I didn't bother going to get him."

"Why would he be going out to be in the garden? It would have been freezing cold and pitch-black. Why didn't you stop him?"

"This is EXACTLY why I didn't want to call you," she squawked. I heard her speak to someone away from the phone's mouthpiece. I could make out a few spat-out words: "Nina," "having a go," "how bloody dare" and "has the nerve."

"Mum," I said, trying to regain her attention. "Mum. MUM."

"WHAT?" she roared.

"I'll get on the train and come to you now."

GLORIA ANSWERED THE DOOR, wearing a grey zip-up hoodie studded in diamanté butterflies. Her overly blow-dried claret-coloured bob was as smooth and bulbous as a conker. She gave me an inappropriately large smile, considering the circumstances of my visit. She was an emotional bollard of a woman, always getting in the way when we were in the middle of a sensitive family situation. When I was in my difficult, argumentative adolescent years, she was constantly at the house collecting all sides of the story like a tabloid reporter. She was in her early sixties, but she still had the air of the all-girls school about her—desperate for gossip, frantic to be the receptacle and dispenser of information in a crisis and strangely fixated on being my mum's "best friend" like two Year 11s with matching tattoos drawn in marker pen.

"Nina!" she said, stretching out her arms and drawing me in for a reluctant hug. "How are you?"

"Worried about Dad," I said, unnecessarily.

"Well—we all are."

"Where's Mum?"

"Would you like a bagel with some sandwich spread?"

"I'm good, thank you—where's Mum?"

"Mandy's in the living room."

"Her name isn't Mandy."

"Her name is whatever she wants it to be, sweetheart. It's Mandy's right to express herself how she likes, and if that's with a new name, it's not our place to dictate to her who we think she is." She had obviously spent hour upon hour bitching about me being difficult about "the Mandy problem" with Mum over instant cappuccinos made from packets of powder, winding her up by quoting a life coach.

I went into the living room, where Mum was sitting in the corner of the sofa, holding a mug in one hand and examining her cuticles on the other.

"Have you called the police?"

"Of course I've called the police."

"Have you told them about Dad's condition?"

"Yes."

"And are they searching for him?"

"Yes, they've made it an urgent case. They're currently checking with all the hospitals, then if there's still no sign of him, they're going to look at local CCTV."

"Okay," I said, sitting down at the opposite end of the sofa. "Well done."

"You don't mean that, you think this is all my fault."

"I don't, Mum, I was just shocked earlier, I didn't mean it."

Gloria walked in. "What's this?" she said.

"Nothing," I said.

"I was just telling her that she made me feel very guilty earlier about Bill going missing."

"Yes, it really is just an unfortunate accident, your mum didn't do anything wrong."

"I think what I was trying to say, Gloria," I said on a long, patient outbreath, "is that we need to look at how we handle and speak to Dad as his condition progresses. We can't carry on as if everything's normal, as much as we'd all like to. I think this is the final warning that something has to change."

Mum was staring ahead blankly at the black TV screen.

"It's just such a waste," she said.

"What is?" I asked.

"It can all be frozen, it can all be frozen," Gloria cooed. She turned to me and spoke in a hushed voice as if Mum couldn't hear. "You mum was meant to be hosting Reading Between the Wines tonight. There was a big group of us who were all meant to come over here and she'd already bought all the food."

"Right, so where have we looked so far?" I said, ignoring Gloria. "Have you rung all your friends in the area?"

"Yes, everyone's aware of the situation," Mum replied.

"What about the golf club? Maybe he thought there—"

"We went," Gloria butted in. "First thing. He wasn't there but everyone knows to look out for him."

"What was the last conversation you had with him? Do you remember what you were talking about last night?"

"We had an argument. And please don't have a go at me about it, you have NO idea what it's been like here, Nina."

"What was the argument about?"

"Urgggghhh," she growled, closing her eyes and shaking her head. "He woke me up in the middle of the night because he was banging about, bringing all the chairs from the kitchen into here and arranging them in a circle."

"Why was he doing that?"

"He said he had a staff meeting the following morning."

"What did you say?"

"I lost my temper, I told him he retired fifteen years ago and there are no staff meetings any more."

"And how did he respond?"

"He got very frustrated. We went round and round in circles for such a long time, Nina, honestly, I thought we were going to throttle each other."

"Have you checked Elstree High?" I asked.

"I don't think he'd be there."

"It's the last school he taught at. He could be mis-remembering that he's retired, so he might have got up early to go to school. Ring Elstree High."

"It's a Saturday."

"It's still worth trying. Did he take his phone?"

"No, just his wallet."

"Okay, so he could have got on a bus or a tube. Or a taxi, even."

I went into my bedroom for a moment of quiet and I sat on the carpet, closed my eyes and tried to imagine where Dad might have felt a pull so urgent he had to get out of bed, dress and leave the house before sunrise. I leant my back up against the bed, my legs crossed on the floor. Whenever I was in a crisis, I found myself on the carpet. I wrote the last two chapters of my book on the floor. Most of my and Joe's break-up conversation took place sitting on our living-room floor. When things became too big, I needed to make myself as small as possible. I thought about sitting cross-legged with my toys under the mulberry tree in Albyn Square. I thought about being there the last time I'd seen Max—how it had felt like I was sucked into it by a life force; how all the markers and memories of time and place had twisted in on themselves like a black hole as I stood in its centre. I thought about Lola's face on the floor of the club toilets the first night we'd met: **I miss home.**

I went into the hallway where Gloria, for reasons I couldn't understand, was applying sparkly lip gloss.

"What was the road Dad grew up on in Bethnal Green?" I asked Mum.

"I don't know," she replied.

"You must remember. Grandma Nelly lived there right up until she died."

"How could I possibly remember the name of that street? She died twenty years ago. Wait until you go through the menopause. You won't be able to remember your own name."

Gloria laughed knowingly, then smacked her glossy lips.

"Don't you have an address book with everyone's old addresses in it?"

"No, not from that far back. It might still be in my Christmas card address book, but I'm not sure where that is off the top of my head." Now was not the time to ask Mum why it was necessary to have both an address book and a Christmas card address book.

"Can you find the exact address for me now? Text it to me? I'll go to Bethnal Green."

"He's not going to be there."

"I just have a gut feeling. It's at least worth checking. Text me the address."

BY THE TIME I ARRIVED at the road where Dad grew up, it was mid-evening and there was still no sign of him. I walked along the row of identical two-bed terraced houses, all with white sash windows and sills that looked like the icing on gingerbread houses. My childhood mind had remembered these buildings as grand and imposing but they were compact and closely packed. Mum and Dad often laughed about the story I once wrote in my school exercise book, in which I described going to my gran's "manshun" at the weekend. I couldn't believe her house had an upstairs and a downstairs.

I rang the bell at number 23. A woman opened the door—she was middle-aged and soft-faced, with hair transitioning from red to white in a chignon, which made it look like a scoop of butterscotch ice cream.

"Hello, I'm so sorry to disturb you, my dad is missing—"

"He's here," she said, ushering me in and closing the door. "He's here, he's safe. Go through." I walked along the hallway, so different to the house I remember, now painted in creams and greys and adorned with the tastes and treasures of another family.

"Dad!" I walked through to him, where he was drinking tea at their kitchen table, reading the newspaper. The sound of Saturday night TV gently bubbled in the background, as comforting as the sound of simmering soup. He looked up at me.

"What are you doing here?" I asked him.

"I'm here to see my mother," he said. "My mother, Nelly Dean, lives here."

"She used to live here."

Dad sighed. "Christ on a bike—this is her bleeding house! I know it like the back of my hand. I'm not leaving until I see her."

"But the problem is, Dad—"

"Would you like a drink?" the woman asked.

"I'm okay, thank you." I imagined the long night ahead, trying to convince Dad to leave this stranger's house. The woman beckoned me back into the hallway where we stood by the door. "I'm sorry. It's his memory, he—"

"My dad had the same," she said, putting her hand on my shoulder in a gesture that I found so disconcertingly caring, it made me realize how much I yearned for maternal solace. "I understand. It's not a problem, don't worry. It was clear as soon as he arrived what was going on. We haven't told him that his mum doesn't live here, we've tried to distract him."

"That's so kind of you. When did he get here?"

"A couple of hours ago. He was very sweet and polite. Once we worked out what was going on, we made him a cup of tea and rang the police to let them know his full name and that he was here."

"Thank God you live here. There are so many people who would have turned him away and he would have been wandering around out in the cold with no phone."

"He was clearly just confused."

"He was born in this house. He grew up here with my grandma and his brother. Then my grandma lived here until she died."

"How did you know he'd be here?"

"I don't know," I said. "I think the memory of your childhood home is impossible to destroy. I can imagine it becoming even sharper and clearer to someone in his condition. I don't know how I'm going to explain what's going on to him."

"I'm not sure how far into this you are, but something we learnt with my dad is that it was much easier for him if we didn't argue with any of the illusions he found himself in."

"I have tried to do that sometimes. Didn't you feel like you were lying to him?"

"A bit," she said with a shrug. "But there's a way of

not contradicting what he's saying without encouraging it either."

"That's good to know."

"You will feel a bit silly. But it's a bit of discomfort for you that will make such a huge difference to him."

I nodded, relieved to finally have someone to talk to about this, without everything I said being dismissed.

"Do you have kids?"

"No."

"I was going to say, think about how you'd speak to your child if they had an imaginary friend, or they believed something to be true that wasn't, but it brought them comfort. Going along with it rarely does anyone any harm. And then they get to the end of the thought at some point."

We went back into the kitchen where Dad was looking in the cupboards.

"What are you after, Dad?" I asked.

"A tin of sardines. She keeps them in here usually. I fancy some sardines on toast."

"Why don't we head back to Pinner and I can make that for you. Nelly's obviously out today, so maybe it's best if we head off. You can tell me all about your mum and this house on the way home."

Dad frowned for a moment, then turned to the woman whose kitchen he was rifling through.

"Will you tell her I was here? Will you tell her I dropped by to say hello?"

"Of course, Bill. I'll be sure to pass on your message."

He nodded, then closed the cabinet door.

I ORDERED A TAXI to take us home and put up with the extortionate price of the long journey to avoid agitating Dad further on a busy tube on a Saturday night. I rang Mum to tell her what had happened and she was relieved. We spent the majority of the journey in silence, Dad staring out of the window, hypnotized by the A40.

"I don't know why my mum wasn't there," he said.

"She was probably just busy doing some errands or meeting people today."

"My dad wasn't there because my dad left."

"That's right."

"He left when I was ten years old, for Marjorie who lived on the next road along. They've both moved away now."

"Yep," I said, remembering Dad's childhood photo albums that had fewer than ten pictures of the grandfather I never met, then a space for a missing man in every other image until the pages ran out. "They have."

"But my mother is still waiting for him," he said. "She will keep waiting and waiting for him for ever, I imagine. She stands at the letterbox every day when the post comes, but nothing ever comes from him. He's not coming back. We will never see him or speak to him again."

"HOME AGAIN," I said cheerily as I opened the front door, trying to gently re-root Dad back in reality. "That was a nice bit of nostalgia, wasn't it?"

"Nostalgia," he repeated, hanging his charcoal coat on the hallway wall hook. "Greek. Conjoining of **nostos** and **álgos.** Gorgeous." He smiled at me. "I must go to bed, I'm spent."

"All right. I'm going to stay tonight. I'll see you in the morning."

"Goodnight," he said, and went upstairs holding the bannister with every step.

IN THE PREDAWN HOURS of the next morning, unable to sleep, I went to Dad's bookshelf and picked up his dictionary of English etymology. I sat on the floor, cross-legged, with my back pressed against the sofa, and flipped to N.

Nostalgia: Greek compound combining **nostos** (homecoming) and **álgos** (pain). The literal Greek translation for nostalgia is "pain from an old wound."

## 10

THE DOORBELL RANG. It had been a few days since Dad had gone missing, and I'd stayed at the house since I'd brought him home. Mum and I had been sitting nervously at the kitchen table. Dad was busy upstairs sorting through books in his soon-to-be-converted study.

"Okay, remember to be as clear and detailed as possible with her about all the information," I said. We both stood up to go to the door.

"Yes, I know."

"We're incredibly, incredibly lucky to have been assigned an Admiral nurse. We have to make the most of her being here. Please don't brush over things when you're talking about Dad."

"All right, all right."

We opened the door to a woman in a bright-red duffle coat with cropped grey hair. She was short, even shorter than Mum and me, with small, round, sparkling brown eyes, a button nose and a girlish gap in between her two front teeth.

"Hello," she said in a voice tinted with a Midlands accent, "I'm Gwen."

"Come in, Gwen," I said.

"Thank you. Blimey, it's cold, isn't it!"

"It is," I said. "I'm Nina." I put out my hand. She took off her fleecy glove before she shook it. It was a sweet and old-fashioned gesture, and it made me like her instantly.

"Nina, lovely, and you are?"

"Mandy," Mum said.

"Mum."

"Stop it," she hissed.

"Her name is Nancy," I said.

"My name is **Mandy**."

"Okay, just to be clear for any documentation or paperwork, her real name is Nancy but she inexplicably wants everyone to call her Mandy."

"What a great idea!" Gwen said, taking off her coat. "I'd love to change my name, I've always thought Gwen was so dull."

Mum looked at me, eyes wide and face indignant. "Thank you," she said triumphantly.

"Lovely name, Mandy. My favourite aunty was Mandy. Such a fun lady."

"It's a fun name," Mum said proudly.

"It is!" she said.

"Gwen, can I get you a cup of tea or a coffee?"

"Oh, tea, please. Milk and one sugar if you have it."

"Coming up," I said. "Shall we all talk in the living room?"

"Yes," Mum said.

"I actually might talk to just the carer first. Who's the carer?"

Mum and I looked at each other. It was a word neither of us had ever used, let alone discussed. Gwen had been here for less than two minutes and she had already made it clear quite how badly we were managing. Mum's face had arranged into an uncharacteristically crestfallen expression. Neither of us said anything for a moment.

"I suppose," she said quietly, "I suppose I am."

"Lovely, how about we have a chat first, just the two of us? Then, Nina, you can join us in a bit."

I SAT IN THE KITCHEN and listened to the clock tick as I tried to make out the conversation in the room next door and heard nothing. I kept recalling Mum's face when Gwen had said the word "carer." My mum wasn't a carer. She was so many things—efficient, organized, managerial. A reliable mother, a fun friend, a loving wife. But she would never be a carer. She had been so young when she'd met my dad—their dynamic had always been somewhat dictated by their age gap and he had always been her great protector. It irritated me when I was younger—Dad was forever defending Mum's slightly unreasonable behaviour. He was devoted to her. He was the one who cared for her. I had never, in all my life, imagined a time when he might be the one who had to be protected and defended by her.

AFTER ABOUT AN HOUR, Mum came into the kitchen and asked me to come through. We sat next to each other on the sofa and Gwen sat in Dad's armchair.

"Did you tell her everything, Mum?"

"Yes."

"About the stroke, about everything the doctor said? Did you give her all the medical letters and the notes from the hospital?"

"Nina, stop talking to me like I'm a child."

"She has, Nina," Gwen said. "She's been very helpful with informing me on all of your dad's medical history."

"Because I feel like I've been left to be the only repository of information throughout this whole thing and I can't be that any more, I can't. I'm so scared something's going to happen to Dad and someone's going to ask for all the facts and I'm going to forget something or miss something out and—"

"Since when have you been the one with all the information? You're never here!" Mum said.

"Exactly! That's what worries me! I'm never here and I'm the only one who seems to be taking this seriously!"

"Hang on, hang on," Gwen said. "Your mum is taking this very seriously, and we're all going to make sure that we keep a record of important information from now on. Nina—tell me what your biggest concern is at the moment for Bill."

"My biggest concern is that Mum's going to let him wander out of the house again in the freezing cold and this time he won't be so lucky to meet people who are understanding and nice."

"Okay," Gwen mediated. "The front door. This is a very common problem and there are a number of things we can try."

"I'm not putting some huge lock on my door and making my home feel like a high-security prison!" Mum squawked.

"There's lots of things we can do before it gets to that. How about a curtain? If you hang a curtain in front of the door, he won't feel so compelled to go to it."

"What sort of curtain?"

"Now is not the time to be worrying about interior design, Mum."

"Just a plain dark curtain," Gwen said. "And the other thing we should sort out is something called the Herbert Protocol. It's a form we can fill out now and keep updating as Bill's condition changes, then we have it on hand to give it straight to the police if he ever goes missing again."

"Okay, that's good," I said. "Let's do that today."

"Is there anything else you wanted to talk about, Nina?"

"Yes," I said. "Dad is misremembering things. It used to happen a bit, but he was mostly very lucid. Now he's often lucid, but the imaginings are happening more and more. He'll get people's stories confused. Or the timeline of his own life muddled. He starts talking about things that aren't happening or people who aren't here and I think the best way to deal with it is to go along with it."

"Absolutely not," Mum said.

"Someone told me it's the most effective solution. And that there's a way we can avoid contradicting his story while also not encouraging it too much."

"I just don't see how that's going to help anyone," Mum said.

"He's getting frustrated because he thinks he's telling the truth. Imagine how frustrated you'd get if someone kept saying you were wrong about something you knew to be a fact."

"That's right," Gwen said. "And as Nina suggests, there's a way of doing it sensitively. What's a recent example of this behaviour?"

"He thinks his mum is alive, but she died twenty years ago," I said.

"Right, so, next time that he talks about his mother, instead of telling him that she's dead, try asking him to share some happy memories of his childhood. Or look through a photo album together and talk about the photos of her."

"Can you do that, Mum?"

She was picking at her cuticles, which looked red and angrily shredded, and refused to make eye contact with me.

"Yes," she said.

GWEN STOOD IN THE HALLWAY and retrieved her coat from the hook.

"Now, you have my number and email address to get in touch whenever you need me."

"Thank you," Mum said.

"And I'll check in again in a week."

Dad came down the stairs and, before Mum and I had a chance to work out what to say, Gwen walked towards him with an outstretched hand.

"Ah! Good afternoon, Bill," she said with sunny, crisp formality. "I'm Gwen. Lovely to meet you."

"Pleasure to meet you," he replied.

"I hear you were a teacher."

"Yes."

"And what did you teach?"

"Children, mainly," he said.

Gwen laughed. It felt good to see Dad back in the role of being the dispenser of comedy rather than the accidental subject of it. Gwen said goodbye to us, then left. Shortly afterwards, I left too. Mum promised to speak to me every day to keep me updated on how Dad was.

I didn't tell Mum about Max. I had started making childish bargains with the laws of fate, and decided that the more people I told about Max's disappearance, the less likely it was that he would come back. I was doing everything I could to keep him alive with me—I had started reading our early messages like they were the pages of a play. I preferred to live with a half-alive version of him than admit he was gone for good.

I picked up ingredients to make tomato soup that night for dinner—it was a particular kind, the recipe for which I'd spent some time perfecting for the new book. A sweet, smooth, infantile soup that replicated a tin of cream of tomato. It's what I craved when I was low; when I wanted to remember a time when someone pressed their cool hand on my forehead when they were worried about my health or gave me a time I had to go to bed so I didn't have to think about it myself. On the way into the supermarket I saw the homeless woman who once told me she liked Party Rings when I asked her if she'd like anything from the shop. I always picked up a packet for her if she was there. A stooping elderly man with a spine arched like a crescent moon unloaded his trolley in front of me at the till: a bag of cat food and three miniature trifles. I wondered if his mum had given him trifle when he was little. Sweet, smooth tomato soup, sugary round rainbow biscuits, mushy ambrosial custard and jelly. The contents of supermarket baskets are surely evidence that none of us are coping with adulthood all that well.

THAT NIGHT, while I was slowly simmering butter, onions and tomatoes in a pan, I heard a loud noise rise through the floorboards. It was a continuous roar, an animal sound. It sounded like rage and resentment—like a war cry and war wounds. Like red-faced football fans of a losing team flooding into a tube carriage after a match. Heavy metal music.

Outside Angelo's door, the sound was deafening— firework bangs of drums, fingertip-bleeding guitar strums and the cries of monsters and demons. I banged on the door, but the music was so loud even I couldn't hear the sound of my knock. I could hear Angelo's voice shouting along to the non-existent melody. I used the soft side of my fists and banged harder, but there was no reply.

I went upstairs and knocked on Alma's door. She opened it and smiled—her hazel eyes sparkling, her heart-shaped face swathed by a black headscarf covered in blue flowers.

"Hello, Alma, how are you? How are your chillies?"

"Both of us feeling the cold weather, but fine otherwise. How are you?"

"I'm well, I'm well. Are you being disturbed by the noise downstairs?"

"What noise?"

"Angelo, the guy who lives on the ground floor. He's playing really loud music, can you not hear it?"

Alma leant out of her door frame and turned her head quizzically towards the stairs.

"Ah, yes," she said. "Now I can hear. But not inside. I'm lucky, I think, because I have an extra apartment below me to absorb it."

"Yes, exactly, I'm absorbing it."

"Oh dear," she said.

"I'm absorbing too much of it, of him. Have you been woken up by him before?"

"No, never heard him. This is the good thing about being old and deaf."

"You're not old," I said. "But I'm glad you're a bit deaf, for your sake. He makes so much noise and he's been so uncooperative whenever I've tried to speak to him about it."

"What can I do?" she asked. "How can I make this easier?"

"Oh, Alma. You're so lovely."

"If the noise becomes too much, you can always sleep on my sofa."

"Thank you."

"But I suppose you will go to your handsome boyfriend's house instead," she said, her irises catching

the hallway light like gemstones. "How is he?" Alma
had become obsessed with Max after he once carried her shopping up the stairs for her. Since then,
every time I saw her she told me how lucky I was to
be with him—what an extraordinary man he was.
I decided not to point out that he too was lucky to
be with me, a woman who had carried Alma's shopping up the stairs more times than I could count.

"He's fine," I said.

"Soon he'll be your husband!"

"Oh, I don't know about that," I said with
a chuckle.

She chuckled knowingly too. "It's wonderful,
being married."

"I know," I said. "I mean, I don't know. But it
seems great."

"I miss my husband every day. He was not like
your lovely boyfriend, he was very set in his ways.
But he brought me a cup of coffee in bed every
morning until the day he died. Fifty-eight years of
being woken up with fresh coffee. Aren't I lucky?"

"Very," I said. "Very, very lucky."

"You tell me if you want to stay here, if the
noise continues."

"Thank you."

WHEN I WENT BACK TO MY FLAT, the music was
even louder. I tried putting my headphones in and
listening to a podcast as I ate dinner, but I could

still hear and feel its vibrations through the floor. I opened my laptop and looked up when exactly I could call the council with a noise complaint. I then sat on my sofa, flowering in fury, watching the clock until exactly eleven o'clock when I rang noise patrol, gave them my address and asked them to deal with Angelo. I opened the curtains, stood by the window watching the road and waited for them to arrive. I imagined this was what spinsterhood might be like and I really did find it thrilling.

At 11:20, two figures arrived at the front door. I went downstairs, opened it to them, showed them the entrance to Angelo's flat then hurried back up-stairs. I locked my door and sat on the floor with my chin resting on my knees and waited—they knocked, but he couldn't hear them. Then they used their fists to bang, but I think he assumed it was me so ignored it. Finally, they shouted repeatedly that they were from the council and, very suddenly, the music stopped and I heard the squeak of his creaky door open. I pressed my ear against the wall and heard the jumble of hands-off, bureaucratic non-threats that belong to the vocabulary of local councils. From Angelo, I heard just one question, which he asked over and over again: "Was it her?"

I heard noise patrol leave and waited for Angelo's door to close, but there was silence. I heard him walk up the stairs. I wished that I had turned all my lights off to make him think that I was asleep. He reached my flat and stood at the door—I could see the shadow of his feet block the hallway light through the crack above the carpet. He remained there, saying nothing, until the hallway self-timer turned the lights off and I lost the outline of his feet. He stayed for a few minutes—in the absence of shadows, my ears attuned to the sound of his breathing. I wondered how long he would stand there, why he stood there, whether he would say anything and if he knew I sat inches away from him. I was too scared to move in case I made a noise, but I also feared I would be sitting in a silent stand-off with him all night. After another minute or so, I heard him walk downstairs and the door to his flat close.

I thought about the day I had moved into this flat. In the first month of living there, I had experienced such deep daily contentment in knowing these square metres were all mine. But now, I felt the omnipresence of an intruder. I felt unwelcome and unsafe in its walls. I felt like I had been infested with cockroaches and there was nothing I could do to get rid of them. I had to either live with it or move. It was then I knew that there are a handful of situations that, regardless of how happy you are without a partner, loot your single status of all its splendour. One of them is dealing with a nightmare neighbour on your own.

I wanted to call Max. I wanted to talk to him. I wanted his straightforward, tough advice and his firm, unrelenting affection. I picked up my phone to call him, but instead I read through our old messages to each other and watched how he had suddenly grown cold and formal before he disappeared. I went to his name and number in my phone contacts and stared at it, looking for a sign of animation, like I was watching someone in a coma, waiting for a sign of life.

I walked around my flat and searched for evidence that he'd been there. I held the copy of the book he'd left on the bedside table the last time he stayed. I touched the set of drawers he had helped me put up in the bedroom. His red woollen hat was in the cupboard. I turned it inside out and put my face into it—my knees reacted to the instantly recognizable scent of him. I hated him for making me a woman who breathed in an absent man's knitwear like it was a reviving salt. But every day since he'd disappeared, I'd needed proof he had existed. Yes, he had been here. His trace was here. I hadn't dreamt him at all.

But finding proof of his existence meant I had to ask myself a harder question: if he was real, but he was gone, had I dreamt our relationship? Had I invented what we were to each other? The magic that I had felt when he'd picked me up and kissed me on the dance floor the first night we met, "The Edge of Heaven" our soundtrack, was that one-sided? Did Max make everyone feel like that? Was he an illusionist? Was this a show-stopping, spangled deception he could perform on anyone? The love I'd felt, the details of him I'd studied like an academic, the future I'd tentatively begun to think about—were they sleight of hand and tricks of the mind? Had I fallen for it?

I wondered how long I'd be waiting for an answer. I thought about Grandma Nelly and how she waited for her husband who never returned. I tried to recall being in her house when I was little and what she'd look like in the morning when the post came. Had she really stood at the door and waited every day for his handwriting on the front of a letter?

There was so much I thought I'd known about Max, but now I questioned whether we had been perfect strangers in a pretence of togetherness. We had first met as five photos and a few words about our respective hobbies, jobs and location. Our meet-cute of Linx profiles was anything but spontaneous—it was curated and censored, enabled by an algorithm, determined by self-selection. We'd read the signage of each other and we'd filled in the rest with our imaginations. Had I created kismet from coincidental—from the fact that we'd both grown up to the sound of a Beach Boys album, which was probably the favourite album of every baby boomer alive? Had I applied more soul to him than he possessed, because of the vintage concert posters on his wall? Had I trusted him too quickly and fallen too deeply, because I'd projected my own version of his personality into the holes of my knowledge of him?

As I stood in the chasm between who I thought he was to me and the reality of a person who never wanted to speak to me again, I realized just how much we hadn't known about each other. I didn't know what his handwriting looked like if he sent me a letter; he wouldn't recognize mine. He didn't know the name of my grandparents; I didn't know the name of his. We'd barely seen each other around other people, apart from waiting staff and strangers in queues. I'd never met any of his friends—I hardly heard about any of his friends, which, for some reason, had never seemed strange. On our first date, he'd told me how untethered he was and I hadn't taken that as a warning. Nor did I question why he spent most weekends by himself in the countryside. I didn't know why his dad moved so far away when he was so young. I didn't know if his mum was waiting for a letter too. He didn't know my dad before my dad started leaving the house at six a.m. to go look through the kitchen cupboards of a stranger's house he thought was his. And now he never would.

I deleted Max's number along with all our messages and I knew then that I would never see or hear from him again. I accepted it. It was over. He was gone.

TWO

"Love looks not with the
eyes, but with the mind,
And therefore is winged
Cupid painted blind"

**A Midsummer
Night's Dream,**
WILLIAM SHAKESPEARE

## 11

THE LAST MONTHS OF WINTER marked the beginning of the most tyrannical of pre-spring rites: hen dos.

I didn't want to go to Lucy's hen do. I barely wanted to go to my actual friends' hen dos. At thirty-two, I had been to plenty—I'd sat through enough Mr. and Mrs. videos to know that every man's favourite sex position with his future wife is either doggy style or girl on top. I'd sipped through enough penis straws and blown up enough flamingo balloons to create 150 tonnes of plastic for landfills. I'd declined every invitation to hen dos from the age of thirty onwards. But Joe had pleaded with me to go—he said that it would make Lucy feel more "comfortable" about me being part of the "wedding party" if she felt I was there for both of them rather than just for him. Katherine dropped out at the last minute, as she was feeling a bit too pregnant to spend the weekend whooping on command. Thankfully, Lucy invited Lola in her place—she was often the first reserve for hen dos of women she'd only count as an acquaintance. She was also regularly invited to the evening-only, post-dinner portion of a wedding reception of couples she didn't know that well. I think the reasons for this were threefold: she was fun, she always bought a present from the gift registry and she was always single. And single women at a thirty-something party carried the same calibre of entertainment as a covers band. We weren't pregnant so we'd always drink, we had no one to go home to so we'd always stay out late and we might get off with someone which gave the evening some narrative tension for everyone else. And best of all: we were free!

LOLA WAS APPLYING MAKE-UP at a café in Waterloo, next to her monogrammed wheelie suitcase. She was wearing a floor-length Navajo cardigan, a denim rompersuit and a pair of white cowboy boots. Plaits as thin as embroidery silk threads ran through her masses of blonde hair and half-a-dozen pearly clips kept it pulled back off her face. Lola still wanted to look like the girl her fifteen-year-old self had wanted to look like.

"I'm going mad, Nina," she said as I approached her and she pulled me in for a hug with the hand not holding a mascara tube. "Absolutely fucking mad."

"Why?"

"Andreas. The architect from Linx."

"Let's get to the platform and you can tell me what happened."

"I need to finish my make-up."

"Do it on the train," I said impatiently. Lola was infuriatingly laissez-faire about transport.

"Let me just finish my eyes," she said, aggressively thrashing the mascara wand through her eyelashes over and over again.

"No one remotely fuckable is going to be on a train to Godalming, trust me," I said.

"Okay," Lola said, doing one last thrash on each eyelash before putting away her make-up bag and standing up with her suitcase. "So, we've been on about five dates now. Things are going really well. But I know he's sleeping with loads of other women and, while that hasn't bothered me before, it's starting to make me feel insanely jealous."

"Okay, firstly—how do you know he's sleeping with lots of other people?"

She retrieved her phone from her handbag as she walked, opened WhatsApp and presented me with the screen.

"See? Online. He's always online."

"So? He could be talking to a friend?"

"Men don't talk to friends, that's not how men work, they're not like us. And if they do, they message things like: **See you there at four, mate.** They're not glued to their phone for hours and hours of the day."

"I don't know if that's true. Joe was on loads of WhatsApp groups that just traded rubbish gifs and memes all day."

"What kind of groups?" she asked immediately, her eyes twitching from what looked like little to no sleep.

"Oh, you know, like footie practice. Or Ibiza 2012, which just rumbled on and on."

"But he's on it all night every night. It's the night shift that really worries me. Men aren't online until two a.m. talking to anyone else other than a girl they're trying to have sex with."

"How do you know he's online until two a.m. every night?"

"Because I basically just sit there with our chat window open on my phone not talking to him but watching him be online. I cancelled dinner with a friend last night to do it."

**"Lola."**

"I know. Pretended I had a cold. Had to post an Instagram story of me fake-drinking Lemsip to support my alibi."

We put our tickets through the barrier machines and walked along the train platform.

"Why don't you ask him about it?"

"What would I say?"

"Say that you've noticed he's online a lot on WhatsApp, make a joke about it."

"No, he'll know what that means. I don't want him to think I'm trying to control his sex life or be possessive."

We boarded the train and sat on the nearest free seats next to each other.

"Okay, then you have to stop thinking about it for now and then have the exclusivity chat when you feel that it's appropriate to have it."

"Yeah," she sighed, looking out of the stationary train's window. "When will this all end? I just want someone nice to go to the cinema with."

"I know," I said.

A man ran along the platform for the train with a baby strapped to his chest. He held its head protectively. The train guard blew a whistle to signify its imminent departure and the man put his foot into our carriage's door.

"Come on!" he said with a grin. "You can do it!" A woman ran towards him, luggage in both hands. She approached the doors. "YES! MY WIFE!" he shouted triumphantly, holding both arms aloft in celebration as if she had reached the end of a marathon. They both stumbled on to the carriage and caught their breath. They laughed.

"Good job, mate," she said. They found two seats, still breathless and laughing, and arranged their bags and baby paraphernalia around them in a sprawling mess. I realized I was staring when they both caught my eye inquisitively. I jerked my head away and looked out at the passing city. Lola squeezed my hand. I smiled at her and squeezed it back. I'd never felt more grateful for her friendship than since Max's disappearance.

Max may have no longer been in my life or on my phone, but he was everywhere I went and in nearly every thought I had. I had spent Christmas at home, staring at my phone like it was 2002. I had spent New Year with Lola, clanking our glasses together for meaningless toasts about hating all men. I had spent January writing the first few chapters of the new book, grateful to have a new work project and a deadline on which to focus. I hadn't experienced this type of pervasive love sickness since I was a teenager—it was impossible to rid my thoughts of him. I'd notice a knot in the wood of a table that looked like his nose in profile. When two of the letters M, A or X were adjacent on a page, my eyes would instinctively dart to those words first. I heard him in song lyrics, I saw him in crowds on tube platforms. It was bone-achingly tiring and oppressively dull. Daydreaming of him, while previously satisfying when we were together, was now like MSG for the mind. It expanded in my brain, making me feel momentarily full, and then quickly disappeared, making me feel horribly empty. An abundance couldn't satiate me and none of it felt nourishing. And yet I couldn't stop. Lola told me there was no way to bypass this stage of a break-up and I had to go through it. My fear was that the feeling would linger because there was nothing final to mourn.

"Right, what are we expecting from this one?" Lola asked, while looking in a monogrammed compact mirror and loading more make-up on to her already plenty-adorned face. "Stripper?"

"No, definitely not, Lucy's a prude."

"Prudes love strippers though."

"That's true," I said. "And chocolate body paint. And massage oils. Classic sign of someone who doesn't enjoy sex that much, if they own massage oils."

"So, no stripper," she said. "What else do you think they've organized?" I took out my phone and opened the hen do WhatsApp group named LUJOE HENS! which had been pinging incessantly since its inception six weeks ago.

"There'd better be a lot of booze for the amount that we've had to contribute for food and drinks."

"There never is," she said. "It will be one bottle a head for the whole weekend and one slice of overcooked lasagne."


WE WERE THE LAST ONES to arrive at the large house in the Surrey countryside that was rented for Lucy's hen do. Most of the twenty-five—

twenty-five—women who were attending had opted in for the full three-night stay, whereas Lola and I were only coming for the Saturday night and Sunday daytime. We were greeted by Franny, the maid of honour, Lucy's best friend and a professional soprano, which I have always found is an entire genre of woman. They were normally in possession of very large breasts, which they'd developed at a young age and therefore had a quiet sense of imperiousness in any all-female group. They were angry at everyone while also being jolly about everything. They also wore silver Celtic jewellery and floaty dresses and blouses that, quite rightly, exhibited their impressive cleavage. Franny, immediately, met all those expectations.

"Hello, latecomers!" she trilled merrily. "Nina and Lola?"

"Yes! Here we are! So happy to be here!" Lola said with a huge smile. She was so good at this; at throwing herself into any uncomfortable situation with enthusiasm: immersive theatre, stand-up comedy shows, hen dos organized by bossy sopranos. I was in awe of her.

"Hello!" I said, comparatively weakly. "I'm Nina." I shook her hand formally.

"And I'm Lola!" Lola said, embracing her.

"Well, lovely, so glad you made it in one piece. Why don't you pop your things upstairs in your room, you'll see your names on the door. Then head back down for a glass of fizz and we can get going with today's activities!"

"Great!" I said.

LOLA AND I carried our bags upstairs and walked along the winding corridors until we reached a twin room with our names written on a sign in swirly glitter glue.

"He's still online," Lola said, throwing her bag on the bed and staring at her phone screen. "I mean— what woman has the time to sit on WhatsApp all day talking to him endlessly? It's an uneconomic use of time. They should just meet up and shag."

"What **man** does, Lola? Don't blame the woman."

"True. Also, I think he might be spreading it out. I think there might be a handful on rotation, so they each get a few hours of his time per day on a schedule."

"Wow, what a treat for them," I said, scraping my hair back off my face into a topknot. "I'm so gutted to be a straight woman. It's all just so gutting."

"LADIEEEEES!" we heard Franny wail from downstairs. "Time for some fizz!"

"Fizz," I said. "That word is only ever used in a room of women who all secretly hate each other."

"Oh, Nina, cheer up."

"If today is terrible can we leave early tomorrow? Can I make up a reason for us and we can leave?"

"Yes, but try to be nice. Remember you're doing this for Joe."

DOWNSTAIRS, the other twenty-three women were all milling around the kitchen. Franny was fussily pouring supermarket prosecco into everyone's glasses and Lucy was sitting on a dining chair with a gold crown on her head and a huge badge on her chest that said THE HEN.

"Nina!" she said, standing as she saw me. "And Lola! Aw, so glad you're here, lovely girls." She pulled us both in for a three-way hug. "This is a new hairdo," she said, pointing at my topknot. "Love it, very practical."

"Happy hen do!" I said. "Are you having a lovely time?"

"Yes! Have you met my very bestie, Franny?" She beckoned Franny over, who brought two glasses for us.

"Yes, she's been such a superstar organizing everything," Lola said.

"She's the greatest," Lucy said, putting her arm around her. "So organized. Führer Franny we used to call her at school!"

Franny was beaming, standing with extraordinary posture, her back overly arched in a balletic way.

"How do you all know each other?" Franny asked.

"So, Lola and Nina are university friends of Joe's,"

Lucy said. "Nina is actually going to be an usher at the wedding!"

"How funny!" Franny said. "A girl usher. Why weren't you a bridesmaid instead?"

"Oh, because she's Joe's best friend," Lucy said breezily. "Besides, Nina's not very into dresses and things, are you?"

"Right, I think it's time for our next activity, Lulu," Franny said, clapping her hands together.

I took a big gulp of prosecco and held my breath, but it made no difference—when would I be allowed to stop drinking this thin, sour, fruity venom of terrible parties and terrible conversation?

"EVERYBODY!" she shouted suddenly, pulling up a chair and standing on it in an entirely unnecessary gesture of a town crier. "QUIET, EVERYONE! If you could each take a chair and arrange them in a semi-circle. We're going to ask our hen to sit in the middle of us and we're all going to make a collage of her! We've got lots of different materials and pencils and chalks for you to play with here, so just have some fun with it and we'll see what we come up with!"

"Are we all doing one big collage?" one woman asked.

"No, no," Franny said with slight panic, as if the whole plan was already coming apart. "No, ONE COLLAGE EACH. EVERYONE, LISTEN. ONE COLLAGE EACH. There's plenty of paper for everyone."

"What's Lucy going to do with twenty-four collages of herself?" I asked Lola under my breath.

"Wallpaper her downstairs loo?" she replied.

I laughed and swallowed some prosecco the wrong
way, which made me splutter.

"Oh dear, you all right, Nina?" Franny said from
on high.

"Yes, fine, sorry."

We dutifully assembled in a semi-circle around
Lucy, who showed not a shred of self-consciousness
at being stared at by twenty-four women as their
subject. I have yet to encounter a more widely ac-
ceptable exercise of extreme narcissism than that of
being the protagonist of a hen do.

"So sorry, can I just ask one more question?" one
of the women asked.

"Yes?" Franny said impatiently.

"Is the collage just of Lucy's face and body or is it
more us . . . capturing her personality?"

"It's whatever you'd like it to be—it can be symbolic and abstract or it can just be a straight, ob-
servational piece," Franny said while handing
out pieces of dry penne and glue. "Here you go,"
she said, passing me a handful of pasta and a few
feathers. "For texture." Lola's cowboy boot pushed
against the edge of my trainer to suppress a deadly
bout of laughter.

If the activity itself wasn't humiliating enough,
we had to stand up and present our collages to the
group and give an explanation of its artistry and

meaning. While each woman stood up and spoke fawningly about Lucy's kindness and beauty represented by cut-up bits of magazines and doilies, Lola and I descended steadily and surely into drunkenness, digging the edges of our shoes further into each other as we went.

"Right, so mine's a map of Surrey," I said, pointing at the tangle of wobbly crayon lines on a big piece of pink cardboard. "Because you're from Surrey, and you're getting married in Surrey." Lucy smiled. "Which I copied from Google Maps. And I've written all the towns, you see," I said, holding it close to everyone's faces as I moved around the semi-circle. "And next to each town I've done a different type of shoe, because you really like shoes. So, look, there's a mule next to Dorking and a stiletto next to Bagshot and a big boot next to Egham and a flip-flop next to Chertsey and a—"

"Aw, really lovely," Franny said, before silently signalling at the heavily pregnant woman next to me that it was her turn to present her collage. I sat back down in my chair. She heaved herself up and stood in the centre with her large, heart-shaped collage.

"So, my name is Ruth, for anyone who doesn't know me already, and this is a bit of an in-joke!" she said, turning it to Lucy who immediately covered her face with her hands in pretend horror. "I happen to know Joe and Lucy's nicknames for each other are . . ."

"Badger and Horse!" Franny finished competitively.

"Yes!" Lucy said. Everyone fell about laughing.

"Why Badger and Horse?" one of the women asked.

"It's so silly, it's because for our one-monthaversary dinner I had got a bad highlights job that day and when I turned up he said I looked like a badger!"

"And why Horse?" Lola asked.

"Oh, because he eats like a horse," Lucy said.

"What's a monthaversary?" I asked. Everyone ignored me.

"So that's why I've drawn a little badger and a little horse as a bride and groom," Ruth said, showing everyone her drawing. There was a collective saccharine sound of approval and a round of applause.

Monthaversary dinner. In seven years of Joe and I going out, I don't think he remembered our actual anniversary once. How did these women do it? What was their secret? What unexpected, mystical orifice on their body did they allow these men entry to that in turn made them do whatever unreasonable thing they wanted? Or was it that they simply told them what to do and when to do it, and the imposed restriction of choice made their boyfriends feel safely shepherded rather than ready for slaughter? Had I been treating men too much like adults and not enough like little directionless lambs?

We were instructed by Franny to stay in our seats for the next activity, which was one I was, regrettably, familiar with. A ceremony of heteronormativity; a coronation of sovereign naffness; a whooping, winking ritual of humiliation lacking irony, decency and taste: the knicker game. "Think we'll need some more fizz for this!" Franny said, disappearing into the larder where I had now realized no one else was granted access.

"There isn't enough fizz in the world to get me through this," I whispered to Lola.

"Right," Franny bellowed. "I thought it would be fun if, while we were playing the knicker game, we all did a reading from"—she picked up a paperback and showed the cover to the group—**"How to Please Your Husband!"** It was a title all women of my generation were familiar with. A definitive 1970s manual on marriage that may have been on our mothers' shelves in earnest but had since been claimed by us in satire. The group made groaning sounds of recognition while they sat back in their seats. "For anyone unfamiliar with the knicker game," Franny said, while dispensing more dribbles of prosecco in our glasses, "Lucy opens this big box, filled with the knickers you've all bought her, and she has to guess who bought each pair."

"What happens to the knickers at the end?" Ruth asked.

"Landfill," I said.

"No!" Franny said, with a sarcastically appeasing tone. "They go in her trousseau!"

"What's a trousseau?" I asked.

"It's what a bride takes away on her honeymoon," Lola said.

"Twenty-four pairs of knickers?"

"Yes!" said Franny. "Well, you'll probably be needing a lot!" Everyone cheered at this meaningless innuendo. Prudes love innuendo.

"What have I bought her?" I asked Lola from the side of my mouth.

"You bought her some purple lacy French knickers that were a two-for-one offer with the leopard-print ones I got."

"Lovely," I said. "Thank you."

Lucy sat back in the middle of the semi-circle and adjusted her crown. She was presented with a large box.

**"How to please your husband,"** Franny warbled. **"A checklist. Number one: make sure the house is clean and tidy when he gets home, that dinner is in the oven and you are in a gay and pleasant mood."**

"Gay and pleasant mood!" Lucy squawked. "Joe's lucky if he gets a hello!" She plunged her hand into the box and pulled out a black satin thong. Everyone made the **ooh**-ing noises of a daytime chat-show audience. "Now, who could this be?" She scoured the room with narrowed detective eyes. "Someone a little bit naughty."

"But classy!" Franny chipped in.

"Yes, definitely classy. I think it's . . ." She caught the coy smile of a woman wearing a felt fedora hat indoors. "Eniola!"

"Yes!" Eniola exclaimed. "I chose them because I

thought they captured your elegance, but also the fact you've got a bit of a dark side." Everyone made perplexing sounds of agreement. Lucy with the dark side. Lucy who once offered me a mug with PARIS IS ALWAYS A GOOD IDEA written on it when I was at her flat; Lucy who owned a Ragdoll cat named Sergeant Flopsy; Lucy who had all the dark side of the Milkybar Kid.

"Lovely," Franny concluded, passing the book to Lola. "Your turn to read."

**"Number two,"** Lola read in her best Speech and Drama voice. **"Make sure you hide all your sanitary products (used and unused) and dirty undergarments out of the eyeline of your beloved."** This divided the room into two camps of horror—those appalled at this domestic anachronism and those appalled simply by the thought of used sanitary products. I remembered, suddenly, that afternoon in 2013 when I thought I had lost a tampon while wearing it and Joe had had to spread me open on our bed and shine his iPhone torch inside me. My muscle tissue twinged at the memory of this impossible intimacy.

"Who could these be from?" Lucy said, swinging a yellow gingham thong from her fingers. "Wholesome, bit naughty . . . Lola?"

"No!" Lola said.

"DRINK!" Franny shouted, showcasing her professional vibrato. Lucy took a delicate sip of her prosecco.

"Hmm, let me think." She looked at the knickers, then up at the circle. "I think it might be Lilian."

A woman grinned proudly. "Yes! How did you guess?"

"I don't know!" Lucy said. "I suppose because they're quite sunshiney and you're quite a sunshiney person." Lola passed the book to Lilian.

**"How to please your husband, tip number three,"** she read. **"Don't bother him with emotions. If something is upsetting you, speak to your girlfriends. Women are good for talking things through, whereas men are straightforward problem-solvers."**

"Well, I've certainly earned my stripes as your friend there!" Franny laughed. I saw, for a nano-second, something in Lucy's eyes that looked murderous, before she forced herself into a guffaw. She pulled out a pair of purple knickers and Lola nodded to let me know they were my offering.

"Oooh, purple," Lucy said. "Lacy, very nice. French knickers which, as it happens, are my favourite type of knickers. So it must be someone who knows me very well. Is it . . . Franny?"

"No! Drink!" she yelped robotically, like one of those talking baby dolls that had only three phrases. "Remember, it might be the last person you expect!"

Lucy's face immediately turned to me. "Nina?" she asked tentatively.

"Yes," I said. There was some inexplicable applause.

"See! I told you! The one you least expect!" Franny

said, her face glowing in self-satisfaction. "It happens every time I play the knicker game."

"Well, I bought these for you, Lucy, because I've always thought of you as being very . . ." I looked at Lola for help. "French, actually."

"I love France," Lucy said. "I'm a real Francophile."

"Yes, I thought you might be. And also I thought you were quite . . . flammable."

There was a pause while Lucy tried to make sense of me.

"Forever the writer, Nina!" she said with a laugh.

I excused myself from the room, saying I had to nip to the loo and instead went upstairs to my room.

"WHERE THE FUCK did you fuck off to?" Lola said, standing over my bed an hour later.

"Sorry, it was making me feel bleak. That book. I know it was meant to be funny, but I just couldn't bear to hear any more. The way it described jollying your husband along into fancying you like forcing sulky children to eat their vegetables. I didn't think anyone would notice. Did you only just finish that game?"

"Yeah," she sighed and flopped on to the single bed next to me. She took her phone out of its charger and stared at the screen.

"Online?" I asked.

"Yeah," she said sadly. "Why isn't he outside? This is the first winter sunshine we've had in ages, he should be enjoying it, not wanking on WhatsApp to all and sundry."

There was a knock at the door. Franny peered her head into the room.

"Everything okay, Nina? We missed you for the end of the knicker game."

"Yes, sorry, Franny, had a bit of a headache."

"Maybe take a break from the fizz this evening," she said, screwing up her face with false concern.

"Mmm," I replied.

"So, we're all going to have a little downtime then back downstairs for dinner in an hour."

"Great!" Lola said with what seemed like genuine verve. "I can't believe it's six o'clock already!"

"I know," Franny said. "Time passes so fast at the moment, doesn't it? I don't know about you but these days I feel like I wake up on Monday morning then I blink and it's Friday."

"I have the same!" Lola said. I watched this back-and-forth of empty phrases purpose-built for a female vocabulary to make everyone feel comfortable. Lola was so skilled at it—it never made her feel silly. When there was an awkward pause in conversation in the pub, she could state, "There's nothing like a cold beer," without irony. I once heard her say to my mother, "Photos are such a great way of capturing memories, aren't they?" at a family party and Mum positively shone from the effort of this banality then glared at me, wondering why I had never been capable of the same. I didn't know whether this was learnt behaviour as little girls, or whether it was in our DNA—passed from generation to generation of women who have entertained husbands' colleagues and impressed boyfriends' friends and arranged platter after platter of crudités and dips. The Nothing Like A Cold Beer gene.

"I think we're the only single ones here," Lola said after Franny left, turning over so she lay on her stomach.

"Where, this party? Surrey? Earth?"

"All of the above."

"I like being single," I said. "I'm not sad to be single. I'm sad to be without Max."

"Try doing it for over a decade."

"What do you think they talk about?"

"Who?"

"Lucy and Joe. I'm trying to remember what Joe and I talked about when we were together, and I can't imagine him and Lucy having the same conversations."

"I don't know, I haven't seen them talking together all that much."

"I have, but when I do, it's always about practical things. What time they're leaving, where they parked the car. When they should set off in the morning to get to someone's parents' house. It's like their bond is reliant on the organization of things."

"Maybe that's what they both want."

"Joe and I never talked about the organization of things. Or if we did it was just me telling him off for being useless. He must have been so unhappy with me if this is what he wanted."

"He probably didn't know what he wanted until he was told it was what he wanted." Both of our phones were letting off loud dings. It was the LUJOE HENS! group, sending photos from the afternoon's activities and desperately trying to erect a castle of in-jokes and catchphrases from the paltry few bricks of this weekend's experience.

"Why are they still messaging each other?" I asked. "We are all under the same roof, we don't need to message each other any more. We can just go into a room and say what we need to say." Lola wasn't listening, she was hypnotized by her phone screen. "I think I should take your phone from you."

"Do you think something might have happened to his phone, some technical glitch which means it shows that he's online on WhatsApp all day, but actually he isn't? Do you think that could be possible?"

"Honestly?"

"Yes."

"No, I don't think that could be possible."

DINNER HAD A DRESS CODE of dresses and heels which I, unsurprisingly, resented. I wore the plainest black dress I owned as a small act of protest and Lola forced some red lipstick on me, which made me look like a vaudeville performer.

"I've never seen you look so glam!" Lucy said as we

entered the dining room to take our seats for dinner. "You should wear lippy more, it looks so good on you." Lucy was wearing a white minidress with a rah-rah skirt of white tulle, just in case we forgot the reason twenty-five women in their thirties were gathered in a rented house for the weekend.

"Everyone in their seats!" Franny shouted. She was wearing an apron over her dress to mark herself as head chef and head bridesmaid. "I've done a **placement,**" she said, in a French accent.

"A what?" I asked Lola.

"It means a table plan," she said.

"You're like my Google Translate for Middle England." I found my name, next to a pregnant woman named Claire. Lola was sitting opposite me, next to pregnant Ruth.

"Nice to meet you," Claire said. "How do you know Lucy?"

"I know Joe," I said. "From university. How do you know her?"

"We used to work at the same PR agency," she said.

"Right," I said. I had nothing left to ask. I glanced over at Lola, already merrily chatting away to Ruth about where to visit in Florence. I offered a glass of wine to Claire, who declined while rubbing her stomach. I poured myself an extra-large one for the both of us.

"Right, we've got some Middle Eastern sharing platters to begin with," Franny said, ushering in some hen-do-participants-turned-handmaidens who carried large plates. Nothing made my heart sink more than a person telling me they've made Middle Eastern sharing platters, code for: heated-up supermarket falafel and a can of chickpeas blended with some bland oil and repurposed as homemade hummus. "So it's very relaxed. Everyone just tuck in." My section of the table politely divided up the plate between us, leaving us with a grand total of two falafel balls, a tablespoon of tabbouleh and a teaspoon of tzatziki each.

"Do you have children?" Claire asked.

"No," I said.

Claire nodded. "Would you like them?"

"Yes," I said. "I don't know if the process of getting there looks especially appealing at the moment."

"Does your partner want children?"

**Partner.** I noticed people often assumed this was a word I used when they spoke to me. I think my lack of make-up suggested I was more humourless than I am.

"I don't have a partner."

"Oh, I see," she said.

"I did have a partner. Well, a boyfriend, until about six weeks ago. Then he disappeared." I looked over at Lola's wine glass. It was diminishing as rapidly as mine.

"Where did he go?" she asked.

"I don't know. He just stopped talking to me."

Her eyes widened in horror. "Could something have happened to him?"

"No, no, he's definitely still alive," I said. "Lola and I collected sufficient intelligence to prove he's alive."

Lola's head turned towards me on hearing her name. "What's this?"

"I'm just saying that we have reason to believe Max is alive," I said across the table.

"Oh, he's definitely alive, yeah."

"Who's Max?" Ruth asked.

"Man who ghosted Nina."

"Oh, I've heard about this ghosting," said Ruth excitedly. "It happened to my sister recently."

"Yeah," Lola said. "London is basically one big haunted house fairground ride for me now."

"Are you both single?" Ruth asked.

"Yes," we said in unison.

"And are you both putting yourself out there?"

Lola topped up her wine glass. "Yes. It's all I've been doing. I hate that phrase, like I'm a worm on a hook."

"If I were you," Claire chimed in, "I would just enjoy being single and relax. There's no rush for starting a family." I don't think there's anything I found more galling than an expectant mother, who already had two children, in a long-term relationship telling single women in their thirties to relax about starting a family. "I mean, my God, enjoy your freedom!"

"What are your kids called?" I asked.

"Arlo and Alfie," she said.

"I have two godsons called Arlo," Lola said. "Can you believe that? From two different mothers." I have never loved her more.

"Yes, it's very popular now, it was hardly known when we chose it," Claire said. "It was between that and Otto."

"Otto's on my list!" Lola said, retrieving her phone from her pocket. I knew her baby-name list off by heart. "Let me read it to you, hang on." She unlocked her phone screen and tapped. "Nina."

"Yeah?"

"He's still online."

"Who? Max?" Ruth asked.

"No, this is a man I'm seeing who is always online on WhatsApp."

"So?"

"It means he's talking to other women all day," I said.

"Can I tell you my secret?" Claire said.

"Yes," Lola enthused.

"You've got to show him what he's missing." She left a dramatic pause. "That's the key—he's got to always be aware of what he could be missing."

"How do I do that?" Lola asked, leaning across the table.

"Number of ways. Men just have to be reminded of how lucky they are all the time."

"What, do you do that even now?" Lola asked

reverently. All at once I realized she was prime for a cult.

"Every day," Claire replied.

"Grim," I said under my breath, pouring more wine in my glass.

Dinner continued with both themes—unappetizing catering from Franny in small portions and unappetizing advice from married women in large portions. Lucy made an hour-long speech in which she went around listing everything she loved about each hen-do attendee—she did a gallant job by managing "a great sense of humour" when it came to me. Franny pretended we'd run out of wine allocated for that day and instead suggested we help ourselves to the gin-flavoured chocolate truffles. We all took turns to do some karaoke around a machine plugged into the TV, then everyone was upstairs in their rooms before eleven.

"I THINK CLAIRE IS RIGHT about showing him what he's missing," Lola said as we changed into our pyjamas. "I might get you to take a really flattering photo of me tomorrow morning when the light's good so I can post it on Instagram. Andreas is always on Instagram."

"No," I said. "I'm not having any of this. Women shouldn't have to trick men into keeping their attention."

"I know you're right." She got into bed and

unlocked her phone, her blank expression lit up by the white glare of the screen. She shoved another gin chocolate into her mouth in one.

"And if he has to be reminded of what he's 'missing,' then he's not the man for you. Now please put down your phone or I will have to confiscate it."

Lola gave a defeated smile and put it on the floor next to her. I turned off our bedside light and we lay silently in the dark.

"Problem is, it does work," Lola said. "Posting a hot photo on Instagram. I've done it before, and it always gets their attention."

"Do you really want that from these men? Their attention?"

"No," she said.

"What do you want?"

"Their love."

LOLA AND I left the next morning after breakfast of undercooked sausages, with the lie of respective family events in the afternoon. Lucy was gracious about it—if anything she seemed a little relieved—and Franny didn't give us much grief but for a few passive-aggressive comments about making sure they had an even-numbered group for the "rap battle in the paddock" later.

"I don't want anything like that when I get married," Lola said as we sat opposite each other on the train and looked out on the nondescript fields of

Home Counties England. "You'll be organizing it all, so just to let you know I don't want anything like that."

"Good," I said. "Glad you cleared that up."

"I want something very casual, very me," she continued. "Not a weekend away anywhere, just a weekend in London."

"**Weekend** in London?"

"Yeah, so like, a Friday night just my bridesmaids, maybe a dinner you can host at your flat or my flat, with all my favourite dishes. Then you can give me my something old, something new, something borrowed, something blue and a sixpence for my shoe." I couldn't be bothered to ask for the translation of this. "Then Saturday-morning brunch somewhere. Then afternoon activities with all the other hens, then a dinner, then a night out, then a Sunday with everyone at a spa. And we should include family members for the Sunday—my mum, my mother-in-law and sisters and sisters-in-law, if I have any."

I always forgot that, despite her occasional company in the stalls of cynicism—watching the show with one eye as we made wry observations to each other—Lola wanted a part in it. She wanted the whole production—the full regalia. She wanted the attention, the gift registry, the hymns, the hen do, the marquee, the multi-tiered cake of fruit, coffee, lemon and chocolate sponges. She wanted a man to ask her dad for permission to pass her over to him. She wanted to discard her surname in favour of one that proved someone had chosen her. When my friends first started getting married, Dad used to tell me, "You never know someone's true politics until you go to their wedding." How right and wise he was. Lola—a girl so outwardly preoccupied with wokeness; who only read overhyped memoirs written by women under thirty having feeble epiphanies about themselves; who had "she/her" written in all her social media bios despite very clearly never being in danger of being misgendered—well, all she really wanted was to walk down an aisle wearing a £2,000 dress and a sixpence in her shoe.

"I've got something for the Schadenfreude Shelf," she said.

"Go on," I said. "I need it."

"So my cousin's best friend, Anne, had always wanted to fall in love and get married. She was a bit like me, never had a boyfriend, thought she'd be alone for ever."

"Right."

"Until one day when she's in her late thirties she meets this man on a dating app and they have an amazing first date. He's a lawyer, really kind, really lovely man. After about six months they move in together—it's a bit whirlwind, but it's like we always say: as you get older things move faster because when you know, you know."

"Sure."

"After two years of being together, they got married."

"Yes."

"And now she's dead."

"What?"

"Completely dead."

"Oh my God, how did she die?"

"Pancreatic cancer."

"Okay," I said. "So those two elements of the story aren't related."

"Perhaps they are, perhaps they aren't."

"That's a slightly false crescendo to the anecdote, I think."

"All I'm saying is, she thought all she wanted was a marriage, she got married and then she got ill and died."

"We need to work on what stories are eligible for the Schadenfreude Shelf," I said. "We need to reassess the vetting process. That hasn't made me feel better about anything."

"Really? Oh, it has me," she said, gazing out at the approaching brown bricks of Guildford. "Poor Anne, I think about her often."

THAT NIGHT, I was grateful for an evening at home rather than the "indoor rounders with inflatable bats and balls" as listed on the hen-do itinerary when the noise began again. It started at exactly seven o'clock—the same roar at the same volume that made it impossible to do anything but listen to it through the floor. It was the first time it had happened since the night I had called noise patrol before Christmas and Angelo had lingered menacingly outside my door. I opened my laptop, brought up the number for the council and waited for the eleven o'clock curfew. I tried to distract myself, but my eyes were fixated on the slow-moving hands of the clock.

Then, at exactly 10:59, the music stopped. At first, I thought his speakers must have cut out or that he was changing music. But a minute later, there was nothing—not a sound, not even his footsteps.

And I realized: 10:59 was not a coincidental time for Angelo to stop making a noise that he knew I hated. He must have read the rules of antisocial neighbourhood behaviour online like I had. As long as he was quiet at eleven p.m., he wasn't eligible for any reprimanding. There was nothing I could say to him—there was no one I could call. This was a torture game of egos. This was a non-verbal proposal of warfare.

At 11:01 I realized I was sitting in a noise that was harder to ignore than anything I had heard all night. Silence.

## 12

PERVERT," Dad announced. "But a ruddy talented one."

We were standing at the centre of a Picasso exhibition, in front of his 1932 portrait **Nude Woman in a Red Armchair.** Dad had loved Picasso since he was a student, and I thought that seeing some of his works in the flesh might stimulate the part of his mind that made him feel knowledgeable and confident. My hunch was right—the art seemed to be able to penetrate through the increasing thick clouds that passed through his brain. It seemed as though he and the works were in a conversation I didn't understand that he could explain to me, rather than the other way around. While Dad was housed in the mind of a cubist—where there were no rules for reality; where the morphing and merging and reversing of structure was beautiful and celebrated—he was right at home.

"They met at an art gallery," he said. "He and Marie-Thérèse. She was seventeen and he was married."

"How many portraits did he paint of her?"

"Over a dozen. Some of his best."

"Did he leave his wife?"

"No. But he moved Marie-Thérèse on to the same road as his family home. He got far more from the relationship than she did. She arguably revived his career."

"How awful."

"Yes. Wrong'un. A very brilliant wrong'un."

I didn't know how much of what Dad was telling me was fact according to history or fact according to him, but I was so enjoying returning to the parental dynamic in which he was the person with more information and insight than me.

"Do the transgressions of the artist undermine the pleasure to be found in the art? If you could answer that, you might solve the internet, Dad."

We both stared at the lilac-grey curves of her body and the brown swirly arms of the chair that held it.

"Maybe I'll meet a nice lady here and move her into the house," he said. "What would your mother say to that?" I laughed. "I'm going for a wander."

He placed his hands behind his back and walked slowly along the gallery, gazing up at the paintings as he went.

"All right," I said, watching him intently, like a child I didn't want to lose. "See you in a bit."

I stayed in front of Marie-Thérèse in her red armchair and examined every part of her exquisitely scrambled form. The impossible positioning of her breasts stacked on top of each other, the surreal placement of her mismatched shoulders. How her face was split into two parts, one half of which could be another face kissing the other in profile, if you looked for long enough. Was the second face that Picasso saw symbolic of Marie-Thérèse's hidden multitudes? Or was it his profile—did he imagine he dwelled within her, his lips on her cheek wherever she went? What would it be like, I wondered, to be seen through such adoring eyes, that they could not only capture you in a painting, but rearrange you to further exhibit who you were? I stroked the rounded right angle of where my neck met my shoulder like it was the hand of a lover and thought about being put inside a Rubik's Cube of someone's gaze. I couldn't imagine ever being studied and known like that.

As soon as Dad and I left the gallery and stepped out into the rush of central London, I could see his brightness and confidence diminish and be replaced with confusion and fear. It was hard to know if it was a symptom of his illness, or whether that was simply a result of old age. Dad—a man who had never lived anywhere but London; who had known its streets off by heart from cycling through them as a boy and striding across them as a man—now looked nervous.

We went to a Hungarian bakery that was a short walk from the gallery. He'd taken me there a few times in my childhood—he loved the wood-panelled walls, the coffee cakes, the surly waitresses he could charm and the fact that it was an institution nearly as old as he was. We sat at a table by the window, and I could see he was hypnotized by passing strangers as he gazed out of the window quietly.

"What do you fancy?" I asked. He glanced down at the menu and didn't respond. "One of the coffee cakes?" I knew not to give him too many options to avoid risk of further confusion.

"I don't know," he said.

"I'm going to get a coffee cake. Why don't I get us two? And some Earl Grey." His eyes looked past me and over my shoulder, widening slightly in awe.

"Goodness gracious."

"What?"

"Don't look now, but three of the Mitford sisters have just arrived." I felt a thud of disappointment and hated myself for it. I knew what I had to do in these situations—Gwen and I had spoken about it a number of times. But I didn't want to play along with an imagining today. I didn't want to spend this precious time with my dad in a sad reversed parent-child dynamic in which I knew what was real and he didn't. I wanted the vital, exacting Dad who could tell me about Picasso's French chateau and exactly what cakes we should order from his favourite bakery. The charming, silly Dad who'd order chips and put one on his shoulder—a daft gag for weary waiting staff. The Dad who'd draw maps on paper tablecloths. The Dad who'd catch the waiter's attention at the end of the meal and use his finger to mime writing. I couldn't remember the last time I'd seen him do that.

"Really?"

"Yes!" he said, with gleeful mischief. "Right, have a look now." I dutifully turned around to see three women who looked nothing alike, other than they all had grey hair, standing at the counter and examining the cakes through the glass.

"Ah yes," I said meekly.

"Nancy, Diana and Unity. There they are."

"There they are," I repeated. "Right. Tea?"

"Nancy must be over from France. I would so love to talk to her. Wonder what she'd make of a Non-U like me."

"Mr. Dean?" We both turned around. A man stood by our table—forty-something, soft-faced with masses of thick brown hair and round tortoiseshell glasses. "It's Arthur Lunn. I was one of your pupils, years ago. At St. Michael's." Dad stared at him blankly. "There's no reason why you'd remember me. You gave me extra help when I was applying to Oxford. I'm pretty sure it's the only reason I got in."

"So lovely to meet you," I said. "I'm his daughter, Nina." Dad was visibly distracted by the three women at the counter. "What Oxford college did you go to?"

"Magdalen. I was miserable for most of it, but still, it's probably the happiest my mum has ever been, the day I got my acceptance letter, so I have a lot to thank you for, Mr. Dean."

"Call him Bill," I said. Dad snapped his head back round to us briefly.

"Yes, Bill's fine," he said.

"Bill. Feels weirdly overfamiliar to call your teacher by their first name, even as a forty-four-year-old man."

"Yes, it's strange that," I said, grasping at platitudes.

"I was going to try and get hold of you, actually, to let you know there's a Facebook group in your honour, where lots of your old students talk about you and share stories and memories of you as a teacher. Some really nice old photos as well from results days. I'll have to tell them that I saw you."

Dad continued to study the three women.

"Dad," I said gently, trying to get his attention. He focused on us.

"Did you ever read **Love in a Cold Climate?**" he asked.

Arthur politely tried to hide his bafflement. "No, I don't think I did."

"You must."

"What are you doing now?" I said, my small talk trying to paint over the cracks of Dad's conversational logic.

"I'm a lawyer," he said. "Which is probably a waste of an English degree. But I think maybe every job is a waste of an English degree."

"Yes," I said. "I think you're right." I was desperate to explain to him that Dad was ill—I was desperate for his long-held memories of Mr. Dean inspiring and encouraging him not to be replaced by this disconnected man who could barely say hello.

"Well, I'd better go, I'm here with my family." He pointed over to a woman at a table, getting ready to leave with two preadolescent boys in navy puffa jackets who had their dad's abundance of brown hair. "It was so lovely to see you again. I think about you every time I start a new book. You always told us that literature belongs to everyone and that we should never feel intimidated by it. I say that to my two boys now they're just starting to love reading."

Dad smiled at him and said nothing.

"Thank you so much for coming over," I said.

As I watched Arthur and his family leave, I realized he must have been in the photo that I found in the box of Dad's documents at home—the one of the smiling boy with his parents on graduation day at Magdalen College. I wanted to run after him and explain what was going on. But Dad was too disorientated to leave in the café on his own, and

I was worried he would try to speak to the three tribute act Mitford sisters he was so entranced by. So instead I watched Arthur and his family walk out of the bakery and along the road until they disappeared. And Dad and I talked about nothing but the Mitford sisters sighting all the way home.

Mum answered the door in yet another workout ensemble of purple flowery leggings and a grey vest top with a matching zip-up hoodie. On the back of it was an outline of a Buddha in metal studs.

"Hello, lovey," she said to Dad, kissing him on the cheek. "How was the exhibition?"

"Wonderful," he said.

Mum placed a precise, glossy-lipped kiss on my face.

"We both saw **The Dream** for the first time, which I think might be my favourite of his paintings," I said. "The colours were incredible in the flesh."

"Yes, and we only bloody spotted three of the Mitford sisters! Diana, Nancy and Unity," Dad said, while sitting on the stairs to take off his shoes. "Wanted to eavesdrop to see if they were talking politics."

"Aren't they all—" Mum started. I glanced at her, reminding her of our agreement. "Right. That's exciting."

"And we went to that Hungarian bakery Dad loves," I said, trying to subtly switch topical gears. "Ate some coffee cake."

"Sounds like you had the time of Riley," Mum said.

"Life," Dad replied, holding on to the bannister as he stood up.

"Sorry?"

"Living the **life** of Riley," he said. "Or having the time of your life. You can't have the time of Riley."

Mum hated being corrected—I inherited this trait from her.

"Yes, all right, Bill," she said.

"Do you want a cup of tea, Dad?"

"Yes please, Bean," he said, walking into the living room.

"Gwen's here," Mum said when he'd shut the door.

We went into the kitchen. Gwen was sitting at the table, reading through her notepad with a pen poised in one hand and a mug of tea in the other. She looked up and gave me a reassuringly wide smile.

"Nina, how are you?"

"I'm good, thank you, how are you?"

"Very well. I was just catching up with your mum."

"I was telling Gwen about how he's still getting up in the middle of the night."

"Which is very normal at this stage," Gwen said. "His internal clock will be altered and his sense of time will be all over the place which, as you can imagine, is very confusing. He won't understand why it's dark outside when it's the middle of the night, because he feels like it's the morning and he's just woken up."

"Yes, which is why he bangs about downstairs every night at three a.m.," Mum said.

"As long as he's staying in the house," I said. "Although I appreciate that must be very annoying for you, Mum."

She nodded gratefully. I'd learnt through Dad's illness that so often all she needed was acknowledgement of the difficulties she was facing.

"Are there any other new behaviours that you'd like to talk to me about?" Gwen asked. "How are the imaginings?"

"They're about the same," Mum said. "Most of the time he's just in a different time, thinking he's still working or that his mum's still alive. Occasionally they're more far-fetched."

"I think it's because of all his reading," I said. "He's spent his life immersing himself in other worlds—conjuring images from what he's read on the page. I'm sure that must have given him a wealth of stories for his mind to draw on."

"Absolutely," Gwen said. "And as we've discussed before, if going along with it has a calming effect, then you should absolutely go along with it."

"The only problem is," Mum said, going to the side table in the kitchen where the phone and a pile of notebooks sat, "he's started marking." She opened her page-a-day diary, which was covered in Dad's handwriting, crosses and ticks.

"I've had an idea," I said, putting my handbag on the table and pulling out some old workbooks. "I found a few projects from my old pupils when I taught English. I think I could easily find some more. So we can give them to him to mark." I looked at Mum, who was clearly uncomfortable at the thought of using props to placate Dad's imaginings, but wanted to seem calm and cooperative in front of Gwen.

"Great idea," Gwen said, finishing the last of her tea. "No harm in trying."

"HOW'S EVERYTHING ELSE BEEN?" I asked Mum once Gwen had left.

"Oh, same old same old. Gloria and I did Pilatus this morning," she said.

"Pilates," I corrected. Why did I have to correct her? Would I have done the same to Katherine or Lola? What was it about mothers that lowered a woman's irritation threshold by a metre just from speaking?

"Yes, that's what I said, Pilatus."

"And how was it?"

"It was fine—I mean, I do wonder how much good it does, lying on our backs splaying our legs around every which way with a lashing strap. How are you, darling?" she said. "I've been thinking about you a lot."

"I'm okay," I said.

"No word, I gather?"

"Nope, no word, but there we go," I said, aggressively stoic. "How's Gloria?"

"She's fine, she's worried about you too. It's just so strange for our generation. In my day—if you said you were going to be somewhere, you were going to be somewhere. You'd say, 'I'll meet you outside Woolworths at seven,' and if you weren't outside Woolworths at seven, you'd leave the other person standing in the cold. And it was unthinkable to do that to someone. I blame all this constant communication, everything has become too casual. When we were young, there were no mobiles, no social media, no MyFace," she said. I couldn't be bothered to correct her. "So you had to stick to a plan and stand by your word. Where's the sense of honour gone?"

"Why were you going on a date to Woolworths?"

"Fine—you don't want to listen to me."

"No, I do, I do."

"All I mean is—I think there is a lack of duty to each other now."

"But love shouldn't be about duty, Mum," I said, splashing milk into a cup of tea to make it an exact shade of tawny brown.

She gave a theatrically knowing laugh. "A lot of love is about duty, Nina." Dad shouted from the living room, asking if I could bring him a glass of water as well as tea. Mum smiled in acknowledgement of his unwitting comic timing. "Thank you for today."

"My pleasure," I said. "We had a great time."

"Do you want to stay for dinner? I've learnt how to make low-carb tagliatelle just from a celeriac and a potato peeler, it's amazing, you won't believe it."

"I'd love to, but I've got a thing tonight."

"A date?" she asked excitedly.

"No, Mum, not a date."

"I'm only teasing. We do a singles night at church, you should come. We need some more heads. They're dropping like flies at the moment."

"You're doing a lot at church recently," I said, taking the tea with one hand and a glass of water with the other.

"I'm applying to be social secretary."

"Do you even believe in God?"

"You don't have to believe in God to have a good time," she said as we walked into the living room. Dad looked up from his book.

"You certainly don't!" he boomed. I handed him his mug and he pulled himself up in the chair by his elbows.

"Right, I better go," I said, putting a hand on Dad's shoulder and giving it a squeeze. "I've got a question for you both."

"Go on," Mum said.

"What is the most annoying song you think you've ever heard?"

They both looked into the middle distance and searched through their invisible Rolodexes.

"Anything by the Steve Miller Band," Mum said.

"No, not abrasive enough, I need something more universally annoying. Something that would make you prefer to have your ears hacked off with a blunt knife than listen to it."

"Little orphan fella," Dad said, taking a slurp of his tea.

"Oliver?" I asked. He put the mug down and returned his eyes to the book. "Do you mean the musical **Oliver!**?"

"Little friend of yours. Ginger hair, very shrill. We should have thrown him in a freezing-cold lake, quite frankly, he's never coming here again."

"Friend of mine?"

**"Annie!"** Mum said suddenly. "He means **Annie.** Remember we took you to a production of it one Christmas when you were little and your dad hated the songs so much he left in the first half-hour and waited for us in the foyer with the newspaper." Mum was laughing as she recalled the memory, Dad was happily no longer listening.

"Genius," I said. "Thank you."


ALMA WAS ALREADY at her door when I went upstairs to pick her up at eight. We had organized it the previous week—I told her I'd take her out for dinner wherever she liked, we'd just have to make sure we were out until just before eleven. She answered the door wearing a plum-tinted lipstick and amber perfume.

"You look lovely," I said.

"I don't think I have been taken out on a date for about twenty years, Nina," she said as she held on to the bannister and walked down the stairs to my flat.

"Right, hold on one minute." I went into the living room where Joe had set up his enormous, cumbersome sound system the day before. I put the **Annie** soundtrack into the CD drive and turned on the setting that would play the album on a loop, exactly as Joe had instructed me to. The bombastic opening strings and drum of "Tomorrow" reverberated around the room, then the singing began. Nasal, high-pitched wailing and a wobbly vibrato poured out of the towering speakers like a sonic flood. The bones of the flat shuddered from the volume. I winced as I returned to my front door and locked it on my way out.

"What is that noise?" Alma said as we descended the stairs to leave the building.

"It's the **Annie** soundtrack. It's a 1980s musical."

"It doesn't even sound like singing!"

"I know, it's perfect, isn't it?"

"Perfect," she said with a mischievous smile.

She chose a Lebanese restaurant in Green Lanes. Over a long, languid feast—sumac-scattered salads, richly spiced dips, lentils and lamb, soft, pillowy pittas, lemony broad beans and delicate rosewater pudding—we talked about family, love, her grandchildren, my parents, Lebanon, London, cooking and eating. I paid the bill and got us a taxi back home just before eleven o'clock and when I opened the door into the hallway, I could hear the jolting orchestra and piercing, jeering chorus of "It's the Hard Knock Life." Angelo's front door was ajar and when he heard us arrive he bolted out of his flat wearing a white vest and grey tracksuit bottoms. His hair seemed more flyaway and his toffee eyes more bulging than usual.

"What is this?" he said, gesturing up at my flat.

"Hello, Angelo."

"Have you been out all night?" he asked.

"Nope," I said.

"Yes you have, I've just seen you come in."

"No, we just popped outside. This is Alma, she's your other neighbour."

"When I knock on the door, there is no answer."

"That's because you don't answer yours whenever I knock, so I thought that was the rule between us now."

"Goodnight, dear!" Alma said as she climbed the stairs.

"Goodnight, Alma! Thank you for a lovely evening. The music will be off in—" I checked my watch, 10:56—"four minutes."

"Okay, my dear," she said.

"You cannot make noise like this."

"Why not? It's just as loud as the noise you make."

"You don't even want to listen to this," he said. "You just play it to make me angry."

"I do want to listen to it, it's my favourite album." The infantile cries of "Dumb Dog" were tumbling down the stairs. "Look, Angelo. I always wanted to be polite to you, I wanted us to get on. I didn't want to be mates or anything, but I think it's important to be civil with your neighbours. I tried to be reasonable, I was very patient. But you fucked it, mate. You completely and utterly fucked it."

"I play my music because I have no one below me. You have someone below you."

"You have someone above you. Then another person on top of that. And whether you like it or not, all three separate households are paying a ridiculous amount of money to live in a carved-up home that was once designed for one family."

"What does this mean?"

"It means we are technically all sharing a house, so we have to be as considerate to each other as possible. And if we can't do that then we should leave London."

He shook his head. "If you play that sound again, I call the police."

"Great. It'll be off before eleven."

"Don't play it again," he said, turning back into his flat.

"I won't play it if you don't play that death metal racket. That feels like a fair deal."

"Pathetic," he said, before shutting his door.

"YOU'RE pathetic," I shouted after him.

I WENT UPSTAIRS and turned off the music. What I wanted now, more than anything, was an ally. Someone to pick apart the dispute with in a hushed voice. I wanted co-conspiring, giddiness. I wanted to be the couple on the platform at Waterloo station who cheered each other on. The only time I found myself missing Joe romantically was when I thought about what a good teammate he had been when we were together. In every situation, we noticed all the same things. I would never feel as close to him as when we'd both overhear someone in the pub say something particularly moronic and we'd give each other a smile across the table that said: **You, me, bed, one a.m.—full debrief commences.**

My solitude was like a gemstone. For the most part it was sparkling and resplendent—something I wore with pride. The first time I met with a mortgage adviser, I told him my financial situation: no parental help, no second income from a partner, no pension, no company that permanently employed me, no assets and no family inheritance in my future. "So, it's Nina against the world," he said offhandedly as he shuffled through my bank statements. **Nina against the world,** I'd hear on rotation in my head whenever I needed emboldening. But underneath this diamond of solitude was a sharp point that I occasionally caught with my bare hands, making it feel like a perilous asset rather than a precious one. Perhaps this jagged underside was essential—what made the surface of my aloneness shine so bright. But loneliness, once just sad, had recently started to feel frightening.

Unable to sleep, I turned on my bedside radio and tuned in to a classical music station. "Good evening, night owls," I heard in a voice as sugary and slow-moving as caramel. "Some of you might just be getting into bed, some of you might be well on your way to sleep. Some of you, I know, are just starting your shift at work." I recognized her instantly, although she sounded lower and slower than I remembered. "Wherever you are, whatever you're doing, I send this ultra-relaxing Brahms . . . straight to you." She was the top drive-time radio DJ on the most popular pop station when I was a kid—as famous for her raucous off-air partying as she was for her wacky phone-ins. My dad and I used to listen to her when he drove me to school every morning in his blue Nissan Micra. I stopped listening to the show in my mid-teens, when breakfast pop radio stopped being cool. But I returned to her again years later when I was a student, tuning in daily to her afternoon show on a try-hard indie station that played newly signed, little-known bands. And here I'd found her again, doing a late-night slot on a classical station. How strange, to have her age with me—to be able to mark the decades of my life by her transition through various music genres. Everyone gets old. No one can stay young for ever, even when youth seems such an integral part of who they are. It's such a simple rule of being human, and yet one I regularly found impossible to grasp. Everyone gets old.

I wondered if Max ever thought of me before he went to sleep. The drifting, floating seconds right before blackout—when thoughts start turning inside out and synapses turn psychedelic—are when I felt his presence most. It felt like I was reaching out to him, waiting to feel his hand touch mine back. I hoped, that night, that I could go meet him somewhere while we were both asleep—that I could speak to him without seeing him, somewhere in the London night sky.

I turned my phone over as soon as I woke up the next morning. There were no new messages.

## 13

I KNOCKED ON THE MAHOGANY DOOR next to mine on the long, dark corridor.

"Come in," he croaked. Joe stood in his socks, boxers, shirt and two components of his three-piece navy suit. He fiddled with his tie in the mirror.

"I don't want to be cruel on your wedding day," I said. "But I don't know if you've got the legs for that."

He sighed. "They're in the trouser press. They're all crumpled and Lucy will lose her shit if she sees creases in them when I walk down the aisle."

"Why are they all crumpled? I told you to hang them up when we got here yesterday."

"**Because,**" he said stroppily, "when I got into the room last night I had a shower and got confused and used the trousers as a towel then chucked them on the floor."

"You shouldn't have been chucking a towel on the floor even if it was a towel."

"Nina. Please."

"I am so glad you're getting married and someone else can manage your cavalier attitude to towel storage for ever."

His face looked pale and fragile, like unshelled crab meat, and his eyes were beady and small, making him look even more like a crustacean. We were both very hung-over. The ushers' dinner had taken place downstairs at the pub the night before and had ended at half three in the morning with all of us doing a cheerleading tower in the car park. "How are you feeling?"

"Terrible," he replied.

"Okay, I can expertly make you look and feel incredible, having been a bridesmaid four times already. What can I get you? Face mask? Green juice?"

"Quarter pounder with cheese."

"No, I'm not getting you that, you just had a massive fry-up."

"Maybe a cheeky half."

"Okay, I think that's allowed. Hair of the dog," I said. I took his trousers out of the press and rehung them correctly. "When are the ushers' photos?"

"Dunno," he said. "Like, half an hour, I think."

"And is there anything else we need to do to get you ready for that?"

"What would I need to do other than get dressed?"

"I can't believe this is what it's really like on the other side," I said. "For all these years, I've wondered. While all the brides I know have been on juice diets and sunbeds in the run-up to the wedding and have woken up at six a.m. on the morning for hair and make-up, the men have been down the road in a pub getting pissed and eating fried food and having a great time."

"Please don't have a femmo rant on the morning of my wedding."

"I'm not, I'm just saying, it's nice to finally know what it's like to be a boy. To have one small insight into it for a day."

"You've always wanted to be a boy, deep down," he said. "Peter Pan."

"I don't think a man will ever know and understand me as well as you do, Joe."

"Yes, he will," he said. "And I'm glad it's not that fifty-foot cunt."

"Joe."

"I'm sorry, but I am."

"I knew you didn't like him that night you met him. You were rubbish at hiding it."

"Can I ask you something now that it's over?"

"Yes."

"How big was his cock?"

"I'm not answering that."

"I'm not jealous or anything, I'm just intrigued because sometimes those big blokes actually have quite stumpy ones. But then maybe they only look stumpy in comparison to the rest of their body when they're naked, and actually they're normal sized?"

I stood in front of him and adjusted his tie like a mother sending her son off to his first holy communion. "His cock was as big as your heart, my darling Joe."

"Oh, shut up, mate," he said through a guffaw.

"I'm not that bothered by big cocks anyway. Only prudes claim to love big cocks."

"So true," he said. "And massage oils."

I was regularly reminded when I spoke to Joe of how much of ourselves we had created together. In pubs, on our sofas, on long car journeys in those seven years of our relationship, we devised language that was so deeply embedded in our brains, I couldn't trace which jokes were his and which ones were mine.

"Now," I said, holding his shoulders, "I get the feeling Lucy doesn't want people to know we were together, so when people ask me how we know each other today, what do I say?"

"Tell them the truth," he said, putting his arms around my waist. "Tell them we grew up together."

We held each other tightly. It was a rare moment of unguarded sentimentality for Joe and me.

"This is exactly how it was meant to turn out."

"It was," he said, placing his lips to my cheek and holding them there for a few seconds before giving it a parting kiss. "And I wouldn't change any of it."

WHEN WE ARRIVED AT THE CHURCH, Franny was already there performing unnecessary maid-of-honour duties. Lucy was apparently worried the ushers would "hand out the order of services wrong," so instructed Franny to go ahead early and oversee us. Franny acted out how to pass an order of service to each guest to the four hung-over ushers. When guests started trickling into the church, she stood next to me to monitor the first few and make sure I was getting it right.

"This is very fun," she said, brushing the lapel of my navy suit that I'd matched with a pale-blue silk shirt.

"Thank you."

"I can't get away with tailoring, sadly, too busty." She pushed her breasts out a little further. She was swathed in long, floaty grey viscose. "Right, I better get going."

"When does the bridal party car arrive?"

"Cars," she said. "Five cars."

"Why five?"

"There are fourteen of us bridesmaids."

"Fourteen?"

"Yes. Lulu's got a lot of best friends. We're very much a sisterhood."

"Seems it."

"See you down the aisle!" she said.

KATHERINE AND MARK were among the first to arrive. Katherine looked exquisite in high-necked pale-yellow silk that poured over her pregnancy bump like hollandaise on a perfectly poached egg. Olive was with Katherine's parents for the weekend, but she stressed that it was only because she "might make a noise in the service" and not because she didn't want her there. Mark told me he definitely didn't want her there and had, in fact, already drunk two tinnies in the passenger seat on the drive here. Dan and Gethin arrived shortly afterwards, their baby daughter attached to Dan's chest. Both of their faces were heavy with exhaustion and bliss, languor and panic, which I had come to recognize as the expression of new parenthood.

Our uni friends trickled in, most of whom I now only saw at weddings, and, as always, I remained perplexed at the cruel lottery of male hair loss. The boys who had once arrived in halls with luscious great big handfuls of golden hair had ended up with flaxen mist passing over their heads. Men who had full coverage at the last wedding suddenly had a perfectly circular patch of bare scalp positioned neatly on the top of their heads like a skin yarmulke. It was almost enough to make me think women have an easier time of it.

Lola was one of the last to arrive, wearing a neon tangerine maxi dress with a matching floor-length cape that made her look like a Hogwarts pupil at a 2006 new rave party. There were large artificial gardenias positioned in her hair. She had been to a speed-dating event the night before that had ended with no matches but instead all the female attendees going to a nearby bar until four a.m. Andreas, while remaining WhatsApp's most active member of the community, had started ignoring her messages—the speed dating was to open up her options again.

The ushers took their pews and Joe stood at the top of the aisle, shifting his weight from foot to foot and nervously adjusting his tie. I mouthed at him to stop fiddling. And then, the wedding march began. Seven rows of two bridesmaids, in various arrangements of the same grey viscose, came down the aisle carrying pink peonies, all looking incredibly pleased to be in the chosen cohort. **We're very much a sisterhood**—I could never get on board with this sort of girl-gang feminism, the groups of female friends who called themselves things like "the coven" on social media and exhibited moral superiority from simply having a weekly brunch with each other. Having friends doesn't make you a feminist; going on about female friendship doesn't make you a feminist. I tried to calculate the original line-up of So Solid Crew, the UK garage band played at my noughties school discos, and I think that Lucy's array of bridesmaids was the exact same headcount.

Lucy looked like the perfect classic bride—angelic, feminine, in love and expensive. She wore a cream strapless dress with an enormous A-line skirt that looked like it could house all fourteen of her bridesmaids in its diameter. Over the top, she wore a cream lace jacket as a gesture of modesty and her hair was wavy in a precise way. Her father—rough-skinned, overly roasted from Marbella sunshine and with a squashed face—grasped her hand with his. He lifted her veil at the end of the aisle and kissed her on the cheek, his face pinched with withheld tears. He held on to her hand a little while longer, then she turned to Joe with a smile.

I still didn't know whether I ever wanted to get married. I did know that if I did, the likelihood was my father wouldn't be there. Or if he was still around, at that stage he'd probably be unable to process what was happening. Getting older was an increasingly perplexing thing, but these moments—understanding that potential future memories were being taken from you year on year, like road closures—were the very worst of it.

I wiped under my eyes with the flats of my forefingers and Joe did the same as he wept and Lucy beamed. She held his hand to steady him. The rest of the wedding was as protracted and anticlimactic

as every other English church wedding I've ever attended. An old priest who knew nothing about the
bride other than she'd been christened at the church
thirty years ago made some strange jokes. Everyone
ignored references to God and that the couple
should inexplicably love God more than they love
each other. Everyone giggled at that weird bit in the
vows, which I've never heard a priest pronounce as
anything other than "**seksual** union." There were
some forgettable readings from some freckly cous-
ins. There was one terrible music performance,
which made everyone's sphincters clench on the
cold wood of the benches (Franny, a capella "Ave
Maria"). Hymns were pitched too high and col-
lectively sung in a feeble, reedy voice. We chucked
some pink and violet confetti that had the texture
of gerbil bedding at the exiting bride and groom.

LOLA WAS ALREADY HOLDING two glasses when
I saw her on the lawn of Lucy's family home at
the reception.

"It's real champagne," she said. "How amazing is
that? Here, have one."

"This is quite a pad," I said, looking at the large
white 1920s house in front of us.

"Her dad paid for it twenty years ago in cash,
apparently. Gangster."

"No, he's not."

"Yes, he is."

"You're being a snob because he wears gold jewellery."

"Nina, I'm being serious, ask anyone who knows her. There are photos in the downstairs loo of him with the Kray twins. And he disappeared for six years in the eighties after he killed a man."

"Gangsters don't live in Surrey."

"Are you joking, they **all** live in Surrey. That's why they do what they do. So they can send their kids to a school with a tennis court and have a Jag XK8 parked on a gravel driveway." Lucy walked past us and waved regally. Lola beckoned her over. She gave us both a delicate kiss on the cheek so as not to ruin her immaculate make-up.

"How are you doing?!" I asked.

"Doing great, thanks," she said. "Really enjoying the day."

"Where did you get your dress from?"

"Little boutique not too far from here, actually. Never thought I'd go for strapless, but there we go."

I could tell she was keen to move on, but she was graciously giving us our allotted three minutes. I realized the tone of our conversation was not dis-similar to two showbiz journalists interviewing a movie star on the red carpet outside a premiere.

"I've got to go say hi to some people, but I'll see you later." She glided away, the train of her skirt looped around her wrist like Cinderella.

"How was this morning?" Lola asked.

"Great," I said. "Really fun. You should see it from the other side, Lola. You wouldn't believe it."

"Tell me **everything.**"

"Stayed up and got really drunk last night—sang some sea shanties and everything. Woke up at eleven. Ate a massive fry-up. Had showers, got changed, did ten minutes of photos and then came to the church."

"Oh my God."

"I get why men always say they had so much fun on their wedding day and so many women I know have breakdowns."

"That's so unfair."

"And I don't think that men know what happens on the other side either. I don't even think they know about all the matching dressing gowns with the names of the bridesmaids embroidered on the back."

Lola sighed. "I'm going to go get more drinks. Sometimes they only do champagne as the gateway for the first half-hour before they wean you on to the harder street stuff."

"Cava?"

"Yeah."

I went over to Katherine, who was standing with Meera and holding her one-year-old baby boy, Finlay. I bent down and looked into his large chocolatey eyes, twinkling from the residual tears of his last tantrum.

"Where's Eddie?" I asked Meera.

"Oh, he and Mark are smoking weed in the car park," Katherine said with a sigh.

"We've been at the reception for less than an hour."

"Yeah," Katherine said. "Spot the new dads out on the razz."

Meera noted the judgement in my face. "I'm sure I'll get to have some fun later," she said.

"Do you want to have a cuddle with Aunty Nina?" Katherine said to Finlay in a sweet, high-pitched voice, before passing him over to me. He wriggled into my arms and his warm, calming weight made my feet feel fastened to the ground.

"How have you found it this time?" Meera asked Katherine.

She stroked her tummy. "Wonderful, actually. I adore being pregnant."

"God, you're lucky. I hated it. I had to give up all my favourite things—wine, fags, caffeine, nice cheese."

"I don't mind that at all," Katherine said, adjusting her sunglasses. "I love giving my body a full detox. I don't miss any of it."

Lola came over, holding three glasses of champagne. She passed one to me.

"Oh my God, Andreas's parents are here."

"What?" I said. "How do you know?"

"Who's Andreas?" Katherine asked.

"A guy I've been dating."

"Are you dating now?" Meera asked.

"No, not really."

"Hold on," I said. "How do you know they're his parents?"

"Because I've obviously looked at every Facebook album he's ever uploaded and I recognize them from there."

"Are you sure?"

"Positive. Oh my God, what are the chances? They must be friends with Lucy's parents." She knocked her head back and took a thirsty gulp.

"Okay, don't stress about it, they won't recognize you, so you can just ignore them all day," Meera said.

"I don't want to ignore them all day. I want to make friends with them."

"Why?" I asked despairingly.

"Because, if I make friends with them, then next time they see Andreas they might say, 'We met this charming girl at a wedding called Lola, she's exactly the sort of person you should be with,' and THEN he'll realize what he's missing."

"Can we please ban the phrase 'what he's missing,'" I said. "I'd like to issue a house-style guide for talking about being single, and 'what he's missing' is strictly forbidden."

Katherine put her arm around Lola. "Darling, are you sure that's a good idea?" she asked.

"Yes, or—OR—I could befriend them and then

post a photo of us together on Instagram? That would really give him the willies!"

"You'll look like a stalker," said Meera.

"No, but he doesn't know that I know they're his parents. As far as I know, they're just a lovely couple in their sixties who I met at a wedding and who have invited me to stay at their house for the week-end this summer. Then he wouldn't be able to ghost me, would he?!"

"I think you should hold the baby," I said, passing Finlay over to Lola. "He's very soothing."

She positioned him on her hip and swayed from side to side. He gurgled and giggled.

"You're a natural," Katherine said.

Pathetically, I noticed that she hadn't said that when I was holding Finlay. Performative, public baby-holding had become a competitive sport for childless women at events over the last five years. We all hoped for those three words to be passed over to us by an Adjudicator of Maternal Qualification like Katherine. **You're a natural.**

"Ladies!" Franny said as she bustled towards us and beckoned with her hand. "We're doing a group photo for all married or engaged girls. So, Lola, Nina, you stay put, but you two, you'll need to come with me."

"Are you **fucking** joking?" Lola said.

"I know," Meera said. "But I feel now is not the day to protest."

"We'll look after the baby," I said. Meera and

Katherine walked towards the front of the house where a collection of women gathered.

"DO WIDOWS COUNT?" a frail-looking great-aunt with a neat silver bob and a walking stick shouted.

"Yes, as long as YOU HAVE A RING ON YOUR FINGER!" Franny shouted across the lawn as the great-aunt hobbled towards her hurriedly. "IF IT'S JUST A RINGLESS OR THEORETICAL PROPOSAL, YOU DON'T NEED TO COME JOIN US."

The grass where we stood was now covered only in suits and a handful of women who smiled sympathetically at one other—we had been marked. The photographer, scurrying back and forth across the line of women, asked them all to reach their ring-finger hands forward.

"That's it!" he shouted. "Now look happy, you're all in love!"

"Are we?!" Franny shouted, before waving at her husband and getting a cheap laugh from the crowd.

"This is what they fought for," I said. "All those women before us who were married off and locked up in a house with no voice or vote or money or freedom. This is what they wanted. For a group of professional women to all wave their engagement rings around like it's a Nobel Prize."

"I think Franny might be a total cunt, you know," Lola said.

———

I WAS PUT ON A TABLE with Meera and Eddie, Mark and Katherine, Franny and her husband, Hugo, and Lola. Since Joe and I broke up, Lola and I were regularly grouped together as a counterfeit couple. Like all weddings, the drinking-on-the-grass portion of the day had gone on for an hour too long and everyone was a bit too drunk to be sitting down for dinner. Mark was pawing at the miniature bottle of damson gin party favour, trying to open it and drink it in one. Eddie's face was pink with booze and excitement as he explained to the table why he thought there were so many eligible thirty-something women who were single.

"It's the Blair Bulge," he asserted, leaning across the table to fill my glass with white wine. "I'm convinced of it."

"What's the Blair Bulge?"

"Women with degrees will only rarely marry men without them, but men are less fussy," he explained. "Because Tony Blair made more people go to university, there are loads of university-educated women who struggle to find suitable long-term partners. This cohort is the Blair Bulge."

"So basically, we've become too smart for marriage."

"Precisely!" he said.

"I mean, that's sort of encouraging."

"Where's Lola?" Katherine asked. The seat next to me was empty.

"I'm not sure," I said. I glanced around the marquee and saw her standing by the table plan, looking like a giant orange-flavoured ice lolly, laughing and talking to a couple in their sixties. "Oh God. I think she's talking to Andreas's parents."

"I've got a question for all you fellow old marrieds!" Franny piped up. "Sorry, Nina."

I shook my head. "Really, no offence taken," I said.

"I want to know what your love language is."

"What's a love language?" Mark asked.

"Oh, Mark, you must know about it! Katherine, do you know about it?"

"Yes, I did the quiz online."

"So did I," Meera said.

"Right, so, listen carefully, boys," Franny said. "There are five different ways of expressing love and every person's is different. It was so useful for us to work out what our ones are, wasn't it, darling?"

"Yah," Hugo barked, stuffing a bread roll in his mouth.

"So, mine was 'acts of service,' which means someone doing considerate things for me, like running a bath or cooking dinner. Whereas Hugo's is 'affirmation,' so he needs compliments and positive reinforcement."

"Mine was 'affirmation'!" Meera said.

"Mine was 'quality time,'" said Katherine.

I looked around the table; the three husbands were checking their phones or staring drunkenly into the middle distance. Was it only women who had the capacity to find their own relationships this fascinating? To make a project and personality from the man they loved? Lola sat down next to me and removed her neon cape.

"Lola, what's your love language?" Franny asked, her chin coyly resting in the palm of her hand.

Lola shrugged. "I don't know. Anal, probably." Franny sat back in her chair, struggling to conceal her horror. "Right, so I've done some groundwork with Andreas's parents. Such a nice couple. They know Lucy's parents from when their kids were all at primary school together and they've remained friends. I said, 'Oh, how many kids have you got?' and they were like, 'Two sons, Andreas and Tim,' and I just smiled."

"Do you feel better?"

"Of course not."


THROUGHOUT THE THREE-COURSE DINNER, there was a roaming lounge singer with a mic, going from table to table crooning the Great American Songbook, a juggler and a palm reader. I've never understood why wedding receptions required this level of multi-sensory entertainment from beginning to end. Lola flagged down the passing palm reader as soon as she could, meaning I had to make conversation with Franny's husband, Hugo, who worked as a press officer for the Conservative Party.

"I'm fiscally conservative but socially liberal," he said within the first two minutes of me asking him about his job. I wouldn't be surprised if right-leaning thirty-somethings received a script in the post to prepare them for social situations.

"I'm not sure if I believe that really exists," I replied. "I know what you're trying to say. But 'I love the gays but don't care about the poor' can't be described as liberal in any sense."

"I do care about the poor." Katherine looked across the table at us. She hated anyone talking about politics. "I just think that politics can't be governed by emotion, progression happens when effective economic systems are in place."

"You're lucky," I said.

"Why?"

"To feel unemotional about politics." My eyes were distracted by Katherine, who picked up her glass and put it under the table, next to her chair, and nodded at Mark. He filled it with white wine. "That's a luxury."

"It's not a luxury, it's a choice. Of rationality."

"What are you two talking about?" Franny asked, leaning across us.

"We're talking about Hugo's job."

"Oh, isn't it fascinating? I can't hear enough about it. Makes me wonder what I'm doing with my life, singing useless arias. Have you told her about that new environmental scheme you've been developing?"

"I'm not going to bore Nina with that," he said.

I smiled gratefully and turned to Lola, who was shovelling tempura prawns into her mouth while talking at Eddie.

"I just wish there was, like, a baby overdraft, you know? I wish I could buy an extra ten years of time that I could dip into if I end up needing it. I don't understand why the bank of life can't give that to me. I'd happily pay interest every month until I'm fifty, just to ensure it's there." Eddie was nodding slowly, his tie now at half-mast. "I feel a bit tricked, to be honest. I've been told that I can buy anything I want. Or work for it. Or control it on an app. But I can't buy love. I can't get it on an app."

"I thought you could get it on an app?" Eddie slurred.

Lola forked Eddie's starter off his plate, shaking her head. She leant into him conspiratorially, holding the prawn slightly too close to his face. "Lies," she hissed. I tried to remember what we all used to talk about at the first batch of weddings in our mid-twenties.

The Father of the Bride speech came first, which included a long list of all Lucy's various school sporting achievements and a full breakdown of her impressive GCSE results. The grand finale came when he revealed that his present to the couple was waiting on the driveway. The wedding guests dutifully migrated outside where a navy Audi sat, tied with a lilac bow. Joe and Lucy jumped up and down like they were winning contestants on a game show while the rest of us applauded.

"I've just realized I haven't got them a present," Lola said as we made our way back into the marquee.

"That doesn't matter," I said.

"Yes it does, I've never forgotten to get one before."

"Go on the gift list, I'm sure there's something left you can buy." She pulled her phone out of her orange clutch bag and went into her emails to find the link for the registry. "Not **now,** obviously."

"No, I need to do it now, how embarrassing."

The Best Man's speech was given by Joe's childhood friend who, regrettably, was in an improv sketch group in his spare time, which explained the numerous wigs and props that he used over the half-hour telling of a collection of rambling anti-anecdotes. When it was Joe's turn to speak, he stood up as tall and proud as a Steiff bear on a collector's display stand. I could tell he had been watching how much he drank because he spoke with formality and reverence, diligently thanking every family member, every bridesmaid, every usher and wedding supplier. He gave a loving tribute to his parents, whose marriage he said had been an inspiration to him. Then he turned to Lucy, who gazed up at his face adoringly.

"On our first date," he said, "I asked you where you wanted to be in two years' time." He turned to the audience for a knowing aside. "A little bit of a job interview question, sure." He waited for the polite laugh. "And you said to me: 'in love.'"

I glanced over at Lola, who was scrolling through the online gift registry.

"Nothing's left but the salad spinner," she whispered.

"Shh," I said.

"I'd never in my life met someone so sure of what it is they not only wanted but what they deserved. I knew then, on our first date, that you were the only person I wanted to be with. You inspire me, you organize me"—another mischievous glance to the audience—"you help me strive to become the best man I can be. I once read that the definition of love is 'being the guardian of another person's solitude.' Lucy, I promise that for the rest of my life—which is as long as I will love you—you will never, ever be alone." Everyone clapped as Lucy used her napkin to wipe away tears from under her eyes. Joe bent down to her face, which he held, and they kissed.

I had imagined this moment before, years ago, during our final break-up conversation. As I'd looked at Joe on our living-room floor, our faces inches away from each other, I had experienced ter-minal lucidity. For a few sudden seconds, I remem-bered what I saw when I'd first fallen in love with him. I knew someone would love him like I had, and that he would love again.

"NOW LET'S DANCE, BITCHES!" he shouted

suddenly, before dropping the mic on the table, which caused an almighty bang so loud all the guests flinched. The DJ fired up the twinkling intro of "Everywhere" by Fleetwood Mac. Joe and Lucy took to the dance floor and began a slick routine of twirling, dipping and lifting that had very obviously been choreographed in their living room weeks before, but was charming nonetheless. Everyone formed a circle around them and clapped in time to the music. At the chorus, Joe signalled for us to join them. We poured on to the dance floor and Lola merrily bopped over to Lucy and Joe in time with the music.

"I GOT YOU THE SALAD SPINNER!" she shouted in their ears, producing her phone and showing them proof of purchase, before enveloping them in a group hug. "I HOPE YOU ARE VERY HAPPY!"

"Ladies and gentlemen," the DJ said into the mic, "I hear we've got someone at this wedding who is named after a Mr. George Michael so, George, this one's for you." The intro of "The Edge of Heaven" played. Joe was the other side of the dance floor, pointing at me with one hand, clicking theatrically with the other. I mimed casting a fishing line out and he immediately hooked his mouth with his own finger—I yanked the invisible rod towards me and he bounced forward in time with the music. We met each other in the middle and Joe picked me up, flinging me over his shoulder and spinning around.

I stretched my arms out like a child pretending to be a plane. Lucy danced over to us.

"YOUR SONG!" she shouted. Joe put me down.

"YEAH!" I replied. I leant in to speak in her ear. Her hair smelt of Elnett hairspray and jasmine perfume. "YOU REALLY DO LOOK SO BEAUTIFUL, LUCY." She smiled and gave me a hug, which we held for longer than we would have done sober, and swayed in time to the music. Joe took us both by the hand and twirled us around—him the maypole, us the flailing ribbons. We picked up speed—he spun us both out to the side of him and when we reeled back in we collided, ricocheting off each other and falling on the floor. He bent down to help us up, and Lucy yanked his arms so he fell and lay prone on top of us. It was unexpected and ridiculous, to have found ourselves in this tangle. All three of us couldn't stop laughing.

## 14

KATHERINE'S BABY BOY was born in early April. The night of Olive's birth, I had dreamt that Katherine was in labour. Her low cries of pain woke me up at exactly 4:12 a.m. and I knew her baby was here—I turned on my bedside light and wrote down the time on a piece of paper. The next day Mark texted me a photo of newborn Olive, black-eyed, rosy-lipped and puffy-cheeked, informing me that she had been born at four that morning. I gave Katherine the piece of paper—she put it in the back of a framed photo of Olive. This time, when I received the text from Mark telling me their six-pound son, Frederick Thomas, was born just after midday, I'd had no premonition he was here. It was like an invisible psychic string between us had been severed.

I got the train out of London and went to their new house a week after his birth, taking pre-prepared trays of homemade lasagne for Mark and Katherine and brownies for Olive. When I arrived at the large house that was exactly as purpose-built as it looked in the pictures, I heard a familiar toddler racket seep out of the door. Mark answered—Olive was sitting on the floor behind him, crying.

"Nina!" he said, giving me a hug. He had the sunken, small-featured face of someone on a handful of hours' sleep. "It's a bit of a madhouse here this morning."

"I like madhouses," I said, moving into the hallway and crouching down to give Olive a hug.

"Look, Olly, Aunty Neenaw. She's come to see us. That's nice, isn't it? Will you give her a big hug hello?"

"I DON'T LIKE YOU, AUNTY NEENAW," she shouted, pointing at me as she wrinkled her face up in vengefulness.

"Oh dear," I said, stroking the top of her head. "Now, I just don't think that's true at all."

"It is, Neenaw, it is, I don't LIKE you."

I laughed and Mark took my coat. "I'm so sorry, this is a new thing she's saying to everyone. You mustn't take it personally."

"Please. She's a toddler."

"I know, I know, but it's just so embarrassing. It started about a week ago, when"—he glanced down at Olive, who had stopped crying and was now listening intently—"when our new friend arrived."

"Got it," I said, walking towards the living room. "Well, that's to be expected. And she can get lots of attention from me today."

"Thanks, Aunty Neenaw," he said, briefly placing his palm on my back. I always preferred Mark softer—I'd forgotten a newborn and no sleep did this to him.

Katherine was sitting in the corner of the sofa, her legs folded under her body in her neatly feline way, and a small cotton-swathed bundle in her arms.

"Oh hello," I said in a hushed voice, taking a seat next to her. I kissed her on the cheek and gazed down at the tiny sleeping baby who smelt of warm milk and warm laundry.

"Hello," she said with a smile. Her face was bare, her lids were heavy. She looked ethereally gorgeous. "This is Freddie. Freddie, this is Aunty Nina."

"I DON'T LIKE HER, GO AWAY, AUNTY NEENAW," Olive shouted from the hallway.

"Olive's having a difficult week," Katherine said.

"Don't worry, I've got brownies and I'm going to use them tactically."

"Clever Aunty Neenaw."

"Look at this perfect little boy," I said, gently stroking his cheek with my forefinger. "Brand new."

"Guess his life expectancy? Mark and I couldn't believe it when the doctor told us."

"What?"

"One hundred and twenty years old."

I gasped and put my face closer to his, to examine every micro-pore. "Magic baby dinosaur."

"Isn't he?"

"I hope you're reserving your energy, little Freddie. You're going to need it."


I MADE US ALL TEA and heard the birth story, well paced and succinctly told, having had a number of performances, with Mark and Katherine taking a line each. There had been a two-day labour, forceps and bruised—yes, **bruised**—labia. For someone so otherwise reserved, Katherine never spared any detail of birth. I loved hearing about it—it's strange how quickly you can become a natal connoisseur by proxy of those around you. Five years ago, I could have barely differentiated between a one-year-old and a one-day-old baby. Now, I knew about Braxton Hicks and mastitis and pre-labour perineum massage. I knew about sleep training, growth spurts, teething and potty training. The lexicon of our peer group morphed in every decade. Soon I would know about school-catchment areas, then university applications, then pension schemes. Then care homes, then the name of every funeral parlour in my postcode.

I TOOK OLIVE OUT for the afternoon. We went to the park, then the soft-play—she was calm and distracted, her little squeaky voice overexplaining everything to me solemnly. "This is the cars, Aunty Neenaw, and they drive you," she said as we walked hand in hand down the road. "This is the grasses and they are green," she said in the park, crouching down to collect a blade and examining it closely. "And sometimes you can eat them like the cows and the snakes but not every day." We came home in time for tea, which was fish fingers, peas and oven chips.

"Nutrition is out the window this week, I'm afraid," Katherine said as she squirted a small puddle of ketchup on Olive's plate. "Will only be for a week though."

"Relax, Kat," I said. "It's fine."

"I am relaxed!" she said. "I'm just saying don't judge us for dinner out of the freezer."

"I wouldn't judge you for anything you gave me for dinner."

"What time is it, Mark?"

"Six."

"Right, feeding time for you," she said, scooping her swollen breast out of her bra and attaching Freddie's mouth to it.

"It's so weird that newborns basically just eat all day," I said. "It's like they're permanently on a long boozy lunch, like a PR girl from the 1990s."

Katherine laughed. "Sounds like a nice life. Speaking of which, how is Lola?" It was a joke I would have found funny from anyone other than Katherine, who I knew thought all childless women did was have long lunches.

"Fine, I think. Weirdly, I haven't really seen or heard from her the last month. I hope she's okay, I think she's just busy."

"How often do you speak normally?"

"Every day," I said. "And we see each other at least once a week, so it's been a bit strange, actually."

"Wow, that's a lot. I'm surprised you don't get sick of each other!" She'd made comments like this before—hinting that my and Lola's relationship was intense or untenable, when we'd been friends now for just shy of fifteen years. She'd had to be sceptical about the omnipresence of Lola to normalize the fact of her own increasing absence. There was a loud bang and we turned to see Olive had accidentally bashed her face on the side of the table while enthusiastically trying to hoover up the peas with her mouth. She had the foreboding wide-eyed expression of a toddler in pain.

"Olive," Katherine said calmly, "darling, you're going to be a brave gir—" But before she'd finished her sentence, Olive was on the kitchen floor banging her fists on the tiles and letting out siren sounds. Mark went over to comfort her.

"Don't pick her up," Katherine said. "She won't like it. When she gets like this you just need to sit close to her." Mark lay next to her on the floor as she wailed, barely able to breathe as her face reddened in overexertion. Mark breathed deeply and slowly to calm her and said the same sentence over and over again: "It's okay, I'm here. It's okay, I'm here. It's okay, Olive, I'm here."

Eventually, Olive recovered. She stood up slowly, holding on to the chair as her little legs wobbled. "Good girl," we all said to congratulate her standing up again. "Good girl, what a good girl." How do we ever manage our emotions single-handedly when this is the introduction to the world we're given? Where do we learn to do it? How do we find a way to cry quietly on our own, in showers and loos and into pillowcases, then stand up again unassisted and with no words of encouragement?

"Let's put on **The Lion King** soundtrack, hey?" Katherine said, removing the baby from her breast and tucking herself back into her bra.

"PLAY **LION KING,**" Olive shouted at the sound system, still sniffing in the aftermath of her violent sobs. The opening chants of "Circle of Life" began.

"LOUD," Olive shouted again and the song boomed off the kitchen tiles. Mark went to turn it down.

"Let her," Katherine said.

"Dance, Neenaw," Olive demanded as drums reverberated around the room. I crouched down and held her hands to twist her back and forth. She grinned.

"Dance, Mummy, dance, Daddy!" Mark rolled his eyes and stood up, swaying enthusiastically in time to the music. "MORE!" she shouted and Mark waved his arms around in the air with un-coordinated gusto. I laughed and scooped Olive up, hoisting her on to my hip and sashaying around the kitchen. The chorus built and Katherine lifted Freddie up above her head, like Rafiki holding Simba to the sky. Olive broke into giggles. Freddie made a burping noise and white spittle dribbled down his chin.

"Chuck me a muslin, babe?" Katherine said, resting him back on to her chest.

"DON'T STOP DANCING, DADDY!" Olive shouted. Mark dance-walked to the cupboard and picked up a cloth that he threw across to Katherine, who grabbed it with her free hand. The choreography of well-coordinated parenthood—they'd never know what those brief moments were like to watch, from the outside looking in. It was worth spending an exhausting day of tantrums and stinking nappies with a young family, just to get a glimpse at these short-lived shooting stars of togetherness.

I left after "I Just Can't Wait to Be King," slipping out as quietly as possible so as not to aggravate Olive. As I closed the front door, I was illuminated by the golden light of Saturday dinner time streaming out of their front window. The cacophony of laughter, shouting, clattering plates and "Hakuna Matata" faded as I walked down their road. I knew the deal—shortly after I left, there'd be the struggle to get Olive into the bath, then calming her down before bed, then storytelling under the covers while they longed for a glass of wine. There'd be washing-up and breast-pumping and sterilizing bottles. Mark and Katherine would be in bed before ten and one or both of them would silently recollect all their past Saturday nights of total freedom. I didn't romanticize child-rearing—I couldn't, having spent so much time observing it close-up through my friends over the last few years. But I didn't need to. Katherine was so desperate to hide the mess of her home life from me, little did she know it was the mess that I longed for. It was not the domestic, cuddly quiet I envied—the sleeping baby in the pram or the perfectly arranged family portraits on social media. The shambles of raising children was what I craved—the toys on the floor, the Disney soundtrack filling a kitchen, the rainfall of tears followed by the rising steam of laughter, the wet jumper after bath time with a wriggling, splashing toddler. My flat had begun to feel so quiet—my shelves too neat, my surfaces too crumbless, my diary pages too blank.

I tried to call Lola on the train home to see if she was free and fancied meeting up, but I went straight to her voicemail. I scrolled through my phone-book to see if there was anyone who might like to go for a drink, but they were all tied into un-written contracts of relationships and families, which meant I'd have to confirm a night with them a fortnight in advance.

I GOT HOME, noticed that Angelo had put a black bin bag in the recycling bin again, ignored it and went upstairs. I didn't have the energy for neighbourhood warfare tonight. I opened my laptop and worked on the new book. Almost immediately I turned away from the manuscript and googled Max's name, which I now did about once a week. Like always, I stared at the one small picture of him that existed online—the LinkedIn profile photo of him in a white shirt and green tie that became pixelated if I zoomed in on it. I had recently abandoned my other bizarre habit of going on to the LinkedIn profiles of his colleagues, to see if they might have information on where he went to. They didn't, they just had lots of information about their client experience and relationships with HMRC and Treasury. I wondered how long I would be indulging in this ritual—Max and I had now been apart for as long as we'd been together.

I googled Freddie's full name. There was, of course, nothing. He was seven days old. If only he could know how lucky he was, to exist on a blanket of untouched snow, with not one footprint yet to be found. If only he could consciously savour this period. What would appear when you typed his name at the end of his estimated 120-year-long life? What mess would he leave?

I typed "Bill Dean secondary school teacher" into Google. Up came the familiar results purpled by the exhaustion of my countless previous clicks. There was an interview with Dad in a local paper about being a headmaster, which he did when he retired. There was a photo of him from another newspaper article in the early noughties, about his support of a national literacy campaign. But just like Max's online edifice, crudely constructed and bare, there was little to excavate. The vast majority of Dad's life had happened in a world that wasn't yet on-line. Now my dad was fading, I wanted to keep in touch with as many past versions of him as possible. But the internet had failed me—I could look up the full names of all of the parents of the cast of **Friends,** but I couldn't find one photo of my dad as a student. I could get a street-view photograph of a road on the other side of the world that I'd never visit, but I couldn't find one video of my dad. I remembered meeting Dad's former student in the bakery after the Picasso exhibition and what he'd said about there being a Facebook group in his hon-our. I typed "Bill Dean teacher" in the Facebook search bar, but nothing came up. I tried "Mr. Dean teacher St. Michael's" and there it was—"MR. DEAN WAS A LEGEND" and a photo of my smiling dad as I remembered him in my childhood, thick salt-and-pepper hair like a Border collie, skin wrinkled but capillaries yet unbroken. Eyes as dark as molasses, alert and bright. I went on to the description: "For anyone who went to St. Michael's and was taught by the LEGEND Mr. Bill Dean."

I scrolled down the wall of the group to find discussions of Dad's unusual snacks that he'd eaten during class (smoked oysters from a tin with a cocktail stick, pickled walnuts wrapped in foil) and his unusual lessons (the derivatives of cockney rhyming slang, Leonard Cohen lyrics as poetry). There were photos of him dressed up as Huckleberry Finn for World Book Day. There were numerous posts from ex-pupils who said Dad's enthusiasm for literature had ignited their love of reading. The latest post was from Arthur, saying he'd bumped into Bill Dean recently and that, while he'd seemed a little older, he looked exactly the same. He made a self-deprecating joke about the fact Dad hadn't recognized him and said this was understandable as he must be the favourite teacher of any kid who was taught by him, he couldn't be expected to hold every single student in the same regard. I logged into Facebook and wrote Arthur a direct message.

Dear Arthur
My name is Nina, I'm Bill's daughter. We met very briefly in a café a while back. I just wanted to drop you a message because, understandably, you might have

thought that my dad was behaving strangely that day.
I wanted to let you know that he's suffering from

I sat back in my chair. My dad had always been open with his students—he thought it was important for them to know his interests and passions. But he was private. He said there was a fine line between showing the kids the humanity of who you were and telling them who you were. He was strict in his avoidance of the latter. He felt that making himself too known to students was not what they, or he, needed. Which was surely one of the reasons this Facebook group existed—speculating on who Bill Dean was other than the man who had been completely focused on their education. How much of this message to Arthur would be to save my father's pride, and how much was it to preserve his legacy according to me? I exited Facebook without sending the message and closed my laptop.

I unlocked my phone and downloaded Linx, which I'd done a few times since Christmas. I knew I had to "put myself out there," like the worm on the hook Lola had talked about, but I was still too attached to whatever it was that Max and I had created together. Every man looked exactly the same: "Tom, 34, atheist, London, likes: reading, sleeping, eating, travel"—it reminded me of the biology GCSE syllabus and being taught what living organisms need: "movement, respiration, reproduction, nutrition, excretion." With every bland profile, I was reminded of a specific memory with Max. The playlist he'd made me called "Happy and Sad Men With Guitars." The vodka tonic he brought me during every evening bath and how he'd sit on the side of the tub and talk as I washed my hair. The time he brushed the conditioner through it and he felt like my mother and I felt five and for some reason that nearly made me cry as I faced away from him, looking at the shower screen. Fucking clumsily while we were both still wearing jumpers after a long, cold walk along the canal—how we'd spent the last rushed mile telling each other in quiet voices exactly what we were going to do when we got back to the warmth of his flat. The thought of trying to replace that closeness with one of these anonymous organisms seemed an impossibility.

It was strange, to have all your screens finally fail you. I didn't know where to get the delicious chemical hit psychologists always warned against— I couldn't seem to feel it, as much as I clicked. Google wasn't giving me the content I wanted, neither was Linx. Perhaps this was why Lola was always online shopping and sending everything back, like a retail bulimic—to feel something even for just a second. I fell asleep on the profile of a 5 foot 10 man called Jake who lived in Earlsfield and liked Japanese synth music.

———

ON MONDAY MORNING, I was recipe-testing in the kitchen when the doorbell rang. It was a man who worked for an international delivery service holding a square parcel.

"Hi, I've got a package for Angelo Ferretti on the ground floor. Would you mind taking it for him and signing for it?"

I glanced at the recycling bins, which had not been emptied by the binmen that morning because Angelo had filled them back up with black bin bags.

"He actually doesn't live on the ground floor, he lives on the first floor," I said. "With me."

"Oh, really?"

"Yes," I said, impressed with the ease of my improvisation. "For some reason people seem to get the ground-floor and first-floor flats confused. Angelo lives with me. He's my husband."

"Oh right, okay," he said, handing the parcel over. "No need to sign then."

"Great. So, ring the first-floor doorbell from now on, if you have any packages for him. Don't want to disturb the poor guy in the flat below."

"Will do, thanks," he said, walking away. I put my ear to Angelo's door and heard nothing—he was out at work.

I went upstairs to my flat and into my kitchen. I pulled up a chair beneath the useless cupboard above the oven—too hard to reach to store anything for cooking—and opened its doors. I slid the package straight in and decided it was now the vestibule for hoarding all of Angelo's packages. No one would ever know. I didn't feel guilt or fear or even excitement—I felt a calm sense of justice. I was the building's legal system now—I was the clerk, jury and judge. Someone had to be. I didn't want to cause him any harm or distress, I just wanted him to feel as frustrated and confused as he'd made me feel. It was what he deserved.

LOLA FINALLY CALLED ME BACK the day before **The Tiny Kitchen**'s book launch, asking if she could take me out for a drink before the party. I wore a backless cream silk blouse and black trousers. She wore a skin-tight flared jumpsuit in fuchsia satin, with a high frilly neck and huge puffed sleeves voluminous enough to rival Henry VIII's, and a high, padded headband in matching pink, which looked like it had been swiped from Anne Boleyn. Large dangling pearl drops hung from her ears. I stood up as she walked in the bar.

"Don't tell me," I said. "**Tudors Go Dating.** A brand-new historical re-enactment reality show for those looking for love, tonight at ten on E4."

"I'm more dressed up for your book launch than you are," she said as she pulled me in for a hug. "Do you want me to change? Shall I go buy a plain black dress quickly?"

"Lola, you're always more dressed up than anyone,

anywhere," I said, breathing in her overwhelming perfume as we hugged. "And that's why we love you." We sat down and the waiter came over.

"Dry Vodka Martini with an olive for her," she said. "And a Moscow Mule for me, please."

"Coming up," he replied.

"Who's going to be there tonight? Mum? Dad? Katherine? Joe?"

"None of them," I said. "It's going to be low-key."

"Oh no, why?" she said, visibly distressed. Lola was a woman who referred to her "birthday month" and its accompanying multiple ceremonies every year with no irony.

"Katherine can't leave the baby, Joe's away for work and . . ." I hesitated. "And I told Mum and Dad there wasn't a book launch."

"Why?"

"Because Dad's often quite confused at the moment and I didn't want him to say strange things and for people to pity him. So I just pretended there wasn't a party for this one. Do you think I'm a terrible person?"

"No, the opposite," she said. "I'll be your mummy tonight. And your daddy. And your husband. And your ex-boyfriend."

"Four kinks in one. You're multitalented, my girl." She laughed. "Now. Where have you been?"

"What do you mean?"

"What's been happening? I haven't seen you since Joe's wedding."

"Oh, nothing, really, just had some new stuff I've had to focus on."

"What new stuff?"

"I'll tell you another time!"

"Tell me now!"

"No, it's your night!"

"Lola."

"What?"

"Tell me."

"I've met someone."

"What! When?"

"A couple of days after Joe and Lucy's wedding."

"Where?"

"An event that my company produced. He was performing at it."

"Musician?"

"Magician."

"What's his name?"

"Jethro."

"How old?"

"Thirty-six."

I was struggling to put together sentences—the day had finally come. I knew it would. Someone had realized how loveable Lola was. "Can I see a picture?" Lola took her phone out of her bag and showed me her background screen. It was their faces pressed together, their hair wet with rain, their cheeks flushed with adoration and vitality, their eyes bright from cold air and morning orgasms. His face was sharp and Hollywood handsome, softened and anglicized with a blanket of freckles. His nose was narrow and reptilian. His red hair was cut and styled in a way that suggested an East London barber with a large Instagram following.

"Lola, he's gorgeous. Where are you?"

"At my mum and dad's. We went last weekend."

"Oh my God."

"I know."

"Did they like him?"

"Loved him."

The waiter brought our drinks to the table and I grabbed the Martini from his hand before he had a chance to put it down.

"So. Sorry, I'm just trying to get my head round this."

"I know."

"Tell me what happened."

"I was working at this event—big brand dinner and a DJ thing—counting the hours until it was over, when he came up and asked if he could do a magic trick on me. Which, as you know—"

"You love magic, yes."

"Exactly."

I sensed that now was not the time for me to put forward my case for magic being a thing that only prudes loved.

"So, he blows me away with this card trick—you're not going to believe it, Nina, the card I picked was **in my handbag which was on my arm.** He was standing a metre away from me! How did it get there?"

"I don't know."

"And then he was like, can I take you out for a drink after this. And I told him I wouldn't be finishing until one a.m., and he said he'd wait. So he waited—**waited for three hours**—can you believe that? Just sat in the green room with a book. Then at one, we went to this twenty-four-hour restaurant and drank loads of Sancerre and ate eggs Benedict. Guess what time we finished?"

"I don't know."

"Seven a.m. We just couldn't stop talking. Honestly, Nina, it was like something out of a Fellini film." Since when did Lola watch Fellini films? Or drink Sancerre? "And then we kissed on the bench outside and I went straight into the office!"

"You must have been exhausted," I managed to muster.

"I felt so awake. So alive! Then he rang my office at lunchtime and asked for my home address."

"That's . . . full on."

"And when I came back to my flat that night, he was there on the doorstep with the ingredients for lasagne and a bouquet of lily of the valley because lasagne—"

"Is your favourite meal."

"And lily of the valley—"

"Are your favourite flowers."

"Not even in season," she said with pride to rival a recently qualified Greek doctor's mother. "Paid extra for a same-day delivery service from the Netherlands."

"So then what happened?"

"He came in and made lasagne. And that was a month ago and basically he never left."

"You're living together?"

"Well. Not officially. He's got his own flat. And he's travelling a fair bit with his job. He's the Magician in Residence for a chain of private members' clubs around the world. Oh, Nina, he's so talented. I know you don't really like magic—I've already warned him, I said: my best friend doesn't really like magic!—but I'm desperate for you to come to one of his shows." She put her phone on the table and presented me with his Instagram page. JETHROTHEMAGICMAN was his handle, Model/Magic Maker/Dream Weaver was his tag line, 33,000 followers. "Some of the stuff I think you'd like is the more stunty bits, like just really amazing physical strength work." She clicked on a video of him juggling loaded guns in a black studio while dramatic violin music played over the top. "Look, look at this bit," she said excitedly, her finger pressing on the screen. He pulled the triggers of the guns as he caught them in each hand. "Isn't that amazing?"

**"Amazing."**

"So anyway. That's it. That's where I've been."

"That's a lot of very exciting information," I said. "Magician. Jethro. Living together for a month."

"I know, and if this was the other way around I would be sceptical. But you just have to trust me when I say that this is the real deal. I know my instincts are right."

"I don't doubt that at all. You seem so happy."

"I am," she said. "It was all worth it. All those dates. All those hours staring at WhatsApp. That man who claimed to be allergic to my vagina acidity. I would do it a hundred times again if I knew it all ended with Jethro. It's like I've woken up and everything is technicolour."

"Wow."

"I know. I'm sorry. I'll stop now."

"No, don't stop," I said. "This is everything you deserve. I can't wait to meet him."

"Thank you, Nina," she said. "And I know this is coming for you too. I promise—it's on its way."

"I don't know," I said, taking another gulp of my Martini. "I don't know if I want a flowers-sent-from-the-Netherlands-wake-up-in-technicolour love again. Think once was enough. Don't know if I have it in me."

"Yes you do," she said. "Just not right now."


THE LAUNCH was in a bookshop in Soho. It took place during a strict two-hour window and there was a conservative amount of red wine, white wine and beer, provided by my publisher. There were under thirty guests—a mix of people who worked for my agency and publisher and some journalists. I signed books, I circulated with Vivien's strict instructions—telling journalists about the story behind **The Tiny Kitchen** and making my desperate availability for potential events clear to the bookshop manager. Vivien made a short but characteristically charming speech about **The Tiny Kitchen** and why its subject matter was timely. I stood up to say just two sentences: thank you to Vivien for making this book happen; and thank you everyone for coming.

**Taste**'s book launch had been a different night. I'd organized a whole floor in a fancy bar for free in exchange for doing a series of speaking events. Lola had used her events expertise to help me engineer a party on a small budget. All my friends and family were there, as were all my colleagues and bosses from years of teaching. I made a long speech, name-checking everyone who I'd worked with at the publisher, thanking my friends, family, my old colleagues who had always been so supportive of my moonlighting as a food writer while I was teaching. Mum was there, with trusty Gloria in tow, both of them wearing beaded "serapes"—a word to describe a type of unnecessary evening shawl I'd never heard outside of Pinner. Dad was there, circulating the room all night with a glass in his hand and his best questions and anecdotes in his pocket.

I stood outside to smoke a cigarette as the book-shop closed so I could say goodbye to everyone as they left. Vivien gave me a particularly long hug goodbye, perhaps because she'd noticed that I was without my mum or dad, and told me how much she was enjoying the new chapters I'd sent her. Everyone had trickled out within ten minutes. It was eight thirty and the sky was still light enough to frame the outline of Soho's roofs and chimneys. Spring had flung its door wide open. Summer soon. Long days, long nights, light at all hours, illuminating everything. Nowhere to hide.

"Right, where are we going next?" Lola asked, the last one out of the shop with a bag full of signed copies of **The Tiny Kitchen** and two self-help books called **The Power of Maybe** and **I Came, I Saw, I Ordered the Cookie.**

"Home," I said.

"I'm coming with you."

"Honestly, you don't have to."

"You've just published your second book!" she said. "I'm buying champagne from the corner shop."

"You really are the best husband." I linked my arm in hers as we walked to the tube.

"And I'm staying at yours tonight. I know you don't like sharing beds and I know you don't need me to stay. But I'd like to." I didn't protest—I knew this was Lola's way of delivering me a clear message in a partially concealed way: **I may have left you**

**as the last single woman we know, but you're not alone. I am still here.**

A bottle of corner-shop champagne and half a bottle of back-of-the-freezer toffee vodka later, I was hearing about all of Jethro's favourite cookbooks. Lola had a bad case of mentionitis—when thoughts of a lover are so pervasive, they find their way into every topic ("Jethro has the grey version of your bath mat!" she said at one point, like she'd discovered we shared a grandmother). A diagnosis of chronic mentionitis—that another human has bought a permanent property on a road that goes right through the middle of your soul—means that you are truly, irreversibly, horrifically in love.

We were both leaning out of my living-room window to smoke a cigarette when the front door opened. Angelo shuffled out in a dressing gown and a pair of slippers. His long hair was tied into a feeble plait, as thin as a ragged friendship bracelet belonging to a teenage girl. In each hand, he held a bulging black bin bag. He opened the green recycling bin and shoved both bags in.

"YOU FUCKER," I shouted. "They won't collect any of our rubbish if you do that! Take it out!" He didn't even answer me with a middle finger—a new habit he'd adopted. I got nothing as he inhaled deeply on his fag and lugubriously shuffled back into the house.

"Alma saw a rat climbing out of our bin last week

because his rubbish had been sitting in it with the lid propped open for so long."

"Do you think he's getting worse?" Lola asked.

"He's caring even less," I said. "It's like, I can't find any consequences for him. Nothing bothers him. He doesn't care who he upsets or how he embarrasses himself. It's so difficult to manage— I never even taught teenage boys this bad."

"I don't know how you're staying sane."

"I don't think I am."

"I think you are."

"I don't think I am, Lola," I said. I put out my cigarette and took a swig of toffee vodka from the bottle, which felt like hot syrup as it slipped down my throat. I stood up to go to the kitchen and beckoned her. She followed.

I climbed on a chair and opened the cupboard above the cooker.

"Look," I said. Lola stood on her tiptoes. "I've started taking his packages. I pretend to the delivery man that he lives here."

"Why?"

"To make him go mad, like he's made me go mad."

"You're a genius. An unhinged, evil genius."

"Do you think so?"

"Yes. How many have you got so far?"

"Three."

"Aren't you worried he's going to find out?"

"I don't think he will. The tracking will say that it was delivered. I haven't had to sign for any yet.

He will go insane, trying to prove to the delivery company that the packages aren't at his flat."

"Hours on the phone to customer services," Lola said, smiling.

"Hours and hours and hours. And imagine the conversation."

"It's been delivered, sir."

"No, it hasn't."

"Yes, it has."

"Well why isn't it here?"

"It **is** there, sir, we have proof it's been delivered," Lola said, her volume increasing with excitement.

"Shh!" I said through laughter. "He might be listening. He stood silently outside my door once, the creep."

"Let's open them," she said, with sudden verve.

"No, we can't."

"Oh, come on! Don't you want to know what's in them?"

"No, it will be something boring. He has no life. He only leaves his flat to go to his job and I've only seen him with a friend once. It will be new Hoover bags."

"I'm doing it," she said. "Pass them down."

We sat cross-legged on the floor with two pairs of scissors and cut open the taped-up boxes. The first, the heaviest, contained two large metal hooks.

"What are they for?" Lola asked. "S&M props?"

"No, no way he's that fun," I said, picking one up and examining it. "I have no idea." I unwrapped another package that contained a large, heavy plastic case of white powder. I held the label up close to my face. **"Potassium nitrate,"** I read, examining a hazardous symbol. **"Warning: powerful oxidizer. Keep away from flames."**

"That's very weird," she said, opening the third package. "What's this?" She unwrapped a long object covered in bubble wrap. Something bright silver glinted as it caught the kitchen overhead light. She revealed a large thin blade, around fifteen inches long, with a slightly curved tip and a dark wooden handle that looked like the base of a pistol.

"Oh my God."

"What the fuck is he going to do with a machete?" Lola asked. I held the handle and brought it close to my face to examine. "Nina?"

"I don't know," I replied.

Lola unwrapped another knife, this one with a longer, thicker blade. She placed it on the floor. On the handle was a small carving. "I think this is Japanese. That means he's in a Yakuza gang," she said. "I watched a documentary about it years ago. It's Japanese organized crime—they have slicked-back hair and they cut off their own fingers. You have to report him."

"I can't," I said. "I've stolen his things."

"He can't buy machetes."

"I think he can, I think it's legal to buy them. I think you just can't carry them."

"Where would he have bought them online?"

"I don't know. One of those online black-market places."

"Clearly he's planning to kill someone. Or at least cause some proper harm."

"We don't know that."

"Yes we do—the disconnected, strange behaviour. The poison, the knives, the fact he never leaves the building. He's preparing for it. It's literally the plot of **Taxi Driver.**"

"Put them back in the package," I said, passing her the knives. "I don't want to look at them. I'm going to throw them out."

"You can't, they might be evidence down the line."

"Don't be ridiculous."

But I didn't know if Lola was being ridiculous. I didn't know whether to tell Alma what I had found, or the police. I didn't know what my responsibility was.

I knew that I would now probably feel safer living above this man if I had two knives stashed in my flat. I knew that I was grateful not to go to sleep alone that night. I knew not to shout at him about recycling any more. And I knew now that I wasn't just living above a nightmare neighbour. I was living above a psychopath.

## 15

M ATTERS OF THE SARTRE," Mum announced. "Isn't that good? For our next literary salon."

"So the theme is?" I asked.

"Existentialism!" Gloria replied. "I'm coming dressed as Nietzsche."

"Did you find a moustache big enough?"

"I did in the end," Gloria said, topping up her glass of white wine. "Brian had an enormous one left over from a Freddie Mercury costume."

"When did you dress up as Freddie Mercury?" Mum asked, passing round a platter of devils on horseback.

"New Year's Eve do a few years back," Brian said.

The five of us were sitting in Mum and Dad's garden around a table on plastic chairs to celebrate Dad's seventy-seventh birthday. Mum had reluctantly agreed to let me organize the menu as part of my book research—I'd chosen all of Dad's favourite dishes, particularly the ones he talked about from childhood. But Dad was distracted—he had barely responded to any of us when we tried to speak to him and when he did he seemed agitated.

"Who else is everyone coming as?" Gloria asked.

"Annie is coming as Simone de Beauvoir, Cathy is coming as Dostoyevsky if she can find the beard and Martin is coming as 'existence,' which I thought was quite fun."

I looked at Dad to catch his gaze and laugh, but he was silently staring ahead into nothingness. His mouth was horizontal, his eyes unblinking. His face looked as if the plug that connected him to the world had been yanked out of its socket.

"Now, Mandy," Brian said, helping himself to another prune wrapped in bacon, "how's it all going at the church since you've become social sec?"

"Oh, it's all politics, politics, politics, as is always the way with these things."

"What have you got lined up for the next quarter?" Gloria asked.

"We've got a Widows and Widowers mixer happening next week, which I think will be a laugh. When it gets a bit warmer we've got a whole lot of outdoor things happening—Boules and Bake-off,

Volleyball and Vol-au-vents, that sort of thing. A lot of activities."

"A lot of alliteration," I said.

"Where's my mother?" Dad asked suddenly. "Where is she? We can't start lunch without her."

"I don't think she's coming today, Dad," I said. Mum looked nervously at Brian and Gloria.

"Of course she's coming! I'm her son, it's my birthday."

"I'd like to talk about her, though," I said. "Shall we look at some pictures of Nelly?"

"Why would we look at pictures of her, we'll see her shortly."

Mum remained quiet and took a sip of her wine. Brian stared at the table and Gloria fiddled with her necklace.

"I'm going to give her a call." He stood up from the table and walked into the house. I followed him.

He stood in the kitchen and picked up the landline phone.

"Now," he said, holding the phone away from his eyes to focus on the numbers, then began pressing the buttons. "Oh-seven-one—"

"Dad—"

"Shush," he said, flapping me away irritably. He continued to punch in numbers before holding the phone to his ear with one hand and leaning on the table with the other. "Oh, bloody hell."

"Is it not working?"

"No."

"She must be out, Dad. Or on her way. We can save her some food." He hung up the phone and put it back in its cradle. "Tell me about the last birthday you spent with her." I walked back out to the garden and he followed me slowly.

Mum and I brought lunch to the table—pork chops with green beans and mashed potato. Dad held the platter of pork chops up to his face and gingerly examined it.

"What's this?" he asked.

"It's pork chops," I said. "Like you ate when you were a kid."

"I never used to eat this."

"Yes, you did, Bill," Mum said. "They've always been your favourite."

"It is not my favourite, I can't bear the taste of pork chops. I've never liked them."

"I've always enjoyed them," Brian said, merrily reaching for a piece by the bone. "Like to eat them with mustard."

"Well, bully for you, but I can't stand pork."

"What would you like instead, Dad? It's your birthday, you choose."

"Anything but pork chops."

"Do you have eggs, Mum? I could make him a quick omelette?"

"No, no, I don't want fuss," he said. "I'll just have to eat around it."

We served ourselves and there was little noise other than crockery clatter, sounds of appreciation and some discussion about what a mild spring it had been, as bland as the pork chops, which Dad ate with laborious chews and flared nostrils.

"Where were you born, Bill? Which hospital?" Gloria asked.

"Homerton," Mum answered.

"Was it Homerton?"

"Yes, Grandma Nelly showed me your birth certificate once. Homerton Hospital, May third, 1942. William Percy Dean."

"Percy!" Gloria said. "What a lovely middle name. Mine's boring old Judith. What's yours, Nina? I can't remember."

"George."

"Oh, that's right."

"Because Wham! were number one the day I was born."

"Wham! weren't number one the day you were born," Dad said, putting his cutlery down.

"Yes they were," Mum said.

"The song that was number one when you were born was 'Lady in Red' by Chris de Burgh."

Mum laughed. "Very funny, Bill. Now—how is everyone for drinks?"

"It was!" he said.

"No it wasn't, it was 'The Edge of Heaven' by Wham!, which is why we gave her the middle name George. Now—drinks."

"Oh, for CHRIST'S SAKE," Dad growled and

slammed his fists on the table in uncharacteristic frustration. "Why does nobody sodding LISTEN to me any more?"

"I'm listening, Dad," I said.

He closed his eyes and spoke in a quiet voice to calm himself. "The day you were born, 'Lady in Red' by Chris de Burgh was number one in the singles charts and I remember it very clearly because it was playing in the Nissan Micra when we drove you home from the hospital."

"Oh, I loved that Nissan Micra!" Gloria said through a mouthful of mash. "So dinky. You looked hysterical driving that thing, Bill. Like Noddy in his little car."

"You're getting muddled again," Mum said, loading more green beans on to Dad's plate.

"I am NOT. And I do not want ANY MORE bloody beans so stop FUSSING."

**"Bill,"** Mum pleaded.

"Okay, Dad, I'll look it up, don't worry." I took my phone from my bag. "Here we go, there's a website that lists all the UK number ones since the 1950s."

"Oh, look up ours when you're done!" Gloria unhelpfully chirped.

I scrolled down to the 1980s to find 3rd August 1986.

"Mum, he's right."

"Thank you!" he said triumphantly.

"No, he can't be."

"He is. From the second of August to the twenty-third of August in 1986, the UK number one was 'Lady in Red.'"

**"I've never seen you lookin' so lovely as you did tonight,"** Brian crooned, closing his eyes and swaying in his seat. **"I've never seen you shine so bright, mmm hmmm mmm."** I suddenly realized that for all my life, I had always hated Brian.

"When was 'The Edge of Heaven' number one? The week before you were born?" Mum asked.

"No, miles out. It was number one from the twenty-eighth of June to the twelfth of July."

"That's not miles out, that's the same summer."

"But why have you always told me that it was number one the day I was born?"

"I don't know, I must have remembered it wrong."

"Why didn't you name me after Chris de Burgh?"

"'Lady in Red' is a terrible, terrible song. You would have hated for that to be the song you were named after. I love George Michael, I love Wham! and I love 'The Edge of Heaven.'"

"You should have seen Mandy dance to it on our wedding day," Brian said. "She nearly took my brother-in-law's eye out with her high-kick!"

"Who is Mandy?" Dad asked.

"I am," Mum said.

"She is not Mandy, Dad, she is Nancy."

"This again," she said, looking at Gloria for support.

"You can't change the course of history because it suits your own story," I said.

"Course of history!" she said through a hoot of a laugh. "Listen to yourself, Nina, how over the top."

"Do you know what 'The Edge of Heaven' is about, Mum? Have you ever actually listened to the lyrics?"

"Of course I have."

"I don't think you have because if you had you would realize it's a completely inappropriate song to name your baby daughter after."

"No it isn't! It's a great, upbeat, dancey song." Mum started clearing the plates in an attempt to finish the conversation.

**"Screaming to be set free, I would lock you up."**

"Are those the words?" Gloria said. "I always heard it as I would have **laughed** you up. But now that I think about it, what would that mean?"

**"I would lock you up,"** I repeat.

"What are you getting at?"

"It's about BDSM, Mum. It's totally fucking weird that we listen to it all together as a family every morning of my birthday."

"The driving school?" Gloria asked, her nose twitching.

"No, not the driving school. Sadomasochism."

"Don't speak like that in front of your father."

"I'm enjoying it!" Dad said.

"Bill—be quiet."

"Don't tell him to be quiet, he's the only one talking any sense."

"Gloria, Brian, am I going mad? I just don't understand what the problem is here."

"Gloria, Brian, with all due respect, this has nothing to do with you."

"You're being incredibly rude, Nina."

"You have lied to me for thirty-two years about who I am."

"It's not who you are, it's who you're named after."

"Those are the same things."

"Don't be ridiculous. You've been filling in too many of those dating app profiles."

"I'm not on dating apps any more."

"Fine, MyFace. All of those websites that make you obsess over 'who you are' and how to explain it to everyone. You don't need to explain it to everyone all the time! In our day, 'who you are' was just the thing that happened when you got out of bed and got on with the day."

Gloria gave a sage nod of agreement.

"I'm going for a walk," I said, standing up from my chair. "I'll help you clear up when I'm back."

"Okay, darling!" she said lightly. "Come back in time for cake."

I RETURNED WITHIN HALF AN HOUR—enough time to walk to the corner shop, buy a packet of cigarettes and chewing gum, smoke two fags and chew through half the packet of gum to disguise the smell. When I returned, calmer and determined for Dad to have an enjoyable, relaxing birthday, I found him alone, reading in his armchair.

"You okay?" I said. "Where are the others?"

"They're outside, er—" he said, putting his book down and taking off his reading glasses. "Um." He screwed his eyelids together tightly. "Forgive me, what is your name again?"

"Nina, Dad," I said, nausea grabbing me by the throat.

"And we've met?"

"Ninabean. I'm your daughter."

"Of course you are!" he said. "Of course. How are you?"

"Generally?"

"Yes."

"Fine. Got a lot of work on at the moment, but I'm enjoying it."

"I'm so glad you're enjoying it," he said. "You're so good up there in your room, revising and revising. It will all pay off on results day, promise."

"Not my GCSEs. My job. I have a job now. I worked as an English teacher like you and now I'm a journalist and a writer. I write about food." Dad stared at me with a frown. I didn't know what else to say. The rhythmic ticks from the mantelpiece clock seemed to be so loud they echoed. Dad put his reading glasses on and turned his attention back to the book.

"The others are outside," he finally said.

———

I WENT INTO THE GARDEN, where Mum and Gloria were discussing the merits of reserving used Christmas gift tags to repurpose for the following year's homemade cards.

"Why is Dad in there on his own?"

"He just wanted a bit of time to read, he's finding it harder and harder to concentrate on a whole book these days," Mum said. "We mustn't baby him, Nina, he really hates that."

"You're right, sorry," I said, sitting down at the table. "He's very agitated today. What do you think has caused it?"

"There's going to be days when he's fine and days when he's not fine, just like Gwen said."

"The memory-jogging-through-food thing didn't work, did it?"

"No, but his appetite just seems to be changing, I wouldn't worry about it. It happens with age."

"What's the memory-jogging-through-food thing?" Gloria asked.

"I'm writing about food and memory. My next book is all about how taste aligns with nostalgia."

"Oh, that's a nice idea," Gloria said. "You know, whenever I eat a Tunnock's Tea Cake, I think of the Girl Guides."

"Did you eat them when you were a Girl Guide?"

"No, I was never a Girl Guide," Gloria said. "I just think of them for some reason."

We heard a noise from inside the house—sudden, sharp, high-pitched. We all got up from the table and rushed into the house.

Dad stood over the kitchen sink with blood dripping from his hand. He looked up at us with a confused expression that made him look disturbingly childlike.

"What happened?" Mum said, running over to him.

"I was trying to open a tin of beans," he said, wincing as Mum touched his hand. I glanced at the kitchen counter—there was the tin with a small slit pierced through, a chopping knife next to it and large splashes of blood leading to the sink.

"Why were you trying to open it with a knife?!"

"I have always opened tins with a blade," he said.

"You use a tin opener, Dad, it's right here."

"I don't know what to do," Mum said. "I can't see how deep it is."

"Let me have a look at it." Gloria leant down to examine him. "I'm First Aid–trained," she boasted.

"Should we go to a hospital?" I asked.

"No, I don't think so."

"It really hurts!" Dad yelped earnestly, like a little boy persuading his mummy that he's worthy of a cuddle. He was suddenly seven years old. Cowering into himself. Clinging on to Mum. My dad, so curious and confident, my father the headmaster— I had never seen him this tiny.

"I think it just needs to be cleaned up and some

dissolvable stitches," Gloria said. "I'll pop home to get them and come back. Until then, just apply pressure with a tea towel."

Dad said nothing for the rest of the afternoon. He said nothing when we tried to distract him with tea and talk while Gloria got her first aid kit. He grimaced silently when Gloria applied the dressing to his cut. He said nothing when we sang "Happy Birthday" to him. He didn't eat the banana cake with condensed milk icing. When I said goodbye, he remained still and stiff as I wrapped my arms around him in a hug.

I wished there was a way I could access the filing cabinet of his mind and keep track of which memories were being lost and when. I knew there was no way of retaining them on his behalf, but I longed to understand what version of the world he was seeing at any given moment. If he thought I was a fifteen-year-old preparing for summer exams, what else in the seventeen years of our relationship since had been wiped? So much of the love you feel for a person is dependent on the vast archive of shared memories you can access just by seeing their face or hearing their voice. When I saw Dad, I didn't just see a seventy-seven-year-old man with black-and-grey hair, I saw him in a swimming pool in Spain teaching me how to front crawl and I saw him waving at me in a crowd on graduation day. I saw him dropping me off for my first morning of primary school and leading a conga line around the living room at a Christmas Eve drinks party in our flat in Albyn Square. But what would happen now that only I could access that shared archive of our history? What would he feel for me and what would I be to him as these memory files dwindled from his side? Would I become just a thirty-two-year-old woman with brown hair and a vaguely familiar face, standing in his house, offering him food he didn't want?

I walked to Pinner station. The next train wasn't for fifteen minutes, as was characteristic of London zone five tube stations. I sat on the platform bench, took my phone from my bag and redownloaded Linx, desperate for a distraction. I flipped through 2-D humans like pages of a catalogue, reading meaningless declarations of identity: "love socialism, hate coriander"; "SARCASM IS MY RELIGION"; "always big spoon ;)"; "Mancunian Aquarius"; "my weakness is an inteligent women"; "is it weird that I always brush my teeth in the shower?!"; "next on my bucket list: the Grand Canyon"; "dogs are better than humans!!"; "I have a thing for girls with their hair tied back"; "interesting fact about me: I have never been on a tram"; "COYS!!!!!!"; "love me some pubbage on a Sunday"; "would rather die than eat a mushroom"; "I have lived in ten countries and thirteen cities"; "when people ask if I'm a legs or a boobs man—I'm a pussy man!!!!"; "working in the emergency services but also writing a sitcom"; "Carpay Deium is my mantra x"; "DETOX TO RETOX";

"Korean cinema, rainy days, strong tea"; "msg me if u got a fat ass and tiny titties with puffy nips"; "pineapple does NOT belong on a pizza!"; "poly, pansexual sex+"; "NO REMAIN VOTERS, PLS."

All these hobbies and preferences and politics and history—were those the essential ingredients of a human? Were those the pillars of ego and id? If these declarations were the construction of a self, then Dad was in the long, slow process of dismantling and destroying his. He couldn't remember where he was born or his favourite meal, his daughter's name or the students he'd taught. What would be left of him as the knowledge, predilections and memories accumulated over a lifetime—so precise and vivid—were removed? I thought about what Mum had said—that who you are is just what you wake up and do every day. I hoped that she was right.

I TOOK THE TRAIN from the suburbs into central London where I was meeting Katherine for dinner. It was the first time I had seen her since I'd gone to her house to meet the baby. She had since been mostly unresponsive to my texts and ignored all my calls. Once every ten days I would get a message that was frantic in tone with no punctuation and many typos which, cynically, I suspected to be strategic to further make a point of how rushed and stressed she was. She claimed that messaging had become "impossible" because she never had any hands free now she had both a toddler and a new-born. Her Instagram content, however, continued to thrive daily.

She was sitting at the table when I arrived, scrolling on her phone, her face tight and twitchy. She looked up and gave me a thin half-smile.

"Hi, I'm sorry I'm late," I said, leaning down to kiss her cheek.

"You're half an hour late."

"I know, I'm sorry. I did send you a text to let you know. I've come from Mum and Dad's and you know what the trains are like."

"I've come from Surrey."

"All right, mate, I'm sorry, as I said. You know me, I'm never late normally."

"I'm never ever late for you either."

"That's because you can't be late because we usually meet up at your house, so you never have to go anywhere." Her head jolted as if caught by a cold gust of wind—she was unused to this sort of candour from me. "Which is understandable, of course, because you have young kids but just . . . can you give me this one, please? It won't happen again. I've had a really horrible day."

"What's happened?"

"I'll bore you with it later, I need a glass of wine first. Shall we get a bottle?"

"I'm not drinking."

"Okay."

"You go ahead."

"I will." I caught the waiter's attention and ordered a large glass of Chenin Blanc. "Sure you don't want one?"

"Yes, Nina, I'm sure."

"I was just checking."

"You're not really meant to while you're still breast-feeding. And I've just really enjoyed my body feeling clean and pure during pregnancy, so I thought I'd carry on."

"Is Mark drinking?"

"Of course he is," she said.

There was a slightly too long pause. I wracked my brain for a question to ask, but thankfully she got there first.

"How was the launch?"

"It was nice," I said. "You were missed."

"Yes, I'm sorry I couldn't be there, I just couldn't get out of Anna's birthday."

"Who's Anna?"

"You've met Anna—Mark's school friend Ned's wife. They're local to us."

"I thought you said you couldn't leave the house while Freddie was that young?"

"I could for a few hours, Mark's mum babysat him. I just couldn't come into town."

The waiter placed the glass of wine in front of me.

"What are you doing on July the sixth?" she asked.

"Don't know," I said, taking a large sip and letting the cold, honeysuckle liquid anaesthetize me back into trusty, taciturn passive-aggression.

"Okay, can you check when you're in front of the diary because we'd like that to be the date of the naming ceremony for Freddie and Olive."

"Will there be a sorting hat?"

"What do you mean?"

"Nothing, it was a joke. Sounds like something from **Harry Potter.**"

Her face was expressionless. "It's just a secular christening."

"Okay."

"Can you let me know tonight as soon as you're home? Because I want to be able to confirm all the godparents can come before I book the venue."

"I will do."

"So what's up with you, anyway?" she said, opening her menu. "Why have you had a horrible day?"

"It was Dad's birthday lunch and he was in a bad way. Didn't recognize me at one point. Kept asking for his mother, who's been dead for twenty years. Then he tried to open a tin with a chopping knife and cut his hand, there was blood everywhere. Thankfully, he didn't have to go to hospital."

"Oh dear, everything's very dramatic with you at the moment, isn't it?"

"What do you mean?"

"Every time I meet you it seems there's another big drama." She looked up from her menu.

"Katherine." I took a deep breath. I couldn't believe I was finally going to say it—the speech I'd been angrily rehearsing for months, that I never thought would be spoken anywhere other than when I was alone in the shower. "I may not have a baby. But I do have a life."

"Of course I know you have a life."

"No you don't."

"Yes I do."

"You don't. You don't ask me about it, you don't take it seriously, you don't come to my home, you don't take any interest in my work, you couldn't even come to my book launch when I had no family there. You're my best and oldest friend and not only did you not want to be there, you didn't even feel a sense of obligation to pretend to want to be there."

"I've told you, it's because I couldn't come all the way into town for the evening."

"So you thought you'd go to a party where you could talk about babies and weddings and houses all night. Because not everyone wants to talk about babies and weddings and houses at a book launch."

"That's not true."

"It is true. You couldn't just be my friend for one night, celebrating my work. I have to celebrate when you get your kitchen retiled, but anything I do is trivial and meaningless because I'm not in a relationship and I don't have children. I don't know what's happened to make you so relentlessly dismissive of anyone whose life isn't exactly like yours, but you need to sort that shit out." I slammed my glass slightly too dramatically on the table and wine spilt.

"I don't need you to celebrate everything in my life!"

The waiter came to our table with a grin as wide as a canal. "Would you like to hear the specials for this evening?"

"Can you give us a few minutes?" Katherine said. He reluctantly nodded and walked away.

"And actually—yeah, things are dramatic at the moment. And I'm sorry if that's not what you fancy right now. I'm sorry that I have a terminally ill father and a mother who is clearly not coping. And that I had my heart broken by a man I'll never see or speak to again. I'm sorry if that's not quite cashmere-socks-and-pastel-coloured-ceramic-tableware enough for you. But you can't phase me out of your life because I'm a bit too messy for whatever aesthetic mood board you're currently living in. That's not how friendship works."

"I don't think you're messy, I think there's just a lot going on."

"Yes, there is. And you just can't be bothered to support me through it?"

"You don't get it, Nina!" she said, raising her voice and eyebrows at unnerving speed. "I don't have the headspace for it! I can't be that for you any more, that's what Lola is good for. You'll understand when you have kids."

I looked at her, completely unable to access my Katherine memory archive—unable to recall how and why we'd been friends for twenty years. I signalled to the waiter for the bill.

"I don't want to have dinner with you. And you certainly don't want to have dinner with me. I don't know why we put ourselves through this any more."

"I've come all the way from Surrey."

"YES, I KNOW," I barked. "No one asked you to fucking live there, Katherine. You're not seventy. You're not a conservatory salesman. You're not a retired **Question Time** presenter-turned-gardening columnist."

"Lots of people have to move out of London, you don't need to act like it's some enormous betrayal."

"Are you only going to want to be friends with me when I get married and have a kid and own a big house? Is that when you'll decide you love me again? When I do all the things you've done so you can feel like you were right all along?"

Katherine took her jacket off the back of her chair and picked up her handbag. Her face had reddened and she was chewing her top lip with fervour. "I'm going. Don't call me or message me," she said, shrugging on her jacket and pulling her hair out from under its collar. "I don't want to talk to you."

"You haven't wanted to talk to me in years," I said as she stood up from the table and left.

———

I PAID FOR MY WINE and left the restaurant. It was early evening on a Saturday night and I didn't want to go back to the flat and sit alone with my rage and the rage of my terrifying neighbour lurking beneath me. I walked, eastwards, not knowing where I would end up. I walked through the inexplicably busy cypher of Holborn and its countless sandwich shops. I walked past St. Paul's Cathedral with its silvery dome hat like a steel combat helmet, then the Bank of England with its grand Grecian pillars. I walked past the crowds of twenty-something girls in chokers and too much eyeliner smoking outside the basement bars of Aldgate, then the elderly smokers outside the pubs of Stepney Green who wondered why twenty-something girls in chokers were spending so much money to be there. Finally, just under two hours later, I saw the cream-tiled front of Mile End tube station. I made my way by memory to Albyn Square and climbed over the railings into the communal garden, like I had done the last time I saw Max. I sat on the bench cross-legged, my plimsolls tucked underneath my thighs. I could see the door to our basement flat, and the road where Dad's blue Nissan Micra used to be parked.

"Love is homesickness," I once read in a book. The author's therapist had told her that the pursuit of love in adulthood is just an expression of missing our mums and dads—that we look for intimacy and romance because we never stop wanting parental security and attention. We simply displace it. My dad was nearly eighty and he was still missing his mother. He'd found a way of concealing it for all of his adult life and now, as the facade of togetherness was being slowly taken apart without his knowledge: the truth. All he wanted was his mum. I would make a strong case for the argument that every adult on this earth is sitting on a bench waiting for their parents to pick them up, whether they know it or not. I think we wait until the day we die.

I remained in the square a little longer, waiting for someone to get me. Waiting for my mum to call me into the flat for tea. Waiting for a Nissan Micra that no longer existed, that would never come to pick me up again. I wondered who lived in our basement flat now. I wondered where the Nissan Micra was—the safety of my childhood. Now scrap metal somewhere.

I looked into the windows on Albyn Square, some of them lit up with scenes of a household—human Punch and Judy shows. A woman worked at a desk, a man poured a kettle in his kitchen. It was just before midnight. It was cold. I was an adult woman with a mortgage, a career and a life full of responsibilities. I was a little girl with a dying dad. And I didn't know where I wanted to go.

"I miss home."

I miss home.

I miss home.

———

I TOOK THE LAST TUBE back to Archway. The streets were scattered with groups of human-ravens, drunkenly flapping at each other—squawking as they pecked at polystyrene boxes of grey kebab ribbons and chips cemented together with mayonnaise. I made my way to my street lined with a few recently planted spindly trees surrounded by their circular black railings and budding with baby leaves. There was one directly in view from my kitchen window. Every morning as I drank my coffee I imagined how big it would be by the end of my lifetime.

I approached my building and saw that someone was sitting outside the house on the ground, back slightly hunched, long legs splayed outward. I couldn't make out the face but I could see they were tall and male and wearing boots. I instinctively knew it was Angelo, and I readied myself for an unpleasant conversation.

But when I got to the front door, I saw someone else. I stood still and took in the sight of him, barely able to believe he was real. There he was.

Max. Smoking a rollie. Sitting on my doorstep.

## 16

ELLO," HE SAID. I had thought about this exact moment for five months. So many times, the bell had rung and I'd gone to the front door, or I would turn the corner on to my street, and imagine he would be there. In my fantasies, "Hello" is exactly what he'd say first. It had the classic cadence of romcom dialogue—uncomplicated and yet loaded with subtext. One word that stated cool, stylized offhandedness, assuming that all would be forgiven and forgotten. A greeting that marked a new and simple beginning. I couldn't remember what my answer had been in my many imagined versions of this exchange. If I had been in a romcom, I would have rushed towards him, thrown my arms around his shoulders, kissed him and said nothing but a one-line statement of relieved gratitude like: "I knew you'd come back." I wouldn't bother him with my questions, I wouldn't demand an explanation, I wouldn't burden him with the facts of his betrayal, I wouldn't scare him off with my anger.

"Where the fuck have you been?"

"I know," he said, discarding his rollie and standing up. "I want to explain everything." He walked towards me.

"No, no," I said, holding my arms out to keep him from coming too close. "I want you to tell me where you've been." He stood still. He looked scared of provoking me. "Where have you been, Max? Where the fuck have you been?"

"I've been here."

"I thought you'd died."

"I know, I can't imagine how stressful it must have been for you."

"What have you been doing here?"

He looked confused, like a schoolboy who'd been hauled into the headmistress's office and would say anything to stay out of trouble. "I've been waiting for you."

"No, HERE, in this city we both live in, for all this time. What have you been doing that meant you couldn't call me and let me know you're alive?"

"I have wanted to, so much. Just because I

haven't called you doesn't mean I haven't wanted to every day."

"Why haven't you?"

"I was scared, Nina. I just got so, so scared and so confused."

**"Scared?"** I said mockingly. "And **confused**?"

"Yes."

"How do you think I felt? A man who I've shared my life with almost constantly for months—who I trusted, who I was vulnerable with—tells me he loves me then never sees me again. How do you think that made me feel?"

Max shrugged remorsefully. I had never known him this quiet.

"I can't imagine."

"A little bit fucking scared?" I said. "Really, really fucking confused?"

He nodded and took another step towards me.

"Can I hold you?" he asked. "I really want to."

"No," I said. "I don't care about what you want."

"Can I come inside? Can we talk?" he asked. I knew I would let him in and I knew that we would talk, rigorously and deeply, into the night. But I saw the words of every sassy self-help book sloganism I'd heard second-hand my whole life: **play hard to get, make him wait, show him what he's missing.** I pretended to be in conflict about my decision and continued the silent stand-off for a minute. Then I walked to the front door, turned the key and entered, feeling him close behind me.

When we got into my flat, I was surprised at how dangerous it felt to have him in my home again. This was a man who was directly responsible for so much of my pain. And I had invited him in, to stand in my living room, both of us either end of the dining table leaning awkwardly on a chair.

"I hate that I put you through this," he finally said.

"I don't think you know what this has really felt like."

"I do know."

"You don't. Because if you did you would never have done something so cruel. I don't think you have really properly thought what it was like or how you would have felt if I'd done this to you."

"I think about it all the time. I would have been absolutely devastated, obviously."

"You made me beg for you to speak to me, to even acknowledge I existed. You made me feel desperate and deluded. You made me feel like you didn't exist, like I'd made it all up." He held his head in his hands. "And I couldn't say anything because whenever I questioned your coldness, you made me feel like I was crazy. You tried to convince me that it was abnormal that I wanted to speak to a man who'd just told me he was in love with me. I can't believe you made me think I was crazy, what the fuck was the matter with me."

"It moved so quickly and it felt so intense so fast," he said. "When in reality we didn't really know each other that well. It derailed me, just for a bit."

"You were the one who made it intense. You were the one telling me you wanted to marry me. Or that you couldn't stop thinking about me. You rang me twice a day. You insisted we spent every other night together. I just wanted to hang out and get to know each other. You decided the entire pace of this relationship then you slammed on the brakes when it suited you. It was like I was just a lucky passenger along for the ride."

"I fell in love with you very quickly, I couldn't help it. I wanted to spend all my time with you, so I did. I should have taken it slower."

"You weren't in love with me."

"I was completely in love with you."

"Being in love isn't a notion. It's not a theory. It's a connection you have to someone. If you were in love with me, you wouldn't have been able to be apart from me. Fucking hell, didn't you **miss** me? What's wrong with you, Max? We saw each other so much, we spoke every day and then there was nothing. Why didn't you miss me?" I was aware how hysterical I sounded now, but I didn't care.

"It was too painful to miss you, I found a way to distract myself."

"With what? Other women?"

His gaze broke away from my mine. "You know what I'm like, I'm scarily good at compartmentalizing things. I can put the blinkers on and hide from all the really difficult things I need to address."

"By which you mean: **I can think only about myself. That comes very easily to me.**"

"No, it's not that. It's why I've always been in a career I hate, it's why I never talk about my family. I can live in denial very comfortably."

I wasn't going to let this become a sympathetic psychoanalytical study of who he was. "What do you want?"

"I love you and I'm unhappy without you. I've been doing everything I can for months to avoid the fact that I know we're meant to be together."

"I don't believe you," I said, sitting down on the chair. "At all. I don't think you actually care about me. I think you care that an experience that might be good for you has ended."

"I know it would take a lot for you to trust me again, but I really, really would do anything for you to consider it. I don't mind how slowly we go, or how long it takes." I stared at the table. "Have you been happy without me?"

"Of course I haven't. It's been terrible."

He tensed his features in pain. "I hate that."

"I've known I'll be fine. It's easier, being heart-broken in your thirties, because no matter how painful it is, you know it will pass. I don't believe one other human has the power to ruin my life any more."

He came over and sat on the seat next to mine. "How unromantic," he said.

"It was so needlessly dramatic, Max. I don't understand why you had to end it in such an extreme way. You could have just told me you were having doubts, or even just broken up with me."

"I couldn't face it. I was too cowardly to look at what was really going on, so I just deleted you."

The brutality of this admission shocked me, despite having known for some time this was the reason for his disappearance. "You can't 'delete' a human you love. I'm not a picture on your phone," I said, sitting back in my chair and rubbing my eyes with the heels of my palms. I was so tired. "Or maybe that's exactly what I am to you, maybe that's what happens when you meet someone on a dating app."

"It was nothing to do with you. I know you're smart enough to not need me to tell you that."

I hated how my body reacted to these glowing paternalistic assessments of my intellect that Max occasionally dispensed. "What was it to do with then? I really need to understand."

He leant on the table and rested his head on his hand. "I was so unhappy when I met you, I realize now. I was a mess. I absolutely hate my job, but I don't know what else I want to do. I hate living in London, but I don't know where I want to go. I have next to no relationship with my family. All my friends have their own proper adult lives that keep them occupied. I don't have any sort of settled life. Then I fell in love with this woman who was so together and focused. Who is successful, who's happy, who has all these meaningful relationships. Even with her ex-boyfriend. And I knew that if I was going to properly commit to you, I'd have to become the man I've been putting off becoming. And I wasn't ready to. I wasn't ready to grow up."

"I didn't ask you to change."

"I know."

"And I am not 'so together.' Everything's coming apart. My dad has got really bad—he keeps having accidents and forgetting who I am. Mum and I argue all the time. We've had to get a nurse to help us. I don't know when or how we need to get more help. I can't seem to write about anything other than about him. Katherine and I had an enormous row. I'm scared of being in my own home because I'm pretty certain my neighbour is really dangerous. And I'm alone." My voice wavered. Max reached his hand out towards mine on the table and held it. "I am really fucking alone."

He knelt on the floor in front of me, held my chin in his hands and tentatively kissed me. He smelt of tobacco—like wood and raisins. He stroked my cheek with his thumb and clutched the back of my head with his palm. I slid off my chair and sank to the floor, so we were both on our knees. We undressed each other and he lay on top of me, pressing his heavy warmth against my body and opening me up, firmly and slowly. And then it was urgent—as if we were now both worried the other would disappear. Only one part of me remained in my skin while other Ninas detached and circulated the room. There was one who was a spectator of the clawing and clinging; who couldn't believe Max was inside my home and inside me—that I could not only look up to see his face but feel his body temperature permeate mine. One Nina rejoiced, another one was scared. Another Nina examined him—every move and every sound—to find evidence of where he'd been since I'd last seen him. **I've missed you,** he said to me as we fought for breath. **I've missed you so fucking much.**

We lay naked on our backs, side by side on the living-room rug with only our fingertips touching. I stared at the long thin line that stretched across the plaster of my ceiling like a crack in dry soil.

"I want tea," I said. I went to stand up, but he tugged my hand.

"Stay here with me a bit longer." He turned me on my side and wrapped his arms around my body. I felt the sweat on his skin against my back. "I'll make us one in a minute."

"How many women have you been with since me?"

He buried his face in my hair and breathed deeply. "Do you really want to know?"

"Yes."

"Why?"

"Because if we are going to be together again, I need to know the whole truth of when we were apart."

"And you're not going to torture yourself with it?"

"No, of course not, this isn't a jealousy issue. I've assumed you've been with other women."

"Okay," he said. "One."

"One? I don't believe you."

"Just one."

"You've had one night with another woman since me?"

"Not one night."

"How many nights?"

"I don't know, I didn't count."

I turned to face him. "Were you in a relationship with her?"

"No—I mean"—he looked to the ceiling to avoid my eyes—"we were seeing each other, but we weren't together."

"When did you start seeing each other?"

"I don't know exactly."

"Max."

"Maybe a month after we finished?"

**We finished** was such a dishonest retelling of how we'd ended, implying consent and communication, but now was not the time to debate wording.

"How did you meet her?"

"Linx."

"Did you delete me as a match? Because when I redownloaded it, you weren't there."

"I don't know. Maybe. I think I probably didn't want to see when you'd last been online because I didn't want to think of you dating again."

"Who was this woman?"

"Her name was Amy."

"What does she do?"

"She's temping at the moment."

"How old is she?"

He paused.

"Twenty-three."

I did a silent calculation in my head, ready to weaponize against him when the time called for it. Fourteen years.

"And she finished with you, so you decided to come back to trusty old me? The service station you can pull into for a break."

"Nina," he said, kissing my forehead. "No. You couldn't be more wrong."

"I don't understand why you started seeing someone immediately after me if what you were scared of was commitment. Your reason for vanishing would make sense if you then went on some sex spree."

"I just needed to distract myself so I didn't think about you. And I can't do sex sprees, so I accidentally fell into something regular with someone."

"How did it end?"

"I finished with her."

"By which you mean you 'deleted' her?"

"No," he said, somewhat irritably. "We ended amicably. I told her I was in a very confused place and she understood."

"All these women who end up as the collateral

damage of your confusion, Max. What are you so confused about?"

"I'm not confused any more," he said, gripping me tighter.

WE GOT INTO BED just as the sky was turning the lilac-blue of predawn.

"Tell me again why you stopped talking to me," I said as we faced each other, our heads on the pillows. We spoke softly, as if trying not to wake anyone else up. "And don't speak abstractly or philosophically. Tell me, clearly, why."

"I knew that I wanted to commit to you, but I was scared to. Committing to you meant looking at the kind of life I really want. And I wasn't ready to. I was a coward."

"And how do I know the same thing won't happen again?"

"Because I know I don't want to be without you now."

"You have to promise me you'll never, ever disappear again."

"I promise," he said, using his knuckles to gently stroke my cheek. "I fucked up once and I've learnt my lesson. I don't care how long it takes to re-earn your trust."

I closed my eyes, failing to will myself to sleep. "I tried to speak to you, sometimes. At night, when

I got into bed. That's really properly desperate behaviour. That's someone who's lost it. I'd concentrate really hard and try to send you messages. But
I don't suppose you ever heard from me."

"I'm here now," he said. "Nina, I'm here now."

Our breathing slowed in tandem. I heard the
tinkling morning call of the blackbirds outside
my window.

"Have you really missed me? Or have you missed
how I made you feel?" My body felt cold and my
head felt light, the prelude to unconsciousness.
I heard the lethargic murmur of his voice.

"They're the same things."

MAX STAYED EVERY NIGHT FOR A WEEK. We
talked—about what we had been together and
what we had been apart. The talking was not
charged with emotion but logic—the conversations
felt like a safety measure. Two dignitaries meeting after global disaster, analysing the chaos and
its after-effects, discussing preventative measures.
Our conversations were tinged with a new-found
sincerity, which I found exhausting but essential if
I were to ever trust him again. We made a promise to be as honest with each other as possible—no
matter how uncomfortable it might feel. I warned
him that his actions had left me uncharacteristically
anxious—that I associated him with pain and pre-
cariousness, that it would take time for me to relax

back into our relationship. I told him I wanted reassurance without asking for it, as much time as was necessary and allowance for anger and interrogation when I needed it. He said he understood, that he would feel the same and that I was entitled to whatever I wanted. As long as I'd try to trust him again.

He told me more about Amy. He told me how surface-level and tenuous their connection had been and I hated myself for how comforting I found the comparison between us, like we were contestants on a dating show of women competing to win one worthy bachelor. I hated myself even more when we laughed about the grimy graduate house-share she lived in and her love of bottomless Buck's Fizz brunches and the fact she had never heard of John Major. I informed him that the embarrassment was not that she hadn't heard of a man who became a member of parliament in the late seventies, but the fact he was romantically involved with a girl who was born the same year as the Spice Girls' first number one.

I told him about Angelo's knife collection, Joe's wedding, Lola's first love, my and Katherine's fallout. He read the new chapters of my book. I updated him on Dad's waning health, but briefly and sparing any detail but the necessities. I still couldn't talk about Dad in any real depth, or in the context of emotion rather than practicality, to anyone. Gwen was the closest thing to a confidante, and even then, when she asked in our many phone conversations how I was, all I could manage was: "a bit sad." I wanted to open up to Max about it—I craved his comfort and advice—but I found the visits home to be increasingly distressing and I wanted to keep them separate to the rest of my life. The only way I had managed to not think all day every day about my dad and his brain—his beautiful, big brain being unassembled and laid in front of him like flat-pack furniture—was the fact that no one knew the details of it. So, no one thought to ask me about it.

In the weeks that followed the night I'd found Max on my doorstep, we talked about things we'd never spoken of before. There was a gentle attentiveness to us—we were less eager to make each other laugh, his bravado quietened, his swagger softened. I was more myself than I ever had been—uninterested in the pursuit of retaining his attention. He told me he loved me, prudently and sporadically, keen to prove he was being thoughtful; that he wouldn't frighten himself with his own extremity again. I kept a running tally of when he said it. Once, whispered in my ear on the tube during morning rush hour as we were surrounded by crotches and armpits and drowned in garish light. Another time during a particularly bad hangover when we were eating chicken nuggets in bed. Another time as we queued for drinks in the pub, when I asked him if he wanted pork scratchings. I often said it back, but never said it first. I pressed the home button on his phone when he was out of the room to see Linx notifications or messages from girls—signs of a secret life that I still suspected he harboured. There was never anything there but the background photo of his car.

I was unused to his presence, which continued to feel like intrusion as well as security. I woke up every morning and checked my phone hoping for a message from him, as I had done for months, and in a half-asleep state would feel disappointment. Then I'd turn to see him lying asleep next to me— a pile of sinewy limbs and golden curly hair. I had the flesh and blood version of Max, but I still felt like I was being haunted by the virtual one.

Lola, who I barely saw since she had emigrated to the land of love and secured a permanent visa, was happy for me. She was monogamy's greatest advocate now, an ambassador for relationships. If she could have done, she would have quit her job and become a missionary for it, knocking door-to-door and handing out literature on how you too can be saved with the right romantic partner. She persistently asked when we could all do a double date, and every time I managed to put her off with a vague excuse. What Max and I had rekindled felt fragile and I wanted to momentarily protect it from outsiders. I could tell Joe thought getting back together with him was a terrible idea, but diplomatically said I should trust my instincts while remaining cautious. Mum was delighted and desperate to meet him—she had a new recipe for carrot spaghetti that she wanted to try out on the both of us. I couldn't tell Katherine, because Katherine and I still weren't speaking.

Eventually, the darkness that preceded our re-union began to disappear and what remained was what I had loved about him, about us, before. We talked—openly and intensely—we laughed, we listened, we got drunk, we were spontaneous and filthy and domestic and peaceful. I remembered the surplus focus and energy that being with Max gave me—I lived every day wanting to do things, see things, learn things and achieve things that I could go back and share with him. And I did, most nights. At his flat or at mine—I gave him a key.

A MONTH AFTER we started seeing each other again, we went away together for the first time. It was set to be a hot June weekend so we hired an almost sickeningly chocolate-box cottage that had ponies roaming around it and a stream running through the back of its garden for three nights. And seeing each other outside our city felt like it would confirm us as a couple, taking us out of the interim state of "seeing each other" again.

We drove down in his car and arrived Friday afternoon. Sleeping in a new place that wasn't his or mine, but ours—even just for three nights—felt like we were playing house. As we unpacked our bags and put groceries in the fridge, we seemed like two children pretending to be adults. It reminded me of the first night Katherine and I spent in our first flat-share as graduates. "Grown-ups now," she said through a smile as we ate beans on toast while sitting on the stained carpet in a living room with no furniture.

In the late afternoon on Saturday, he went for a run. When he returned, pink-faced and damp-haired, I was making pastry for dinner. He stood, leaning in the kitchen door frame, catching his breath.

"Fuck."

"What?"

"This is all I want."

"What is?"

"Walking into a room to find you doing something with flour and butter."

I laughed. "Really?"

"Yeah." He made a lustful groan. "That's exactly what I want. But I also want you to have some flour on your face, just like a streak on your cheek, that would make it perfect."

"Women only bake with a perfectly placed streak of flour on their face in films. All domestic fantasies are a lie in films—we don't drape a sheet around ourselves in the morning. And we don't wear our boyfriend's shirt and nothing else when we're doing DIY."

"Just put a bit of flour on your face, c'mon," he pleaded. I reluctantly smeared some on my cheek.

"Perfect. And I want you in a really big kitchen, maybe a barn kitchen."

"Okay, into that."

He walked towards me and wrapped his arms around me from behind. He spoke into my hair. "And you'd be totally naked other than an apron." He kissed my neck. "And I'd obviously have to pinch your arse." I turned around to face him. "And you'd say, 'Not in front of the kids.'"

My heart double-pirouetted. I had been betrayed by my biology, which was a bandersnatch, a sneaky, fast-moving nuisance that was indifferent to logic. It would be a terrible idea to have a baby with Max any time in the near future—it was inappropriate to even talk about it. And yet, my body reacted to the thought of it as if it were the only solution. His joking words awoke an insatiable craving—deeply embedded desires that were placed inside me without my approval. Who had put them there? Had I inherited it? Was it my mother? Or my grandmother? I hadn't made this choice. I got to choose the number of espresso shots in my coffee, the colour of my light switches and the accent and gender of my satnav's voice. I was tirelessly in charge of every single tiny decision I made, every single day. So who had decided I wanted a baby, more than anything, on my behalf?

"Why would I be cooking naked if I was in front of children?"

"Shh," he said.

"You're conflating two fantasy narratives that should be kept completely separate."

"Fine."

How easy it was for him to play this game. How enjoyable it must be, to throw these hypothetical scenarios into conversation, knowing the primal panic it might ignite in a woman over thirty. How powerful he must have felt. This was not the first time we had done this sort of wholesome role play and every time he pushed it a little further, to see how deep into the fantasy we dared to go. It was the dirty talk of this decade—when once couples whispered in each other's ears about going out and picking up a girl who we'd take home and have a threesome with, now we talked about baby names and whether we'd have sons or daughters. Who cared if we'd ever see it through? That wasn't the point of the game. It was exciting enough just to hear the words being spoken aloud.

"And, Max," I said with a reprimanding tone, "watch yourself. Remember, I'm not saying any of this, it's you. We don't want you getting all confused and scared again." We had finally got to a point where we could laugh about what had happened, as it no longer threatened to repeat itself.

"I know, I know," he said, giving me a playful spank and leaving the kitchen. We didn't talk about it again.

———

WE SPENT THE FOLLOWING AFTERNOON in a local pub. When he came back from the bar with our third round, he had a packet of salt-and-vinegar crisps in his teeth and the newspaper and supplements in his hand. He dropped them both on the table.

"You're in today's, aren't you?" he said.

"Yes," I said. "Column about rhubarb. And an interview with a chef."

Max opened up the magazine and flipped to find my pages. He pointed at my severe by-line photo. "Look!" he said.

"Yep."

"I can't believe it."

"Really? It's not that big a deal. You've read my work before."

"Yeah, but it feels so much more real and im-mediate sitting with you now, knowing that these words are reaching thousands of people today as they drink their pints or ate their breakfast."

"I suppose—"

"Shh," he said, putting his hand over my mouth while keeping his eyes on the page. "I'm reading."

I'd never watched Max read my words before. He nodded occasionally, he sometimes laughed. I knew he would have had thoughts that weren't all positive—he was always observing and analysing. But I could tell that we were experiencing a rela-tionship milestone—when you see the person you love through the eyes of strangers for the first time.

As he read me, he could imagine other people reading me, and remember what it was like to see me and speak to me that first night we met.

He put down the magazine.

"I don't think you know how envious I am of you, Nina," he said, knocking back the last of his beer. "This pays your mortgage. Your interests pay your mortgage. It's amazing."

"Well," I said, "interviewing a hero is a particular highlight and doesn't happen that often. It's not all like that. Last week, thousands of people wanted me dead on Twitter because I miscalculated the ingredients for a recipe and said it needed ten kilos of Cheddar, rather than a hundred grams."

He laughed into his pint.

"And a huge portion of my days are spent on the phone to accounts departments, asking to be paid for work I completed months ago. And I had an argument with a really difficult food stylist on a shoot last week."

"But you love your job."

"I'm very lucky. For the most part, I love my job."

"You're not just lucky, I know you've worked hard for it."

"Lots of people work very hard and they still hate their job."

"Like me," he said, spinning his circular beer mat on the table.

"Do you really hate it that much?"

"Hate it."

"There has to be something else you can do that uses your skills and makes you all right money that you don't dread every morning." He nodded. "We're all going to live for much longer than ever before, so we're going to be working for the majority of our lives. We can't hate the majority of our lives."

"I know," he sighed. "Trust me, I think about it a lot."

"I have an idea!" I said with drunken enthusiasm. "Let's make a list of all the things you like doing. Have you got a pen?" A waiter walked past. "Excuse me, could I borrow your pen, please?" He pulled a biro from his pocket and handed it to me. "Thank you."

"Nina—" Max protested.

I took a notepad out from my handbag.

"Right, let's make a list of everything that you love and everything that you hate. Can be big or small, professional or completely random. Even if it doesn't feel relevant, we should still write it down at this stage. So. What makes you happiest?"

"I don't know."

"I do. Being outside. Nothing makes you happier."

"Can we not do this?"

"Come on, it's only between us."

"Can you please stop acting like a school careers adviser?" he said. "Sorry. I know you're trying to be helpful. But it makes me feel like a child."

"Okay," I said. "Don't worry," I said. I finished my wine and we left.

———

MAX WAS MOSTLY SILENT on the walk back to the cottage, it was only me who spoke with enforced, drunken jolliness, desperate to keep the light mood of the afternoon afloat. I had never seen him so absorbed in his own thoughts and unresponsive to me. Eventually I stopped trying to make conversation.

"Why did you do that stuff with the condensed milk company?" he asked.

"You know why," I said. "I've told you about it before. Those jobs pay the bills."

"You shouldn't do them any more. It's really clear that your writing is best when you actually believe what you're saying."

"I always actually believe what I'm saying, otherwise I wouldn't say it. I'm not that much of a sell-out."

"Like me?"

"Max," I said, stopping on the empty, winding lane lined with foxgloves. He stopped walking as well. "Do you want to talk about this or not? I'm happy to talk about your job, but please don't say you don't want to talk about it then make passive-aggressive digs at me."

"I'm not being passive-aggressive. I'm giving you constructive feedback."

It was the first time I'd seen any sign of insecurity in him. For a moment, his carapace of cool masculinity had cracked. I saw him without his props.

Without the big salary and the sports car, without the Americana on vinyl and the Bob Dylan CDs in his glove compartment, without his weathered knitwear and the desert boots caked in mud. The bricks of self had fallen, just for a few minutes, and all I could see was a nervous little boy who had been hiding underneath. I could forgive, just this once, his belligerence.

"THIS NOSE," I said as we lay in bed that night. I dragged my finger along the hard curve of it. "It's the most assertive nose I've ever seen. That nose has never been wrong about anything."

"I have my dad's nose."

"Do you look like your dad? I've never seen a proper photo of him other than that one in your flat."

"I don't think I have one," he said. "But yeah, I do look like him. A lot like him." He ran his fingers through his hair. "I once read Freud say that when two people have sex, there are at least six people in the room. The couple and both of their parents."

"What a thoroughly unenjoyable orgy."

"I know."

"Do you think that's true?"

"I think my dad is always going to be a missing piece for me, in every situation. No matter how much I talk or think about it, no matter how much

I analyse it. It's always going to torment me in a very quiet way."

"Boys and their dads," I said. "I don't think there's a parent-child dynamic that's more potent."

"Yeah," he said, rubbing his head as if to iron out the uncomfortable creases of his thoughts.

"Why did he leave your mum?" I asked. "We don't have to talk about it."

"He met someone else."

"How old were you?"

"Two."

"I'm sorry."

"It's okay."

"How did your mum cope with it?"

"Emotionally, she never really gave anything away. She just got on with it. Financially, it was tough. I remember, when I was eight, she gave me a fiver to get some milk from the shop in the village. I bought her a box of chocolates as a present, because I was aware she didn't have a husband like the other mums, and when I got home and gave it to her she burst into tears. It was only recently she told me the reason she was crying was that was the last five-pound note she had to feed us for a week."

"God, Max. That's a horrible memory, I'm sorry."

"I think that's why I feel so wedded to a job I hate. Because I don't ever want to worry about money like that."

"How old were you when you met your dad again?"

"Nine. I came home and Mum told me he was waiting in the living room. We had nothing to say to each other, he didn't know how to talk to me."

"What's your relationship like now?"

"We don't have one. He still doesn't know how to talk to me. He sent me an email for my birthday last year two months late, wishing me a happy thirtieth."

"Jesus."

"I worked out a long time ago that the best way to not be disappointed is to not give him a chance to disappoint me."

"Is he with the woman he left your mum for?"

"No. He left her when she was pregnant."

"Has he been with anyone since?"

"Yeah."

"How many?"

"Lost count," he said.

"Did he have more than one child after you?"

"Yep."

"How many?"

"Lost count," he said with a defeated laugh.

"Do you worry you're like your dad?" I immediately regretted the question—it was goading and seemed to relate his experience back to me.

"We're all like our dads," he said. "Come on then, what ghosts are you bringing to the orgy?"

"I don't know, really. My parents' relationship is very boring. I don't think they're soulmates, they're so disconnected in so many ways, but they're complementary to each other. And they're best friends, they really have a good time together. Well, they used to. It's hard to remember what their relationship was like before Dad got ill. His behaviour is so different now, obviously, but so is hers. I can't remember her being this self-obsessed. And there must be a reason for it—but I can't work out what it is. I think she is just pretending what's happening isn't happening. Or maybe she doesn't want to care for Dad any more, I know how upsetting it must be. Maybe she just finds it too hard." Max had become completely quiet as I spoke. We had never talked about our families like this. "It was always Dad and me who were the closest—he was the one who I talked to the most when I was a teenager. He taught me how to drive. He taught me everything. Mum and I were never like those mums and daughters who are best friends. But I've never felt quite so distant from her as I do now. And that scares me because Dad's not going to be here soon. I don't know how soon, it could be years and years, but sooner than I thought. And it will just be me and her. That will be my whole family. And I don't know how I'll have any sort of relationship with her when he isn't here. I think Dad is the only thing we have in common." My words hung above the bed. More silence. I couldn't work out exactly when he'd fallen asleep.

———

WE DROVE BACK TO LONDON on Monday morning in contented quiet. We had entered the stage of our relationship where not every journey had to be filled with conversation, where we weren't greedily trying to eat each other up, as if we feared we had a use-by date. We knew we had time now. It stretched ahead of us endlessly like the tarmac of the motorway. My palm rested on his leg as he drove. Hot, thick sun poured over us, warming the leather of his car seats.

He dropped me off outside my flat. His car ignition gave a leonine roar as he drove away down my road. I stood on the doorstep to wave him off—romantic and corny, but the kind of gesture he appreciated. I blew him a kiss. He held his hand aloft, waving goodbye without looking back. His car turned left and he disappeared.

17

WHEN I AGREED to meet Jethro and Lola at the pub, I knew that I was in for quite an afternoon. Their continuous stream of social media posts, captioned with long declarations of love and littered with in-jokes, had foreshadowed this lunch. But I hadn't anticipated quite how oxytocin-drunk the pair of them would be. When Jethro saw me, he opened his arms wide and embraced me for longer than I was comfortable. "Nina," he said, on a deep outward breath. "Nina, Nina. At last we meet. How long I have waited." The whole thing felt unnecessarily ceremonious, like I was the wise, elderly leader of a tribe and Lola had returned with a partner for approval. Lola was no better—every time Jethro said anything, even something as innocuous as "I live in Clerkenwell," she would look to me with an expectant smile as if to say **Isn't he amazing?!** and wouldn't break my gaze until I gave her a grin or a nod to confirm that, yes, he really was amazing. The pair of them finished each other's sentences so smoothly it felt choreographed and, on the rare occasions they interrupted each other, they'd touch hands and say: "No, you go, darling, I'm so sorry, I spoke over you. No, I insist, my love, you go first."

They loved explaining things about each other to me: "Jethro doesn't need much sleep whereas I, as you know, need nine hours"; "Lola is someone who very much carries the emotions of others"; "More and more, we are seriously considering a move to Mexico City." Lola kept finding ways to join us together with tenuous links, whether it was what food we ordered or what we both laughed at—she would turn to Jethro and say, "See? What did I say? Like twins, you two," and he would nod with knowing gravitas.

They also loved telling stories that either heavily hinted or explicitly described how much sex they were having. Jethro was clearly a man who thought he knew the female body better than any woman; that it was not only his job but his gift to the world, to educate us on how it all worked.

"Any woman can have an internal orgasm if their

G-spot is stimulated correctly," he told me as he tucked into shepherd's pie.

"They can, Nina, they really can," Lola said excitedly. She had not only lost her mind, but all sense of social appropriateness.

"Very interesting," I said. When Lola wasn't hinting at the sexual awakening she was currently undergoing, she relished telling me the mundane details of their cohabitation. She told me about the surprising amount of grooming products he'd left in her bathroom; how annoying it was that he filled the fridge with green smoothies. This was something she'd never experienced before—she'd never been close enough to a man to do the "him indoors" bit. She was not only in love with being in love, she was in love with finally being able to complain about someone. It would have been churlish of me not to allow it.

"How was your weekend away with Max?" she asked.

"Ah, yes, the great, hunky Max!" Jethro said. "I've heard all about him."

"It was lovely," I said. "I think the more we spend time together, the more I realize how unsatisfied he is in so many ways. And I really want to help him, but I also don't want to be smothering. So I'm just trying to work out that balance at the moment."

"Yeah, I mean, I don't know. Darling, what do you think, from a man's perspective?" she said, turning to Jethro, who immediately launched into a speech about the misconceptions of the male psyche. I arranged my face into an expression that seemed engaged while allowing me to not listen to a word he was saying—the one I used at most birthday parties—and instead thought about the fact I hadn't heard from Max since we'd come back to London. It had been four days. I texted him the day after he dropped me off, to see how he was, and I got no reply. I'd called him this morning and he didn't pick up. A sense of dread had returned like a recurring injury.

"Do you like him?" Lola asked, when Jethro went to the loo.

"Really like him," I said, searching my brain for specifics, because I knew she would not rest until specifics were given. "He's very open, which I think is great. Really good hair. Love a male redhead. Very confident. Very warm."

"What else?" she demanded gleefully.

"Obviously adores you."

"You think?"

"Yes."

"We're moving in together."

"I thought you already live together?"

"Yeah, well, we basically do, but we're going to buy a place together."

"Buy a place, why?"

"Because we want to have somewhere new that is both of ours."

"Definitely rent together first, don't buy."

"Renting is a waste of money."

"No, it's not, that's a thing our parents say. Renting is the best money you can spend, you get a home in return."

"He doesn't want to rent."

"Can you afford to buy?"

This question irritated her. "He's going to buy then we'll split the mortgage."

"But then you're not buying a place together."

"I don't want to waste any more time," she said. "I've been waiting my whole life to live with a man I love, I want to just get on with it now."

"Okay," I said. "I get it." I did not get it.

In a classy move that proved to me that Jethro really was desperate for my approval, he paid for the bill without saying anything on his way back from the loo. I thanked him, we hugged goodbye, he told me we were "family now," which felt almost like a threat, and I told him I looked forward to spending more time with him. Lola hugged me and told me she'd call me to arrange dinner that week. I knew she wouldn't—having seen her with Jethro, it was confirmed that she really was on an indefinite holiday now, and I knew from experience that it was hard to get in touch with anyone who was staying where she'd checked in. I didn't mind. I was happy that she'd finally got what she wanted.

I walked the two miles home and called Max. He didn't pick up. I tried again—no answer. I walked past a sports centre that had outside courts. A group of teenage girls were playing netball. Netball reminded me of Katherine—we were in the team together when we were at school. She was so good at it—her body was factory-built for netball—long, quick, light on her feet. She was Goal Defence, I was a Wing Attack. Even in adulthood, we still employed the insult "she has such Centre energy" as the worst aspersion you could cast on a woman. I stood at the side and looked through the metal net and thought of all the matches my dad came to—how surprisingly blood-thirsty he became at the sidelines for such a mild-mannered man. I wondered if Katherine remembered it too. She was my only close friend from childhood—one day I would be the only member left of my triumvirate family and she'd be the one person who could travel into my memories with me. I found myself missing her more than I'd ever missed her.

I watched one of the girls glide into the air to catch the ball and gallop her feet down in two neat steps. What a prissy sport it was. No touching, one foot glued to the ground, no obstruction, no holding the ball for more than a few seconds. I watched the girls pivot balletically and wave their arms like an arabesque and was reminded of the day when we swapped all our sports lessons with a local boys' school. They had a horrible time playing netball—unable to summon the emotionless, no-contact control the game required for which we had been so well trained. Whereas we all had the best day of our lives on their football and rugby pitches—kicking things and throwing each other to the ground and getting covered in grass and mud. Only now, watching teenage girls in prim bibs play netball so precisely and perfectly, did I realize that I wanted to scream on their behalf. I wanted to scream for all of us.

I sent Max a text.

"I think you're doing it again."

Ten minutes later I sent him another one.

"You promised me you wouldn't do this again."

WHEN I ARRIVED HOME, I could hear shouting as I approached the building. I stood in the hall-way and pressed my ear against Angelo's front door. There was arguing in Italian, first from him and then from a female voice. They shouted over each other—both of them raising their voices to defeat the other one in a tireless battle. I heard the female voice scream and something smash. There was a brief pause and then the shouting started again, from him, beginning slow and menacing and build-ing to a crescendo so loud his voice broke from ex-ertion. I banged on the door.

"Hello?" I yelped. I didn't know what else to say. I only needed to know she was safe. "HELLO?" I said, banging the door. "ARE YOU OKAY?" She started shouting again, so I banged the door harder. "I'll call the police, Angelo," I shouted. "If you don't open the door I'm going to CALL THE POLICE." The door flung open. A woman stood in front of me—short, hard-featured, dark-eyed. Over-plucked, feathery eyebrows. Thin, almost invisible lips, quivering in anger. Her shoulder-length hair was that bottle-burgundy you saw a lot of in the mid-noughties, thick and crisp from straighteners.

"WHAT?" she shouted, lightly spritzing me with her spit. She had a silver hoop through her septum.

"Are you okay? Just tell me you're okay and I'll leave you alone. You can come sit in my flat if you need to." I looked behind her and saw Angelo standing in his dressing gown, blank-faced, his hands swinging uselessly by his sides. She turned and asked him something in Italian. He shrugged and muttered something back. She gave a snort of laughter, then slammed the door. When I got upstairs I wrote the time and date on a scrap of paper, along with a description of what had just happened, in case it ever became important information.

A WEEK LATER, still having heard nothing from Max, I decided to keep my phone at home when I left the flat. I had already wasted enough of the last year staring at my screen, waiting for him to appear. If he really was ghosting me again, this time I wanted the exorcism to happen as quickly and painlessly as possible. When I returned home one afternoon and picked up my phone to find five missed calls from my mum, I knew one of two things must have happened—a divorce within the royal family, or Dad was in trouble.

"Nina?" she squawked when she picked up after half a ring.

"Yes. Hi. Is everything okay?"

"I've been trying to get hold of you all day," she said.

"I'm sorry, I'm trying to leave my phone in the flat when I'm out."

"Why the hell would you do that?"

"Because—" I couldn't face telling her that Max was ignoring me again—"of my . . . mental health," I finished feebly. She'd know immediately this was not a phrase I would ever use. **My mental health.** Like it was a pet dachshund.

"Oh, for God's sake."

"What's happened?"

"Your dad's had a fall," Mum said.

**A fall.** Something happens when people become clinically vulnerable, they stop "falling" and they have "a fall." "Dad's fallen over"—how harmless that would have been ten years ago. A couple of bruises, a comedy retelling of the anecdote. "Dad's had a fall" flicked panic on inside me like a fluorescent strip light.

I TOOK THE LONG TUBE JOURNEY up to the suburban hospital where Dad had been taken to A&E.

I had only ever been in a hospital twice: once, when I fell out of the mulberry tree in Albyn Square and needed stitches on my knee; the second, to say good-bye to Grandma Nelly. I had forgotten how enormous hospitals were—how impossible they were to navigate, signed with too much information and yet not enough information. I spent half an hour unable to get hold of Mum, walking through various indistinguishable zones with names of different colours, trying to find someone who might be able to help me. But there were no passing staff to help me because such was the nature of a hospital—it wasn't a hotel.

After finally locating one of two lifts in the entire building, I found the reception for A&E and was taken through to the cubicle where Dad was lying in bed, Mum standing by his side. I found myself petulantly withholding a hug from her, and I wasn't quite sure why.

"Has anyone seen him yet?"

"No," she said. "I think we could be waiting a while."

"What do they want to check?"

"I don't know."

"Do they know about his condition?"

"Yes," she said impatiently. "I'm going to get a coffee. Bill—I'm getting a coffee, would you like one?" He didn't answer. She kissed him on the head and he didn't respond, then she left. I approached the bed—there was a background noise of conversations and commands that I could tell was unsettling him. The air was sickly—a mixture of sugar, antibacterial liquids and the soggy potatoes of school dinners. It was the smell of both institution and dereliction.

"Does my mother know I'm here?" he asked.

"Yes," I said, sitting down in a chair beside him and reaching for his hand with mine. He was indifferent to it.

"When is she coming to see me?"

"I'm not sure, Dad," I said. "I know she's keen to know how you are."

"Go fetch my mother and she can find out how I am."

I wanted to cry. "Tell me what you've been enjoying recently, Dad. What music have you been listening to? Have you seen anything interesting in the paper?"

"I want to speak to her." He was spitting his words out now. He was frustrated. And why wouldn't he be? I was dismissing his questions and trying to distract him. I couldn't think of anything I would find more exasperating. "I WANT MY MOTHER!" he shouted unexpectedly, discarding my hand. I thought of Olive and the last time I had seen her—how anxious and infuriated she had been, how Mark had soothed her from a distance.

"It's okay, Dad," I said. I tentatively reached to touch his arm and gently placed my hand on the fabric of his shirt. "It's okay. I'm here, it's okay."

"No one listens to me any more."

"I will always listen to you. I will always listen to you, and I will always take everything you say seriously. I promise."

"I just want to speak with Mum, that's all," he said diminutively. "I want my mum." I continued to stroke his arm until his breath deepened. He closed his eyes and eventually fell asleep.

Mum returned with two black coffees and I quietly ushered her out of the cubicle so Dad could try to rest. We went out to the hallway beyond the reception.

"We need a carer," I said.

"Don't be dramatic. People his age have falls all the time."

"This isn't ageing or an accident. It's a progressive disease that is only going to get worse."

"I will keep a closer eye on him."

"That's not going to work any more. You can't give him the sort of support and attention that he needs."

"So I'm not doing a good enough job? That's what you're actually saying? Any opportunity to have a go at me. Well, why don't you move in and have a go instead, be my guest, see what it's like."

"I'm worried you're not taking this seriously."

"I am taking it seriously!"

"You're not, and I don't know why. I've tried to work out why, I've tried to be as understanding as I can. But I still don't get why you seem so unbothered

about the fact your husband is confused and angry
and vulnerable—"

"How dare you say that to me," she said, gripping
one of the metal chairs that was against the wall
and gritting her teeth. "I am not. Unbothered."

"Why won't you get extra help then? I'll help you
with the applications. I'll talk to Gwen. If we need
money, I'll rent out my flat, I'll move in with you
if I need to."

"It's not about that," she said quietly.

"It doesn't mean we're defeated. It doesn't
mean tragedy."

"YES IT DOES!" she screamed, slamming her
hands down on the back of the chair. Its front
legs lifted and clattered back down to the ground.
I flinched.

"Why?"

"Because it means we're old. And I don't want to
be old yet, I'm not ready."

"You don't want to be **old**?"

"It's okay for you—you're in your thirties, you
don't have to think about this stuff. You don't know
how morbid it is, to meet up with people and all
you talk about is bad knees and cancerous moles.
Your father and I go to more funerals now than
birthdays and I don't want this to be my life." I had
no idea what to say or how to comfort her. "I know
I'm lucky and the alternative is worse, but I don't
want the alternative either. I don't want to die and
I don't want us to be getting close to dying. It's all

shit, it's all SHIT," she shouted, slamming the chair legs down to the plastic flooring again.

"But, Mum—"

"I'm not meant to say any of this. I'm not allowed to. And I'm definitely not meant to be saying it to my child. But . . ." Her voice wavered. She pressed her lips in on each other. "There's so much left I want to do and see with your dad. I don't want to be in the last bit with him. I don't want a dying husband, I don't want him to die." She covered her eyes with her hands, like she was trying to hide from me. She became short of breath as she tried and failed to hold back tears. "I don't want my husband to die." I went over to her and sat her down in the chair. She sank her head down, curling in on herself, and sobbed into her knees. I sat cross-legged next to her on the floor and stroked her back. After a few minutes, she straightened herself up, breathing out through the controlled circle she'd made with her mouth. Her cheeks were stained with the grey tears of too much mascara.

"He is going to die, Mum." She closed her eyes and nodded furiously. "But we don't know when—it could be years and years. So, we need to do everything we can to make it as easy as possible."

"I don't know who I'll be without him," she said in a voice so small it sounded like a squeak.

I wished, selfishly, that I was little again. That I didn't have to see all the humanity of my otherwise steely mother explode out of her like a geyser.

I wished this hospital visit had been like the last time I'd seen Grandma Nelly, when I came in, read her a poem, kissed her velvety cheek that smelt of pressed powder, and was protected from the trauma and admin of illness.

"I know, Mum. It must be very frightening for you."

"I've been with him since I was a girl, Nina. He's my only boyfriend." **My only boyfriend.** These words threw open a box of ideas I hadn't let myself contemplate until now. "I don't know who I'll be without him."

"You'll be social secretary of the church and running all those literary salons and coming up with puns for them."

"I only do all that because I'm trying not to think about what's going to happen to Dad," she said. "I might not even want to do it any more when he's gone."

"You'll be a great friend. Life and soul. Everyone's matriarch, sorting everything out like you always do." She relented to this truth with a shrug. "And my mum."

"Yes," she said, putting her arm around me and pressing her mouth, hard, to my forehead. She had never been partial to affection. I stayed completely still and savoured these few seconds of physical closeness. "I'm going to do this better."

"Really?"

"I promise."

"We're doing it together. It's going to be traumatic and stressful and sometimes it's going to be very fucking weird and funny." She laughed, wiping away the mascara on her cheeks. "But no one is going to get what it's like other than you and me. So we have to be on the same team."

"I know," she said, composing a defiant smile.

Gwen's number appeared on my phone—we had been trying to get hold of her.

"Hi," I said as I picked up and signalled to Mum that I could take care of this call.

"Hello. I'm so sorry I've only just been able to get back to you. I've been with a patient this afternoon."

"That's okay. Dad had a fall and we've come to A&E."

"Ah," she said, like she had found the glasses she'd been looking for under the sofa cushion. She was so hard to faze or shock, and it was deeply reassuring. "Has he been seen yet?"

"No, they've said they want to do some checks? But we're not sure what checks."

"It will be a physical and blood pressure. They'll be trying to work out if he fell and hit his head or if he had a mini-stroke and that was the reason for his fall."

"Okay."

"He'll be out by tonight. And I'll be round at the house first thing in the morning and we can talk it all through."

"Thank you, Gwen. We've decided we need some

more help. We want to know our options for hiring a carer."

"Of course," she said. "We can look at all the care agencies in your area and work out which one will be most suited for what you need."

"Great."

"Is everything all right between you and your mum?" she asked.

"It wasn't," I said, looking up at Mum who was diligently reapplying concealer under her eyes. "It is now."

"Okay, that's good," she said. "Do you know, Nina, I've been doing this job a long time and if there's one thing I've learnt, it's that when someone stands at the end of an aisle aged twenty-seven and says 'in sickness and in health,' and they mean it with all their heart, no one specifically imagines this."

"You're right," I said.

"Take it easy on her."

"I will." Mum gestured that she wanted to speak to her. "I'm going to pass you on to Mum now. I'll see you in the morning."

When I returned to the cubicle, Dad was sitting up in the bed. His eyes were brighter.

"How you doing?" I asked, sitting by the side of the bed and passing a paper cup of water. "Bit better for having had a nap?"

"Yes," he said. "But how are you?"

"I'm okay," I said, removing the lid of the cold, bitter coffee and taking a sip.

"No, come on, tell me everything, I want to hear it all," he continued. "Because the last time I saw you, you were Peter Pan." I laughed. He looked surprised. Then he started laughing too—big, bellowing guffaws that turned into wheezes. Every time the laughter subsided, we'd catch each other's eye and laugh some more. He laughed so much he did his hissing Muttley cackle through his teeth. I knew why I was laughing—because of the absurd mess we had all found ourselves in; a chaos we could have never predicted. And though he didn't say it, I knew that's why he was laughing too.

As I watched him surrender to the silly, untameable joy of hysterical giggles, I realized that while the future might strip him of his self, something mightier remained. His soul would always exist somewhere separate and safe. No one and nothing—no disease, no years of ageing—could take that away from him. His soul was indestructible.

"Oh dear," he said, after our laughter had finally quietened. "You seem fretful. Why are you so fretful?"

"Can I be honest?"

"Yes, please do be honest."

"I've found everything really difficult recently. And I can't work out if this is just a tricky period or whether this is what adulthood is now—disappointment and worry."

"What are you worried about?"

"I'm worried I'm not going to live the life I always

thought I'd have. I'm worried I have to come up with a new plan."

"There's no point coming up with a plan," he said, shaking his head sternly. "Life is what happens . . ."

"I know, I know," I said, acknowledging our favourite Lennon line—as glib as it was profound. "I know that clever women aren't meant to worry about having a family. And I know I still have time. But I'm scared that if I don't plan for it, it will never happen."

He shrugged. "It might not ever happen."

I found the starkness of this fact strangely comforting. No one had ever said it to me before. Everyone had always said, in one way or another, that I could have whatever I wanted.

"Now look," he said, "you got a distinction for your grade seven violin exam."

"That's right," I said, unsure of where this fact would take us.

"You know you can't pass grade seven in all this," he said, presenting me with one of his riddles with which I had become so familiar. I knew, if I thought for long enough, I could find the logic within it— I always did. "Listen to me: you will not be able to get a distinction with all of this," he said slowly. "And that's half the experience. That means everything's going right. Do you understand?"

"Yes, Dad," I said. "I understand."

## 18

THE DOORBELL RANG at ten o'clock on a Friday night. It had been three weeks since I had last seen or heard from Max and, just like last time he disappeared, every time there was someone at the door, I would walk to it saying a silent incantation: **Please be him. Please be him. Something terrible happened and he couldn't get hold of me. But now he's here. Please be him.**

I opened the door to find Katherine. She was leaning against the wall and everything about her looked a little skew-whiff—slightly bloodshot eyes, stringy hair overdue a shampoo. She carried a blue corner-shop plastic bag in her hand.

"Nina!" she cried joyfully.

"Hi," I said, unsure of whether she was here for confrontation or reconciliation. "Why are you in London?"

"Seeing you! I miss you!" she said, lunging towards me with open arms and pulling me in for a hug. She let herself in and walked up the stairs, the plastic bag swinging in her hand. "I had a free night without the kids and I thought: where do I want to go, who do I want to see? I want to get pissed with my best and oldest mate, that's what I want to do." She was talking to herself, wittering aloud the way Olive did when she played with her toys. She was either in the midst of a breakdown, or spectacularly drunk. "Because how long has it been since I got pissed? Er: a hundred years, I think! And how long has it been since I've seen my best friend?"

"About two months," I said humourlessly as I led her into the flat.

"God, I bloody love this place!" she said, flinging the plastic bag on the sofa, along with herself. I hadn't seen Katherine like this in years—sloppy and enthusiastic about everything. It was rare she got drunk—she always liked to be in control of herself—it was even rarer she got **this** drunk.

"Where's your handbag?" I asked.

"Don't need one, FUCK handbags! It's like our whole lives we're . . . carrying things? As women? You know? And we just don't need to."

"Where are the kids?"

"Ugh," she said, throwing her head back on the sofa. "With Mark."

"Is he . . . all right with them?" I realized how ridiculous this question was as I asked it.

"Of course he's all right with them, he's their fucking father, not their teenage brother. Although, you wouldn't know it." She took two gin and tonics in a can out of the clanking plastic bag and threw one to me. She cracked the other one open and took a swig. "Do you know, when Olive was one—ONE—I had my first night away from home for a friend's hen do. Mark was so nervous about being on his own with her, I had to write him this long bloody manual on how to operate his own bloody daughter, like she was a new iPhone. Anyway, I didn't hear anything from him all night, I was so pleased it had gone well. The next day I find out he'd hired a babysitter."

"Did he go out?"

"Nope. Just sat in the next room, watching **A Question of Sport.**" She tipped her head back to drink more from the can and its contents spilt down her chin. She wiped it with the sleeve of her blouse without acknowledging her clumsiness. She sank further into the sofa and splayed her legs as far as her skin-tight jeans would allow. "Have you got any weed?"

"Of course not."

"Let's buy some! Let's take some weed!"

"Katherine, last time you and I 'took' weed we

both vomited. We're not party girls and we never will be."

"Speak for yourself, maestro!" she shouted. **Maestro?** "Right, we're going out dancing." She stood up purposefully and walked out of the room. I didn't know how to respond to any of this. She was clearly too drunk to talk about our friendship in any meaningful way, but I felt too unsettled by our argument to pretend we were fine and have a big night out together.

I followed her into my bedroom, where she was standing in front of my full-length mirror.

"I hate all my fucking clothes," she said. "I look like a soon-to-be-retired school registrar all the fucking time. Can I borrow something of yours?"

"Sure," I said, sitting on the bed and observing her. She took her peach blouse off and lassoed it round her head. She went to throw it on the bed and it got caught in the lampshade, which she found implausibly funny. I laughed along for the appropriate amount of time, while she continued for longer and louder than was necessary. Her face fell when she caught mine.

"Oh, come on, Nina, HAVE A LAUGH!" she shouted wearily. Was there anything more annoying than someone so drunk they could barely stand up telling you what was and wasn't funny?

"I **am** having a laugh," I said unconvincingly.

"Get another drink down ya!" she said, throwing open my wardrobe and flipping through my clothes like pages of a magazine. I decided she was right and went to the kitchen to pour myself a whisky. I needed to smooth the edges of this jagged encounter.

I came back to find her in my black swimsuit with cut-outs revealing bare skin at the sides.

"Love this top," she said, hopping up and down as she yanked her jeans on over her thighs.

"That's a swimsuit."

"Perfect."

"Do you really want to go out wearing a swimsuit?"

"Yeah, come on. Upcycling. Haven't you heard? The end of fast fashion! Austerity Britain!" She guffawed at her own non-joke that made no sense. "See? You think I'm some provincial potato-head who doesn't read the **Guardian** but I **do read the fucking Guardian.**"

I took another large mouthful of whisky, which burnt deliciously as it slid down my throat.

I TOOK HER TO THE INSTITUTION. The last time I'd been here was on my first date with Max, at the end of last summer. Here I was again, at the beginning of this summer. I imagined going back to myself as the ghost of summer future, telling that girl in her high heels and jeans what this first online date with a man would lead to. I wondered how long she might have stayed. I considered floating this observation to Katherine then decided not to. She was at

a level of drunkenness where I had to assess everything I was about to say, to work out whether she'd
understand it or if the act of explaining it would be
more hassle than it was worth. We queued at the
busy bar while Katherine's bare shoulders bopped
up and down in front of me in time with the music.

"Max and I came here on our first date," I said
into her ear.

"Oh yeah?"

"Yeah. We got back together, by the way."

She turned to face me. "What? When?"

"That night I last saw you, actually." I waited for
her face to register an emotion at the mention of
our argument—nothing.

"And?" she said. "How's it going?"

"It was going great, but he's ghosted me again."

"No!" she cried. "When?"

"Few weeks ago. It's completely my fault. I'm an
idiot for taking him back."

"Hey," she said, holding me by both of my arms.
"You are not an idiot." I was about to be hit with a
series of meaningless declarations about how amazing I was, I could tell. These drunken niceties are
what these once-solid-now-flimsy female friendships relied on. They were the string that kept us
connected, as thin as dental floss. "You are an amazing woman, Nina. No, honestly. You've got a great
career, loads of friends, a flat, you're gorgeous. He
was very, very lucky to have known you, let alone
been with you!"

"Thanks."

"Right, what are you drinking? Shots? Shots." She leant over the bar and shouted into the server's ear. "TWO VODKA TONICS PLEASE. DOUBLES. AND TWO SHOTS OF TEQUILA." She turned to look at me and winked, then turned back to the barmaid. "FOUR, FOUR SHOTS OF TEQUILA. FIVE! ONE FOR YOU, LOVE." The shots were lined up on the bar, along with a saucer of lemon wedges and a shaker of table salt. "HERE'S TO MEN BEING TWATS!" she shouted, clinking her miniature glass against mine and then the one belonging to the exhausted-looking barmaid.

I tried to quickly catch up with Katherine's drunkenness as we sat in a booth by the bar, gulping down our drinks.

"So what's actually happened with you and Mark?" I said. "You seem angry at him."

"I am angry at him," she said. "We had a big row."

"When?"

"Tonight."

"And then what?"

"And then I came to see you."

"Does he know where you are?"

"Nope!" she said, popping the "p" enthusiastically.

"Should I let him know where you are?"

"No fucking way. I never misbehave. I always do what he wants. I took his stupid surname, I moved to stupid Surrey, I go on all-inclusive holidays with his stupid friends and their stupid wives and children. He can do what I WANT for a change. And what I WANT is to make him worry I'm DEAD. That's what I want! That's my new favourite hobby!" She cackled manically. "It used to be spin classes and now it's making my husband worry I'm DEAD."

"Katherine," I reasoned, unsure of what to say next. It was impossible to feel drunk around her. Everything she said made me feel sober and concerned.

"Oh my God, Nina, listen! Listen!" The bassline of "The Edge of Heaven" reverberated from beneath us. "IT'S YOUR SONG!" Before I had a chance to protest, she yanked me by my hand and pulled me downstairs and on to the dance floor.

I had forgotten what a terrible dancer Katherine was. I always found this particularly endearing about otherwise very beautiful and elegant women. It might have been the sexiest thing about her, in fact—the only wonky, weird physical flaw you could find. She had absolutely no sense of rhythm and moved herself with wild, jerky abandon. The longitude of her body stayed still and stiff while her long, gangly limbs moved like cooked spaghetti flailing around a colander. She bit down on her bottom lip and would only open her mouth to sing the wrong lyrics.

"THIS ISN'T ACTUALLY MY SONG," I shouted over the music as we danced.

"WHA?" she shouted back.

"THIS ISN'T MY SONG."

"YEAH IT IS. IT WAS NUMBER ONE WHEN YOU WERE BORN."

"NO, IT WASN'T," I said, my throat scratchy from straining my voice. "MY MUM LIED. 'LADY IN RED' BY CHRIS DE BURGH WAS NUMBER ONE WHEN I WAS BORN."

Katherine stopped dancing and looked aghast.

"Oh fuck," she said, putting her hand over her mouth.

"I KNOW," I said, continuing to dance. "I COULDN'T BELIEVE IT."

"I THINK I'M GOING TO BE SICK."

I took her hand in mine and pulled her off the dance floor as fast as I could. We rushed upstairs as she clasped her palm to her mouth, gagging as she went. As soon as we were outside and engulfed by the cool night air, she folded in on herself and vomited. I held back her hair and she gripped on to my arm. We were by a long queue of people waiting to get into The Institution. All of them laughed or grimaced.

"Oi," the bouncer said. I looked up at him.

"I'm sorry," I said. "New mum. First night out since she had the baby." I gently guided Katherine to the side of the building, on to an empty street.

"I love you, Nina," she slurred, in between retches.

"I know you do."

"I really love you."

We both sat on the pavement in silence, waiting

for the sickness to pass. Hiccups came in its place. I ordered us a taxi back to mine.

WHEN WE GOT INTO MY FLAT, I had to help her up the stairs. She leant on the corridor wall for support.

"What would you like?" I asked.

"Water."

"Okay, I'll get you a glass of water."

"No, on my body!" she protested. "Water all over my body!"

I'd forgotten how melodramatic people this drunk could be.

She lay on my bathroom floor and I undressed her. The overhead spotlights robbed her of all her dignity as she thrashed about unselfconsciously. I manoeuvred her into the bath, where she lay sprawled and half asleep. I held the showerhead and tested the water on my hand. When it was warm enough, I hovered it above her body and moved it from her head to her toes. She shut her eyes and gave a sweetly satisfied smile—with her dark wet hair slicked back, she looked like a baby otter. It was the first time I'd seen Katherine naked since she'd had babies. I noticed changes I could never have seen through her clothes. Her hips had expanded, magically, like a sponge blooming in water. Her tummy—formerly so taut and hard—had softened and, in one part, slightly crinkled. Her nipples were pinker and swollen; her breasts were big enough to lie down on her ribcage, whereas before they'd never touched it. She'd made two lives in that body. It was a reminder of the changes she'd been through, that perhaps I would never understand. I felt a pang of guilt.

I gave her a pair of cotton pyjama shorts and a mug of black coffee. She got into my bed and sat upright against the headboard. The shower and caffeine had straightened her out. I perched next to her on top of the duvet.

"Are you okay?" I asked.

"I don't know," she said. "I don't think so."

"Talk me through it. You can tell me anything."

She put the mug down on the bedside table. "I'm just so tired this time round," she said. "I'm so tired I feel like I'm losing my mind. I can't remember what happened when I was awake and what was a dream, I can't remember whole conversations I have with people. I can't seem to keep Olive happy and look after Freddie. She's taken it so badly. I'm worried she doesn't feel safe and loved."

"Of course she's taking it badly, she's a toddler. Every toddler goes mental when a new baby arrives."

"I'm a bad mother, Nina," she said, her eyes becoming glassy. "I'm not doing a good enough job." Tears fell down both her cheeks, dappled pink as they always were when she cried.

"No, you're not. I know what sort of mother you are. You can lie to yourself, but you can't lie to me."

"The other day, I was going so fucking insane, I went outside, locked Olive in the house, sat on the side of the road and didn't go back in for fifteen minutes. When I came back, I found her in the bathroom, drinking the juice from the loo-brush holder like it was a beaker." This image made me desperate to laugh, but I managed to stifle it. "I was lucky. Anything could have happened."

"It's okay, she wasn't hurt."

"And last week, I was making her tea while Freddie was sleeping in his basket. When I wasn't giving her enough attention, she went to hit him."

"What did you do?"

"What I swore I'd never do, I grabbed her and I shook her. I was so angry."

"That's understandable."

"No, it's not, I'm the adult, I'm meant to know better. I'm not meant to lose my temper like a toddler." She looked to the ceiling and more tears spilt from her eyes. "All I am at the moment is a mother. I'm not interesting, I'm not engaged with the world. My whole life is feeding and changing and bedtime. If I'm not even doing that well, then I truly am totally fucking useless."

"Katherine, listen to me. I love your daughter— I would do anything for her. But Olive is, plain and simple, being a cunt." Katherine let out a piercing yelp of laughter. "She herself isn't a cunt, she's a delight. But at the moment, she's behaving like a cunt. And that would test the patience of anyone."

"She is," Katherine said, wiping her face. "My daughter is being a cunt."

"Well done."

"My daughter is being a total and utter cunt."

"There we go."

She retrieved her mug of coffee and leant her face into the warmth of its fumes.

"You have to be able to talk to me about this stuff, Katherine. You've got to drop the Stepford act, it does no one any good. It annoys me and it makes you feel isolated."

"I know."

"If we have to pretend to each other like we pretend to the rest of the world, then we might as well not bother with the effort friendship takes."

"I know," she said. "I'm sorry. I've been an unreasonable bitch."

"Yes, you have."

"I haven't been here for you at all."

"No, you haven't."

"Are you okay?" she asked.

I hoisted myself under the duvet, still facing her so we could natter into the night, resuming the position of all our childhood sleepovers.

"I think I will be," I said. "Mum and I might have turned a corner, which I hope will make everything easier. I think now Max is out of my life for good, I'm realizing that being in love with someone who was so clearly dangerous was a distraction from the actual tragedy in my life."

"Which is?"

"Saying goodbye to Dad."

She reached her hand out to mine. "Do you think you really loved Max?"

"Yes, I really did," I said. "I don't know if he loved me. I think he thought he did. But it's like he imagined me—I provided him with a feeling that he enjoyed. But he couldn't quite see the actual outline of me. I don't know if it counts as love if it was genuinely felt on my side but imagined on his."

"But—" She stopped herself.

"Go on," I said.

"Well, whenever you've described him to me, it sounds like you're imagining him a bit as well. He sounds sexy and interesting. But other than that, he seems pretty unfeeling and self-obsessed."

"Yeah," I said. "I think I have to accept some responsibility with what happened. I wonder how much I really wanted to actually get to know the real him, and how much I wanted a storybook hero."

"What happened wasn't your fault."

"But I think you might be right, I think I've created a version of him too. Or maybe that's all love is. So much is how we perceive someone and the memories we have of them, rather than the facts of who they are. Maybe instead of saying **I love you** we should say **I imagine you.**"

She wriggled down into the bed and pulled the duvet up to her neck. "Do you think we'd ever be friends if we met now?"

"No, I don't think so."

"Me neither."

"Sort of magic, isn't it? To know that we could meet the most exciting person in the world, but they'd never be able to recreate the history you and I have. What a unique superpower we have over each other."

"It is," she said, turning off her bedside light.

"Is that how you feel about Mark?" I asked.

"I don't know," she said, turning her head on the pillow to face me. "I don't know what I feel about Mark at the moment. It's like we just share a house and a schedule. Maybe that's having kids. But then again, it's never been some big romantic love story. That's not who we are."

"What do you mean?"

"I don't think I need the sort of passion other people need. Do you remember how he asked me to move in with him?"

"Yeah, he sent an email to your work address with the subject heading 'Next Steps.' I think about it at least once a week." We both laughed into our pillowcases.

"I know he can be a bit clueless, but he's a good dad," she said. "And he's always got my back."

"You two are so solidly on the same team."

"We are," she said, closing her eyes.

I turned off my bedside lamp. "Sounds pretty romantic to me."

"It is," she said quietly, before falling almost instantly asleep.

I sent Mark a text.

"Kat's with me. She is well and fine and all is good. Call me if you want to talk x"


WE SLEPT IN THE NEXT MORNING. I awoke, dry-mouthed and nauseous from spirits that left a sticky ring-mark in my head, to a text from Mark that I read aloud to Katherine: "Thank you for letting me know. Please tell her there is no rush to come home. I've got it covered—and I can take a day off work next week and look after the kids. She deserves a break. Mark x"

We celebrated her first hangover in nearly four years by behaving like we did every weekend afternoon of our early to mid-twenties. We put on tracksuits, I made us toad-in-the-hole with peas and mash, we heaved the duvet on to my sofa and watched three musicals back to back. After the credits of **West Side Story,** her third helping of mash, two glasses of red wine and a bath, she left at ten p.m. to catch the train back to Surrey. She hugged me, thanked me, told me she loved me and that she'd call me the following week.

I went to the kitchen and filled the sink with water, soap and washing-up. I tied my hair in a ponytail and switched on the radio to the soothing classical Saturday-night show with the radio DJ I liked. An operatic piece reached its denouement with settling strings and a soaring male tenor. There was a brief silence. "That was from the little-known cantata 'The Spectre's Bride,'" she said—the voice I'd been listening to since the year-seven school run. "And it's a reminder to all us ladies that sometimes when your ex-boyfriend gets back in touch, really, he's just trying to take you down with him to the grave. I think we've all been there, haven't we!" She chuckled to herself. "Just a little joke there for the hard-core Dvořák fans. And now—for something a bit more mellow. A seasonally appropriate number from Vivaldi's . . . **Four Seasons.**" I snapped the rubber washing-up gloves over my hands and sank them into the hot water, contemplating which station she'd end up at next. Where do you go after a late-night classical music show? The shipping forecast? And where would I be listening to it? This flat? A family home? A retirement bungalow?

I heard a knock on the door and knew that Katherine had realized in the hallway that she'd left something.

"Come in!" I shouted down the corridor. "Door's open, Kat, sorry. Just doing the washing-up." I heard footsteps approach.

"Where are my packages?"

I turned around to see Angelo, unusually fully dressed in a T-shirt and jeans. I stood with my back against the sink.

"You can't barge into my flat."

"Where are my packages?" He stood in the doorway; his face and voice were calm and still.

"I don't have your packages."

"Yes, you do," he said, walking towards me, stopping about a metre away by the cooker. "I see the delivery man today out of the window and I run down the road and ask him where he puts the packages for Angelo Ferretti and he say, 'I leave them with your wife on the first floor.'"

I quickly spun through a choice selection of excuses, but I could find nothing. I had not thought of an alibi. "I don't know what you're talking about," I said breezily, using my elbow to brush my fringe out of my face while my hands were still in washing-up gloves.

"WHERE ARE MY PACKAGES?" he shouted.

"Angelo, just get out of my flat and I will leave them by your door. I will leave them there right away."

"No. Show me where they are."

I gestured to the compartment above the oven fan. He was so tall he could open it on his tiptoes. He reached in, pulled out the three parcels one by one and put them on the floor. He spluttered bemusedly in Italian. "I only took three," I said, like a surly teenager defending something indefensible.

"You opened them?!"

"Yes," I said.

"You went through my things?"

I had angered a psychopath who now had direct

access to a handy selection of machetes. I allowed my eyes to quickly flicker to the knife block on my kitchen counter to assess whether I could reach for it with one quick motion.

"I didn't have any other choice. You made everything so difficult for me, I wanted to make something difficult for you."

"What is the matter with you?"

"What is the matter with YOU?"

"You cannot steal things!"

"You wanted me to do this."

"AH?!" He snarled in confusion.

"Yes. You did, you wanted me to lose it. And I did. I snapped. You win."

"I did not do this."

"This is all because of you!" I said, flinging my be-gloved hands into the air and inadvertently spraying him with drops of water. "This is ALL your fault. Why have I never ever, ever had a problem with my neighbours before I lived above you? Why did I use to love living here and now I dread coming home?"

"You," he said, pointing at me with narrowed eyes, "are crazy."

"No I'm not."

"Yes you are."

"It means nothing when a man says that to me any more because I know the truth. You can say it as many times as you like, it will have no effect on me."

"You're crazy."

"It means nothing, Angelo. I know the truth. I know what happened. I know how you behaved. The more you say it, the saner I feel." I pulled the rubber gloves off.

"Fucking crazy."

"Don't believe you," I said, edging closer to him. He stepped back like a frightened animal.

"You're FUCKING CRAZY!"

"I KNOW WHAT HAPPENED. I KNOW THE TRUTH. I AM NOT FRIGHTENED OF THAT WORD ANY MORE."

"YOU'RE A CRAZY FUCKING BITCH," he shouted.

I pushed him and he stumbled backwards into my fridge. I heard pickle jars clank as he landed against it. He straightened up—I was inches away from him and looking at his eyes, bulbous in shock. He smelt of a recent shower and the toiletries that teenage boys find in their Christmas stocking in a gift set. I searched for evil in his face—for signs of violence, detached cold-bloodedness. The push had felt good, but I needed more. I wanted to use more of my anger on him, more of my body on him—show him that he couldn't scare me. Show him that this was my home as much as his—that he couldn't force me out. I wanted to hit him—swipe my hand cleanly across his cheek, to both leave something on him and take something of his. But I'd never hit anyone before.

I pressed my mouth up against his, so hard that I pushed through the cushion of his plump lips and could feel the bone-hardness of his gums. I pulled away, horrified, and examined his face like a stab wound.

He pushed me back towards the sink as he kissed me. His hands grasped both my cheeks, then his fingers dragged through my hair, pulling it out of its ponytail. He kissed hungrily along my jaw, my chin, then moved down my neck. He tugged my vest top off, threw it on the dish rack and pressed me in towards him, running his hands up and down the juts and curves of my bare shoulders and spine. He kissed me, slower, making noises of satiation that echoed as a hum from my mouth into my ears. He was warm and pulsing and moving. He was flesh and blood. He was breathing. He was steadfast—he lived below me. He never left. He was here. He wouldn't disappear. He couldn't disappear.

I wanted to feel more of him. I hurriedly pulled off his T-shirt—his chest was hard, his skin the colour of almonds. It hugged round the surprisingly muscular curves and hollows of his shoulders and arms that were lean and coltish, at odds with the sallow weariness of his face. He dropped to his knees as he pulled down my tracksuit bottoms so they bunched at my bare feet, which looked laughably adolescent, and turned me around by my hips so I faced away from him. He took a mouthful of my thigh in between his teeth as I heard him clumsily unbutton his jeans. He held on to the counter as he stood up and pushed himself inside me. I leant forward—we were completely still and breathed slowly as my body got used to him. The steam rose from the sink and on to my face as I felt him move. My hands slipped and plunged into the water, splashing suds on to my bare skin. I felt his laughter reverberate through me, which made me laugh too. He leant down so his stomach pressed against my back and the thin silver chain he wore around his neck tickled my spine. He lifted my hair so it spilt over my face, the tips of its strands dipping in the water.

My hands, wearing soapsuds like lace gloves, reached behind and grabbed on to his forearms, like I was checking he was still there. I dug my fingers into him and let out a guttural noise of relief. I didn't fragment and travel the room, every part of me remained in my body. I kept my eyes wide open, staring at glasses with red wine sediment and crusty forks that lurked beneath the water and knocked against each other. I felt him slow, stop and shudder. He gasped. We were still again. It had been brief and uncomplicated. Unplanned and ungainly. And real. Soapy, dirty, clattering, awkward. Real.

We sat opposite each other, half dressed on my kitchen floor, his back against the oven, my back against the cupboard under the sink.

"I thought we hated each other," I said.

"What?" he said, his vowels stretched in out-rage. "No!"

"Why have you been so rude to me?"

"It's not you—fuck." He looked at the floor. "Do you have water?"

I nodded and stood up, aware I was now topless in tracksuit bottoms like a brickie on a warm day. I took a tumbler from the cupboard and put it under the tap while strategically using my arms to cover myself, suddenly self-conscious.

"I struggle. This year," he said slowly, presenting chunks of thoughts to me like Scrabble tiles.

"With what?"

"Living."

"I'm sorry," I said, handing over the glass and joining him on the floor. I thought of his dressing gown. His vests. How he'd ignored me. How he'd seemed to ignore everything—rules, light, time, bin collection, manners, the world outside his flat. "Can I ask why?"

"My girlfriend, she was living here."

"Is she the woman you were having the argument with?"

"Yes," he said, nodding. "She cheat on me last year. I forgive her, she stay a while, but then she leave anyway."

"I'm sorry," I said again.

He shrugged as he took a sip of water. "I try all this year to be better but now there is no . . ." He put his glass down to avoid my gaze.

"I understand," I said. "No purpose. No fun. No point."

"Same for you?"

"Yeah, he disappeared. Stopped speaking to me."

He nodded sympathetically, like we were strangers in the same community support group. Which I suppose we were. I thought of the three flats on top of each other, how they each housed a broken heart. Betrayal, disappearance, grief. Cuckolded in the basement, abandoned on the first floor, widowed on the top floor. "You know you will be fine again, Angelo," I said. "We were fine before and we'll be fine again."

He pushed the side of his hand methodically along the floor, like he was cleaning crumbs. The overhead kitchen lights illuminated the skin at the back of his head where his hair had become diaphanous.

"I'm sorry," he said, looking up at me with a repentant smile that seemed painful for him to hand over.

"Thank you," I said. "I'm sorry I took your packages. That's a completely unacceptable thing to do. I didn't realize you were in so much pain, I thought you were just horrible."

"It's okay," he relented. He finished the glass of water in a gesture of finality. "I think perhaps it is not a good idea to . . ." He motioned between us.

"All right, all right," I said. "I don't think we should do that again either."

"Why did you say you're my wife?"

"For no other reason than to steal from you, don't worry."

"Ah."

"But I do think we should be friends," I said. "I think we deserve some peace."

"**Sì,** peace," he said with a sigh. "Peace. Piece of cake."

"Good idiom."

"Idiom?"

"It's when a phrase means something in a language, but it doesn't have any literal meaning."

"I see."

"Teach me an Italian one."

He leant his head back against the fridge and searched his thoughts. **"Hai voluto la bicicletta, e mo' pedala."**

"What does that translate as?"

"You wanted the bicycle, now pedal it."

"And what does that mean?"

"It means, you must face the consequences of your desires."

"I see. We have 'You've made your bed, now lie in it.'"

"Yes," he said. "You have your beds, we have our bikes."

"Where are you from? I know 'Baldracca' isn't a place, you piece of shit."

"You liked my joke!"

I scowled.

"I'm from Parma."

"I've been there. I went for work a couple of years ago."

"You did?" He looked delighted.

"Yes, I write about food. I was writing a piece about protected-status food products in Emilia-Romagna. It was about vinegar in Modena and Parmesan cheese and the ham in Parma."

"No!" he said. He excitedly dragged one of his cardboard boxes open and took out one of the long knives. "From my mother."

"Why?"

"To make prosciutto."

"Oh."

"What?"

"I thought—" I brought my head to my knees and breathed into the fuzzy softness of my tracksuit bottoms.

He craned his head to look at me. "What?"

"I thought you were going to kill someone," I said, snapping my head back up, my gaze meeting his limpid amber-brown eyes, now wide in shock. "I'm sorry."

"What?" He shuffled back very slightly, as if I were now the threat.

"I thought you were a psychopath. I thought you wanted to hurt someone," I said, glancing at the packages.

"No! She sent me this to make prosciutto. She hangs it in our garden. I will hang in the garden here," he said, opening the box and showing me the hooks.

"What's with the poison?"

He rolled his eyes. "**Poison.** It's to help the meat. Colour the meat?"

"Cure it," I said. "Of course."

"Poison?"

"Fuck off," I said as we both laughed. "I was told that it's the air in Parma that makes it taste so good. Might not be quite the same in Archway."

"Yes," he shrugged. "Maybe."

"I've got a good butcher for you to go to if you need one. For pigs' legs."

"Yes?"

"Yes. How long will you hang them for?"

"A year maybe?" he said. "My mother hangs it for two. I miss it."

"Ham?"

"Home."


HE LEFT SHORTLY AFTERWARDS. He kissed me, formally, on both cheeks and we exchanged numbers. I heard the door open to his flat downstairs, then I heard him walking through to his kitchen, whistling as he went. I heard him make himself something to eat as I had a shower, a metre above his head. He did the washing-up and listened to the radio as I brushed my teeth. I fell asleep while he was watching TV. I slept soundly through the night.

## 19

LOLA AND I had an emergency code word—
penguin. We had employed it just twice in our
fifteen-year-long friendship. The first: when she accidentally uploaded a naked photograph of herself
to a shared album where all the godparents to a
baby called Bertram were meant to post photos
of him. The second: when I thought that I'd seen
Bruce Willis in a phone shop, but it turned out to
be a similar-looking bald man. When I received an
emoji of a penguin, then a pub location, date and
time, I knew there was only one thing she had to
tell me: she was engaged.

I pre-emptively ordered a bottle of champagne

and waited at the table for her. She arrived—yellow polka-dot halter top, black-and-white stripy shorts, heeled silver clogs and a floppy straw hat on a decidedly unsunny day. She sat down at the round table without hugging me hello and removed her Jackie O sunglasses and hat.

"Jethro," she said.

"He proposed!"

"He's gone."

The waiter came over and popped the champagne cork ceremoniously. Lola flinched.

"For you?!" he said, beside himself with excitement that a customer had finally ordered the champagne.

"Yes," I replied.

"Fabulous. And are either of you lovely ladies celebrating anything special?"

Lola pressed the heels of her hands into her forehead.

"No, don't worry," I said, gently prising the bottle off him. "I think we can . . . sort it from here. Thank you so much." I put the champagne into the ice bucket and he left.

"What happened?"

"Everything was completely normal until a couple of weeks ago. We were having loads of fun, we had some flat viewings lined up for this week, we were really excited about properly moving in together. He'd started talking about marriage." She registered the judgement on my face. "I know, I know. It seems mad now. Then on the Sunday evening he said he had to pop home to pick up some stuff and then he'd come back to mine. He'd been gone for a few hours so I texted him to check if he was okay—he said he was going to stay there. He said he'd realized that everything had been moving too fast and he needed to 'put the brakes on.' I asked him if he knew he was going to say this to me when he left the flat and pretended everything was fine and he said no. But of course he did. He was just avoiding having a difficult conversation."

"Then what?" I said, pouring the champagne, now mocking us.

"We decided to have a few days of not speaking, have some time to ourselves, think about what we want then meet up to talk."

"Have you heard from him?"

"No. Not for over a week. At first I thought he must just need some more space, which is fine, but he's not even responding to my messages." Her husky-blue eyes filled up with tears and they spilt down her cheeks. She was so desperate to love someone. It seemed like such a simple, singular thing to ask from this life.

A sensation rose inside me—one that had been long-repressed. Something I should have expressed, fully and freely, when Max first disappeared, but instead I had hidden everywhere else, to be a good girl. I had turned it in on myself, to examine all my possible imperfections. I had let it rise like hot air into my brain to analyse and pathologize needlessly.

I had allowed it into my heart and let it melt down into something patient and forgiving. I had distributed this feeling into any part of my body so that it wouldn't escape from my mouth; so that it couldn't catch the air. That way, no one could accuse me of being intense or deluded or crazy. But it was time to breathe it out like fire. I had no interest in retribution, all I wanted was redress.

"Where does he live?" I asked.

"Clerkenwell."

"Right," I said, downing the rest of my glass in one. "Bring that with you." I gestured at the half-bottle of champagne and stood up.

"We're not going to his flat."

"You're not, I am."

"No, Nina."

"Yes," I said. "Real human people can't be deleted. We are not living in a dystopian science fiction."

"What are you going to say to him?"

"Everything he needs to hear."

"Okay," she said, picking up the champagne and taking a swig as we went to the door. "I've got nothing to lose now."

JETHRO'S FLAT was in a warehouse that, even from the outside, looked very pleased with its own conversion. The steel Crittall windows looked like big toothy grins that were smugly congratulating each other. I rang the buzzer.

"Hello?" he said.

"It's Nina," I said flatly. "Nina Dean, Lola's friend."

"Oh." The fuzzy white noise indicated he was still on the line. "Can I help you with something?"

"I just need ten minutes to talk to you." There was a pause, then the flat, obtrusive beep that let me know he'd let me in. I knew he'd cave—these men cared so little about their actions towards the women they hurt, but so much about what people who knew about those actions might think of them. I held a thumbs-up aloft to Lola, who was sitting on a doorstep a few buildings down with the bottle of champagne.

He opened his front door. "Nina, hi, come on in," he drawled in a demonstratively unbothered way, exposing his nerves. I scanned his flat, which was filled with the essential props of a try-hard renaissance man. The exposed-brick wall and original tiles of someone interested in heritage, but only of the building he lived in. Framed Pink Floyd albums, a pasta-making machine, linen cushion covers, a neat row of orange Penguin classics, herbal hand soap in an apothecary-style jar that cost £38 a bottle. There was an oil painting of a nude woman who was very slightly overweight with very slightly pendulous breasts, which probably made him think he was a feminist. He had bought his entire personality from a cobbled side-road of boutiques in Shoreditch.

"How are you doing?"

"I'm fine," I said. "So, you're alive, then?"

"Evidently."

"Well, as long as you're alive and well, that's the important thing."

He leant against the kitchen cupboard, willing this interaction into something friendly and relaxed. "Look, Nina, I get that she's your friend and you're doing this because you love her. But what's happening with me and Lola is really between me and Lola."

"But it's not though, because you're not talking to her, so it's happening between Jethro and Jethro. The two most important people in the relationship."

His mouth opened slightly, then closed. It felt good to catch him out. It was so rare that men like Jethro felt like a woman had the upper hand in a conversation.

"I needed some space, I haven't done anything wrong. You don't understand how intense it's been. We haven't had a day apart, I haven't had a moment to myself to think."

"Who pursued who in your relationship?"

He groaned. "Me."

"And who said 'I love you' first?"

"Me."

"Who suggested buying a place together?"

"I know what you must think of me."

"Was it just a challenge?"

"What do you mean?"

"Was it a game you wanted to complete? You met a woman who had her life together, and you wanted to see if you could pull it apart? You wanted to know that you could get her to fall in love with you, say all the things you wanted her to say, do all the things you wanted her to do, then the game was finished and you could turn it off?"

"Of course that's not what I did. I just changed my mind—people are allowed to change their minds about things."

"You know, every time you 'change your mind' in such an extreme way, it takes something from a woman. It's an act of theft. It's not just a theft of her trust, it's a theft of her time. You've taken things from her, so you could have a fun few months. Can you not see how selfish that is?"

"Yes," he said.

"Do you have any idea how hard she has to work to trust someone? And it's going to be even harder for her to do that now. It's yet more labour women have to put into a relationship that, on the whole, men don't really have to think about."

"Okay," he tried to reason, "I've handled this very badly."

"You said you wanted to marry her. Do you know how **mental** that is, Jethro? How wildly inappropriate it is to say that so early on in a relationship even if you meant it, let alone if you didn't."

"I meant it at the time."

"You do know how marriage and children work, don't you? You know you have to, like, go out with someone first to get to that bit."

"I know. I'm very in love with her. I'm just not ready to commit properly yet."

"You're thirty-six."

"Age doesn't matter."

"And love doesn't work like that, anyway. I can't believe I'm having to explain this to a man in his late thirties."

"Mid-thirties."

"You have to take your chance, it's not like you fall in love with someone every week. How arrogant are you, that you think you're going to feel like this again about someone whenever you decide you're ready on your terms?"

"It's not about her, it's about timing."

"So when do you think you'll suddenly be ready to commit?"

He shrugged and made baffled noises as he searched his thoughts. "I don't know. I can't say. Four years maybe? Five years? I don't know."

"Lola will be nearly forty then. Do you expect her to wait to start a proper relationship with you when she's forty?" I imagined him as a single forty-something, silvery strands streaked through his red hair, gallant crinkles around his eyes, a flat twice the size filled with twice as much detritus of an insecure man with too much money. He wouldn't seem desperate or sad. Men like Jethro got to journey through life and be perceived as lion-hearted, intrepid explorers.

Then I realized—he would be able to decide when

he wanted to fall in love and have a family and it would happen. There would always be a woman who wanted to love him. He didn't have to take this chance at all—he could wait for another chance. Then another one. The female population was just an endless source of chances and he could wait as long as he wanted. There was so little risk involved when it came to who and how he loved. Nothing meant anything to him.

"You won't marry a woman your age," I said, understanding it as I said it aloud. "You'll marry a woman ten years younger than you. That's how this will work. You're right, age doesn't matter. To you." He stared at me, his mouth tight and defiant, and said nothing. "Has Lola left anything here?"

"No," he said. "I don't think so."

"Don't date until you've sorted your shit out." I went to the door. "And don't call Lola again."

I KNEW HE WOULD DATE AGAIN. Probably within weeks, just like Max had done. I imagined all the women Jethro and Max would date, while they were "confused" and "not ready," standing next to each other in a long factory line. Each of them would give these men something—a story, a weekend away, their attention, their advice, their time, a sexual adventure, an actual adventure—then they'd be forced to pass him along to the next relationship. These men would emerge at some point, full of all

the love and care and confidence that had been be-
stowed upon them over the years, and they might
commit to someone. Then, most certainly, another
one. Then another one when that one got boring.
Their greed would not be satisfied by one woman,
by one life. They'd get to lead a great many lives.
Life after life after life after life.

Because these men wanted to want something
rather than have something. Max wanted to be tor-
tured, he wanted to yearn and chase and dream. He
wanted to exist in a liminal state, like everything was
just about to begin. He liked contemplating what
our relationship might be like, without investing
any time or commitment in our relationship. Jethro
liked talking about the home he would buy with
Lola, but he didn't want to turn up to the viewing.
They were like teenage boys in their rooms, coming up with lyrics to write in their notebooks. They
weren't ready to be adults, to make any choices, let
alone promises. They preferred a relationship to be
virtual and speculative, because when it was virtual
and speculative, it could be perfect. Their girlfriend
didn't have to be human. They didn't have to think
about plans or practicalities, they weren't burdened
with the concern of another person's happiness.
And they could be heroes. They could be gods.

It was pathetic.

"WHO ARE ALL THESE FUCKING MEN?" Lola slurred, opening a dusty bottle of Tia Maria. It was past midnight and we'd run out of wine—we'd resorted to liqueurs in the back of the cupboards in my flat. "How do they get to have sex with us? Do they know how lucky they are that they got to have sex with us? They should have had to cut out vouchers from a magazine for a year— A YEAR—and send them off to a PO box number before they were even CONSIDERED as people who might be lucky enough to have sex with us." She poured the Tia Maria into our wine glasses with a wobbly hand.

"PO box number? Mate," I said, "you're showing your age, there."

"I want to show my age. I'm thirty-fucking-three. My age is an accumulation, it's an asset. It's a **furnishing.** It isn't a loss. I'm a CATCH. Why don't they understand I'm a catch?"

"I don't know."

"If I were a boy, everyone would want to be with me. I have a great career, lovely teeth," she said, baring her gums at me. "I have good cardiovascular health. I own a whole set of suitcases I saved up for, with all the separate compartments for underwear and toiletries. One of them even has a frigging USB port built into it to charge your phone. That's an impressive person. Why doesn't everyone want to be with me?"

I opened our second pack of cigarettes and withdrew one. "Beats me."

"We have to download Linx again."

"No," I said, lighting my fag. "No way. I'm done with dating."

"You can't be done with dating if you want a family."

"I was so much happier before this year. I don't want to think about it or look for it any more. If it happens, it happens."

"There's nothing wrong with wanting to love someone, Nina."

"I know that."

"It's not a weakness, to want that for yourself," she said. "I don't want you to give up hope."

"I think that might have already happened." We both leant out of the window, exhaling smoke into the sky. The recently planted tree waved its nascent branches at us in the breeze.

"I know," she said. "You should give your hope to me."

"What do you mean?"

"It's like what Joe said in his groom's speech: love is being the guardian of another person's solitude. Maybe friendship is being the guardian of another person's hope. Leave it with me and I'll look after it for a while, if it feels too heavy for now."

"I can't do that, you're already carrying yours."

"Oh, I've been carrying mine for a decade," she said. "I won't notice if I chuck a bit more in."

I tucked her hair tightly behind her ear. "I couldn't be less of an advocate for relationships right now. But, for what it's worth—I know there is a love ahead of you, Lola. Grander than either of us can imagine. He might not be a celebrity magician. He might not be anything like the sort of man we thought he would be. But he's on his way."

"I know that, Nina," she said. "I've always known that."

"You really have, haven't you?"

"So I can know it for you too. And then you don't have to think about it any more. You just keep writing your books and looking after your dad. I'll keep your hope safe for you until you're ready for me to hand it back."

Angelo approached the front door and saw us leaning out of my window.

"Hello!" he shouted up to me.

"Hello!" I said. "How are the hams?"

"Okay," he said. "I hang them on hooks on the washing line, but I have a problem with flies."

"You wanted the bicycle," I said.

"Ah, yes."

"I have something you can cover them with that will let the air get to them."

"You do?"

"Yes," I said. He smiled and turned the key in the door. I turned to Lola; her face was aghast.

"What. Was that?"

"He's okay."

"The possible-murderer?"

"He's not a murderer, he's a depressed man who has bought knives to take up the art of charcuterie to distract him from his broken heart and remind him of home."

"How do you know?"

"We talked, had it out and came to a truce."

"How?"

"We fucked."

"Very funny."

"I'm actually being serious." Lola's mouth hung open in shock and her drunken, dancing eyes came into focus. "He came over to confront me about the stolen packages, I confessed and we ended up having sex in the kitchen." The cavern of her mouth widened. "I know."

"Will you do it again?"

"No, no. It was a one-time thing."

"Do you fancy him?"

"I don't know. I did, a lot, when it was happening. I think I needed to have sex with someone who couldn't disappear. We live in the same house. We share an electricity meter. I can basically hear his heartbeat through the floor."

Lola thought on this, removing another cigarette. "Lush," she concluded sadly.

WE SAT IN DRUNKEN EXHAUSTION—a mostly silent cycle of pouring, drinking and smoking.

"I have got something new for the Schadenfreude Shelf," Lola said. "And it's the best one yet."

"You say that every time."

"No, trust me, this one really is the best one yet. I heard it a while back and I've actually been saving it up for our lowest low."

"I don't think other people's misery is going to do anything except make me feel more miserable."

"Why don't you try it?"

"Okay."

"Okay, so," she said, bringing her feet up to her chair so she sat cross-legged like an excitable teenager during a secret-swapping session. "Do you remember my friend Camille?"

"Yes."

"So, not Camille, but—"

"Don't believe it, the source has already been weakened."

"We can call her right now for clarification."

"I'm not calling your friend Camille."

"So, Camille's friend Emma moved to California. And in the first month she's there, she decides she wants to take ayahuasca."

"What's ayahuasca?"

"It's a psychoactive drug that's administered by a shaman and apparently it's like doing ten years' therapy in one night."

"Right." It worried me how fluent I had become in Lola-babble.

"So, she's at this ceremony in Joshua Tree with a

bunch of other strangers and they all take the aya-huasca. Emma goes on this crazy emotional trip, like she's gone back in time, and she heals all these awful rifts between her and her mother. She comes out the other side and stands in the desert, sand under her feet and stars over her head."

"All right, get on with it."

"And she realizes she's at total peace for the first time in her life. Then—a man is next to her. This other guy who has taken it too. He holds his hand out to her and she takes it. They say nothing to each other, but she knows she's just met the love of her life."

"Lola, this story is not true."

"Now—**wait a minute.** So. They go back to LA, where he also lives, and they spend the weekend together. She is happier than she's ever been—she has never felt so understood by another human. He moves into her apartment. They have three blissful months together."

"Okay."

"Then—something happens. This guy starts to actually really annoy her. They start having all these fights about things. She says to him: 'I think this might not be right.' He says: 'We just have to go back to the desert to take more ayahuasca.'"

"So it was like a long, low-level hallucination?"

"Precisely. So she says, no, take your stuff, leave my apartment, and he does. Then, about a week later, there's this horrific smell everywhere. In every room, she can't escape it."

"Oh no."

"She gets cleaners round—they deep-clean the whole place, the smell doesn't go. After a month of living in hell, she finally traces where it's coming from."

"Where?"

"He had dismantled the air-conditioning unit, stuffed it with raw prawns, then screwed it back up. The smell dispersed with the airflow."

"Oh my God." I sat with the magnitude of this anecdotal finale for a minute. "That's a really, really good addition to the Schadenfreude Shelf, Lola. Our worst break-up will never be as bad as that."

"What would you have done? If you had been her?" she asked.

I swallowed the last of the sickly sweet coffee liqueur. "I think I might have gone back to the desert," I said. "And taken more."

"But then it would have all been a lie."

"Think about Demetrius and Helena."

"Were we at uni with them?"

"In **A Midsummer Night's Dream.** The happy ending is about two couples who are all in love with the right person. But Demetrius only loves Helena because he's under the cast of an earlier spell."

"Is that really the ending?"

"Yeah."

"Why?"

"There are different theories. Probably because Shakespeare needed to resolve everything, so the story could follow the rules of what made a comedy. It was really hard to explain it to the kids when I taught it—they found an illusion so impossible to accept as a happy ending. They always used to ask me if I thought that Demetrius stayed in love with Helena after the play ended."

"Do you think he did?"

"The question isn't whether he stayed in love, it's whether he woke up," I said.

Lola looked out on to my road, the street lamp bathing her face in amber light, the amber light that had illuminated these late-night scenes of our friendship for so many years. She picked up my phone, unlocked it and went into the app store. The Linx logo appeared with an option to download it.

"I hope he didn't wake up," she said. She placed the phone in the palm of my hand and the screen shone with bright uncertainty.

# Epilogue

IT IS CLEAR-SKIED when I wake up on the 3rd of August. It is the kind of weather that reminds me of childhood—of ladybirds on freckled arms and strawberry ice cream in the park. I know there must have been white-skied and drizzly days in my early years, but I can never seem to remember any of them. I brush my teeth and wash my face and, for the sake of tradition if not historical accuracy, play "The Edge of Heaven" from the living-room speakers. It really is the best song to dance to.

I go for a walk around my neighbourhood, stepping over kebab-shop debris from the late-night moveable feasts. I walk past the flaking red-painted front of The Institution which, in daylight, looks like a kids' party entertainer without its costume. I do my preferred circuit of Hampstead Heath and pick up a flat white on the way home (double shot, full-fat milk).

Angelo's leaving as I arrive. We exchange pleasantries, both smoke a cigarette in the sun, and I tell him it's my thirty-third birthday. He informs me I'm the same age as Jesus was when he died and asks what I plan to do to rival his achievements. I tell him I am sure I can save mankind in the next year. Or if not, I'll definitely donate to food banks more.

In the mid-afternoon, I head to Albyn Square. I wanted a small afternoon picnic to celebrate this year and couldn't think of anywhere lovelier than the road of my first home. I take a rug, some fold-out chairs and a cool box of wine and food. The guest list is just seven: Katherine, Mark, Lola, Joe, Lucy, Mum and Dad.

Katherine and Mark arrive first, Freddie on Katherine's hip, Olive holding Mark's hand, no one complaining about how long it took to get to East London, even though I know that's what they've been talking about on the train journey. I asked everyone to bring their favourite snack from childhood as research for the final chapter of my new book. Kat brings salt-and-vinegar chipsticks, Mark brings Scotch eggs.

Joe and Lucy arrive shortly afterwards, with

packets of Babybels and Jammie Dodgers piled up in their arms. Lucy spends the afternoon going from cheese to biscuit, then biscuit to cheese. At one point, I see her sandwich a Babybel between two biscuits and eat it in one bite. Her bump is showing now and Joe can't stop touching her. He is the sort of expectant father who refers to the birth as a joint venture and knows every answer to every question about pregnancy. They arrive in their new navy car, with Lucy shouting at him about parking. It's already been fitted with a seat for the baby. One day that baby will sit on a bench, wondering if that navy car is scrap metal somewhere, wishing it could come collect them.

Lola turns up with sherbet and strawberry laces, wearing a blue gingham maxi dress and a matching parasol. She has a date later this evening. A man from a new app, which matches you on mutual dislikes rather than mutual likes. They've been talking about their shared hatred of country music and tomatoes in panini for five days solid now. Despite the fact he's a Gemini, she thinks he may be the one. (We persuade her not to take the parasol.)

Dad remembers Albyn Square as soon as he arrives. He remembers teaching me to ride my bike in circles, he remembers the day I fell out of the mulberry tree and needed stitches on my knee, he remembers the bench where they sat with me a few days after I was born. I have given up sifting through the timeline of his memories, trying to work out which is the sediment that will stick. Some days he can't remember who I am, sometimes he remembers the grades of all my violin exams. I like to think of everyone he loves as a gallery of Picasso paintings that hang in his mind—in a constant state of fascinating rearrangement, rather than in the process of erasure.

He sits on the bench and talks to Joe about cricket. Mum sits on the grass and Lola shows her how she's learnt to fishtail braid her own hair. Olive eats all the sherbet while no one is looking.

Katherine's made me a cake—she asks me to sit on the bench next to Dad while she indiscreetly takes it out of its carrier behind Mark's back. It is three-tiered and lopsided and covered in buttercup-yellow icing.

Everyone sings "Happy Birthday." Lola harmonizes badly, Freddie giggles in my lap, Mum takes a photograph. Olive crawls under the mulberry tree. The tree that lives inside me and is impossible to demolish, only hide or lose through ever-moving mists. The tree that grows up through me, the trunk of which forms my spine. Katherine holds the cake below my face and the candles flicker lightly in the still heat of the day. "Make a wish," she says. I close my eyes and think of all the paths that lie ahead, none of which I can see yet. None of which I can plan for, only walk towards with faith. I blow out the candles of my cake for the thirty-third time. Another year begins.

# Acknowledgements

I could write ten pages of thanks to Juliet Annan. For her instincts, wisdom, wit, insight and straight-talking. But she's already had to edit enough of my rambling in recent years, so instead I will say this: I loved every single moment of writing this book. This is entirely thanks to Juliet, who is, I'm pleased to say, right about everything.

Thank you to Clare Conville for her unwavering guidance, passion and kindness. There is no better woman to have in your corner.

Thank you to Jane Gentle, Poppy North, Rose Poole and Assallah Tahir—celebrants and strategists, guardians of my work and sanity.

# Acknowledgements

Thank you to Ruth Johnstone, Tineke Mollemans and Kyla Dean—grafters, go-getters, total and utter dames.

Research was needed to write a part of this story and I am grateful for the generosity of the people who shared their experiences, expertise and information with me. Thanks to Julian Linley, Hannah Mackay, Hilda Hayo, Holly Bainbridge, Howard Masters and Dementia UK.

Thank you to my first readers for their encouragement: Farly Kleiner, India Masters and Edward Bluemel.

Particular conversations with friends inspired much of these chapters—I'm especially thankful to Tom Bird, Sarah Spencer-Ashworth, Monica Heisey, Caroline O'Donoghue, Eddie Cumming, Octavia Bright, Helen Nianias, India Masters, Laura Jane Williams, Farly Kleiner, Will Heald, Max Pritchard, Ed Cripps, Sabrina Bell, Sarah Dillistone and Sophie Wilkinson.

Thank you to Lorraine Candy, Laura Atkinson and the **Sunday Times** Style for their support as I wrote this book.

An ongoing, lifelong thank you to Lauren Bensted, with whom I have been in the middle of a conversation since we were fifteen. Every writer dreams of having access to a brain like yours. I'm so lucky to get it second-hand. Thank you for everything you say at the pub (even the bollocks) and thank you for always letting me write it down.

And thank you to Sabrina Bell, for a great many things—but particularly for always knowing it, when knowing it seemed impossible.